C000036790

Felicity Fights Back

Felicity Fights Back

STELLA SYKES

transita

Published by Transita
Spring Hill House, Spring Hill Road,
Begbroke, Oxford OX5 1RX
Tel: (01865) 375794. Fax: (01865) 379162
email: info@transita.co.uk
http://www.transita.co.uk

British Library Cataloguing in Publication Data
A catalogue record for this book is available from the British Library

ISBN 10:1-905175-27-2
ISBN 13:978-1-905175-27-7

Produced for Transita by Deer Park Productions, Tavistock
Typeset by PDQ Typesetting, Newcastle-under-Lyme
Printed and bound by Bookmarque, Croydon

ABOUT THE AUTHOR

Stella Sykes was born in Scotland a long time ago and was brought up on a farm in Kent. Her many jobs have included being a cleaner, running a marriage bureau, being a photographic stylist and writing fashion copy for an advertising agency. Having lived in Spain and Australia and London she has now settled in Hampshire with her second husband, six dogs, thirteen alpacas and several chickens. She has a son, three step-children and six step-grandchildren and apart from family her interests include skiing, gundogs, gardening, cooking and eavesdropping.

CHAPTER 1

FELICITY FOX HAD JUST HAD a most distressing experience. She had seen what she thought was the reflection of an old bag lady in the plate glass window of Peter Jones, but after a couple of seconds she realised that she was looking at her own image: lank hair, old black jumper and a pair of jeans that had been old when she was thin and they had still fitted her. It had been a long time since she had seen her reflection like that, so much had happened and she hadn't been aware of this physical deterioration.

She had left the house early to try to find some material for her bedroom curtains. Her son Oscar was coming back from New York soon and would be furious if she still had an old sheet covering the window. She had been in her new house for several months now, but there were still a few finishing touches to be done before it would feel like home. Now she could only pray that she wouldn't see anyone she knew. A few minutes later she was skulking in the corner of the fabric department.

'Frumpy. Frumpy Frobisher!' The honking voice seemed to reverberate through the whole department. Hearing her hated, but at the moment painfully apt, old school nickname, Felicity turned round and came face to face with a mouthful of teeth under a mop of wiry grey hair attached to an extremely large body. Felicity frowned, trying to remember who this woman was, as the voice continued.

'Thought it was you Frumpy. It's been simply yonks. Not since Fizz's coming out dance.' Fizz? Coming out dance? A faint memory stirred. Was it possible that this fat, hearty, and frankly, old-looking woman could have been at school with her?

Felicity replaced the roll of fabric she had been examining and tried to put a pleasant expression on her face as she said, 'Gosh, it's been ages.' Then cautiously she tried a question. 'Where are you living now?' seemed safe enough.

'Got a house near Hurlingham, Timmy's retired, back from Hong Kong for good.' At least she didn't call it Honkers. 'Of course you've never met him. Timmy Bignall, that's my husband. I'm Jane Bignall now.' Then, as if sensing that Felicity still wasn't sure who she was talking to, added, 'Plum. That's what I was called at school. Plum Cranford.'

'Of course.' Felicity felt like hugging her, with the relief at knowing her name. Then without thinking she started to speak. 'But you were so ... so ... so ... ' grinding to a halt, realising that none of her thoughts were appropriate. 'Dark,' she ended lamely.

Jane shrugged her shoulders. 'Never seem to have time for the hairdressers. Used to have a figure too, but four children later – what can you do?' She laughed, quite relaxed.

Felicity could remember her now. She had been a big girl, but with loads of style, and a heart-shaped face surrounded by a cloud of dark hair. The years had certainly been cruel. The woman standing in front of her was a good size twenty. She was wearing a shapeless red cardigan, a striped shirt with a piecrust frill, a green dirndl skirt, green tights and loafers. Surely people in Hong Kong weren't still dressing like that. Felicity turned her head away, aware that she was smirking. It was good for her morale to see an old schoolfriend looking dowdy. For a few moments she had forgotten her own appearance, then the memory of her reflection in the shop window came back to her. Turning to Plum, she tried to dismiss the image.

'Do you ever see anyone from school?' she asked. She'd meant to wash her hair last night, with that new colour shampoo, but in the end couldn't be bothered, and this morning she hadn't even put on any mascara. It hadn't really seemed worth the effort. Whatever had she been thinking of, venturing into Sloane Square dressed like that? She'd no right to criticise Plum. Why on earth had she been called that? Felicity was hardly listening as the other woman continued, then she snapped to attention as she heard Plum's voice.

'Sally Pelham was in Hong Kong for a while. She's a great chum. But of course you see her, don't you?'

'Not since she ran off with my husband.' Felicity knew her voice was icy.

'Oh Lord!' Jane wailed. 'Lummy, put my foot in it as per usual.'

Felicity gave a half-smile. 'Don't worry.' She just managed to say it. 'Happens all the time. I thought you'd probably know. Everyone else seems to.' Then to her fury she felt her eyes smart and her lower lip begin to quiver. 'Got to go,' she muttered and felt Jane pat her arm sympathetically as she blundered past her and through the china department out into Sloane Square.

It wasn't just the brightness of the sun that made Felicity fumble in her bag for her dark glasses. All it needed right now was for someone she knew to see her in tears. There were people who managed to look appealing and vulnerable when they were crying, but Felicity wasn't one of them. She walked, hardly knowing where she was going, northwards up Sloane Street.

'Oh fuck,' she thought, but then realised that she must have said it out loud as an elderly couple gave her a disapproving look. 'Sorry,' she muttered to the air, and struggling to keep her thoughts quiet she continued on towards Pont Street. Even in her misery she noticed that summer had finally arrived. The air was warm, the trees were

3

green and young couples in skimpy tops and shorts with long, tanned limbs were entwined on every corner. Enjoy it, she thought bitterly. It won't last.

She could feel her tears turning to anger, which was better, because it made her feel stronger. She debated whether to carry on towards Knightsbridge and the comfort of Harvey Nichols' food department or ring Venetia. Remembering the depressing sight of her too-tight jeans she resolutely got her mobile out of her bag. Squinting at the numbers and then cursing again, but silently this time, she fumbled around for her reading glasses. It wasn't meant to be like this, she thought. She had always imagined that by the time she was fifty-five her life would be a sea of tranquillity. She would be living in a perfect Georgian manor house, with a swimming pool, two labradors and a horse, and a faithful, adoring husband. And indeed she had had that, apart from the pool and the faithful husband. And now she was living alone in a tiny, terraced house in one of the few unimproved corners of Battersea. It all hurt so much and the awful thing was she didn't understand why it had all gone wrong. Sitting on a low wall by the bus stop halfway up Sloane Street Felicity dialled her friend's number. Venetia must have been sitting on top of it because it only rang once when she answered.

'Thank God, you're there. Can I come round?' Felicity gasped.

'You sound frightful. What's wrong?' Venetia was her oldest friend and was instantly concerned.

'How long have you got?'

'I'll open the emergency champagne.'

*

Venetia Kent-Fletcher lived in a tall, narrow house in a quiet Chelsea square with her husband Andrew. Like her house she was tall and slim, but unlike her house this was the result of a

4

great deal of hard work. She was a freelance fashion editor for a fashionable magazine and aimed for perfection in all things. She was waiting by the door when Felicity rang the bell and threw it open immediately.

'Oh Fifi.' Venetia couldn't help raising her eyebrows disapprovingly as she took in Felicity's appearance. 'Bad day?' she said, more as a statement than a question, as she hugged her friend.

'They all seem to be lousy at the moment.' Felicity was aware of an unattractive whining tone in her voice as she followed her friend into her drawing room, but that was how she felt. Venetia redecorated constantly but always, it seemed to Felicity, in the same shades of beige and oatmeal. Now Felicity sank down onto an immaculate wild silk cream sofa and quickly held out her hand as Venetia walked across the room and put a glass of champagne into it.

'Netty you're a life saver.' She managed a weak smile before she raised the glass to her lips.

Venetia smoothed her already perfectly smoothed hair and said, 'Bugger tea and sympathy – champagne and gossip's better.' She eyed her friend warily.

Felicity managed a mirthless laugh. 'The only gossip I want to hear is that Sally's given Henry crabs.'

'I'm sure that could be arranged, sweetie.' Venetia perched on a chair next to Felicity, her cream Armani trouser suit exactly matching the damask of the upholstery. She raised her own glass to her lips and took a small sip before putting it down on the perfectly polished glass coffee table, with its neat pile of this month's glossy magazines. She took a cigarette out of a packet and lit it with a slim gold lighter, and then leant forward frowning as she held out a hand towards her friend and asked, 'Do you like this colour?'

Felicity looked at the bright orange iridescence on her friend's perfectly manicured nails and with the frankness of an old friendship gave a small shudder. 'No. It's simply vile.'

Venetia sighed. 'I know, it was one of these freebies sent to the magazine. It's supposed to be the new Rouge Noir.' Felicity looked blank. 'The "must have" colour everyone was wearing a few years ago.'

'Not in Little Biddlehampton,' Felicity retorted. She tried to sit on her own hands, but Venetia was too quick for her.

'When did you last have a proper manicure?' Venetia grabbed her friend's hand and eyed the nails with distaste.

Felicity looked at the dehydrated reptile on the end of her arm in astonishment. Where had that dead iguana come from? Surely it was only a few weeks ago when the skin on her hands had been young and springy.

'Obviously ages ago,' she replied, 'there doesn't seem much point.'

'It's time we fixed that. And your hair,' Venetia said, averting her gaze from Felicity's head with a slight grimace. 'I'll make an appointment for you with Pelle.'

'I thought he was a footballer. Things must be desperate.'

'Idiot! It's the name of the salon. Pelle Capelli. What about your face?' she continued relentlessly.

'What about my face?'

'What cream are you using?'

Felicity looked sheepish.

'I find those women so scary – they see me coming. I know what they're thinking. Bells ringing – Emergency! Let me through, I'm a beautician. Do you think they put a matt fixative on their faces in the morning after they've made them up – those mask-like faces?' Felicity was aware that she was babbling. She did not like the direction their conversation was taking.

'Don't change the subject. What cream have you got?' Venetia demanded fiercely.

'I can't remember what it's called. All I know is that it cost about as much as a small family car. The woman said something about free radicals. What on earth are free radicals? She sounded convincing at the time but now I come to think, it sounds like a slogan you'd spray on a wall, not the ingredients of a face cream.'

'Are you using it?' Venetia was not to be deflected.

'I did use it couple of times, but it didn't make any difference.'

'You're supposed to use it every day, religiously.' Venetia's tone was exasperated. 'And you obviously haven't been.'

'Thanks a lot.' Felicity flushed and tried to wriggle down into the sofa. 'If you remember, it hasn't exactly been a great year.'

'So. Your husband left you. I don't mean to be harsh, but that's no reason to let yourself go completely.'

Felicity looked round the room, willing herself not to be a wimp. She didn't want to cry again. But it was no good.

'Frumpy,' she wailed. 'I'd forgotten that's what I was called at school.'

'Sweetheart, I'm sorry for you. We're all sorry. But if I'm being strictly honest, you have got a bit frumpy since the dickhead left.'

'Don't call him that,' Felicity said automatically.

'Sorry. You know we all love Henry, but he is being a dickhead and the truth is you had let yourself go before that, hadn't you?'

Felicity ignored the question.

'I understand,' Venetia continued, 'you were doing everything, without much help from Henry. You didn't have much time for yourself, did you?'

'It's all right for you,' Felicity said, gesturing dramatically at the expanse of the drawing room. 'You've got all this and Andrew. What have I got?'

'Your health for a start and your children. Your life. Now it's time to move on. Even find a new man.' Venetia sat down on the sofa and leant forward intently.

'In case you haven't noticed there aren't any out there. I'm fat, fifty-five and flat broke. And I don't think I want a new man. I was quite happy with the old one.' Felicity shut her eyes. Nobody understood how bloody it was.

Venetia took her hand and gave it a squeeze. 'Age you can't change. Although Sally Pelham seems to get younger every year. But flat broke is simply not true. You're much better off without Henry draining the bank account. Fat on the other hand ... '

Felicity opened her eyes and interrupted Venetia indignantly. 'It's not fair. When you're miserable you go all pale and thin, you don't eat and get even better cheekbones. While I get a morbid fascination with contents of my fridge. It's constant graze. The pounds just pile on,' she sighed and added, 'if you're going to keep going on at me I need more champagne.'

Venetia looked at her with the incomprehension of the naturally thin, but she got to her feet and poured them each another glass. Then like a terrier with a rat she continued. 'First your hair, then the gym.' As far as Venetia was concerned all problems were soluble if you looked right.

'I can't afford to go to the hairdresser,' wailed her friend.

'Nobody can afford not to go to the hairdresser,' Venetia retorted, patting her own sleek ash blonde bob. 'I saw Sally the other day and she looks great.'

'Bitch.'

'I know, but she still looks great.'

'I meant you.'

*

'Somebody's been letting themselves go, haven't they?' Roberto, owner and queen of Pelle Capelli, stood with one hand on his twenty-eight inch hips and a faint expression of revulsion on his face as he lifted a strand of Felicity's lank hair with his comb. 'Venetia asked us to look after you, so we'll try and wave our magic wand shall we?' With pursed lips he continued to pick up strands of her hair.

Felicity stared at him in amazement, even though Venetia had already warned her that he was camper than a boy scout jamboree.

'Hmm,' he said. 'I think I'll let Sadie look after you. Sadie, come and see what you can do for Felicity.'

Felicity felt a sense of relief as she remembered what her cousin Rose had said. 'Hope you don't have Roberto, he's such a number. Last time Daisy went there he'd had a row with his boyfriend and she came out looking exactly like Danny La Rue.' Felicity obviously wasn't smart enough for Roberto himself to look after. There were compensations for being a country bumpkin.

'Hi Felicity, I'm Sadie.'

Sitting in front of what she hoped was an unflattering mirror Felicity wondered when hairdressers stopped calling their clients Madame or even Mrs Fox. Then she realised depressingly that she was becoming just like her mother. She looked into the mirror and was confronted by a pierced navel with a silver ring in it. Raising her eyes she took in a cropped black top and then a pretty pale face with pierced lip, nose and ears and white-blonde hair about half an inch long. At first she tried not to stare but then decided that no one would look like that if they were trying to blend into the background. She felt nostalgic for Little Biddlehampton and the familiar smell of perming lotion at Hair Today. Did they even do perms here in this minimalist, cool salon with its décor of square glass vases filled with pebbles instead of the dusty arrangement of artificial flowers that had been the principal decorative feature at Hair Today ever since she could remember.

'Have you been hennaing it yourself?' Sadie's voice broke into her thoughts.

'Yes.' Felicity was forced to confess she had. 'But it seems to have gone a rather strange colour so I stopped doing it.'

'That's because you're reely grey.'

'That's why I've been putting henna on it,' Felicity said patiently.

'Henna on grey makes it go that horrible orange. What I'd like to do,' Sadie confided, as if they were friends, 'is put a vegetable dye on. It's all organic ingredients. It's got papaya and avocado oil in it and it'll give a lovely shine, and a reely lovely colour. Then we'll give it a good cut and get rid of these horrible split ends.'

Felicity could only nod and smile. She wondered as she did so whether Sadie actually believed all that about organic ingredients.

'Why don't you look at a magazine, try and find something you'd like to look like?' Sadie called over her shoulder and she disappeared to mix up the colour.

Felicity idly thumbed her way through a succession of photographs. What on earth made Sadie imagine that even with the aid of a top plastic surgeon she would be able to make a fifty-five-year-old woman remotely resemble any of these swan-necked, pre-pubescent girls? Once again she could hear her mother's voices suggesting a sensible style that was tidy and easy to look after, and when Sadie came back she muttered something about not wanting it too short.

'It's not going to be bright red is it?' she asked nervously as Sadie applied a purple cream to her head.

'No, reely subtle, you'll love it.' She thrust her under a drier, saying she would have her shampooed in twenty minutes. A child covered in more piercings brought her a Capuccino, which made a nice change from Little Biddle-hampton's smartest salon where the instant coffee had always slopped over onto the digestives in the saucer.

Felicity picked up a copy of *Tatler* and began turning the pages. Why was it that the only people she knew in the gossip pages were her children's friends? Suddenly she saw a picture of Upton Court. It was the estate agent's photograph from the sale. Bugger Henry, she thought. Bastard. Why did he have to ruin everything? My language included. Her eyes blurred as the tears came, as they had so often in the last few months. She closed them tightly and tried to force the photograph out of her head.

Upton Court. It had been love at first sight. Already in love with Henry, she'd often joked later that she would have married him anyway to live in the house. It was a medium-sized, Georgian manor house, set in parkland at the end of a long, meandering drive. Exactly the house she'd always felt destined to live in. When they were first married she and Henry had lived in London and Henry's parents had been living at Upton. After a few years they decided they were getting too old and the house too big and moved into the lodge.

Henry and Felicity moved into the main house in those wonderful far off days, when there had been plenty of money, before the disaster of Lloyds. The children had all been born there, first Laura then the twins. It had been tiring of course, but there was Sylvie to look after the babies and Felicity had been able to play house with seemingly unlimited funds. Nothing had been touched since Henry's parents had moved in just after the war and it needed a lot of renovation. A new kitchen and two new bathrooms, then new curtains, loose covers and wallpaper everywhere.

Once the house was done there had been several years of fun. Friends to stay, dinner parties, holidays abroad, the house filled with the children and their friends. Henry had never been the most industrious of men, but he had been good with the children and on the whole they had been happy until the Lloyds mess happened.

Not long after that the children left home and went their independent ways. Henry appeared to lose heart at that point and gave up any pretence of trying to earn money. And then he really did lose his heart – to Sally Pelham, and that had been that. Now the house was sold and that chapter, which she had thought would be the whole book, was over. And here she was sitting in a smart Knightsbridge hairdressers, imagining that a new hairdo would help push her out of her depression.

After twenty minutes the drier pinged and Sadie bustled over to inspect her hair.

'Lovely,' she said and then called across the salon. 'Tracy, will you shampoo the vegetable?'

Felicity gave a weak smile; it seemed a bit too close to the truth. 'I was hoping to be spared for a few more years, before it came to that,' she said feebly, trying to make a joke of it, but Sadie just smiled at her blankly. She does think I'm a vegetable, thought Felicity gloomily. However, Sadie was obviously a serious-minded girl and probably hadn't intended it ironically. And it seemed unlikely that anyone who'd done that to their own appearance would have a highly developed sense of humour.

'You going anywhere nice for your holiday?' Tracy asked as she massaged shampoo into Felicity's hair.

'I'll probably manage a couple of days in Scotland. How about you?'

'Me and my boyfriend are going to Bali.'

'That's nice,' Felicity said absently.

'You been there? Lovely isn't it?'

'No. But I've heard that it's gorgeous.'

'Sright. We've been three times.'

Felicity was amazed. This girl could only be about nineteen and she'd done more travelling than Felicity had at fifty-five. What a lot of ground she had to make up.

When she emerged from Roberto's two hours later Felicity felt quite different. She hoped it was an improvement. At least her hair felt light and she couldn't help running her fingers through it. It shone and had bounce, and it seemed to put a spring into her step. She couldn't resist looking at her reflection in the window of an Italian restaurant. For a moment she stood staring admiringly at her new self.

And then behind the glass she saw, sitting at a table for two, Andrew Kent-Fletcher holding hands with Slutty Sonia. Felicity leapt back from the window and walked hurriedly down the street. She couldn't believe what she had just seen. She was tempted to creep back and have another look, but knew it wasn't necessary. How could Andrew do that to Venetia? Her first thought was that she should ring her friend and tell her. Then she decided it probably wasn't a good idea. She needed time to think. She had just seen her best friend's husband in a restaurant, at four o'clock in the afternoon, with a girl who was known locally as the Lay of the Land. Luckily she was driving down to Wiltshire tomorrow to spend the weekend with her cousin Rose, the very person to give good advice, who would know what to do.

CHAPTER 2

FELICITY WENT HOME AS QUICKLY AS POSSIBLE, her head full of thoughts of Andrew, Venetia and Sonia. She put the key into the lock of her freshly painted, egg yolk yellow front door and entered the hall with relief. Hanging her jacket on a hook, she paused and admired her new hair in the over-large, gilt-framed hall mirror that she had brought with her from Upton.

'It was ghastly.' Felicity was on the telephone to her cousin Rose. 'One minute I was looking at the transformation in my appearance and the next I was crouching down and scuttling away. I was terrified they'd see me, but they were so absorbed in each other, they wouldn't have noticed if I'd been dancing naked in front of them.'

'Might have caused a bit of a pile-up in Knightsbridge though,' Rose remarked mildly. 'What time are you arriving tomorrow Possum?' Rose had spent a number of years in Australia.

'As soon as I wake up.'

'Good. I know the fete's not until Saturday, but there's a lot to do. Got to fly now. Leo's struggling with the marquee. Must stop him before he has a heart attack.'

*

Felicity set off early the next afternoon for Wiltshire. Rose, who was three years older, had always been one of her closest friends and the person she most often turned to when she was in need of advice. She had promised to go down there as usual to help with the village fete and she knew she would feel better as soon as she arrived at Hatch House.

Rose was the person Felicity would like to have been. Although not beautiful she had a distinct presence in a natural

14

if rather unkempt way. Dressed in a pair of overalls and an old jumper, she still managed to look stylish and elegant. She was usually to be found with her hands either immersed in the soil or making pastry. Leo, her second husband, was a farmer, but at heart he was an academic, and had an encyclopaedic knowledge of English country houses. He was much older than Rose, but generally acknowledged by all her friends as the man they would most like to be married to. Rose's first marriage had been to an Australian and she had lived in Sydney with him and their two children for nearly fifteen years. When she discovered that her first husband was conducting a love affair with alcohol she had come back to England with the children and met Leo, a childless widower. Now her children were grown up and back in Australia.

Hatch House was a rambling farmhouse, filled with dogs, wellington boots and the smell of cooking. Felicity always felt a sense of calm when she turned into the drive. The sun was shining and the herd of Longhorn cows, Leo's pride and joy, grazed peacefully under the ancient oaks in a scene that could have been painted by Constable. She drove round to the back of the house, past the heavy oak front door that was only opened for strangers or at party time.

Parking her car next to the stables, above which Rose's half-sister Daisy lived with her two young sons, Felicity jumped out, and dragging her case out of the back of the car she walked straight into the kitchen. A familiar scene met her. The air was filled with the scent of garlic and thyme, mingling with the sweet smell of horse sweat. The sun was low in the sky and flooded the room with light. The old pitch pine table that was the centrepiece of the room was piled with its usual clutter. A pony's bridle had been thrown carelessly into a workbasket, where it nestled on top of a half-finished square of needlepoint. Seed catalogues flagged with fluorescent pink post-its were stacked at one end, topped by a half-deflated football.

Leo was sitting in his usual niche by the garden door reading a book. Rose was stooped over, busying herself at the sink, and her three black labradors lay entwined in an enormous wicker basket at her feet. When she saw Felicity she looked up and a grin spread over her face. She went towards her cousin with arms outstretched and hugged her, making sure as she did so that her floury hands didn't touch her cousin's clean London clothes.

'How lovely, you're nice and early.' She turned to her husband. 'We can have a drink now, can't we?' Leo got slowly to his feet and came across the room to kiss Felicity. 'We're all completely worn out. The vicar's had a fight with the verger over where to put the beer tent, so it's been moved three times.'

'I hope no one's touched the bric á brac?' Felicity looked enquiringly at Leo.

'Don't worry – Daisy's saved you your usual place under the oak tree. In the shade. Been guarding it like a rottweiler. Champagne?' he asked as he opened the fridge door. 'I think your visit is call for a celebration.'

'Leo, you are the nicest man. You do know how to make a girl feel better.'

'Not to mention the need of a restorative after the in-fighting in the marquee.'

'Such a relief to know that nothing's changed here at least.'

'I'm just going to put some more ash round the delphiniums. You've no idea what a ghastly year it's been for slugs.' Rose, giving her hands a cursory wipe on a teacloth, made for the back door.

'Will you sit down and have a drink? Felicity's only just arrived. In any case I thought those chickens of yours were supposed to deal with the slugs.' Leo shrugged his shoulders with an exasperated tolerance.

'They can't do everything, poor little loves. Particularly since the fox got four of them last month. I won't be long,' Rose called over her shoulder as Leo opened the champagne with a tiny, gentlemanly phut. She had just reached the door when it flew open and Rose's half-sister Daisy burst in.

'Can you have the boys on Wednesday? I'm going to London for a shag.'

'We all know what you mean, but it's hardly an elegant way of putting it.' Leo was used to his sister-in-law but raised his eyes heavenwards as he spoke.

'Sorry Leo, didn't realise you were here. But will you?' she entreated Rose.

'All right Possum. But there's a condition,' she replied mildly, pushing an ever-escaping strand of hair behind her ear.

'What's that?'

'Stop letting the chickens into the kitchen, unless you can housetrain them. They keep shitting on the kitchen floor, just when I've cleaned it.'

'Sorry. But they look so sweet pecking around by the Aga.'

Rose aimed a slap at her as she set off in the direction of the garden, calling over her shoulder, 'Are you implying that my kitchen floor isn't clean enough for humans to eat off?'

Daisy turned and shut the door, then came back into the room. Tossing her hard hat onto the table she sat down next to it, one long, jodhpur-clad leg dangling. At thirty-eight, Daisy was startlingly pretty with a tumble of pre-Raphaelite blonde hair and an angelic face which belied the morals of an alley cat.

'I don't know why we keep that horse, it's got a mouth like iron and a foul temper.' And without waiting for anyone to contradict her turned to Felicity and exclaimed, 'Fifi! When'd you arrive?'

Felicity smiled indulgently at Daisy. She loved her dearly even if she did breeze in and out of everyone's life without appearing to give any of them more than a passing thought.

'Just got here. Still trying to acclimatize. Why's the country always so much colder? It was baking in London.' Felicity had plonked herself down in an ancient armchair opposite Leo and was happily sipping her champagne.

Within minutes Rose was back and rushing around the kitchen haphazardly tidying things away. Felicity always made a beeline for the same chair whenever she came to stay with her cousin. It had originally been covered in leather, but this was now completely battered and worn. On top of this was a moth-eaten old rug Leo claimed to have had at school with him and all the family believed it had magical healing properties. It seemed to envelop her like a comfort blanket which at the moment was just what she wanted. She knew it was useless suggesting she helped with anything. Rose was always fiercely independent in her own domain.

'Never thought you'd become such a townie, Possum.' Rose looked at her cousin in amazement. 'It's not cold.'

'It's this kitchen, it's so draughty. They've hardly got single-glazing, let alone double. Rose thinks fresh air kills ninety percent of all household germs.'

'Pretty rich coming from one who never shuts a door,' Rose said indulgently.

Daisy smiled and leant across to the kitchen table to grab a mug, and picking it up took a swig. 'Ugh – it's got sugar in it.'

'I know – it's mine.' Leo leant over and reclaimed it. For the first time in weeks Felicity felt relaxed. The moment she turned off the A303 she had felt the calming effect of this house. She knew the way like the back of her hand. She and Henry had loved to drive over from Upton and escape the B & B guests once in a while – usually in the winter when they had few bookings. The drive was about half a mile outside the village and difficult to find if you didn't know where it was. There was no sign and the lane was an old farm track, which had to be driven up cautiously because of the potholes. The way went through a park with ancient meadows that led down to the river. The house itself was covered in Virginia creeper and a large oak tree grew in the middle of the lawn beside the back door. At the moment a small ancient marquee took up most of the garden.

'How are Laura and the twins?' Daisy asked, leaning forwards, elbows on the table and her head cupped in her hands as she asked about Felicity's children.

'Laura's being Laura – dramatizing everything. Nothing trivial, just Mark working too hard and the au pair's stolen her best bra. Oliver's still suffering from unrequited love.'

'So nothing new there then? And what about Oscar?'

'He's taking great pleasure in annoying his father now he's "come out". Poor Henry's doing his best – it's not that he minds Oscar being gay – he just wishes he'd stay in. Now he's had his nipple pierced and I know he's only done it to aggravate his father. He's still in New York, but coming home soon. He's met this new chap – Barry.'

'What would you all complain about if you didn't have children,' Leo remarked to Rose as he got to his feet and left the room.

As soon as he had gone out Felicity turned to Rose and said, 'I didn't want to say anything in front of Leo in case it upset him, but I still can't believe it. Andrew and Sonia.'

By now Rose was standing at the sink sorting and washing a trugful of vegetables from the garden, but she turned round and faced Felicity. 'I can. Andrew's always been an arch shit. And we all know what Sonia's like. The point is, was it just a lunch or is it a liaison?'

'Who knows? But Venetia loves Andrew. Either way she's going to be desperately upset.'

'And he's quite sexy.' Daisy smiled as if in memory. She picked a copy of *Horse and Hound* off the table and began to thumb through it.

'Daisy. Really. Is that all you ever think about?' Rose took an eye out of one of the potatoes with a small, worn knife.

Felicity, wanting to be fair, added, 'Shit or not Andrew was super to the children when they were young.'

'Probably trying to borrow their pocket money. He's a bounder.' Leo made them jump as he spoke. He had come back into the room while they were talking. He was carrying a book in his hand as he wandered back towards his favourite old armchair. He was a tall, slim man, slightly stooped now in his seventies, but still with a thick head of white hair. Next to his chair in the corner of the kitchen he had created his own space where he had a small bookcase filled with reference books and a table with just room for a lamp and a mug of coffee or a glass on it. Rose smiled affectionately at him.

'You sweet, old-fashioned thing,' she said. 'What a lovely word. Bounder. Nobody says that any more.'

Felicity hesitated. After all Sonia was still married, even if only loosely, to Leo's brother Humphrey. She wasn't sure if she should continue.

But Daisy had no such scruples. She announced, 'Fifi saw Andrew lunching with your ghastly sister-in-law.'

Felicity looked at Leo with a worried frown and before he could speak she said, 'I'm sure he still adores Venetia. I can't believe he's having an affair.'

'How come you stayed so innocent? Andrew's been playing around for years.' Daisy giggled. 'Handy Andy, that's what we used to call him.'

'Daisy! I've always thought most of it was rumour. Anyway, you don't know he is having an affair. It may have been perfectly innocent.' Rose washed her hands briskly and wiped them on her dungarees and said with concern, 'He's frightfully thin. If he was a dog I'd say he had worms.'

'Is a worm more like, not got them,' Daisy snorted at her own joke.

'I shouldn't think Venetia feeds him much. She's always on some sort of diet,' Felicity interjected.

'And he's full of nervous energy,' Rose said.

'That's the strain of living with Venetia I imagine – enough to make anyone lose weight.' Leo shook his head and went back to his book.

If only that were true, thought Felicity, I'd move in with her tomorrow.

'How about Humph? Do you think he knows?' she asked Leo, who politely shut his book and carefully put in on the table before answering.

'Shouldn't think so. Lives in a world of his own. Not worldly like me,' he said finally.

Rose and Felicity exchanged glances. 'I'm not sure how much he cares any more. That marriage was a mistake from day one,' Rose said as she carried a bowl of vegetables across to the table.

'Can I help?' Felicity asked, knowing as she did so what the answer would be. 'I could top and tail the beans or chop the carrots.'

'Don't worry Possum, it'll be quicker if I do it.' As usual Rose competently and speedily started to deal with them. 'But you could just pop out and make sure there's not a bloodbath out there.'

'Right ho.' Felicity jumped to her feet and went out of the back door. 'Coming, dogs,' she called at the pile of recumbent labradors in their basket. One of them raised a lazy head and thumped his tail, but thinking better of it went back to sleep.

*

Outside in the garden all seemed calm. In fact it took Felicity quite a while to find anyone at all. First of all she walked over to the oak tree and stood in front of the long bare table. There were boxes of bric á brac stacked behind it waiting for Daisy and Felicity to set them out in the morning. She remembered last year. Everything had been all right then. Or so she had thought. She remembered it now and with hindsight, she must have been blind. Henry had been helping her set out the stall when Sally had teetered over on her unsuitably high heels.

'Oh, Felicity, you don't mind if I borrow Henry for a bit do you?'

'No. You take him, he's only getting in the way here.' As she thought about it she could hear the complacency that had been in her voice. Why had it not occurred to her that Henry's eyes might have been wandering, that he would fall for another woman's flattery?

'It's just that my car's making a funny noise. And I'm such an idiot about anything like that.'

Sally's voice purred in Felicity's memory. Henry had sprung into action and they disappeared for over an hour. She hadn't thought anything of it at the time. She took a deep breath, turned away from the table with all its memories, and walked towards the marquee. Inside a large trestle table was weighed down by an aluminium barrel of beer. Crates of clean glasses stood beside it. Across the tent another table covered in a white cloth held the tea urn. Felicity spotted Mrs Perkins, the Blighs' daily, bottom in the air polishing tea cups.

'Hello Mrs P. How are you?'

'Oh, Mrs Fox.' Mrs Perkins stood up and, straightening her back, gave Felicity a sorrowful look. 'Mustn't grumble. I was ever so sorry to hear about Mr Fox. Terrible shock, after all these years.' She wiped a cloth thoughtfully round a saucer. 'Must be lonely for you. I remember what it was like when Mr P passed away. It's all right for the young folk, but when you get to our age you can't expect another chance.'

Felicity wondered whether that expensive hairdo had been worth it after all. Mrs Perkins must be nearly seventy. However, she smiled as pleasantly as she could. 'I'm managing fine,' she said.

'Well you've got grandchildren haven't you, they'll be a blessing.'

'Just the one,' she tried to correct Mrs Perkins but she wasn't listening.

'It's all right if you look like Daisy, no problem getting a bloke then. Not quite the same for us. But Mr Fox's new friend's not a young lady, by all accounts. Probably looked after herself though.' She looked at Felicity narrowly, her piercing eyes taking in every wrinkle.

Felicity's lips were beginning to ache with the effort of keeping a pleasant smile on her face.

'Suppose you heard Dr Edwards's wife's left him.' She bent down to pick up another plastic tray of cups from behind the table and plonking them down she continued. 'No good thinking he'd do for you,' she chuckled malevolently, giving Felicity a sly look.

'I wasn't – ' Felicity interrupted, but she was.

'He's not really a ladies' man, if you catch my drift.' Mrs P was unstoppable. 'I told my Cynthia when I e-mailed her last week. It wouldn't surprise me if he was gay. Though gay's not the word I'd use. Gloomy old sod. Always has been.'

Felicity's nails were digging into her palms, so strong was her urge to slap the old woman. She sat down heavily on a red plastic chair.

'Still he was very good when Stan had Colin,' Mrs Perkins continued relentlessly.

'Colin?' Felicity asked, almost certain as she did so, that she wouldn't want to hear the answer.

'His colostomy bag – it was our little joke.' She grinned, exposing a set of dazzling white teeth that owed very little to nature.

Felicity remembered Stan Perkins quite well and all this was rather more information than she wished to know. She gulped and with a weak smile she made her escape before Mrs P got stuck into any more gruesome medical details. She made a quick inspection of the site for the bric á brac stall before she went back into the house.

'I don't know how you put up with Mrs Perkins. Awful old bitch.' Felicity sat down crossly.

'We couldn't get rid of Mrs P. She's been here for ever.' Daisy smiled the indulgent smile of the young and attractive. 'She's amazing, so up to date. She's learnt to use a computer, spends all her time e-mailing.'

'So now her evil tongue has an international arena. She told me Dr Edwards's wife left him 'cos he's gay.' Felicity sighed. 'All these marriages going wrong. This time last year everyone was so happy.'

'Apparently not that happy.' Daisy examined her finger-nails as Felicity glowered at her.

'That's my point, we thought we were happy, but there were all these undercurrents.' Felicity returned to the Venetia situation. 'What am I supposed to say to Netty?'

'Nothing, Possum,' Rose said firmly. 'You never say anything when something like that happens.'

'But I'll have to say something. She's my best friend.'

'Don't be silly. There's no point is saying anything unless you've got some proof that he is having an affair. Even if he is it could well blow over and you'll be the messenger that gets shot.' Rose's voice was sharp. Then she added more gently, 'Oh Fifi, I know you're upset, but telling her won't help. Even if they are sleeping together it may not amount to anything in the long run. I doubt it's the first time.'

'Venetia's so beautiful. How could he?'

Rose got to her feet and looked at the sorry remains of the carrots. She put her hand on Leo's shoulder and he looked up at her with a smile.

'Beauty can be very hard to live with,' he said, putting his hand on his wife's.

'Slightly back-handed compliment, but thank you my love.' And picking up the carrots she walked over to the oven.

'These are only fit for puree, I'm afraid. Terrible trouble with carrot fly this year.' She opened the oven door and a delicious aroma of cooking filled the room.

'Smells yummy. I'm starving. What time's supper?' Daisy asked.

'Are you and the boys staying? Wish you'd let me know. I'll have to do some more potatoes,' Rose said mildly as she disappeared into the larder.

'You don't mind do you? I forgot to go shopping and the boys are sick of baked beans.' Daisy smiled beseechingly at her sister as she returned with a basket full of potatoes.

'Don't worry, there's masses.'

Felicity looked at Rose in admiration. Nothing ever seemed to faze her. 'Let me peel those potatoes. You sit down. You must be exhausted.' Felicity got to her feet.

'Don't worry. I've only got those to do and the bread sauce.' Rose dismissed her with a wave of her hand. 'Of course, I blame slutty Sonia,' she continued as she tipped the potatoes into the sink and turned on the tap. 'She's had the roundest heels in the county since she was sixteen. Roll over onto her back for anyone.'

Leo glanced up with a look of resignation and then turned back to his book.

'Daisy, you were at school with her weren't you? I've just remembered,' Felicity asked while taking a radish from a bowl on the table and crunching it.

'Yeah. And she was frightfully over-sexed even then. Always trying to get us younger girls to look at her tits, we thought it was frightfully exciting. She had great tits. We were really jealous.' Daisy laughed.

'Then she came here as a girl groom. Only lasted about five minutes. Always trying to lure Leo into the stables. I wasn't having any of that,' Rose put in.

'I'd forgotten. I just remember when she ran off with Humph.' Daisy got to her feet and helped herself to a handful of radishes.

Leo looked up again at the mention of his brother's name. 'What's that?' he asked vaguely.

'We're still talking about Sonia.'

'Always been a slut. Can't think why Humph married her.' He went back to reading his book.

Rose shrugged her shoulders. 'I think we do know. Possibly something to do with those tits?' They all sat in silence for a while, remembering the great scandal when Sonia had left her husband to run away with Leo's younger brother when he'd only been widowed for six months.

A few minutes later the kitchen door flew open and two fair-haired and grubby boys came charging into the kitchen followed by a muddy border terrier. The larger of the two was hitting his brother with a stick. The smaller boy shrieked as he saw Daisy.

'Mum, Mum, save me. Tom's trying to kill me.' He darted behind his mother and stuck his tongue out.

'He was riding my bike.'

'Tom, Jono, just shut up. Go and wash your hands. We're staying here for supper.'

'Wicked. Can we watch a video?'

'All right, supper in half an hour.' One of the labradors got to its feet and wandered over to sniff the terrier's bottom.

'Why do dogs smell each others' bums?' Jono asked the room in general.

'It's their way of saying hello,' Leo remarked mildly as he turned a page of his book.

'Jolly glad we don't,' said Tim to his brother. 'I wouldn't want to sniff your bum.'

'Specially not if I had diarrhoea.' They both started to giggle helplessly.

'Or farted,' Leo suggested. They both ran out of the room with shrieks of laughter to watch a video.

'Really Leo. Why is it men never grow up? You're over seventy and still think farts are hilarious.' Rose shook her head in mock bewilderment as her husband settled back down into his armchair with a snort of mirth.

'Savages,' said Daisy affectionately as she turned to her brother-in-law. 'Talking of farting, Leo darling, can I have a glass of white wine? I always fart like mad after champagne.'

'You know where the cellar is.' Leo didn't look up from his book.

'But I'm exhausted,' Daisy wheedled.

'Surrounded by women. Nagged to death.' He heaved himself to his feet again and left the room.

Rose smiled at his back view then she turned to her cousin. 'Your hair looks great Fifi. What've you done to it?'

'Venetia sent me off to Roberto. After what Mrs P said I was beginning to regret it.'

'You were luckier than me. I didn't tell you that Venetia made me see him. About five years ago – he gave me a crew cut.' Rose pulled a face.

Daisy turned to her half-sister. 'You always look wonderful, except when you let Venetia bully you. You two, honestly! Whenever she calls you both jump.'

'She's on a mission to renovate me and find me a new man,' Felicity said sheepishly.

'Why do you need a man? Look at me. Great life, great kids, no man.'

'Well you've got Rose and Leo to help you.'

'What's that?' Leo came into the room carrying two bottles of wine. 'Couldn't remember if you wanted red or white so I brought both.'

'There,' said Daisy putting her arm round Leo. 'The only man in England worth having and he's married to my sister.'

Rose blew her husband a kiss. 'He's perfect most of the time,' she said. Then she turned to look at her sister. 'If you haven't got a man, why are you going to London for this so-called shag?'

'That's not a proper man. It's just a horizontal date. A bit of fun.'

'Horizontal date?' Felicity was puzzled.

'He's married – so we never do anything vertical.'

28

Felicity thought how much the world of dating and sex had changed since she had been out there, all those years ago. She didn't understand the rules now and she supposed she was going to have to learn them. Although it was difficult to imagine herself being horizontal with anyone except Henry.

*

'Morning Fifi. Ready for the fray?' Rose was at her usual post in the kitchen. She was looking tired and Felicity sometimes wondered if she ever slept. The smell of bacon frying sent all Felicity's resolutions out of the window and she allowed her cousin to pile her plate up. It was yet another glorious day and already there was a hive of activity in the garden. After a jolly family evening with Rose, Leo, Daisy and the boys Felicity felt much more cheerful and she had woken this morning ready to face the village. Upton was near enough to Hatch House so that most of the locals would have heard about Henry leaving her, and that made her self-conscious, but she was determined to rise above any pitying looks.

'You don't think Henry and Sally will turn up do you?' Felicity had a sudden horrible thought.

'No chance. Sally's dragged him of to Spain to play golf.' Daisy crammed a piece of toast into her mouth.

'Don't be silly,' Felicity laughed. 'Henry loathes golf. He's always refused to learn.'

'It's true, Oliver told me.'

'Well, I suppose he ought to know what his father's up to.'

'Poor old Henry.' Leo spoke for the first time from the depths of his newspaper.

'Poor Henry! Whose side are you on?' Felicity was indignant.

'Just wait. And remember that I said poor Henry.' Leo raised his magnificent bushy eyebrows.

Felicity didn't have time to think about what he said as the vicar arrived at that moment in a panic about the gate to the park. Last year someone had left it open and the Longhorns had got into the lane and it had taken the Sea Scouts almost an hour to get them all back. Leo got slowly to his feet and went off with the vicar to make sure that the gate was firmly padlocked.

'Fifi, you must wear a hat. It's going to be boiling and you'll get sunstroke if you're out in it all day. Grab one from the shelf by the back door.' Rose gave her an appraising look. 'Pretty skirt. I don't know why I never seem to have time to shop.'

Felicity smoothed her navy linen skirt with both hands. 'You don't think it's too tight over my bottom?' She twisted round to try and look over her shoulder.

'You're so lucky to have a proper bum.' Daisy patted her tiny jean-covered bottom. 'I've got nothing. Just like a boy.'

'Not quite, Possum,' said Rose dryly as she tried vainly to pin up escaped strands of hair. Then the three of them, all wearing suitably-old straw hats, went out into the garden.

'Don't let me forget to take Mrs Brocklebank over to see Phyllis Bide.' Rose paused to glance towards the drive. It was too early for any visitors. The fete wasn't due to open for a couple of hours, but already a steady stream of helpers' cars were bumping their way slowly up the drive.

'Who's Phyllis Bide?' Felicity wanted to know

'Not who, what. It's a rose and Mrs Brocklebank – '

'New arrival in the village. Fancies herself as a gardener,' Daisy interrupted to explain.

'As I was saying, Mrs Brocklebank hasn't got one and she's green with envy about mine.'

Felicity and Daisy busied themselves arranging the contents of the boxes on their stall. Every item had been meticulously labelled by Rose during the preceding week. Now all they had to do was set them out before everyone arrived.

Several hours later the garden was filled with people. The bric á brac stall had been doing a roaring trade and was practically empty. If Felicity attracted any pitying looks she made sure that she ignored them. Rose, as usual, was at the hub of everything. Felicity tried to ask Daisy if she thought her sister was all right, worried she might be overdoing things, but Daisy dismissed her fears.

'You know Rose,' she said, 'never happy unless she's busy.'

Felicity suspected Daisy had made it her mission to keep her in fits of giggles. She was being her usual irreverent self and kept up a running commentary about the lurid sex lives she imagined the oldest and most infirm inhabitants conducted behind closed doors.

'Poor little Mr Perkins, he had an awful time. Mrs P says that she told him on their wedding night that if he wanted any of *that*, he'd married the wrong woman. Apparently she doesn't hold with that sort of thing. Once Cynthia was born that was it.' Daisy stopped talking for a moment as she picked up a little glass cream jug for the umpteenth time and examined it. 'I wonder if I should buy this?' she asked and without pausing for an answer continued discussing the domestic life of the late Mr Perkins and his widow. 'She always said he had his ferrets. What he did with his ferrets, history doesn't relate.'

She was just in the middle of discussing the pros and cons of the organist's organ as compared to the Member's member, when a large, formidable woman approached the stall. She picked up a particularly hideous china ornament of a luridly painted fat child.

'I'm sorry,' Felicity said. 'We've hardly got anything left – only a few bits that no one wants.'

'Five pounds?' she said crossly as she held the ornament up in a gnarled gardener's hand.

'I'm sorry, but it is for the church. It's pretty horrible isn't it? Tell you what, I'll let you have it for two-fifty.' Felicity was amazed that anyone was interested in it at all.

'Two pounds fifty?' The woman's mouth snapped shut, then she took a deep breath. 'Where's the vicar? This is outrageous. It was made by my daughter. Her work sells for a great deal of money. Two pounds fifty pence!'

Felicity had never actually seen anyone bristle with rage until now. 'Oh Lord, I don't seem to be able to do anything right at the moment. I used to be a competent person,' she wailed.

Daisy put a comforting arm round her. 'I bet it's something to do with your aura, it's gone off its axis. Somebody told me about this amazing woman in Saffron Waldon who cleanses auras. I can find out and make you an appointment.'

'No thanks, Daisy. I think I'd better leave my aura alone for the time being.'

Happily for Felicity the vicar had a sense of humour and managed to placate the formidable lady. 'I'm afraid I had to tell her you were a temporary helper and a bit simple. Just a small white lie,' he said with a twinkle.

'Rather too near the truth for absolute comfort.' Felicity started to pack up the few remaining unsold items into a cardboard box.

CHAPTER 3

IT WAS THE MIDDLE OF THE AFTERNOON a few days later when Jane Bignall rang, but Felicity was curled up, fast asleep on the little chintz sofa, in front of the television.

'Jane here. Not disturbing you, am I?' The voice boomed as Felicity grabbed the telephone.

'No, not at all. I was ironing.' Felicity had woken with a start when she heard the telephone and lied automatically. Why on earth did she felt guilty about sleeping during the day? Surely at her age she was entitled to have a short rest if she felt like it.

'Had a terrible job getting your number. Timmy got it from Andrew in the end. Are you doing anything on Friday night?' Jane's voice was as loud and hearty as ever, jolting Felicity out of the last vestige of sleep. She rubbed her eyes and pushed a strand of hair behind her ear as she struggled into a more vertical position.

'Friday. No, I'm not doing anything,' Felicity admitted, her brain still fuzzy, and immediately regretted it; but how could she have asked for time to consider once she found out what Jane was proposing? Her friends kept telling her she must accept any and all invitations.

'Good, I want you to come to dinner. Make up for my bish the other day.'

'Oh, don't worry about that. I'd forgotten all about it. You caught me on a bad day,' Felicity said, lying yet again. She stifled a yawn as she tried to uncurl the telephone wire and wondered why she seemed to be tired all the time. Venetia said it was depression and that going to the gym would cure it.

'Didn't you have a crush on Sally Pelham at school?' Jane asked suddenly.

'I don't think so. I don't remember,' Felicity stammered. She knew it was too much to hope that everyone who had been at school with her would have forgotten her shameful secret, but she was damned if she was going to admit it to Jane, unless absolutely forced to do so.

'I was sure it was you. Wonder who it was then? I'm sure I'll remember if I think hard enough. Not surprising someone having a crush on her.'

'It was a long time ago.' Felicity said feebly.

'Sally was jolly attractive, still is. Oops, sorry! I mean you're attractive too. In a different way. Anyway, back to Friday, we've got a few friends over from Hong Kong,' Jane's voice boomed on. 'It should be rather jolly.'

Felicity's heart sank. She was pretty sure that her idea of a jolly evening was nothing like Jane's.

'Do you know Robin MacKenzie?'

'No.'

'Oh good. You'll simply love him.'

I'll be the judge of that thought Felicity ungratefully. After all it was kind of Jane to think of her.

'He's great fun, and,' she added conspiratorially, 'he's single.'

'Divorced, or widowed?' Felicity enquired.

'No. He's never been married.'

'Is he gay?'

'Lord no. Timmy can't abide poofs.'

'That's a pity. One of my sons is one.' Felicity couldn't help enjoying the gasp at the other end of the line. She could imagine Jane squirming.

'Oh dear, I'm so sorry.'

'I'm not – he's lovely.' She thought fondly of Oscar and how she wouldn't change him for the world.

Jane's voice continued on the other end of the line. 'No, sorry I said anything. Lummy, I've done it again. Can't help putting my foot in it with you, can I? So sorry, I'd no idea.'

Felicity accepted her stammered apologies but once she had put the telephone down she felt a sense of dread at the thought of the evening at the Bignalls. She knew how lucky she was to be asked to a dinner party. Everyone told her that single women of her age were a glut on the market and Jane was doing her best. But Felicity had an awful feeling she was being taken up as a cause. She could imagine Jane saying. 'Poor old Felicity, she's had such a ghastly time. I'm jolly well going to try and find her a man.'

It was humiliating. So stupid and unnecessary. She and Henry had been pottering along all right – after all they'd been married for over thirty years, it was hardly going to continue being love's young dream. But she hadn't thought they had any real problems. She hadn't noticed anything different. Then one day he'd announced he'd fallen in love with Sally Pelham. And somehow it only seemed to make matters worse that not only had she been older than Felicity at school, although now she claimed to be two years younger, but Felicity had had a crush on her. A fact that she had been trying hard to put out of her mind, but it was undoubtedly too much to hope Sally herself had forgotten. The embarrassment she felt was almost as bad as the hurt and the pain.

She wondered idly whether girls had crushes on other girls any more. Probably not – it was all pop idols and real boys by the time they were twelve. Anyone showing romantic feelings towards other girls would be forced to ring the gay and lesbian helpline. It had all been much more innocent in her youth. She could remember Sally's legs as she strode about the school stage as Mr Darcy, but her fantasies had not gone further than imagining a lot of poetry reading and gazing into each other's eyes. Felicity didn't discover what lesbians actually did until she was twenty-four.

She shook her head trying to drive painful images out of her mind. She heaved herself off the sofa. Sleeping there had made her stiff and she tried stretching and bending her shoulders back as she rolled her head round. She could feel the stiffness of old age in her joints. Perhaps Venetia was right and she should join a gym. She smoothed her skirt down and tucked her white shirt back into the waistband, although it seemed more reluctant than usual. Her neck ached; it was probably arthritis or bone cancer, she thought gloomily. She stumbled to the loo and while sitting on the seat looked at her reflection in the mirror. It occurred to her that maybe it was time to remove all the mirrors from the house, seeing the bedraggled face that stared back at her. Her mascara had smudged. The very expensive mascara she had bought last week to cheer herself up. The very expensive mascara that took about twenty minutes to remove at night, but which left her eyelashes and parked itself on her cheeks during a five minute kip on the sofa – well maybe half an hour, but it was still a swizz.

What was she doing with her life, she wondered. It all seemed so pointless. The children didn't really need her. They were kind, rang her and worried about her. But they had their own lives, which was just as it should be. When she'd been married there had never been time to sleep in the afternoon. There was always something to be done, B & B guests to be looked after, the garden, the dogs, even the chickens. All that was gone now. Was it surprising that she felt bitter? She still felt sick when she remembered the night Henry had left her.

There hadn't been a row or anything. But perhaps she should have noticed something was wrong. Certainly Henry had been out a lot, but she had presumed he'd been at the pub. And it was true Sally had rung up several times asking to borrow him for some little job or other. Frankly she'd been glad to get him out her hair, give him something to do and stop him moping round the kitchen, getting in her way. Then he'd announced out of the blue that he was in love with Sally.

After he'd told her she had sat in the kitchen in total disbelief while he went upstairs and packed. He'd come down quite calmly and just said 'Well I'll be off then, old girl.' And he walked out, without a backward glance. 'Old girl,' that had rankled. If that's how he'd thought about her, it was no wonder he'd left. She remembered sitting downstairs in the hall, in the dark, wondering what she felt. Hurt, angry, sad? Stunned was the only word that even came close to describing how she felt. It was as though instead of saying that he was leaving he had hit her over the head with a croquet mallet. She really hadn't seen it coming, how stupid was that? Right under her very nose.

Now what was going to happen to her? What would people say? It was so undignified. She realised she hadn't cried and wondered why not. Was she going to miss him? She didn't know. Was she going to kill him – it was a tempting thought. But how would she do it? Cut the brakes on his car? People in films did that all the time, but how did they know what to do? She could hardly ask Philip at the garage. Had he taken his shotgun? Perhaps it would be possible to shoot him. But Felicity would be the prime suspect and she was damned if she was going to prison for the bastard.

After that it had all been communicating formally through solicitors, discussing what to do with the house. They'd had to sell it, of course. The family home. Thank goodness both his parents were dead, they'd have been heartbroken about the house at least – it had been in the family for generations – if not the demise of their son's marriage. Felicity had felt she'd no choice but to move back to London and start a new life, when she'd been perfectly happy with her old one. But there would have been no point in staying in the area. She didn't think she could face the humiliation of her oldest friends asking her to a kitchen lunch and sheepishly asking Henry and Sally to their dinner parties. No one wanted single women in the evenings, at least not in the country.

Now she had agreed to have dinner with people she was sure she had nothing in common with. The more she thought about it the more certain she was that she had never liked Plum much even when they were at school together. It was going to be a terrible evening. It would have been nice to ring Venetia to discuss the whole thing, but since she had seen Andrew having that intimate lunch, she felt awkward every time she talked to her. She knew she shouldn't say anything, but she had to keep biting her tongue, and she was terrified of putting her foot in it. She wasn't used to keeping secrets from Venetia, but she had no choice. Instead she rang her daughter Laura.

'Hi, darling,' she said with a breeziness she didn't feel.

'Oh Mum, I'm so glad you've rung. I need someone to talk to. You've no idea how tiring Jamie's being at the moment.'

'I think I've got a pretty good idea,' her mother replied more crisply than she meant to, remembering the days when Laura was a toddler and the twins just born. She'd been hoping to discuss her own life with her daughter for a change. But she'd forgotten that parents weren't really people.

'He's spent all afternoon scribbling on his bedroom wall when he was supposed to be having a rest.' Laura was revving up to have a good moan.

'Oh dear, that's three-year-olds for you.'

'It's going to take Concepcion hours to clean it off.' Felicity lay back on the sofa. 'I've only just had his room decorated. And you know how long it took me to find the paper. I don't know if they'll have any more. It's a disaster.'

Possibly not on a world scale, were the words that came unasked into Felicity's mind, as she noticed the television screen flickering in the background showing images of a flattened city.

'Poor you,' she said in a soothing voice instead, wondering as she did so why she had even considered discussing her fears about the Bignalls' dinner party with her daughter.

'It's so exhausting, it takes so long explaining things to Concepcion that I might as well do it myself. And Mark's no help, he's never here when I need him. He's always at the bank.'

'They do pay his salary,' said Felicity mildly. 'Anyway darling, Jamie's going to nursery school next term. That'll give you a bit of a break.'

'Only in the mornings, and we're trying for another baby.'

'That's wonderful.' Felicity was genuinely delighted. It would be good for Jamie to have a brother or sister, although he probably wouldn't think so to start with.

'But we're both so exhausted – it'll be a miracle.'

'Would you like me to have Jamie for the weekend?' Felicity suddenly thought what a wonderful excuse that would be for not going to the Bignalls. Jane would understand that grandchildren took priority and as she didn't have any herself it would give Felicity a point-scoring opportunity.

'Thanks Mum, Concepcion's here. We're going out on Saturday night. Though when I'm going to have time to get ready I can't think.'

'That'll be fun.' Felicity was only half listening as Laura told her in detail what she would be wearing and who was likely to be there. Absently she twiddled with the cord of the telephone that had yet again got itself tied into knots. It was something she did to the wretched thing and it used to drive Henry mad. When her daughter had finally finished Felicity told her news.

'I've been asked to a party too, a dinner party. What do you think I should wear?'

'You've been asked to a party?' There was astonishment in Laura's voice.

'Don't you want to know whose dinner party it is?'

'Of course I do. That's exciting.'

'Not really – it's some people called Bignall. I was at school with her. Bumped into her in Peter Jones the other day.'

'Not Timothy Bignall?'

'Yes. I think that's her husband's name.'

'Wow! Mum! Wait till I tell Mark. He's really important – he ran the whole of Osgoods in Hong Kong. I didn't know you knew them.'

Felicity smiled, she didn't often impress her daughter. 'So what am I going to wear?'

'Why don't you wear your black dress? That always looks nice.' Felicity sighed. She had bought the famous black dress when Laura was about five and worn it continuously ever since. At moments of doubt she had trotted it out. But it was practically transparent under the arms by now and she very much doubted she would get into it. However, it did give her an idea. She would go shopping and find another black dress. Then she would ring Venetia in triumph when she had something to wear. Venetia always loved talking about clothes. Perhaps the Bignalls' dinner party wouldn't be that bad after all.

After she got off the telephone Felicity went upstairs to examine her wardrobe. She stood in the doorway of her little bedroom. The optimistic double bed was covered in a pale pink throw and piled high with white lace cushions. Henry liked the stripes and bold colours that reminded him of school. He probably imagined that if he slept in a frilly bedroom, he'd be asked to resign from his club. Now Felicity had the pastel and white bedroom she had wanted since she was a little girl. Only the curtains still to do and then it would be finished. She opened the doors of the fitted wardrobe and stood looking at its meagre contents in despair.

*

It should be quite easy, Felicity thought, as she lay in her bath the following morning. All she wanted was a simple little black dress to replace her old favourite. Something in a nice fine wool or silk jersey – a very forgiving fabric she always felt, nice and comfortable, and it wouldn't crease too badly. She had in her mind a picture of Joanna Lumley in a Jean Muir dress – that was the way she wanted to look. Well didn't everyone? Perhaps that wasn't realistic, Jean Muir was very expensive and even if there had been time she certainly couldn't afford the plastic surgery. She'd seen a programme about liposuction once and the thought of buckets of fat being removed from her inside, while quite appealing on one level made her feel very squeamish on another. No, what she wanted was a simple little dress falling to just below the knees, skimming her body, covering up a multitude of lumps and bumps. Even at her most optimistic she didn't believe she could lose a couple of stone by Friday. However, she would be starting her diet any day now. All the preparations were made. She had a fridge full of slimming food, plenty of raw vegetables – carrots and celery, skinless chicken breasts, and she had made a concerted effort to eat up all the biscuits and chocolate in the house. She was ready. And she was going to go to the gym – definitely – soon. She had a horrible feeling Venetia would see to that. Even so she had to admit she wasn't in great shape yet. Never mind, she was feeling positive and she would go out and buy herself a new dress.

Venetia had called her yesterday, she had heard somehow about the dinner party and she offered to come along on the shopping trip. Felicity had quickly refused; she had often been shopping with Venetia in the past. She was a wonderful friend, but a perfectionist, and she would have been prepared to spend several days finding exactly the right outfit. In fact she could remember many occasions when Venetia had turned down an invitation because she had nothing to wear. But she had to get something to wear by Friday. Besides which she was not sure that her more than usually fragile ego would be able to stand several hours of trying on one dress after another, being made to stand in front of Venetia and a shop assistant as they tugged at the clothes, pulling her this way and that, discussing her all the while. She would go alone. She got out of her bath and, wrapped in a towel, tried to select a shopping outfit. Something loose and cool – London shops were always too hot – easy to get in and out of, without ruining her hair. Her old button-through denim dress was perfect. Admittedly it didn't scream 'This woman has money to spend', but it would have to do.

Now where should she go? How much should she spend? What about accessories? She decided she would feel better if she made a list. She sat at her little Queen Anne desk, another refugee from Upton, and with a biro in one hand she stared at the notebook in front of her.

CLOTHES TO BUY she wrote in capital letters at the top and underlined it. She sucked the end of the biro for a while until she realised it was leaking. She went to the kitchen sink and washed the ink off her mouth and carrying another cup of coffee she returned to work. Underneath the heading she wrote 1 black dress, then she added a question mark. Did it really have to be black? After thinking for a moment she crossed out the question mark. Next she wrote 1 pair black suede shoes – small heel. Underneath that she added 1 black suede evening bag – small, and 1 pair black tights – 15 denier. She mentally added up what she thought this would cost. It should be quite affordable and it all looked very efficient.

Underneath that she wrote another heading SHOPS. Again she underlined it and then wrote Peter Jones, Harvey Nichols, Harrods. Then she crossed out Harrods – she had a feeling only foreigners went there now. Well, that was great and shouldn't take long. She would just pop over to Sloane Street and Knightsbridge; the whole thing would probably take no more than a couple of hours. Feeling organised and efficient she set off early the next day.

*

'I really don't understand it,' she said to Venetia on the telephone that evening. 'I fully intended to buy a black dress, but I seem to have come home with a pink one.' There was a sharp intake of breath from the other end of the phone.

'It's very pretty,' said Felicity hastily.

'What shade of pink?'

'Sort of bright – shocking I think you'd probably call it.'

'Shocked more like, with your colouring.'

'That's what I thought, but the girl in the shop said that's just old-fashioned. Redheads do wear pink. There's that model, very famous, Karen something.'

'Exactly. Now I've no wish to be unkind, but we have to face facts. Redheads with flawless, porcelain complexions, not blotchy old bags like you, can wear pink.'

'I thought you didn't wish to be unkind.' Felicity voice was waspish.

'It's for your own sake. I wouldn't be your friend if I didn't tell you the truth.'

Friends, especially very old friends, were sometimes a bit too liberal with the truth. Felicity thought that reassuring lies would have been a better option. After all she was just about to face her first solo dinner party.

'What are you going to wear with it?' Venetia changed the subject.

'I was going to buy some black suede court shoes.'

'I'm hearing a but there.'

'High-heeled strappy silver sandals!'

'I've a nasty feeling you're not joking.'

Felicity looked at the carrier bags lying on her bed. The sales girl had been very persuasive – perhaps not surprising in retrospect. Into her mind crept a picture of the girl punching the air and crying, 'YES – I finally sold it!' as Felicity left the shop with the pink dress. Lying bitch, she thought as she remembered her, so sweet and charming, such balm to Felicity, who was exhausted after trailing round what seemed like every shop in London. Her feet were hot, sore and swollen, her hair dishevelled and her face shiny and red. Not the best circumstances for trying on clothes. In the cold light of day she realised she should have retired hurt and started again in the morning.

'Of course we'll have something to fit you. You're not fat, just well built, but well proportioned. How about this? No, it isn't black, but pink is the new black – everyone's wearing it this season … No, it's not tight, it's fitted … that's how they're wearing them this year … it really suits you … not everyone could carry that colour off.' And of course Felicity had carried it off; in a shiny black bag. She was so relieved to have found someone to help her that she happily wrote a cheque for an unbelievable amount. She very much doubted that she would have been able to buy the carrier bag on its own for £150. Then the shoe shop – low-heeled black suede court shoes were

44

apparently not being made this year, certainly not in the civilised world. Of course the sandals would look miles better when worn with a perfect pedicure and not the borrowed grey pop-sock with a ladder in it, and of course she had to have a silver bag to match. Thank goodness she had drawn the line at silver sparkly tights.

By the time she got home she was totally drained. She used to enjoy her bi-annual trips to Cheltenham to replenish her wardrobe. Quiet little shops where the sales assistants were motherly women with ample bosoms who understood that not everyone could be a size ten. Clothes had never been a priority in her life and since she'd been running the house as a B & B she had lived in jeans. They didn't go out much in the evenings, but she had a long velvet skirt and of course the faithful friend, the old black dress which could be trotted out when they went to a dinner party. Their friends' houses were usually so cold that a long skirt was ideal – you could wear thermals underneath. Also everyone knew her in the country, so it didn't really matter what she wore. It was different in London, she had to try and make an impression, and she had a horrible feeling she was going to make one in that pink dress.

*

Felicity allowed herself plenty of time to get ready for the dinner party. The bathroom was her favourite room in the house. Soft apple green tiles on the walls and a blind covered in dog roses gave it a relaxing feel, but even better was the fact that, for the first time in her life, she didn't have to share it with anyone. There were no dirty socks lying accusingly on the floor, no damp towel thrown onto the chair. Felicity poured herself a scented bath, filled with her favourite Floris stephanotis bath oil and lay there for a long time. She washed her hair, dried it carefully and then brushed it till it gleamed. She had already laid her clothes out on the bed. She played soothing music and lit a scented candle. She was doing her best to convince herself that everything was going to be fine. She looked at the medicine cabinet for the third time, wondering whether to take a valium. It might help, but it probably wasn't a good idea. After all she was only going to a dinner party, not about to jump out of a hot air balloon. It was ridiculous to be so nervous. Being divorced wasn't anything to be ashamed of, not these days. She would have to face the evening cold turkey. Well, not quite.

She went downstairs and poured herself a large gin and tonic, which she took back up to her bedroom. She carefully dried, powdered and scented her body and stepped into the expensive, underwired Rigby and Peller bra that Venetia had forced her to buy. Next the tummy control lycra pants, next the pink dress. She turned to examine herself in the full-length mirror.

'Oh fuckadoodledo,' she exclaimed. She looked ridiculous. The bright pink dress matched her bright pink face and clashed with her red hair. Altogether setting off the hot flush nicely. And the sleeves were so tight she'd have to spend the whole evening with them clamped to her side. At least she wouldn't be able to eat much. As for those stupid pants – they pulled her stomach in all right, but it had to go somewhere and that great roll coming over the top wasn't a good look. One thing was certain, she was never going to have sex again. If Robin the bachelor wasn't already gay Felicity was sure that one look at her in her underwear and he certainly would be. She remembered buying it with Venetia and how they had giggled.

'The young think this is a revolutionary new garment, but don't you remember panty girdles?'

'Remember them? They were the only form of birth control we had. There was no way you'd ever let anyone see you getting out of one of those.'

'The only difference is that now they've invented lycra you don't dislocate your thumbs every time you pull them on.'

Felicity noticed that her glass was nearly empty. Oh well, she thought, as she stared at herself in the magnifying mirror. I'd better try putting a face on and see if that helps. She decided another gin and tonic might help settle her nerves. A bit more Dutch courage. Why Dutch courage, did the Dutch talk about English courage?

Back upstairs again she couldn't make up her mind whether it was better to get herself together in a dim light and hope that everyone else would have poor eyesight, or to use the full horror of magnification. Risking the big mirror she found one of those mysterious long hairs growing out of her chin. How did they get there? She could swear it hadn't been there yesterday, but now it was a good half an inch long. If one could work out why, just think what a boon it would be on the head. After several minutes of dabbing and patting the contents of various pots and tubes onto her face she sighed.

'That'll have to do.' She dragged her brush through her hair one last time and turned away from her unsatisfactory reflection. At least when she'd been young, the look might not have been perfect but she didn't actually make people wince, which she felt she might tonight.

'Here we go,' she said to herself with all the enthusiasm of someone on the way to the scaffold, and picked up her car keys from the kitchen table. Why had she agreed to have dinner with Plum? She must have been mad or more probably desperate. The first dinner party she had been to since the rat deserted the sinking ship. She was fed up trying to convince herself it might be fun. People said you often enjoyed parties you didn't want to go to. She hoped it would be true tonight, but she couldn't help looking longingly at her little house. She would have preferred to stay here, tucked up on the sofa with a glass of wine and a good book.

Half an hour later she had parked her car outside their door and was standing inside the Bignalls' drawing room. It was a bland but pretty room in shades of pale apricot. A large vase of lilies stood on top of a baby grand piano, amongst silver photo frames and enamel boxes. Felicity thought that if she had to imagine Jane's drawing room she would have pictured it exactly like this. Now for the guests. She smiled brightly as Jane made the introductions.

'This is Tim.' A fair man, with sandy eyebrows and a ruddy complexion bounded forward as though he was about to catch a cricket ball. His open-necked shirt exposed a tuft of reddish brown hair and freckles.

He held out a large hand, grabbed Felicity's and shook it hard. 'You were at school with Jane? Jolly good.' He made a loud snort, like a pig on a truffle hunt. It took Felicity a moment to realise he was laughing. He waved a bottle of sparkling wine in front of her. 'Fizz?' he asked.

'Lovely,' said Felicity as she squinted at the label and wished she had the courage to ask for another gin and tonic. As soon as she had a glass in her hand Jane grabbed her arm and propelled her across the room.

'This is Robin MacKenzie,' she announced, introducing Felicity to a pale round man with wispy grey hair and watery blue eyes and skin that had the pink untouched look of a newborn baby.

'Robin's the bachelor, the one I told you about,' Jane hissed loudly in her ear, and turning to Robin continued in her normal, loud voice. 'Poor Felicity, her husband's just done a bunk.' Robin looked at Felicity as though he wasn't at all surprised by this piece of information.

Felicity stood, glass in hand, frozen. After that introduction, she couldn't think of a single thing to say. It was ridiculous; she had never had a problem in the past. Why should being minus a husband make her a social outcast? Robin wasn't helping. He asked her if she had ever been to Hong Kong and when she said she hadn't, he turned towards the other guests.

There were two other couples there. One pair had been in Hong Kong with Tim and Jane.

'Heard about Dinks? Run off with an Indian.'

'Good Lord. Poor old Starchy.'

'Some maharajah – she's covered in jewels. Even got her own elephant.'

'In Hong Kong?'

'No, Jaiphur.'

'Strordinary. What about Pots?'

'Bit of bad luck. Quack's warned him off the gin.' And so on.

Felicity tried to fix a grin on her face but soon gave up the attempt. She knew none of these people and if their current conversation was anything to go by she would try to make sure she never would. Mentally berating herself for being a snob, she turned to the other couple who were in London for a couple of nights' break from Scotland. Felicity had at least been there so she felt it might be possible to talk to them, certainly easier than standing with a fixed smile on her face listening to the others gossiping about Hong Kong.

'How's Scotland then?' she asked a toothy woman who she thought was called Cynthia.

'All right apart from the gnats.'

'They are ghastly aren't they? I was bitten to death last time I was up there.'

'Oh I say. Jolly witty,' said her husband, whose name was Angus.

'Witty?'

'Cynthia was talking about those ghastly Scot Nats. Scottish Nationalists.'

'Oh – I thought she was talking about ... never mind.' Felicity gulped her champagne.

Angus continued. 'I simply don't know about shooting Grice this year.'

'Who's Grice – is he a Scottish Nationalist?'

'Hwa, hwa, hwa, jolly amusing. Grice, glorious twelfth, little brown birds. Know what I mean?'

'Oh grou ... grice, right.' Was it possible that grice was the plural of grouse, like mice?

'Where's your hice?'

'Hice?'

'Where d'you live?'

'Oh my hou ... hice. In Battersea.'

'That's nice.'

It was no good. Felicity couldn't deal with any more of this. They obviously thought she was either simple or deaf. She held out her glass for Tim to fill it and turned back to her date, Robin. Desperation putting words in her mouth, she managed to come out with the stunningly original 'Have you been in Hong Kong a long time?' He gave her a bored look as he answered and Felicity decided he was unattractive and rude so she wouldn't bother any more.

The other three women were all wearing a variation of the same theme. Silk brocade jackets over black skirts. Felicity felt extremely out of place and over-dressed in her shocking-pink dress, which was getting tighter by the minute and beginning to feel extremely uncomfortable. Netty was right. She must start going to the gym. And diet too. God it was boring being overweight. Jane was enormous, of course, but she didn't seem to care, and the other two women were pin thin. What was it her mother used to say, 'After forty you've got to choose face or figure.' Perhaps it was true. The woman who'd been in Hong Kong – Angela – had a pale, dry skin that was covered in fine lines like an ordnance survey map. Felicity doubted that being fatter would help. But there was a happy medium and she hadn't achieved that.

'How's your glass?' Tim was at her side bottle waving.

'Oh goody. Yes, please.' Oh goody? Where had that expression come from? She certainly hadn't used it since she was at school. Still one thing about Tim, he was an excellent host. Glasses were replenished as soon as they were half empty. On second thoughts Robin wasn't that bad looking, quite attractive really. Perhaps it wasn't going to be such a ghastly evening after all.

CHAPTER 4

IN THE END IT HAD BEEN A TERRIFIC PARTY. The other guests might not have been very exciting, but they had loved her. She had really sparkled. By the end of the evening they were all hanging on her every word, hardly uttering themselves. Arriving home in a whirl, she realised there was nothing to this social lark. She undressed, flinging her clothes lightheartedly onto the floor, jumped into bed and lay there trying to remember her many witticisms.

It was several hours later when she woke up. She glanced through half-closed eyes at the clock radio beside her bed and saw that it was nearly ten o'clock. She sat up in bed. That was a mistake. Sleep had changed everything. Her head felt as if there was someone climbing up inside it using crampons and a pick, the inside of her mouth tasted as if a small furry rodent had crawled in there and died. She urgently needed a glass of water so she staggered out of bed.

She caught sight of herself in the bathroom mirror and screamed. That was a mistake as the sound reverberated inside her head. But the sight in the mirror was very upsetting. She had gone to bed, as far as she knew, looking like a human being. Granted, she had failed to take off her makeup and the vestiges of it clung to her face in a curious patchwork effect. There were black smudges under her eyes and on her cheeks, but even that didn't explain why it looked as though some sadist had crumpled her skin up into a ball and had the creases badly ironed into it. Her hair looked like a disintegrating bale of hay. If she'd been a dog she would have dosed herself with a conditioning powder. Were there such things for people? Thank God they didn't still have witch-hunts – she'd have been burnt before lunch. She bent down to find an

Alka Seltzer or at least some aspirin in the cupboard under the basin. A rush of blood to the head necessitated her sitting on the floor grovelling for some sort of pill.

'Drugs,' she moaned, 'why aren't there any drugs when I need them?' She pulled out tubes and small jars. A tube of athlete's foot cream – when had anyone in her family last had athlete's foot? Why hadn't she sorted things when she'd left Upton? She'd do it now. Perhaps not. She'd think about doing it after she found an aspirin, several aspirin. Suppositories for haemorrhoids – years past their sell-by date. Boxes of sticking plaster all containing that curiously shaped one that she never knew what to do with. Aspirin! Where were they? Aha. Andrews Liver Salts – they'd do.

She pulled herself up on her knees and fumbled on top of the basin for the tooth mug. She tipped out her toothbrush and toothpaste and, ignoring the grey sediment in the bottom of the glass, she prised open the lid of the tin. She tipped some into the glass, then tipped some more. She added water. Whoa – it was fizzing all over the place. She put her tongue out and licked the foam that poured over the side of the glass. Still sitting on the bathroom floor she shut her eyes and rested her head against the bathroom cupboard.

Her head fell forward as she tried to remember what had happened last night. Mercifully it all seemed a bit vague at the moment. She hoped she hadn't driven home – she thought she could vaguely remember a taxi. She'd have to leave the car for a bit – there was no way she could drive yet – she would be way over the limit. Through the fog inside her head she had a picture of herself trying to fight her way out of the pink dress. She opened one eye and could see it lying in a crumpled mess on the floor of the bedroom, one sleeve hanging off. Of the silver sandals there was no sign.

Felicity had never been much of a drinker, but her new situation made her nervous. She had drunk far more than she usually did, nerves making her gulp when it would have been wiser to sip. What she had thought of as her fascinating and witty conversation of last night turned out in the cruel light of day to be nothing more than the drunken, repetitious babbling of a woman who was old enough to know better. Surely after fifty women were supposed to be growing old gracefully, not getting drunk at dinner parties? No wonder everyone had been silent, they had been stunned. Oh dear, she would have to bite the bullet and ring Jane to apologise and make sure the car was all right. She sat in a stupor trying to remember the details of the dinner party. It was horribly vague, but she felt herself going hot and cold by turns. She had a feeling it was going to turn out to be mortifying. No doubt Jane would be happy to fill in the gory gaps in her memory.

Once she had drained the tooth mug she struggled to her feet and, wrapping her cotton dressing gown round her, she searched for her slippers. Slipping them on she shuffled downstairs, looking and feeling like a very old woman. She could still remember the days when she could party all night and wake up looking fresh-faced and bright-eyed. But that had been years ago, not any more. Like an automaton she gathered the post from the mat, made a jug of coffee and sat at the kitchen table praying that her head and stomach would soon return to normal. Suddenly the telephone rang and she jumped, her heart banging in her chest making her feel she might have a heart attack at any minute. She put her hand out quickly to stop the dreadful noise.

'Hello,' she croaked.

'Hi, Mum? That you? You sound awful. It's me. Oscar.'

'Darling, when did you get back?' Felicity roused herself from her hungover torpor.

'Last night. I did ring but you were out.'

'Don't remind me,' Felicity groaned. 'I've got an appalling hangover.'

'Mum. I'm shocked. Hope it was worth it.' Oscar laughed.

In spite of herself, Felicity felt better. Oscar always had that effect on her. Of all her children he was the one she felt closest to. There were great advantages in having a gay son; it was like having an extra best friend. He had been working in New York for nearly a year and now he was back. She couldn't help feeling a surge of optimism; surely life was about to take an upward turn.

'When am I going see you?'

'How about lunch today?'

Felicity hesitated for a moment. Much as she longed to see him she wanted to look her best, or at least better than she looked at the moment. 'Supper tonight would be better.'

'OK – see you about eight. All news then. Bye Mum.'

As soon as she put the telephone down Felicity got herself into first gear. Pouring another cup of coffee she went upstairs to have a shower. Hangovers were mostly in the mind she thought, as she rubbed herself vigorously with a towel. It's mind over matter she tried to convince herself as she brushed her hair, wincing as she did so. Why should drinking too much make your hair hurt? Had there been any research on this she wondered idly, as she stood vacantly in front of her fitted wardrobe trying to find something to wear. It wasn't that there was a big choice, more that her brain wasn't engaging. Finally she selected an old friend, a faded cotton skirt with a comfortable elasticated waist. She could hear Venetia's voice in her ear as she did so. 'Elasticated waists are the beginning of the end.'

'Bugger that,' she said to the air as she took a blue and white checked shirt from the cupboard, then she slipped her feet into a pair of her favourite navy blue, low-heeled court shoes. Next she put some moisturiser on her face, and as she felt her pores sucking it in, she slapped some more on, but her skin still felt dry and parched. She dabbed some foundation on top, which didn't seem to make much difference. She added some more, but the result wasn't very attractive. If they could put the whole of the Encyclopaedia Britannica onto a CD why couldn't they make an industrial strength foundation that actually stuck to the skin and covered up all the red veins and bags, without making you look like a pantomime dame?

*

Felicity held her breath as she rang the doorbell of Jane Bignall's house a few hours later clutching a large bouquet of flowers. With any luck, she thought, they would be out, and she would be able to leave the flowers with a card thanking them for a delicious dinner and apologising for drinking too much of Tim's excellent wine. Unfortunately, moments after she rang the bell Jane appeared, larger than life and twice as noisy.

'Frumpy!' she exclaimed heartily. Never, Felicity thought, had the name been more appropriate. 'How you feeling this morning? Bit fragile?'

'Me? No, I'm fine,' Felicity lied, wondering why she bothered as it was unlikely Jane would believe her. In any case, fragile was not really the word that best described the feeling of someone sitting on top of her head trying to drive spikes into her skull with a mallet. Fragile was a delicate and attractive word, which brought to mind fine porcelain, not a badly hungover woman well past her prime.

'Come and have a coffee. Timmy's on the golf course as per usual.'

Felicity reluctantly followed Jane into the house. She didn't have the strength to resist, her wit was too dulled to think of a suitable excuse. She was juddering already with the amount of caffeine she had drunk in order to try and feel a bit more human. But Jane was like a steamroller flattening everything in her path. Now she marched purposefully ahead of Felicity into the kitchen. It was a light airy room, filled with sunlight that made Felicity reach into the depths of her bag for her dark glasses.

'Plonk yourself down there.' Jane pointed to a stool at the breakfast bar. The kitchen itself was immaculate. The white counters were spotless and the blue and white tiled floor likewise. Jane went to the cupboard and removed two blue and white flowery mugs, which exactly matched the colour and pattern of the kitchen blind, and Jane herself was wearing a blue cotton shirt-dress. Felicity, who was also wearing blue and white, felt that her red hair created the only discordant note in this perfectly co-ordinated room. Plum had been just the same at school, her crayons carefully colour graded in their case.

'Thank you so much, it was a lovely evening, super food.' Felicity sipped her coffee.

'Glad you got home safely – you were pretty squiffy when you left.'

'Tim's a marvellous host. Hope I didn't behave too badly.' Felicity stirred her coffee making it swirl in the mug.

'Don't worry – I explained that Henry had done a bunk, left you for another woman. Poor you – I'm sure they understood.'

Felicity winced. She tried not to imagine the post-mortem after she had been poured into a taxi.

'Robin was very … um … charming.' Felicity felt duty bound to comment on her potential date.

'I'm afraid you scared him. Just a teeny bit of advice.' Jane lowered her voice and leant forward confidingly. 'I'm not sure female circumcision is a good topic of conversation for a dinner party, particularly when you don't know the other guests.'

Felicity gulped and then felt a blush rising up her neck.

Jane held out a plate of biscuits. 'Never mind, you're probably out of practice with chaps. They like a girl to be feminine.'

Felicity could scarcely believe her ears, this was the way her mother had thought. 'It was an article I read in the hairdressers,' she tried to say by way of explanation.

'It's not just that, Frumpy. You sang *The Good Ship Venus*. Tim says it's a rugger song.'

'But I can't sing.' Felicity was mortified.

'I think you're missing the point, although you were completely out of tune, but you certainly knew an awful lot of the words. And very disgusting words they were.'

'Henry taught them to me years ago. How embarrassing. I'm so sorry.'

'Let's just forget it, but one other thing. Please don't call my husband Dim. It's not funny and it's not true.'

Felicity put her head in her hands. It was worse than she had imagined. As Jane spoke she was getting flashbacks of the whole terrible evening. 'Oh, Jane, I'm grovelling. I don't know what to say. Just sorry again I suppose.'

'Don't worry,' Jane was magnanimous. 'I'm not giving up on you. I'll keep searching around, sure to find someone. Timmy's always meeting men at the golf club. We'll arrange another party. Better go a bit slower on the old vino next time.'

Felicity gritted her teeth. However badly she'd behaved she hated being patronised. Obviously Jane thought anything in trousers would do for her desperate friend.

As she talked Jane was taking pristine, gleaming silver out of a drawer and polishing it. Felicity thought of her own tarnished knives and forks that were stuffed into the back of a cupboard. She'd certainly let her standards slip since she'd moved to London.

'Gosh, I wish you'd come round and clean my silver,' she joked. Wondering as she did so why words like 'gosh' and 'goody' always came out of her mouth when she spoke to the Bignalls.

'Really,' Jane turned to her with the eager expression of a labrador puppy. 'I will if you like. I love cleaning silver.'

'Only joking.' Felicity didn't think her house would stand a cleaning assault by Jane.

'I wouldn't mind. I really don't have enough to do,' she confided, rubbing away at an already sparkling fork. 'Always been a pretty busy person. Never stopped in Hong Kong. We did a lot of entertaining, had so many people to stay.' She breathed vigorously onto the handle of a knife and started to polish it with a cloth. 'Now Timmy's retired he plays golf – morning, noon and night. Children have all left home.' She stopped her polishing for a moment to examine her face in the knife's spotless, silver blade. 'I've done everything I can to the house.' Her shoulders drooped.

'How about getting a job?' Felicity felt herself relax slightly as Jane seemed to be showing a more human vulnerable side.

'Oh no. I don't think so. Getting a bit old for that. I haven't had a job for years and I don't think Timmy would like it. He likes me to be here for him when he gets home.'

'And what about what you'd like, why does it have to be about what he wants?' Felicity was surprised by Jane's pre-feminist attitude, as much as she was surprised by how strongly she felt. She had looked after Henry for all those years and where had it got her. Besides, she had imagined that London women were much more advanced.

'Call me old-fashioned, but I did promise to obey,' Jane said primly, giving Felicity a look that implied if she'd only had been a bit more obedient she might have kept her own husband.

'Anyway, I'm on a few charity committees, that sort of thing. They keep me fairly busy. I'll soon get back into the swing, only a question of time. Just at a bit of a loose end at the moment.' So that was why she had time to meddle in other people's lives. 'But it'll be fine,' she continued, 'I'm just out of touch with all my old chums. There's a school reunion coming up. Be fun to go to that, wouldn't it?'

Felicity thought she'd rather lie down in front of a moving train than face all her old schoolfriends at this moment in her life, particularly if accompanied by Jane and her sotto voce explanations to everyone about Henry's departure.

'I'd like a job, but I can't think who'd employ me,' Felicity persisted, not sure she did want one, but it seemed a safer topic of conversation than her behaviour of the previous night.

'When did you last work?'

'Paid work? Not since before I was married.' Felicity took a sip of coffee from the blue and white mug. Looking round the kitchen she saw a DIY catalogue lying on the counter. 'I read somewhere that B & Q employ older people, perhaps I could get a job there.'

'Don't be ridiculous. You'd never meet any nice men there.'

'I wasn't really thinking about a job as a way to meet men. But I don't think it would be any good, I don't know one end of a screw from another.' And that's almost true she thought. 'But if I'm supposed to try and meet men, perhaps I should get a job in a garage.'

'Being flippant all the time is something most people grow out of.'

Jane was getting cross now, and Felicity knew she should keep her mouth shut, but she couldn't help herself. 'Sorry,' she said insincerely. 'Force of habit, I'm afraid.'

'You could try somewhere like a flower shop. Loads of men buy flowers.'

'And I could look at the cards and see who'd been widowed recently – get in early.'

'Now you're just being plain stupid. It's no good becoming hard and bitter. Chaps don't like that.' Jane started replacing the silver with a lot of clattering.

'Why's it all about what the man wants, what about what I want?' Felicity's head hurt and she wanted to get out of this house. The conversation was beginning to take a rather unsatisfactory turn.

'At your age you can't afford to be too choosy.' Jane looked smug, safe in the knowledge that even if her life wasn't exactly as she would like it to be, she did at least have a husband.

'I don't think I can afford not to be.' Felicity resolved not to come to any more of the Bignalls' dinner parties. If Robin was the best they could do and Jane thought any man would do, she must definitely refuse any more invitations.

'It's all right, I understand.' Jane leant across the table and patted Felicity's hand sympathetically. 'It's been a difficult time for you. But time is a great healer.'

'And time wounds all heels, with any luck,' Felicity said through clenched teeth as she hurriedly got to her feet. She had to get out before she hit Jane. 'Got to go,' she muttered and adding the words 'Peter Jones' like a mantra she fled the house.

CHAPTER 5

FELICITY SANK DOWN ONTO VENETIA'S luxurious cream sofa with a sigh. 'What a ghastly day I've had,' she said.

Venetia reluctantly brought her a cup of strong black coffee. She didn't really approve of caffeine, but she was prepared to indulge Felicity who still looked in need of something.

Felicity sipped it gingerly. At this rate she'd never sleep again. She was no longer sure if she had a hangover or if she was jangling from drinking so much coffee. Venetia poured herself a glass of still mineral water and lit a cigarette, which Felicity knew she didn't approve of either, but until she could be assured that giving up wouldn't make her fat she allowed herself to smoke. As Felicity relaxed back on to the cushions Venetia stood in front of a large gilded mirror that hung between the two windows and examined herself minutely. She turned this way and that tugging at her beige and coffee checked Armani jacket.

Then she turned to Felicity. 'You look terrible,' she said in a conversational tone.

'Thanks, but not as bad as I deserve to feel.'

'That skirt.' Venetia made a disapproving face. 'The one that Oxfam rejected I presume.'

'Don't scrutinise me today. I can't face it.'

'On the bright side, the skirt draws the eye away from your face.'

'If I had the energy I'd throw a cushion at you.' Felicity laughed and then groaned at the effort.

'What happened?'

Felicity gave a brief account of the dinner party as far as she could remember it then she said, 'I had to go round to collect my car from outside the Bignalls' house. I was far too drunk to drive home last night. Honestly, how could I have allowed myself to get into that state?'

'Born again single nerves, I imagine. It must be pretty hard having to strike out on your own.' Venetia gave a sympathetic look and a half smile, but Felicity felt that her mind was on something else.

'I took some flowers round. I was hoping the house would be empty. Unfortunately Jane was there, larger than life, booming away. Horrible expression eating humble pie, but I think that's what I did.' Felicity winced and then continued, 'It was pretty grim.'

Venetia, who had been pacing about the room restlessly moving ornaments from one place to another, paused and spoke. 'What did you wear in the end?'

'The pink dress. And yes, you were right. Of course. It was a very expensive mistake.'

Venetia grinned for the first time and raised her eyebrows. 'You notice I'm not saying anything.'

Felicity looked at her gratefully, and putting her cup down on the table continued, 'Jane gave me an understanding talk about being squiffy. She told everyone what a sad, pathetic person I am.' Felicity paused. 'Do you think I've got a drink problem?' She looked at Venetia waiting for her to say something. By now Venetia was fiddling with her hair, tucking it behind her ears. It occurred to Felicity that her friend was very restless this afternoon.

But then she turned round and said sharply, 'Don't be ridiculous. Of course you haven't. I drink far more than you. That's probably the problem, you don't drink enough, haven't got the tolerance.'

Felicity, who was so full of caffeine by now that she was past caring, poured herself another cup of black coffee from the cafetiere and sighed. 'Honestly, it was awful. She was feeling sorry for me. I can't bear it.' She closed her eyes, remembering the full horror of it. 'Then she told me I'd frightened the bachelor.'

'What'd you do? Stick your tongue down his throat?'

'Good God, I hope not. He wasn't at all attractive, sort of white, doughy and sexless. I think he thought I was a frightful drunken old bag and ran a mile. But I've a nasty feeling that at one point I gave his knee a saucy squeeze.' Felicity gave a small shudder. 'Oh, fuckadoodledo – how embarrassing.' She picked up one of Venetia's beige silk scatter cushions and covered her face. Venetia forced a small laugh and came to sit down beside her. Felicity removed the cushion from her face and sipped her coffee.

'Sometimes I wish I still smoked,' she said. 'Unfortunately Jane hasn't given up, finding a man for me that is, not smoking. It's like a crusade. I think she's bored. Tim plays golf all day. She's on a couple of charity committees helping autistic dogs or something, but she hasn't enough to do. She'll probably drag me off to AA next.'

'Don't be so wet. Just say no,' Venetia said impatiently.

'She's such an exhausting person, I haven't the energy to resist, you've no idea how easy it is to end up agreeing with her suggestions.' Felicity leant back on the sofa and looked round the room. She would never manage to have a place like this. There was no clutter here at all. Every surface was clean, and empty. Above the fireplace were a few smart invitations and on the coffee table a couple of heavy and expensive books of photographs. It was a wonderful, calm flat and Felicity always found it soothing, if a bit sterile. It was difficult to imagine that people actually lived here, with its air of waiting to be photographed.

'Then, as if that wasn't enough,' she continued, 'I had to go and see Aunt Violet – you remember her don't you? Pop's sister.'

'No one could forget her. She was simply terrifying. How is the old bat?'

'Amazing. She's nearly ninety and barmy as a bear, but she looks miles better since she went into the dementia unit.' Felicity paused for a moment remembering the way her aunt used to be not so very long ago. She sighed. There was not much to look forward to if old age was going to bring Alzheimer's. With an effort she pulled herself together.

'Does she know who you are?' Venetia asked.

'I really don't know. I think she does sometimes, other times she thinks I'm a social worker, or sometimes my mother.'

'So what's the point in going to see her?' Venetia's face wore a puzzled frown.

'There isn't anyone else?'

'You and your waifs. You've always been a softie,' Venetia said.

Felicity got to her feet. Talking about it made her uneasy, it was too much like looking into her own future. She paced about the room.

'If I didn't laugh, I'd go mad too. The whole place stinks of cabbage and urine,' she added as an afterthought.

'Is she incontinent too?' Venetia looked appalled.

'I don't think so. I'm not sure, but most of them are.'

'What a lot we've to look forward to.'

Felicity laughed as she looked at Venetia and said, 'Don't – every time I sneeze I wet myself.'

'You don't? How simply disgusting.'

'Don't you?'

'Certainly not.' Venetia looked indignant at the thought.

'That's because you didn't have children.'

'No, and if that's what happens I'm extremely pleased I didn't. You must be able to do something about it.'

'You can do sort of pelvic floor exercises, like the ones we were told to do for better sex, only now it's to stop me wetting my pants.'

'Perhaps you should tell Jane that, it might put her off finding you a man.'

'I thought you wanted me to find a man.'

'Not something found by Jane. Once we get you sorted out, you'll find someone much better than that. Just you wait.'

Felicity was confused, since her divorce it seemed as though all her friends were trying to take her over. Venetia suddenly got up and went out of the room. Felicity stared at the ceiling. It was strange, this being divorced business. She wasn't sure if she missed Henry. Did she love Henry? Had she loved Henry or had it just been habit? She had spent more than half her life with him. Taken him for granted. And then he'd left. She'd been upset, angry, stunned and finally numb. It was a bit like a bereavement, but at least if Henry had died people might have thought she was a brave and noble woman, instead of a poor, sad, old cow whose husband had left her. It was typical of Henry's selfishness not to die. A few moments later Venetia came back into the room with a bottle of Muscadet and two glasses.

'And I've had a pretty bloody day too. Thanks for asking,' she said bitterly as she opened the bottle and poured out two glasses.

Felicity immediately felt contrite as she gingerly put out her hand to accept one of them. 'Netty, I'm sorry. How selfish of me. I should have asked, you've been pacing about, I knew there was something up. What is it?'

'Had a row with the new editor. She's about fifteen – she wears train tracks on her teeth for God's sake.'

For the first time Felicity noticed that Venetia looked tired and not so young any more. She was still immaculate, but there were visible signs of the work that went into her looking that way. She sat down again and concentrated on her friend. 'What did you row about?'

'Did you see this issue? The accident fashion shoot.' Venetia picked up a copy of *Vous* from a small glass-topped table beside the sofa. She passed it across to Felicity.

'You know I don't buy magazines,' she said apologetically as she began to flick through the pages.

'Don't bother. The junior fashion editor has found this new designer, Xulio. Well, she calls him a designer, he's a glorified stylist. His boyfriend's a photographer. Those pages there,' she jabbed an impeccably manicured finger at Felicity. 'They mocked up a motorway pile-up. Bandaged bodies and bleeding limbs sticking out from under cars. The dresses all torn bits of taffeta and the shoes lying in the middle of the road.'

Felicity looked at the pages with distaste. 'It's horrible. And you can't see the clothes at all.'

'I know, but the editor loved it. Trouble is if I say I think it's ghastly they think it's because I'm too old. I've been so depressed by the last few issues, I thought I was going to have to leave the country.'

'Do you have to stay with them? There are other magazines apart from *Vous*.'

'I've been there a long time. Anyway where would I go? All the mags want young people.'

'What about that new one – *After Birth*?'

Venetia managed a weak laugh. 'It's called *Extra Life* – as in get a bit extra out of life.'

'Yes, that's the one. It's supposed to be for the older woman.'

'It is. But for older read over thirty. Over fifty you simply don't exist.' Venetia, who had been sipping from her glass during this conversation, poured herself another drink, and leaning her blonde head back on the cushion she closed her eyes. Felicity did hope that Andrew wasn't having an affair; it was the last thing Venetia needed at the moment.

As if on cue the door opened and Andrew Kent-Fletcher came into the flat. He was running a comb through his thick, unnaturally dark hair and he went straight to the mirror to check his appearance. Like Venetia he strove for perfection. It was strange that two such good-looking and successful people were so insecure they had to cover up all the cracks. Andrew flicked an imaginary fleck of dust off his crease-free, navy linen jacket as he turned reluctantly away from the mirror. His shirt was open a couple of buttons too many, revealing a thickly-haired chest and although he didn't wear any jewellery round his neck, Felicity always felt that he'd like to have a bit of gold glistening there.

'Hello darling,' he said as he pecked the air above Venetia's head and blew a kiss at Felicity. 'Bit early in the day for wine, isn't it?' he said, looking at his gold Rolex as he did so.

'Come on darling, it's nearly six and it is a Saturday. Besides it's medicinal for Fifi. She's got a frightful hangover.'

'I'm feeling much better now,' said Felicity, whose own glass was still full. She didn't want to upset Venetia, but the last thing she felt like at the moment was a glass of wine and she certainly didn't want to have to repeat the whole saga for Andrew. 'How are *you?*' she asked to change the subject.

'Fine. I've just been having lunch with Timmy Bignall. He's putting me up for Tuffnells.'

'How odd. Not about Tuffnells. About Timmy – that's where I had dinner last night. I didn't know you knew him.'

'Met him in Hong Kong years ago. He's a very bright banker. Made loads of money.'

'No wonder Jane hates me calling him Dim.' Felicity gave a rueful smile. She realised she was beginning to feel almost human again.

*

Felicity was feeling decidedly better when she got back to her little house in Battersea. For the first time since moving to London it actually felt like home. As she went up the path she saw a skinny and rather mangy-looking black and white cat sitting on top of one of the white plastic tubs either side of her front door that she had planted with daffodils just after she moved in.

'Hello cat,' she said feeling faintly foolish as it stared coldly at her. Felicity had owned dogs all her life, but never a cat. But it looked so forlorn, she crouched down. It didn't move so she slowly put out a hand to stroke it. The little animal rubbed its head against her hand and started to purr. Felicity felt unaccountably flattered. She tickled it under the chin, but that was going too far and it gave her a contemptuous stare, got up and walked away. Once inside the house, Felicity looked in her fridge for a bottle of milk and placing some in a saucer she left it on the front step.

'What's this?' Oscar arrived promptly at eight o'clock and Felicity, who was waiting eagerly for him to arrive, flung the front door open almost before he had rung the bell. He indicated the empty saucer.

'There was a stray cat here earlier. But never mind that, give me a hug.'

He threw his arms round her and squeezed her hard. Then he put his hands on her shoulders and stepped back to have a look at her. 'Poor old Mum. The hair's great, but the rest of you looks terrible,' he said and gave her a kiss.

'Well that's cheered me up a lot,' said Felicity, aware that although she was feeling a great deal better, she still had the remains of her hangover, and despite a rest and a fresh application of makeup she was not looking her best. Truth be told she had probably looked her best about twenty years ago.

'Sorry.' Oscar patted her arm and together they walked into Felicity's tiny front room. He stood in the doorway and look round. 'The house on the other hand looks great,' he said admiringly.

'So it should – you advised me on all the fabric, and the paint colour. Sending me all those swatches. Must have cost a fortune.' Felicity plumped up an already plumped cushion from the sofa.

'I know, but you've put it together really nicely.' Oscar smiled with approval.

'Are you being patronizing?' Felicity was feeling a trifle sensitive. He laughed and patted the sofa affectionately.

'This looks good here. I'm glad you rescued it from Upton.'

'It was the only one in the whole house small enough to fit into this little matchbox. But that damask you chose looks pretty, doesn't it? Gives it a new lease of life.' Felicity smiled. She was pleased with the room. After nearly a year she was beginning to feel settled and comfortable here. The new curtains of ready-faded chintz provided the finishing touch. On the coffee table Felicity had put two glasses and an opened bottle of white wine in a bucket of ice, together with a bottle of mineral water, and she had filled a couple of bowls with crisps and nuts. She poured Oscar a glass of wine and herself a glass of water and then sat down on the sofa, patting the seat beside her.

'Come and sit down and let me have a good look at you.'

Every time Felicity saw her sons she marvelled that she could ever have given birth to two such wonderful creatures. Although not identical they were nevertheless very alike. Oscar, the older by twenty minutes, was also half an inch taller, but they were both over six feet, with dark brown hair and grey eyes. While Oliver wore his hair quite long, with an unruly hank permanently falling over his right eye, Oscar had had his head shaved while he was in New York and he also wore a gold earring in one ear. He was a designer, and much as the mother in Felicity missed his lovely thick hair, she did understand that it was important to be at the cutting edge, in his case literally, of things. The look was everything and no hair was apparently very 'now'. He was wearing his usual summer uniform of a pristine, white and rather tight T-shirt, which showed that unlike his mother he did use the gym regularly, with black chinos, deck shoes with no socks and today a rust-coloured linen jacket.

It was much easier for men, thought Felicity. It was also much easier being twenty-seven and having a twenty-eight inch waist. Once upon a time she had had a waist herself, but now she was shaped like a barrel. It really wasn't fair – her eighty-nine-year-old aunt had the figure of an eighteen-year-old girl, although to be fair she had the brain of a two-year-old child, which Felicity didn't envy.

Oscar was full of news, bubbling with excitement. He had loved New York, but now he wanted to be back in London. There was a man involved. Barry was English and he had asked Oscar to move in with him. Now he had decided to start his own business.

'There's such a need for it. I can't think why no one's done it before.'

'People always think that about brilliant ideas.'

'All decorating accessories together in one shop – door knobs, picture frames, braid, lampshades.'

'Well, there is Peter Jones.'

'Mum! This is going to totally different – I'll source everything in Italy, India, Bali, all over the world – they'll be really original, beautiful *objets de virtu*.'

'It sounds fabulous darling – really exciting, but ... ' Felicity always tried to be supportive for any of her children's schemes, but naturally cautious herself, she couldn't help worrying. 'Where's the money going to come from?'

'Let's go out to dinner and I'll tell you all about it.' Oscar drained his glass and got to his feet. 'I've booked at @Table.' He mentioned a very new restaurant Felicity had read about in the hairdressers.

She got to her feet and rummaged in her handbag for some more makeup. She wished she was looking better – it would be just her luck to bump into someone she knew. She dabbed a bit more foundation on her face more in hope than expectation and pulled a brush through her hair. She had to admit it did look a lot better since she'd had it properly coloured and cut.

She took her cream linen jacket off a peg in the hall, opened the front door and with Oscar following her walked out into the street. It was a hot evening and the London air felt thick and heavy, with car fumes hanging over the street.

'I hope there's air-conditioning in this place.' The sweat was already trickling down her back by the time she reached the pavement. She sent up a small prayer that in her next life she would come back as a slim, cool blonde.

'Not on HRT yet?' Oscar gave her a concerned look as he took her arm.

'Sometimes it's the weather that's hot – it's not always a hot flush,' Felicity said crossly. 'We can take my car if you like.

I'm not drinking tonight.' She winced as she remembered the embarrassing conversation she'd had with Jane when she went round to collect it that morning.

'As bad as that?'

'Everyone drinks so much in London. People can't afford to do it in the country – taxis are impossible. And no one can manage if they lose their licence.'

'It's your age, you don't bounce back any more,' Oscar teased her as they got into the car.

Felicity noticed, with mixed feelings, that although the restaurant was full, and Oscar seemed to know practically everybody, she saw no one she knew. She realised she hadn't wanted to be seen by anyone, but paradoxically she was irritated no one would know she had been taken there. The restaurant was, as its name implied, very hi-tech, all brushed steel and glass, with one sunflower in a silver flowerpot on each table. The menu was full of things Felicity knew she ought to know about, but wasn't sure, like tahini, polenta and couscous.

'Remind me what polenta is,' she whispered at Oscar.

'A sort of savoury semolina,' he whispered back

'Right. I think I'll have the seafood cocktail and then the lamb chops, they won't be too pink will they?'

'Oh dear, you really are an unreconstructed country girl aren't you? Haven't you been anywhere or done anything since I left London?'

'Well, I've been getting divorced – that's quite time consuming you know.'

'That's over now. Time to move forward.'

'You sound like Venetia.'

'How's my darling godmother?'

'I saw her this afternoon. She's all right, but I'm not sure Andrew's behaving very well.'

'Do tell.'

Felicity told Oscar about seeing Andrew lunching with Sonia. To her horror he shrieked with pleasure. He adored gossip and it wasn't often his mother had any to interest him, but she was rather shocked at his lack of sympathy for Venetia.

'Oh *that* Andrew, he always told us the vilest jokes. Most unsuitable for impressionable children. Poor Venetia, but she's getting a bit past it, even her latest facelift hasn't done much good.'

'I didn't know she'd had a facelift.' Felicity was hurt to think Venetia might have done something so major without telling her best friend.

'Mum!' Oscar raised his eyes heavenwards. 'Have you seen her shut her eyes recently? I bet she has to sleep with them open. Sonia's a bit of arm candy for Andrew's image. She's young, Venetia's old.' He waggled his fingers at a passing waiter but Felicity wasn't sure if he was trying to get him to take their order or pick him up.

'Oi,' she protested feebly, feeling she should be defending her friend more than she was. 'She's the same age as me.'

'That's what I mean – old.'

'You have just become my least favourite child!' Felicity glared at Oscar who blew his mother a kiss across the table and continued. 'Only teasing. But you know what I mean Mum. Everything about him is image – even that stupid name.'

'Andrew?'

'Idiot. Kent-Fletcher. Pure invention. It must be. I bet someone asked him, 'Are you one of the Kent Fletchers?' Just as one might ask if someone was one of the Cornish Trevelyns. He's so bogus.'

'Your father thought it was because he came from the Old Kent Road.'

'Ooh, bitchy.'

'Well he's your father.' Henry had always been able to make Felicity laugh; they had frequently come home from parties in fits of giggles. She did miss that, but she still had Oscar. Felicity thought, as she always did, how much she enjoyed the company of her son, even at his most bitchy. At the same time she felt guilty – this was Venetia, her friend, they were talking about. Had she really had a facelift? How insecure she must have been feeling. Felicity should have noticed. The trouble was, she was so wrapped up in her own problems. She must see if there was anything she could do. Just being there to listen might help a bit.

She looked over at Oscar. How easy it was gossiping away to him. Unlike his sister he didn't make everything into a personal drama and unlike his brother he treated her like an equal, a friend. Oliver was a lovely boy, but he loved his mother as part of his parents and he did not like to think of her as a single woman in London. He was a very proper young man – shades of her own father she often thought.

The rest of the evening flew by. Felicity drank several glasses of mineral water and was feeling much better. Oscar told her in more detail about his plans for the shop and his future, which he hoped would include Barry.

'You must meet him, you'll love him.'

'If he makes you happy darling, I'm sure I will.' Felicity hoped he had found a permanent partner to share his life with. Life was tough enough and nowhere more so than on the gay scene. But for the time being it was enough to have him back in England.

CHAPTER 6

S EVERAL DAYS AFTER FELICITY'S DINNER with Oscar Venetia appeared to collect her.

'What's that?' she asked, pointing to a dish of cat food outside the front door. 'Encouraging the neighbourhood strays?'

'It's a poor little thing, so thin. I think it's been abandoned.'

'Probably got fleas.'

'It hasn't been in the house yet, but it lets me stroke it.'

'You and your lame ducks.' But Venetia smiled indulgently and Felicity realised she would want to keep her sweet today. They got into Venetia's car and she drove across London with the zeal of a missionary. When she parked the car, Venetia got out purposefully. Felicity diffidently followed her up the steps of Bodyworks. Today was the day she had promised to join the gym. At the time it had seemed, if not exactly a good idea, a least a possibility. That had been after a cosy, relaxing supper. Now in the cold light of day she realised that the gym was a terrible mistake. For a start she had nothing to wear. Finally she had gone to M & S and bought a navy tracksuit size eighteen – better to be roomy if she was going to exercise. Venetia had given her several looks out of narrowed eyes but had not said anything as yet.

'I'm not going to do aerobics,' Felicity told Venetia firmly.

'Of course not, that was the eighties. You're going for an assessment and then they'll work out a programme for you to do in the gym. Then you'll probably want to get a personal trainer.'

Felicity was confident the words 'want' and 'personal trainer' used in the same sentence would never apply to her. It all sounded quite terrifying. She had visions of herself lumbering round like a red-faced hippo surrounded by women who looked like anorexic whippets wearing high cut leotards that disappeared like dental floss between their buttocks.

'Hi Venetia.' A toothy blonde, with skin so young and flawless it looked as though it had been computer enhanced, greeted them. Sitting behind a hi-tech reception desk with a bank of VDU screens she smiled warmly at Venetia and raised an eyebrow at Felicity who could hear the unspoken words 'Who's your fat friend?' as she looked her up and down.

Venetia placed her black sports bag on the counter and handed a card to the girl then she indicated Felicity. 'This is Felicity. She wants to join.'

'I wouldn't put it as strongly as that. I'd like to find out a little bit more first.' Felicity was determined not to be browbeaten into anything. She eyed a glass-fronted cabinet displaying fluorescent leotards.

'Well its thirteen hundred pounds for a year's membership.' The girl's voice sounded like nails being filed.

'That's that then. You needn't go any further,' Felicity gasped. 'I'm out of here.' She turned to walk back down the steps.

Venetia grabbed her arm. 'What on earth did you expect it to cost? It's very good value. If you come three or four times a week it's only a few pounds each visit.'

'Three or four times a week? I was thinking more along the lines of popping in for half an hour on the first Thursday of every month with an R in it.'

'If you're not going to take this seriously, I shan't bother any more.' Venetia was beginning to look cross. If there was one thing she didn't have a sense of humour about it was physical appearance.

'How about a month's trial for a hundred pounds?' The receptionist quickly suggested and Felicity felt she had no option but to agree. The girl produced a camera from behind the desk and told Felicity she would have to have her photograph taken.

Felicity glared at Venetia who hadn't warned her about this. As she was coming to a gym she hadn't bothered to put any makeup on this morning. The resulting photograph made her look like the sort of person you would make sure never went near your children. She was then given the key to a locker and grimacing nervously followed Venetia through the double swing doors into the gym.

The last time Felicity had been in a changing room it had been at the local swimming pool, when she had reluctantly taken the children to Puddleducks for their life-saving badges. There the whole area had been awash with water and smelt of chlorine. She remembered the nightmare of trying to dry wriggling children with wet towels surrounded by notices warning of the perils of head lice and verucas. She had naively imagined these changing rooms would be somewhat similar. But how wrong she was. Perma-tanned and highly-polished women stood around in various stages of undress. Others lounged on bleached wood benches exposing areas of their anatomy that Felicity had always imagined people showed only to their gynaecologist. Highly-toned thighs and tiny taut buttocks were on display with not a pubic hair or a vestige of cellulite to be seen. It was worse than she had imagined. These women even sweated in a healthy, glowing manner, unlike Felicity who could imagine herself turning purple in the face, veins standing out like writhing earthworms on her forehead and sweat dripping into her eyes

'This is not for me,' she cried as Venetia thrust a towelling robe into her hand.

'You want a better body don't you?' Venetia still looked disapproving as she started to undress.

'What about liposuction?'

'That's extremely dangerous. Ruth Fletcher had it done at a very reputable place and she got a horrible infection. She lost four stone.'

'That sounds great, give me the address.'

Venetia was standing in front of Felicity now in her bra and pants. She looked fantastic and that reminded Felicity of why she wanted to lose weight in the first place. And although Felicity stared hard she could see no evidence of a facelift. Oscar had undoubtedly said that to cheer her up. With difficulty she bent down over the rolls of fat to tie the laces on her brand new trainers.

Venetia grabbed her arm and sat her down on a wooden bench. One or two people waved at her, but she ignored them and concentrated on her friend. 'I know you're feeling beastly. Henry's run away and you don't think it's worth doing anything about yourself, but I wouldn't be your friend if I didn't tell you the truth.'

Felicity winced. This was going to be nasty.

'You used to be very pretty. You know you've let yourself go. I don't blame you, but it's time to get on with your life.'

Felicity bit her lip. She felt like telling Venetia looks weren't everything and that she wouldn't be so harsh if she knew what her own husband was up to, but this was hardly the time. Venetia was only trying to help, so she shrugged her shoulders, but she knew her bottom lip was stuck out in a silly pout. It was very childish of her, but she'd never been very good at accepting criticism and she felt she ought to have a bit of leeway at the moment.

Venetia, seeing her friend's face, softened. 'Let's be positive,' she said. 'Come on.' She got up and pulled on a shimmering purple leotard and a pair of silver cycling shorts.

Felicity felt both under and over-dressed in her tracksuit, but she obediently followed her into the gym. It was a vast room, with horrifying mirrored walls and full of torturous-looking machines. Most of the machines were occupied by athletic young men and women, all working frantically hard. Felicity wanted to run away, but Venetia had a firm grip on her arm.

'Terry's going to look after you,' she said, leading her friend towards three men wearing navy blue shorts and sky blue singlets. Two of them were tall, young, blond and lean. The third was a small, wiry, old man who looked as if he'd been left in the oven too long.

'I bet I can guess which one's Terry,' Felicity muttered through clenched teeth. Sure enough, she was right, she had been allocated the toasted gnome.

'I'm going to do your assessment, measurements, weight, blood pressure, all that sort of thing.'

He led Felicity into a small private room. At least this wasn't going to happen in front of everybody. Terry was very thorough and talked her through every step as though she was a child. He produced a tape measure and told her to hold one end while he ran round her like a small terrier. Every so often he stopped to make notes of her measurements. Luckily it was all in centimetres, so Felicity was none the wiser, although to judge by the way Terry was sucking in his teeth like a plumber confronted with an expensive job, it wasn't good news. After he had finished he sat her down on a clear plastic chair.

'I'm just going to wrap this round your arm, and then I'll take your blood pressure,' he explained slowly. How he imagined that at Felicity's age she had remained ignorant of the procedure seemed surprising. Then came the weighing which was the worst part. Felicity had been carefully avoiding her bathroom scales that were lurking in a cupboard somewhere, waiting to be unpacked. That way she had almost convinced herself the cleaners were responsible for her tightening waistbands. No longer.

'Oh dear,' she said, 'I hadn't realised I was quite so heavy.'

'The way to lose weight is to take in fewer calories and exercise more,' said Terry earnestly.

'No!' Felicity, suddenly very bored with this whole procedure, pretended to gasp in amazement. 'Why hasn't anybody told me? Does everybody know about this?'

'Oh yes,' he replied solemnly and Felicity realised yet again that the search for the perfect body and a sense of irony did not go hand in hand.

It was far worse than she had imagined. Terry took her round and explained every machine to her. Under his supervision she had to exercise. He wrote out a programme for her that she was supposed to follow every time she came in, then after two weeks she would have another assessment to see how well she was doing. She had quite enjoyed it to begin with. The treadmill seemed fine, she walked along at two miles an hour and even managed to get it up to three and a half miles an hour. She was sweating nicely and feeling quite satisfied with her performance, when a young woman got on next to her and immediately put the dial up to seven miles an hour. Muscular and fit she ran easily, hardly sweating at all. Felicity, who was by now a virulent shade of magenta, was panting and dripping. Terry made encouraging noises, but she could only see the spectre of an imminent heart attack. She was quite sure that whatever Venetia said, she shouldn't be here.

*

'D'you miss being married, Fifi?' Daisy pulled out a chair and sank down gracefully onto it. Pizza Fiesta, the Spanish-owned pizzeria, was almost empty at three-thirty on a sunny afternoon and they chose a table by the window where they could watch the passing people. It was Felicity's local and it was empty quite a lot of the time. Carmen and Manuel, the couple who ran it, were convinced that selling pizzas was a recipe for making money. Maybe, but not the way they made them. The glass-topped tables were made of black lacquer beginning to chip, the walls were inappropriately decorated with posters of flamenco dancers and bullfighters and each table had a single pink carnation on it. Felicity came here a lot because she felt sorry for Carmen.

'I don't know.' Felicity frowned. 'I miss the idea of being part of a marriage, but I'm not sure if I miss Henry. I've always been married and all my friends are married. And I suppose I feel my life doesn't have a focus any more.' Felicity examined the menu listlessly. She always had the Pizza Margharita, which she had discovered by trial and error was the least nasty option.

'Surely not all your friends? You must know some unmarried women.'

'No, I don't – well not of my age anyway. Old maiden aunts of course and one girl I was at school with became a nun. Apart from that they're all married.'

'That's so weird.' Daisy looked mystified. 'Are you planning to get married again?'

'Hardly planning it. I can't imagine it happening, but I just don't know anything else. It sounds ridiculous but it's what I was trained for. And all my friends seem set on fixing me up.'

'So what do you miss about it – sex?' Daisy leaned forward.

'We were married for thirty years, there wasn't much sex at the end.'

'Well, you've always got your vibrator.'

'Shh … ' Felicity glanced round the restaurant horrified. Manuel and his son were glancing in their direction as they leaned against the bar. Felicity was pretty sure the Spanish word would be similar.

'I most certainly haven't got a vib – one of those things, I've never even seen one,' she whispered, nodding her head in the direction of the waiters.

'Good Lord.' Daisy was surprised. 'I'd better give you one for Christmas. I can't imagine life without my jolly green giant.'

'Your jolly green giant?' Felicity gulped. 'I'm afraid to ask.'

'Big green job, I'll show it to you.' She bent down and dived into her handbag. Felicity held her breath in horror, but Daisy reappeared with her diary in her hand. 'Better still,' she said, 'I'm going to an Ann Summers party soon. I'll send you one.'

'If they're so great why d'you need a man at all?' Felicity's curiosity overcame her embarrassment.

'Vibrators don't tell you you're gorgeous and sexy or buy you dinner.'

At that moment one of the waiters came over and took their order. They sat in silence for a moment as they waited for their drinks to arrive.

Felicity, keen to change the subject, spoke. 'It never occurred to me before, but married people are very self-absorbed. Wrapped up in their own world. I suppose I just

83

never thought it would end,' she said as she sipped unenthusiastically from a glass of still mineral water. Terry, her trainer, was adamant she must drink at least two litres of it a day.

She was having a pizza with Daisy, who was in London for a day of sex and shopping and who, having just spent an inordinate sum of money on a pair of Emma Hope shoes, had decided to call a halt to the shopping part of the day. She had rung Felicity on the offchance.

Felicity loved seeing Daisy, whom she adored. But Daisy was an enigma. Too beautiful to be ordinary, she was too unsure of herself to be extraordinary. She loved everyone and no one. She had been sixteen and away at school when her and Rose's father had had a fatal heart attack. Her mother Deirdre had pinned all her hopes on Daisy. Daisy was going to be perfect, and much better than her half-sister Rose in every way. When Daisy had come home and announced she was moving in with a Rastafarian drummer with a reggae group, Deirdre had been horrified, but that was only the beginning. Then Daisy had been convicted of being in possession of cocaine. She had got away with a fine, but Deirdre told her she would never be able to hold her head up in society again. The final straw was when Daisy had rung her mother to tell her she was pregnant and not only did she have no intention of marrying the father, she wasn't entirely sure who he was. That was when Deirdre had thrown her out and Rose had picked up the pieces. Felicity sometimes wondered what her own life would have been like had she looked like Daisy with her tumbling, corkscrew curls, her slim figure with long shapely legs, and her heart-shaped face with wide blue eyes.

'That's quite a generalisation. All married people, or just the neighbourhood of Little Biddlehampton?' Daisy broke into Felicity's thoughts.

'I suppose I meant me. I was so busy I didn't spend time examining other people's lives for cracks. Now I stop and look, all my friends seem to have more cracks than lives.'

'Stop being so gloomy. The glass is always half empty with you. Just because your friends aren't all holding hands like Tony and Cherie doesn't mean their lives are shit.' Daisy leant back and ran her long fingers through her hair, brushing it back from her eyes. Looking down she noticed that she had spilt tomato sauce on her pale pink T-shirt. 'Bugger,' she muttered and dipping her napkin into Felicity's water she started dabbing ineffectually at the stain. Two waiters immediately came over and offered to help.

It was easier to get help when you were under forty and had enormous breasts, Felicity thought. She had been under forty once, but then her breasts hadn't been that big. Now she was over fifty, her breasts had grown along with the rest of her, but even with the help of her heavy-duty, underwired bra, gravity had taken its toll, and she very much doubted the waiters would be queuing up to help her. Daisy flashed a wide grin at Felicity.

'How about other men?' she persisted, returning to her favourite subject. 'You must have had lovers?'

'Never. Henry is the only man I've ever slept with.' Felicity was proud of this fact and happy to tell Daisy, who she felt might be impressed. Not for long.

Daisy's eyes opened wide and her mouth fell open as she gaped at the older woman. 'But the Sixties?' she exclaimed. 'You lot were all so promiscuous. Rose was at it all the time. She's told me. And I bet Sally was too, she's got that much-laid look.'

'Probably, but I wasn't. I met Henry when I was nineteen.'

'You're not going to tell me you were a virgin when you got married?'

'Of course not. We slept together after we got engaged.'
Felicity bridled, but Daisy threw back her head and laughed.

'Darling Fifi,' she said, 'I may be a generation younger, but you're such an innocent old thing. Completely out of the Ark.'

Felicity was hurt, but she smiled and said nothing. It wasn't that she was a prude. She wasn't really shocked by other people's behaviour, more disappointed. Sex had been lovely when they were all young. She and Henry had been quite adventurous when they were first married. She could remember making love in all sorts of places and at different times of the day. But that had all been years ago. For goodness sake, she was a grandmother. She'd resigned herself to the fact that sex would be in the past. She tried to imagine her own grandmother having sex and couldn't help smirking.

'That's better,' Daisy said, 'I don't like seeing you look all sad. I thought I'd upset you. You know we all love you, but sometimes you seem to belong to another age.'

'Because I've only been married once and haven't had oodles of lovers?'

'Yes.' Daisy gave up trying to remove the stain from her front and put her elbows on the table. Resting her head on one hand she listened to Felicity with an amused smile on her face.

'There are lots of people like me. Jane and Timmy, Venetia and Andrew – '

'I thought you said Andrew was having an affair.'

'OK, but they're still married.'

'But that's so hypocritical. Makes me realise why I've never done it.' Daisy smiled at Felicity as if to soften her words as she continued, 'What you're saying is that affairs are all right as long as you stay together.'

Felicity felt rather muddled. She wasn't expressing herself very well. Everything she'd believed for so many years had been turned around. She and Henry had been a couple, and she'd assumed they'd stay like that till the day one of them died. He wasn't perfect, but she had believed she had loved him and he loved her. From that position she'd been able to look down loftily on other people's lives. Now the ladder had been pulled out from under her, she was lying at the bottom of the pile and people like Jane Bignall, who were still up there with the smug marrieds, could look down on her.

'I'm so out of touch,' she said. 'I don't understand how the world works today. Do you still have the three hot dinners rule?'

'What on earth are you talking about Fifi?'

'When we were young, you didn't sleep with a man until he'd taken you out to dinner at least three times, unless you were a slut.'

Daisy looked at her incredulously. 'I thought you said Henry was the only man you'd ever – '

'I wasn't talking about me,' Felicity interrupted her hastily. 'It was a general rule.'

'D'you know, I've no idea. I certainly don't think like that and I don't think any of my friends do. Sometimes it's just a one-nighter. If you fancy someone, why not sleep with them?' She shrugged and started fiddling with the sugar in the bowl.

Felicity could tell she simply couldn't understand what the problem was. Felicity wasn't sure she knew herself. After all it was academic. It wasn't as if there was anyone who had taken her out to dinner even once.

'Forget about it,' Daisy beamed suddenly, 'I've got some gossip.'

'Cheerful gossip, I hope.'

'Not really, but you'll love it. It's about Henry.'

'I'm not interested in Henry.' Felicity could feel herself flush as she spoke.

'Liar. You're bursting to know.'

'Well, you're bursting to tell me.'

'Leo bumped into him in Tuffnells last week. He said he looked awful. Circles under his eyes. Exhausted. Sally's making him work all the time. He's having to do all the gardening.'

'Poor old Henry.' Felicity felt genuinely sorry for him, but at the same time she couldn't help being pleased that he wasn't having too good a time of it.

'Serve him right, more like,' said Daisy. 'I think it's really funny. He's such a lazy sod. You let him get away with murder, running around after him. But Sally won't put up with that.'

Despite herself, Felicity couldn't help smiling. The idea of Henry being bullied by Sally was quite pleasing.

'You're coming down this weekend aren't you? Rose's rounded up this divorcé, she's sure its going to lead to wedding bells. Sweet romantic thing that she is.'

'Wedding bells for whom? You?'

'No, silly. You. She's determined to get you married off to someone in Wiltshire so she can keep you in the fold.'

*

'Hi, Felicity.' Sadie greeted her like an old friend and after three visits to Pelle Capelli, Felicity was feeling quite at home there. 'You look very well,' she added, something that Felicity always suspected was what people said when they thought you were looking fat, but maybe she was being paranoid, after all she had been to the gym again this morning. But as far as she could see all that was happening was the fat getting firmer, which would presumably make it more difficult to shift. However, she was feeling more cheerful, at least she was doing something about her appearance, which she now realised she had neglected for far too long. It might not be doing much to help the world in general and was probably rather shallow, but at this point in her life it was important. According to Terry, her personal trainer, it was all to do with endorphins, whatever they were, affecting her mood.

'Going anywhere special?' Sadie asked as she carefully cut Felicity's hair strand by strand.

'A dinner party,' Felicity found herself confiding unexpectedly. 'My cousin's found a man she wants me to meet.'

'That's nice. What you going to wear?'

'I was thinking of black trousers. I'm going to buy a new pair this afternoon.'

'They've got some lovely ones in Joseph.'

'I might try there,' said Felicity, knowing she would not. She might be feeling better but she didn't need size eight sales assistants sniggering as she looked along the rails for a pair of trousers that she could cram even one leg into, let alone afford. She was actually thinking of the large ladies department in Peter Jones. She had to say that Sadie was an excellent hairdresser and as usual she left Roberto's feeling good. It was amazing how a simple thing like professional haircare could make such a difference to her outlook on life. To her pleasure and surprise she found a well-fitting, reasonably priced pair of black crepe trousers and a cream silk tunic to wear over them. So far things were going well, ominously well in fact and she immediately bought a second copy of the *Big Issue* to placate the god of banana skins.

*

Felicity felt her spirits lift as she left London. At the very least her new life was quite a challenge and she was enjoying parts of it, but she did miss the countryside. Besides, Oliver had been invited down for the weekend too and he was driving her in his sports car. The sun was shining and he had the top down. She wondered about Geoffrey, the divorcé. He was a man and a man Rose and Leo liked. That at least was a good first step. Next it had to be hoped he would like Felicity and, perhaps more importantly, but maybe more likely, that she would like him. Anyway, she was feeling so happy she sang along to the radio as they drove along the motorway, oblivious to the fact that she was completely out of tune.

Her voice blared out and she croaked her way through the Beatles' *She Loves You*. Sitting beside Oliver, him looking just like his father did at that age, she felt young and free, her hair blowing in the wind.

When they stopped for petrol Felicity glanced at her reflection in the wing mirror as Oliver filled the car up. The hair that she had imagined to be attractively tousled, was in fact a matted mess, making her look completely mad. She crouched down in the car to avoid being seen by other drivers and reached for her bag on the back seat so that she could brush it. It was no good, her brush was in the boot. Keeping low she got out of the car and went round to the back.

'What are you doing?' Oliver stared at her.

She stumbled and put her hand on the car just as Oliver was removing the nozzle. Petrol dripped onto her fingers.

'Trying to find my hairbrush.' Without thinking she nervously ran her petrol-soaked fingers through her hair as she spoke. That'll make it smell nice, essence d'essence, she thought, hoping, as she did so, she would have time to wash it before tonight's dinner party. Which meant the expensive afternoon at the hairdressers would be completely wasted, but unless he was a serious car anorak, the smell of petrol on her hair wouldn't be much of a turn-on to the divorcé. She tried to walk nonchalantly to the ladies loo behind the cash desk, studiously avoiding the tempting packets of crisps she had to pass on the way. Then she ignored the stare of the callow youth behind the till, trying to convince him by her calm, relaxed stance that this was the way they were wearing hair in London nowadays.

When she sank back into the car she noticed with annoyance that somehow a large bar of fruit and nut chocolate had entered the car with her. Well, she thought, there was nothing for it but to eat it, otherwise it would melt in the heat. Ten minutes later, feeling slightly sick, she was cross with herself for eating it. And she was quite annoyed with Oliver too, because he had refused to eat half, so she had had to eat the whole bar. Still at least she didn't have to try and cram herself into the pink dress again. That had been an expensive mistake and hung, minus a sleeve, in her cupboard to remind her of a ghastly evening. Tonight, however, was going to be different, she would be wearing the black trousers and a cream silk tunic, very flattering and approved by Venetia. What could go wrong?

*

First of all, cream was a bloody stupid colour. Of course makeup was going to show on it. It was only a tiny spot, or rather it had been a tiny spot before she had tried to remove it, now it was smeared all over her bosom. She thought of covering it with a brooch, but decided that pinned to the end of her tit, it would look a trifle strange. Naturally she hadn't had time to wash her hair, she had only been able to brush it, thus removing quite a lot of it, the hair unfortunately and not the smell of petrol. In the past Felicity had felt herself to be a competent person, not the accident-prone idiot she had turned into recently. Was it the menopause or was it lack of a husband that had turned her into this bumbling, simpleton?

'Are you nearly ready?' Rose's voice sounded from the doorway of her room.

'Had a bit of an accident with the top. It's got makeup all over it.'

'You're supposed to put it on after you've done your face. Haven't you anything else to wear?'

'Not really, only a T-shirt.'

'I'll lend you something.'

'Rose, you're about half my size.'

'I've got a silk shirt that's enormous, completely swamps me, would fit an elephant.' Rose raised her hands in the air, as she realised what she had said. 'Not that you're that big. Oh hell Possum! I'll shut up and get it.'

It was a pretty, dark red silk shirt. On Rose it would have been oversize and appealing. On Felicity it was tight. Not the look she had planned. Now she was flustered and hot. Her face exactly matched the colour of the shirt and clashed quite violently with her hair. Why hadn't she bought six copies of the *Big Issue*? Eventually she managed to calm her face down and re-do her makeup. Her hair now looked all right, just as long as no one got close enough to smell it and she hoped that in artificial light the colours wouldn't react quite so strongly against each other.

'You look nice,' Leo greeted her when she descended the staircase at a quarter past eight.

'Liar,' she said, 'but thank you. I look enormous in this top.'

'Always hated skinny women. Bit of warmth in the winter and shade in the summer, that's what I like.' He took her arm and led her into the drawing room. Daisy and Oliver were standing by the fireplace. Daisy had picked up a photograph of Leo asleep in a chair. Someone had written *Waiting for Godot?* on it.

'What's Go Dot – a new website?'

'No Daisy, it's a play, a very famous play.' Oliver was laughing.

'It can't be that famous, I haven't heard of it.'

'Did you actually have any formal education?'

'I kept getting chucked out of schools. They said I was disruptive.'

'No change there then.' Oliver ducked out of the way as Daisy aimed a swipe at him.

Felicity thought what a handsome couple they made. Even though Daisy was eleven years older than Oliver, in the evening light she looked incredibly young. Her eyes were full of laughter as she looked up at him. Then she leant against Oliver and giggled. Felicity knew they were aware of how good they looked standing there and were putting on an act for the three other people in the room. They were a local couple Felicity had met several times before and a tall, good-looking man with bright blue eyes and a warm smile. He was elegantly dressed in a burgundy smoking jacket. That must be Geoffrey, she thought, and after Leo's kind words she had to admit she felt more cheerful.

'If he's so gorgeous why did his wife leave him?' Felicity asked Rose when she told her about the dinner party.

'She ran off with a local trainer – you know how over-sexed horsey people are. It's all that bouncing around in the saddle.' Looking at him Felicity was quite shocked to realise she was thinking she wouldn't at all mind bouncing around with him. When Leo introduced them he held out both hands and enfolded hers.

'Wonderful to meet you,' he said. 'I was really pleased when Rose told me you were coming. You're Oscar Fox's mother, aren't you?'

'Yes. That's his twin, Oliver, over there,' she pointed towards her other son. Please don't let him be gay, she thought. That would be just my luck, the man Rose produces for me fancies my son.

'Oscar and Oliver?'

'I had a three-month-old baby when I discovered I was pregnant again and then when we discovered it was twins everyone was horrified. We didn't get any congratulations, just people saying "Oh" in a shocked voice. So they became the "Ohs". Do you know Oscar?' she asked nervously.

'No, we've never met, but I gather he wants some additional finance for a shop he's thinking of starting.'

'That's right. It's a really good idea.' Felicity grinned with relief. She loved gay men, but she'd much rather this one was straight. 'Are you a banker?'

'A venture capitalist. We help people find money for projects,' he added by way of an explanation when he saw Felicity's puzzled expression.

'And you're going to help Oscar. How wonderful.' She loved this man already.

'We might. I've got a meeting with him and his partner next week. Why don't you tell me a bit about it?'

*

Leo circulated with a bottle of white wine, but Felicity was taking no chances, she nursed her first glass. She didn't want this evening to be a repeat of the Bignalls. At half past eight Rose appeared from the kitchen and announced that dinner was served. The light outside was beginning to fade and the dining room was softly illuminated with candles, and soft picture lights directed at all the sporting pictures that hung on the bottle green walls.

Felicity was seated between Leo and Geoffrey. The conversation flowed easily. Geoffrey asked her quite a lot about Oscar's new business and to her surprise she found herself quite able to tell him about it.

'It's such a good idea,' she enthused. 'Oscar's got brilliant taste. He loves travelling and he's one of those people who can hunt out beautiful and interesting things. He's got such great imagination.'

Geoffrey laughed. 'I'm not surprised he's got you working for him, you're a good marketing director.'

'Oh, I don't work for him,' Felicity explained hurriedly.

'Well you should do – you'd be a great asset.'

Felicity was enjoying herself. For the first time in what seemed like ages she was having a grown-up conversation that wasn't about her divorce. Perhaps she should suggest herself to Oscar, maybe she could work in his shop. She and Geoffrey were getting on really well. At the other end of the table she could hear Rose discussing the merits of different varieties of Swiss Chard.

'I like the old-fashioned varieties. But it's become the new vegetable. I've been growing it for ages of course, but round here you wouldn't dare admit you didn't have any in your garden.'

Felicity thought how strange it was that this was the sort of conversation she might have been having herself only a few months ago. It was rather liberating not having a garden to maintain, never mind the competition over this year's 'in' vegetable, or decorative feature. Felicity realised to her surprise that she was able to understand her life had changed and moved on and maybe it wouldn't all be bad for ever.

Then while Rose was clearing the pudding and making the coffee, helped by Daisy, Geoffrey turned to her and asked, 'Does Daisy have anyone special in her life at the moment, d'you know?'

'No one special, I don't think,' Felicity replied, quite unprepared to what was coming next.

'I think I might give her a ring next week. She's so attractive, I've always fancied her.'

The rest of the evening passed in a blur. Felicity managed to freeze a smile on her face, even though her jaw ached with the effort. She had completely misread the signals, it had been so long since she had even tried to flirt with an attractive man. She had been a wife for so many years but now she was single again, but it appeared the men out there didn't want someone like her. How stupid she had been to imagine a friendly interest in her son's business meant anything more than that.

CHAPTER 7

'OH, FUCKADOODLEDO!' Felicity muttered to herself when she woke early the next morning. She lay for a while with her eyes tightly closed. She couldn't face getting out of bed yet, or rather she couldn't face going downstairs and seeing everyone's sympathetic faces. She knew she was lucky to have family and friends who loved her, but because they did, they would be feeling sorry for her and she wasn't sure if she could face it. There had been far too much of that sort of thing in her life recently. In the dinner party postmortem last night Felicity had foolishly mentioned what Geoffrey had said. Daisy had staunchly declared she hated him and wouldn't dream of going out with him after he had rejected Felicity. Felicity had tried to persuade her she didn't mind, but had merely convinced everyone she was being brave.

The problem was she had been part of 'Henryandfelicity' for so long she now felt she didn't exist alone, at least not socially. It had all been so easy. People would say: 'D'you know Henryandfelicity?' and 'Ah here's Henryandfelicity.' It was if they were one entity. Parties were fun and relaxing – you could talk to everyone, have a cosy gossip with your friends and observe the goings on of other people, safe in the knowledge that you'd be going home with the same person you'd arrived with. Women were friends not competition. You were invisible to most men – or at any rate neuter. They talked to you about their gardens, or children, they might ask your advice about what to buy their wife for her birthday and occasionally, after too much wine they might give your bottom a squeeze or try for a fumbling kiss on New Year's Eve, but they didn't exactly flirt with you, nor did they expect you to flirt with them.

'I'm out of practice,' she said to herself. They ought to run classes for women, perhaps for men too, who needed to get back into circulation. Actually they probably did, but not for people like her who were just about to get their bus pass. What a grizzly thought, surely it couldn't be happening – it didn't seem a moment ago when she'd been young, with her life ahead of her. Where had it gone? She lay there pondering gloomily for a while, but the desire for a cup of coffee soon came upon her and she opened her eyes. The sun was shining and it was a lovely day. And to her surprise, once she got up she felt more cheerful. Proving to herself yet again that inactivity made her depressed. She had quite liked Geoffrey and would certainly have been pleased if he had asked her out, but the more she actually thought about it the more she realised that deep down she wasn't sure she was ready for another man yet. If one came along eventually, it would be fine, but she wasn't going to go through this ritual humiliation again. She had never been given to introspection. She liked doing things, practical things, but in the past year she had spent far too much time thinking about her life and the things that had gone wrong with it. She got up, had a bath, got dressed and went downstairs. A delicious smell of coffee and frying bacon met her as she entered the kitchen. The room was full of sunlight and through the French windows she could see the table laid on the terrace, under a big, white umbrella. The scent of lilies wafted in from the large terracotta pots that were scattered about the garden.

'Morning, darling. How'd you sleep?' Rose called from the terrace, and putting down her cup of coffee she came into the kitchen and gave her cousin a hug. Felicity hated it when she called her darling, instead of Possum, because she only did it when she thought someone needed a bit of TLC.

'Extremely well,' she answered with a smile on her face. 'I'm starving.'

'I'll get you some breakfast.' Rose looked surprised, but she took a plate out of the warming cupboard and deftly put a couple of rashers of bacon on it.

'One egg or two?' she asked.

'Two please.' Felicity ignored the little voice inside her that was mentally adding up the units of fat and calories. Taking her plate she went out into the garden where Daisy's two boys were throwing a ball for Rags, the terrier. She pulled out a chair and sat down under the umbrella, between Daisy and Leo. The table was laid with a white linen cloth and a pottery jug of sweet peas stood in the middle.

Leo was completely hidden behind the *Times,* but he lowered it and gave her a smile. 'Thought you'd be all right,' he said.

Felicity smiled back at him. Rose stood in the doorway and gave him a silencing look. Felicity could tell she was furious.

'I'm never going to have that man in this house again.' Rose was extremely protective of her family and friends.

'Why not? It's not his fault he preferred Daisy to me. I mean just look at the two of us – what man wouldn't?'

'That's not the point – he was asked for you and he knew that perfectly well.'

'Oh Rosie, you're sweet to worry for me, but honestly it's fine. I felt a bit of an idiot last night, but I feel OK this morning.'

'Good girl,' Leo said from across the table. 'You can do much better than him anyway.'

Oliver came out of the house at that moment. He went over and kissed his mother.

'Honestly Daisy, those boys of yours. We went for a walk by the river and Thomas asked me what a dyke was. I was trying to explain about drainage canals when he said with a knowing look, "That's odd 'cos Mum says Persephone's gonna to be one".'

'They're such eavesdroppers. I was gossiping outside school. Persephone's only seven, such a stupid name, it's asking for trouble – she's built like a tank.'

'I told them to ask you to explain. It's too early in the morning to start sex education. I'm never going to have children. Far too exhausting,' Oliver said determinedly but Daisy laughed.

'I'll remind you of that in a few years time when you're being the perfect snag – doing all those right on things like changing nappies.'

'Snag?' Felicity asked.

'Sensitive New Age Guy. And I'm not going to be one of those,' said Oliver and swiftly changing the subject added, 'I thought you looked smashing last night.'

'Loyal child.' Felicity patted his hand.

'It's true, Possum,' said Rose. 'You did. You get so hung up on being overweight, just because Venetia's been having a go at you.'

'You know Venetia, it offends her sense of propriety to have unimproved people around her.'

Felicity was beginning to realise that being divorced could become a way of life if she wasn't careful. Just as her role in life had once been that of wife and mother it now seemed to be that of woman in need of help.

'I think,' she announced, 'I'll give Geoffrey a ring anyway – he wants to help Oscar start his new business – he should be encouraged.'

Rose and Leo looked at each other across the table. But rather to her own surprise Felicity realised she didn't have an ulterior motive for wanting to ring Geoffrey.

'Tell me darling,' she said turning to her son, 'we've hardly spoken – it's impossible in that car of yours. How's your love life?'

'Pretty moderate. I'm still sort of seeing Frankie, but she's been in Spain all summer, and there's this other girl … '

Felicity smiled. It was all so different for the young. They had choices. In the kitchen the phone rang and Rose turned to answer it. Felicity sipped her coffee contentedly.

'That was Sheila Fletcher on the telephone. She saw Andrew with Sonia last week. It's really too bad of him.' Rose came bustling out of the door carrying a trug. 'I'm just going to pick some runner beans. D'you think someone ought to speak to Andrew?' she continued, looking at Leo meaningfully.

'What's that?'

'Never listens to a word I say.' Rose shrugged at the world in general and continued. 'Venetia, Andrew. Someone's got to do something – talk to Andrew.'

Leo looked grave as he put down his copy of the *Sunday Times*. 'And you think it should be me, I suppose? Let me think about it.' Leo picked up his newspaper again and returned to reading.

Rose, who could never stay still for long suddenly shouted 'Bastard' and rushed into the house. A few moments later she came back out carrying a fishing net.

'What on earth?' Felicity enquired as her cousin charged past her.

'Cock hunt,' Rose called over her shoulder.

'Some alien cockerel has got into the garden and is bonking her beloved Buff Orpingtons, she's off to wreak vengeance.'

'As I sometimes say, fuckadoodledo.'

*

The rest of the weekend passed off pretty smoothly. Some people from the village came in for drinks after church: a retired Colonel and his wife, with their rather droopy daughter who had been at school with Daisy, and the local doctor who was mad on horses and had been a keen member of the local hunt. There ensued a long, and to Felicity, rather tedious conversation about whether there could ever be a future for hunting again. Rose was particularly stirred up about it all having lost another of her precious bantams to a fox the previous week. Then more people arrived for lunch. As usual Felicity was amazed at the way Rose managed to organise food and drinks for dozens of people, apparently completely effortlessly. She never complained, but for once Felicity thought her cousin did look a bit more tired than usual. She always maintained she was never happier than when the house was full of people, but Felicity found her in the kitchen after everyone had left, standing over the sink with stooped shoulders.

'Is everything all right?' she asked and Rose immediately straightened her back and turned round with a warm smile.

'Fine,' she said. 'Just a bit tired. Find the bones creak a bit more than usual these days. And Leo's not as active as he used to be.' She paused. 'I worry about him.' Her face dropped and Felicity could see concern in every line. Grabbing a pair of rubber gloves she propelled Rose gently towards a chair and once she was seated Felicity started to scrub a large Le Creusset casserole dish. To her surprise Rose made no resistance and merely sat at the kitchen table restlessly leafing though a seed catalogue. This was the first time Felicity remembered being allowed to do anything in this kitchen. It was so unusual it made her feel distinctly uneasy. As soon as she had finished scrubbing all the pots she made them both a cup of coffee and they sat at the kitchen table.

'I wish you'd move back to the country. I miss you.' Rose spoke quietly.

'I miss you too,' Felicity said truthfully, 'but I've got to sort my life out and I think it's more likely to happen in London.'

'Why?'

'I'm not just Henry's ex-wife there. And a single woman in the country, especially at my age … '

They were both silent for a moment until Felicity asked, 'Is there anything I can do to help about Leo? Talk to him perhaps, persuade him to see a doctor.'

'No. The silly thing is, I don't think there's anything actually wrong with him, but he is over seventy and I can't help worrying. But there's nothing we can do to stop the passage of time. Trite but true.'

Felicity leant across the table and squeezed her cousin's hand. She opened her mouth to take advantage of this rare opportunity to talk to Rose alone, try to get her to talk about herself for once instead of concentrating on everyone else. However, before she could say anything Daisy and the boys came back from taking the dogs for a walk and loudly demanded tea. Felicity wondered, quite crossly, why Daisy took such advantage of Rose all the time. Why couldn't they go back to their own kitchen over the stables? But Rose revived instantly and seemed genuinely delighted to see them and before Felicity could move she had leapt to her feet, put the kettle on and taken a chocolate cake out of the tin. A few minutes later Leo appeared from his study and suddenly the kitchen was chaotic and full of people again. Felicity tried to push her worries about Rose and Leo to the back of her mind and stayed for a cup of tea and then Oliver drove her back to London. As they left the house, Felicity looked backwards to see Rose, her arm around Leo, waving and smiling. But even that familiar sight didn't entirely reassure her all was well.

'Geoffrey had a mad idea that I ought to work for Oscar,' she said to Oliver as they were driving back. She wanted to see what his reaction would be. When he remained silent she continued, 'It's a pretty silly idea, I haven't worked for ages, don't know how to do anything.'

'That's not true. You ran the B & B guests very efficiently. You had a computer – used a database. I think it's a great idea.' Oliver turned to smile at his mother.

'Actually, you're right. I did manage pretty well. I never thought of it as a business, but I suppose it was. I might give Oscar a ring and discuss it with him.'

'Good for you, Mum.' Oliver took his hand off the steering wheel and gave her hand a squeeze.

Felicity thought she sometimes didn't appreciate this son enough. When he dropped her off later she kissed him and waved as he drove away shouting, 'See you on Thursday.'

The cat was on the doorstep when she arrived and, with the distinct feeling that she might become a dotty old cat woman, she let it in through the front door. But it felt good to have another living creature in the house

*

'Dear lady, let me help you with that.'

Felicity was struggling with a recalcitrant shopping trolley that was refusing rather unreasonably to mount the kerb. She jumped on hearing the educated voice, she had not been aware of anyone near her in the car park. Turning round she saw a very thin man of about her own age, with long, but thinning grey hair. He bowed slightly in her direction and she smiled at him, not sure whether she knew him or not.

'Darcy Fitzgerald at your service,' he said as he grasped the trolley and heaved it, with some difficulty, over the step.

'Voila,' he gasped, making an elaborate gesture towards her groceries.

Felicity, who had been watching him in mild surprise, thanked him and turned towards her car. She didn't want to prolong a conversation with an obvious lunatic. Even though he said his name was Darcy, could he really be named after every woman's favourite hero? For some reason the name rang a faint bell, but perhaps it was just her lifelong passion for Jane Austen.

'May I at least know the name of the fair lady I have been assisting?'

Felicity turned round reluctantly, feeling it was a mistake, but politeness dictated she reply. As she walked towards him she took in the polished but worn brown brogues on his feet, the shabby grey flannel trousers, the frayed collar on his blue and white striped shirt, the stained club tie and the blazer with patches on the elbows. He had obviously fallen on hard times.

'Felicity Fox,' she said and as the words left her lips she wished she had given him a false name.

'Felicity, a beautiful name, and most apposite. I'm sure you spread happiness all around you.' Felicity backed away nervously as he paused and gazed at her. 'I hesitate to ask … don't like to impose on your good nature.' Another pause. 'Would you … could you lend me five pounds? Most embarrassing, I appear to have left my wallet at home. I don't have the money for a taxi.' Felicity realised she had walked right into that one.

'Couldn't you take the bus?' she asked with a short laugh as she clutched her handbag firmly to her side.

'One's not really accustomed … ' he started.

'Well I think it's time one did get accustomed,' Felicity said briskly. The man stood dejectedly in front of her. Feeling sure she had been conned she reached into her purse and reluctantly handed him a pound coin.

'I don't know where you're going, but that should get you most of the way there.'

'As a matter of fact I live in an adjacent street.' His voice was bored now as if he had tired of this game. 'I usually find the ladies who use this supermarket more than willing to recompense me for any assistance I give them.'

'In other words you're a beggar.' Felicity was getting cross.

'Please,' he said in an offended tone. 'I like to think I bring a bit of gallantry into your mundane lives.'

Felicity thought it was more likely they wanted to get rid of him. She sniffed surreptitiously. Was he an alcoholic? She shrugged, it wasn't her problem and she wanted to get home and unpack her shopping. Oliver was taking her to the cinema this evening.

'Well, goodbye,' she said. 'It was – ' but she didn't finish her sentence as Darcy Fitzgerald collapsed in a heap at her feet. She looked down at the crumpled figure. He reminded her of Cat, a pathetic creature rejected by the world. She knelt down beside him.

'Mr. Fitzgerald. Mr. Fitzgerald,' she spoke his name urgently as she tried to feel for a pulse. Suddenly his eyes opened.

'Darcy, or Sir Darcy, but please not Mister,' he said.

At that moment Felicity knew exactly who this man was. He had been staying in the villa next door to them in the South of France years ago when the children were little. He had had a wife then, Tamsin, Teresa, Thomasina, that was it, Thomasina was her name. It was all coming back now. They had spent a fortnight in each others' pockets and parted with promises to keep in touch. Had indeed sent Christmas cards for a couple of years, even had dinner together once and had then lost touch. How strange to find Darcy here lying at her feet.

*

A couple of hours later Felicity was regretting the fact that her sense of humour had got the better of her. But seeing him lying there on the ground she hadn't had the heart to leave him. She realised it was foolish of her to have brought him home with her, but she really didn't know what else to do. Besides, she didn't think he would be strong enough to mug or rape her and she had nothing much to steal. And she did know him, after a fashion. She had no cash on her, and would keep her credit cards close by her side, but although he was obviously down on his luck she didn't think he was likely to be a thief. As far as she could remember they had one or two friends in common. While not necessarily giving him a watertight reference this was vaguely reassuring. In any case she could hardly have left him lying in the middle of an empty car park.

She had driven him to her house and taken him inside. He was rather shaky on his feet and was limping badly. She wondered how he had managed to lift her loaded trolley on to the pavement. A supreme effort required by desperation. Taking his arm she noticed he was painfully thin, and the image of a Donald McGill postcard popped into her mind as they walked arm in arm into her house. Once inside she propelled him gently but firmly towards an armchair. He slumped down, and taking her handbag with her she went into the kitchen and put the kettle on to make him a cup of tea.

'You are too kind.' Darcy put his cup down and rested his head on the cushion.

Felicity was relieved to notice that his hair, though thin, looked quite clean.

'I really prefer China tea, but under the circumstances ... '
he muttered, but left the sentence unfinished as he caught
sight of Felicity's expression.

'Beggars can't be choosers,' Felicity finished the sentence
for him.

An hour later, he had eaten half a loaf of bread and cheese
and was lying on the sofa with his feet up, Cat sleeping
peacefully by his side.

'What happened since we last met?' Felicity wanted to
know his story. What had taken him down to the gutter? But it
was obviously going to be a terrible story.

'Thomasina left me. Perhaps you heard. Once I had
inherited the baronetcy but without the money, she was off.
Lady Fitzgerald ... ' he gave a bitter laugh. 'Death duties of
course. Eldest son of an old but impoverished family. Not
always thus – should have gone to Eton had things been
otherwise. Any spare money father spent on horses.' It had the
ring of a much-told tale.

Felicity tried to think back to the last time they had met.
What had his circumstances been then? They had been living
in a borrowed house, certainly, but there was nothing strange
about that. She forced herself to smile with sympathy that
masked a slight sense of nervousness.

'Spell in the army ... married the wrong woman ... very
pretty ... oh, yes, social mountaineer, I'm afraid ... unfortunate
incident.'

His voice droned on and Felicity's mind kept wandering.
Once started the man couldn't stop. How foolish she'd been to
ask him about himself. She was probably the first person to
have done so in a long time. She thought she would have a job
removing him from her house now he was actually in it. Why
on earth had she let him in in the first place? Casually she
glanced at her watch and realised with horror that it was 6.30.

Oliver would be here in an hour. She had to do something about Darcy immediately. She put her hand up.

'Excuse me a second, fascinating though this all is, I must make a call.' She dialled Oliver's number. Damn, she'd got the answering machine. She tried to make her voice sound feeble. A headache seemed a reasonable excuse. She really didn't fancy him finding Darcy here. She couldn't think of a reasonable explanation to give him. Perhaps because there wasn't one.

'Have you got anywhere to sleep tonight?' she asked, knowing the answer as she did so.

'My apartment is in the process of being refurbished at the moment. I've been staying with a friend, but a slight disagreement leaves me without a bed for the night.'

'Isn't there anywhere else you could go?' Felicity was getting desperate.

'There's always the park, I believe it's possible to find a suitable bench.'

Even though it was a warm night he might die of hypothermia, he was so thin and frail. Felicity didn't want that on her conscience. 'You'd better stay here,' she muttered reluctantly, half hoping he wouldn't hear what she said.

'You're too kind, dear lady.' He seemed unable to talk like a normal person and his flowery speech was curiously irritating. Had he always been like this or had he become more eccentric with age? Her own memory was failing with age that was for sure, as she simply couldn't remember whether he had spoken like that or not.

'But only for tonight. Tomorrow you'll have to find a hostel or something.' Felicity relented. She didn't think she would be able to sleep if she imagined him wrapped in an old copy of the *Times* on a hard, wooden bench.

'Of course.' He gave her a hesitant smile. She had acquired another stray.

'My son may be coming round at any minute. We were supposed to be going to the cinema, but I'll make some excuse and send him away. But he's bound to come in for a drink, so don't make a sound – he wouldn't approve of my bringing you back here.'

'Why not?' he asked, bristling with indignation.

'Well he doesn't know you, and I haven't seen you for years.'

'It must be obvious that I am, if nothing else, a gentleman. Your son should appreciate that. Doesn't he expect you to have friends?'

'Friends yes, not people I pick up in supermarket car parks. He's very protective.' She smiled fondly.

'You appear eminently capable of looking after yourself if I may say so. You're certainly big enough,' he added a trifle waspishly. Felicity glared at him. He appeared to realise it might be the park bench after all. 'My apologies, I did not mean to offend you. But you look like a capable woman.'

'Maybe, but if you're going to stay here, I'd like you out of the way before my son arrives.' With that she got to her feet and pointed to the door.

Darcy smiled ingratiatingly at her and got to his feet. He stood up shakily and holding onto the arm of the sofa, steadied himself for a moment before following Felicity upstairs. She found him a towel and after burrowing in a bag of jumble she had inexplicably brought with her from Upton, she found an old pair of the twins' pyjamas.

'Here,' she said. 'Put these on.' She left him in her bathroom while she went into her tiny spare room. Strange to think her first visitor would be an old down-and-out from her distant past.

After his bath and once he was safely covered in Oliver's striped pyjamas and an old towelling robe Felicity showed him to the spare bedroom.

'Now not a sound. D'you understand?'

'I don't suppose you'd be kind enough to indulge me with a small whisky? Just to take the chill out of my bones.'

'I should have spotted that one. It's August, Darcy, not exactly bone-chilling weather.' But he looked so pathetic she weakened and brought him up a glass with a large measure of Scotch in it. With any luck it would send him to sleep.

Was he an alcoholic? Had he been one when they had known each other in another life? They had been young then and often stayed up half the night drinking. Would she have noticed if he had a problem?

*

Oliver arrived half an hour later, without having received her message, but after she had managed to remove any evidence of Darcy from downstairs.

'Darling, how lovely to see you.' Felicity greeted her son with a hug and a kiss and led him into her living room. 'Have a drink. Scotch?' She fetched him a glass with some ice and sat down on the sofa opposite him.

'Have you rung Oscar about this job?' Oliver was keen to know.

'No, but I rang Geoffrey; they've got a meeting next week. And Oscar and I are having coffee tomorrow morning.'

'Good. Are you all right Mum? You look a bit strange.'

'Got a bit of a headache, had it all day. Would you mind awfully if we didn't do the cinema tonight? I did try to leave a message.' She had no intention of leaving Darcy alone in the house.

'Poor you. Have you taken anything?' Oliver was all concern. He got up and sat down beside his mother on the

111

sofa and gently patted her hand. Unfortunately at that moment Darcy decided to have a coughing session upstairs.

'The cat!' Felicity cried wildly.

'You've got someone here? You should have said. I'll leave immediately.' Oliver could be quite pompous, particularly as far as his mother was concerned.

'Don't be silly darling, it's not what you think … '

'Mother. I don't need to know any more. I'll leave immediately.' Oliver's face had turned pink.

'Darling,' Felicity said quite firmly. 'I've got a friend staying, completely platonic, not a lover or anything.' She laughed.

'Mother!' Oliver's voice was full of horror. 'As far as I'm concerned you had sex twice, with father, we were the result, and that's that.' He was smiling, but with teeth clenched as he made this remark, and Felicity knew it was meant half-seriously. He got to his feet and walked towards the door.

'I hope your headache gets better,' he said stiffly and giving her a little wave he left the house.

After he had gone Felicity wondered why the thought of their parents having sex was so repellent to the young. She hadn't thought about it much herself for the last few years, but now, single once more, she had to admit that the possibility if not the reality had crossed her mind.

*

Felicity was upset and cross with herself. The evening, which she had been looking forward to, had gone horribly wrong. It was her own stupid fault for getting carried away and then forgetting her date with Oliver until it was too late to stop him. Her children had their own lives, they were busy, so she cherished any time spent with them and now she had ruined this evening. She had never been able to resist helping waifs and strays. Recently it had been Cat and now Darcy. She hated

112

living alone. She had only been trying to help someone, a stranger in need; surely she deserved some credit for being kind. Instead Oliver had gone home and she was here all by herself. A tear trickled down her cheek.

'Come now. Don't cry, dear lady. It can't be that bad.' Darcy's voice made her jump. He was standing beside her, dressed in her son's old pyjamas, holding an empty glass in his hand.

'It's your fault,' she said angrily. 'My son's gone off in a huff. He heard you coughing and got the wrong impression.'

'What business is it of his, pray?'

'He's my son, it's natural he should be concerned about me.'

'It sounds positively Oedipal. He should be delighted for you to have a new friend. Unless of course, you're still married to his father.'

'No. We're divorced.' Felicity snapped. 'And you are *not* my friend. You are a dubious acquaintance.'

Darcy looked peeved. He sat down heavily in the armchair and tried another tack. 'If you are divorced, you are a free woman. If I may say so, you are an attractive woman. Your son will have to accept you are going to have lovers.'

Felicity felt rather cheered by this remark. She had considered the possibility to be unlikely in the extreme, but now a man, even if he was the next best thing to a tramp, was saying he considered it to be quite possible. Although she was certain of one thing, Darcy was never going to be her lover.

CHAPTER 8

FELICITY DID NOT SLEEP WELL THAT NIGHT. She kept her bedroom door locked and one ear open for any strange noises, but a combination of exhaustion and whisky had sent Darcy straight to sleep. In the morning she had given him breakfast and then sent him off to sort himself out with a bed for the night. He looked so wistful she had foolishly said that if he didn't find anywhere he could come back. She was expecting him back.

Oscar arrived at ten-thirty looking tanned and healthy. It was a terrible shame for the female sex that he preferred men. He handed her a bunch of roses. Proper old-fashioned, scented roses.

'Darling, they're gorgeous.'

'From Barry's garden.'

'Is he a keen gardener?' Felicity distractedly put them into a bowl.

'I told you. That's how we met. I was doing up this house and he was doing the garden. Let me have them.' He took the flowers from his mother and in a few deft movements they were transformed from some haphazard flowers in a bowl into a bouquet.

'Yes, I remember now. My mind was on something else.'

'The lover, I suppose?'

Felicity gulped. But Oscar laughed and put his arm round his mother's shoulder. 'I had Oliver on the phone last night. Tell all, I'm aching to hear.'

So Felicity explained as best she could about Darcy. Oscar was clearly disappointed his mother hadn't embarked upon a torrid affair, on the other hand he didn't seem to think it was such a crime, or even particularly dangerous to ask Darcy to stay. He claimed to remember him from their French holiday, but as Felicity worked out he had only been three years old at the time she was not sure she believed him. Oscar was more amused by his brother's reaction than anything else. After that Felicity relaxed and, changing the subject, she began to talk to her son about the possibility of her working for him.

'Right,' he said. 'Sell yourself to me.'

Felicity looked startled, she hadn't been expecting this. She sat for a moment chewing her lip.

'That's a point against you for a start.'

'What?'

'Nervous ticks. Nibbling your mouth like that.'

Felicity stopped and examined her nails for a few seconds, then she cleared her throat. 'I'm good at organising things. I managed the B & B guests. I used a computer. Had all their details on it. Did the books. I ran the village fete. What else?'

'You tell me.' Oscar wasn't giving his mother an easy time.

'Furnished all the rooms. Stocked everything from the cash and carry.' She ground to a halt. 'I don't know darling. This is hopeless,' she sighed.

'You're doing fine. You don't have to be nervous. I just wanted to know what you think you can do. Give me a few days to think about it and I'll get back to you.'

'Don't do it just to be kind.' Felicity was mortified. The last thing she wanted was his pity.

'I won't. This is a business. I've just got to go away and work out what I need, what sort of job there might be for you.'

'Fine, I'm off to see Aunt Violet.'

'It's very sweet Mum, the way you go and visit her all the time. You can add that to your CV – good with old people.' Oscar smiled affectionately at his mother.

'Only when they're so dotty they don't know who I am,' Felicity reflected as she ushered him to the door.

*

'I don't suppose you remember the name Darcy Fitzgerald? Henry and I met him in France years ago. D'you know anything about him?' Felicity asked Venetia cautiously when she telephoned her a day or two later.

'Of course I do. Everyone knows Darcy.'

Felicity gave a small sigh of relief as she realised that at least one thing he had told her was true.

'He said he knew you and Andrew, but I wasn't sure whether to believe him. He saw that photograph of us all in Ibiza,' she said

'Where on earth did you find him? I thought he was in prison, or drying out.'

Felicity could hear Venetia was intrigued. And she wasn't really surprised. Darcy was a most unlikely person. 'Let's just say I bumped into him.' Felicity didn't feel like telling Venetia the details of her trip to the supermarket at this precise moment. 'Is he really Sir Darcy? I don't remember that.'

'Oh, I think so. I believe his father was a very respectable old baronet. Lived somewhere in Wales in a rambling old ruin. Leo went to visit him once.'

'So Rose knows him.' Felicity felt instantly relieved.

'Not as far as I know. I think Leo went alone and I don't think Darcy was there. He's a completely urban being. Can't imagine him in the country.'

'But you said Leo ... '

'It was his father's place once. Leo was doing some sort of research on the house.'

Felicity was lying on her bed, fully dressed, talking on the telephone in her bedroom. Darcy had gone out armed with a list and a small amount of cash to buy some household essentials. It was in the nature of a small test. He had been in the house two days now and this was the first time Felicity had let him out alone with any money.

Oscar had rung the day after his visit and offered Felicity the job of managing his shop. She had been so excited she had forgotten to ask him about salary, hours or anything practical. She had a sneaking suspicion he was desperate as he had asked her if she could go in his place to visit a possible shop today. He had an appointment with a very important potter in Wales and Felicity knew that would appeal to him much more than going over some dusty old premises. However, he needed someone to be there when the architect arrived to measure up. Felicity had taken Darcy with her and he had been surprisingly helpful. He had happily held the tape measure and had gone across the road to fetch coffee for everyone.

Felicity had spent a couple of evenings talking to Darcy, but was finding it difficult to sort fact from fiction in his life story. It was quite possible he had been at school in, if not at, Harrow, even remotely possible he had climbed Everest, but she did consider it unlikely in the extreme he had been a Colonel in the SAS. Even in his prime, she doubted he could have passed the physical. All that seemed certain was that Thomasina had left him with nothing. Every morning they had a conversation about his finding somewhere else to stay, but inevitably it had come to nothing. And there was something childlike and charming about him that brought out all Felicity's maternal instincts.

'But you don't think he's dangerous?' Felicity cautiously asked Venetia. She didn't really think he was, but she knew she should be careful. He seemed to have become more of a Walter Mitty character than anything else.

'I wouldn't lend him money or give him the key to the wine cellar. Why?'

'It's a long story, but he's living here.'

'You're living with Darcy Fitzgerald? Are you mad?'

'No. We're not *living* together. He's just staying here for a few days.'

'You *are* mad. You'll never get him out. You and your lame ducks.'

'He's so skinny, I think I could throw him out if I had to.'

'There you are,' Venetia said triumphantly, 'the gym's working already.'

Felicity stretched a leg out in front of her. It was true it was more muscular now, although if she were going to find a new man she wasn't convinced that thighs honed like steel hawsers were necessarily an asset.

'The point is,' she continued, 'I've got to take a man to a party.'

'Darcy isn't the sort of man you take to a party, Sweetie. If you remember you go to parties to meet men.'

'Henry's going to be there with Sally and my invitation says and Guest.'

'Ah.' Venetia understood immediately and after a minute she added, 'Do you have to go?'

'I want to, it's the Camerons' party, everyone's going to be there, all my friends.'

'Yes, of course. We're going. I see the problem. But you can't take Darcy.'

'I don't know who else to take. Jane saw the invitation and she offered to find me someone – but I'm not that desperate.'

'Yes you are.'

'OK, but I'm bloody well not going to be patronised by her any more.' Felicity remembered Jane's visit of the day before. She had breezed into the house, claiming she was just passing and wanted to drop off an invitation to some dreadful coffee morning in aid of the NSPCC. Darcy had gone out, ostensibly to check a new hostel, so Felicity felt obliged to ask her in. Jane immediately pounced on the invitation standing by itself on Felicity's mantelpiece.

'I didn't know *you* knew the Camerons?'

Felicity wasn't keen on the emphasis in that sentence but she was quite good at social tennis so she volleyed. 'Henry was at school with Christopher. I didn't know you knew them.' Thirty all.

'I've known Belinda for yonks. We went to flop and drop together.'

'Excuse me? Flop and drop?' Felicity raised an eyebrow in incomprehension. Thirty-forty.

'Ante-natal classes. You must have gone to them. Wonderful place to make friends.'

All Felicity could remember about her ante-natal class was that Henry had come to fathers' night, rather drunk, after a long liquid lunch at his club. He had thrown up when the instructor started to explain about the waters breaking. Felicity never went back. Jane had undoubtedly won the set. Now she asked her if she had someone to take, as it appeared Tim had met a lonely soul at the golf club and Jane was longing to introduce him to Felicity. At this Felicity panicked and told Jane she already had a date. Now she had to find that someone and was rapidly coming to the conclusion it would have to be Darcy.

'On the plus side, he does know how to behave. Whether he will or not is another matter. But you must keep him away from the champagne,' Venetia eventually conceded.

'His clothes are the real problem – he looks so frayed,' Felicity continued.

'Oscar,' Venetia said suddenly.

Felicity frowned. A son wasn't a satisfactory date under the circumstances – she knew too many people, they would know he wasn't her toy boy.

'At the party?' she asked.

'No – to dress the dreaded Darcy. He'd enjoy it and he wouldn't be stuffy about it, would he?'

'Good idea, I'll give him a ring. He might be able to lend him an old suit. Although Darcy's so thin it'll probably swamp him.'

'You've got to think about this carefully Fifi – he can't wear just any old thing. You don't want him to look gay.'

'Certainly not, anyway Oscar doesn't look gay, whatever that means.' Felicity bristled, immediately defensive.

'Oscar's perfect. We all know that. The apple of his mother's eye. On the other hand you know the look I mean – too well-dressed for an Englishman.'

'OK. So what look should I go for?'

'Not too smart or expensive looking – anyone who knows him will think you've been buying him clothes. Help the Aged.'

'Are you talking about the shop, or are you making a suggestion?'

'What?'

'Help the Aged. Never mind. It's a good idea, then I won't have to get Oscar involved.'

'Does he know about your latest domestic arrangements?'

'Yes. I told him and he's fine about it, but Oliver was taking me to the cinema the day I met Darcy – now he thinks I've got a lover.' Felicity heard Venetia laugh and hoped it wasn't at the idea or her having a lover, but rather at the thought of Oliver's reaction.

'What about Laura?'

'I haven't told her yet. I'm going to tea with her on Friday to see Jamie.'

'Don't mention it. I love your daughter, but she's a frightful prude.'

Although Felicity denied this hotly to her friend, she had to admit to herself it was true. However, at the moment she had the more immediate problem of brushing Darcy up so that he was a suitable escort for the Camerons' party.

Before Darcy had returned from the shops and she had had a chance to tackle him, the telephone rang. It was Oscar.

'How's lover boy?' he asked.

'He is not my lover. You know that perfectly well.'

'Oliver still thinks he is and I bet Laura does too.'

'You haven't told her about Darcy?' Felicity groaned. She was not feeling strong enough for a lecture by her daughter.

'Calm down. Ollie did. But I rang her and explained. It's cool.'

'I'm going to take him to the Camerons' party. I don't suppose you've got an old suit he could wear?' She certainly wasn't going to add anything about it not being too gay.

'If you're desperate I might be able to find something. How tall is he?'

'On second thoughts it was a stupid idea. He's much too short – he'd be swamped by anything of yours.' Felicity got off the bed and sat at her dressing table gazing morosely at her expression.

'Are you sure you still want to work for me?' Oscar changed the subject.

'Of course. You haven't changed your mind have you?' Felicity was immediately worried. Had she not checked the measurements properly?

'No, Mum. I haven't changed my mind, but we've got to put the whole thing on a proper footing.'

Felicity hugged herself. This was the first piece of really good news she'd had in ages. They arranged to meet to discuss all the details, and although she was nervous, she did think this was something she would be able to do.

As soon as she got off the telephone Felicity forced herself to concentrate on Darcy. She had heard him come in while she was talking to Oscar. Now she had to sort him out. Pulling on a pair of comfortable trousers and an old sweatshirt she went rushing downstairs without even bothering to brush her hair. There were two carrier bags on the kitchen table together with her list, with all the items neatly checked off, and there was even a pile of change. Glancing through the window she saw a figure moving about.

'Darcy,' she called as she went through the French windows into her postage-stamp sized garden. 'Are you there? I need you.'

Darcy's head appeared from behind a large ceanothus. He had a trowel in one hand, a trug in the other and a smug expression on his face. 'I've been working ceaselessly on your behalf. Look, I've dug up these onions – I thought I'd cook supper. I'm known for my onion soup.'

'Very possibly, but those are daffodil bulbs and they're poisonous,' Felicity snapped impatiently. She had spent hours planting them in the autumn as her one concession to her new garden. If she hadn't needed him for the party she would have been very tempted to let him poison himself. Remembering what she'd been about to ask him, she forced herself to smile. Darcy looked at her warily, as a stray dog might when expecting to be kicked at any moment.

'I need you to do me a little favour. Nothing too onerous,' she added hastily. 'I want you to come to a party with me on Saturday. Looking smart.'

Darcy's expression changed as he raised a supercilious eyebrow at Felicity.

'I'll be looking smart too,' she said, aware that at the moment this seemed unlikely. 'I'll buy you a suit.'

'That's most generous.' His face broke into a smile that quickly disappeared when Felicity mentioned the charity shop aspect of their shopping trip. He began to mutter something about not being accustomed to that sort of thing, but catching sight of Felicity's expression the words 'Savile Row' dried on his lips.

*

The next morning they set off for a row of charity shops in Battersea. Felicity wasn't quite sure how he did it, but Darcy managed to look both shabby and grand at the same time. He refused to try anything on in the shop, so Felicity was reduced to holding things up in front of him and doing her best to imagine what it would look like and if indeed it would fit. He was slightly mollified when they did eventually find an extremely nice suit in a very fine navy blue worsted, by Gieves and Hawkes, who, to Felicity's complete disbelief, Darcy maintained were his tailors.

*

Over the next few days Felicity spent several hours instilling into Darcy the importance of his behaving himself at the Camerons' party. She was aware that he was drinking, but it didn't seem to be excessive, and he was trying to be helpful around the house. Not always successfully. He had already broken the hoover, pulled the blind off the bathroom window and spilt a glass of red wine on the drawing room carpet. He offered to cook her supper on three occasions and seemed quite hurt when she refused, so finally on Friday when she was going to tea with Laura she agreed he could make spaghetti that night.

Felicity dithered for quite a while trying to decide what to wear for tea with her daughter. It was quite ridiculous, but since the divorce she had found her only daughter quite intimidating. She had been such an adorable baby and it only seemed a moment ago that Felicity was powdering her dear little pink bottom after her bath. But since the divorce Laura had developed a way of looking at her mother through narrowed eyes with a slight sneer on her face. Felicity wasn't sure why, but she knew it had something to do with Henry leaving home. For some reason Laura blamed her mother for breaking up the family home, even though it was Henry who had left. Apart from that she wasn't looking forward to being given the third degree about Darcy.

Finally she chose an A-line denim skirt and a pale blue cotton jumper – quite flattering and tidy and more important, washable. She doted on her only grandchild, but his table manners left a lot to be desired. Laura and Mark lived in a large house in Putney. They had bought it when they first got married and Felicity had been horrified when she heard what it cost and the size of their mortgage. Mark, who worked in the City and earned a fortune, seemed quite relaxed about it and Laura had never bothered her pretty head about money in her life. She had had a few half-hearted jobs before she met Mark, but had given up work with great relief the moment they got engaged.

'Hello darling,' Felicity greeted her daughter enthusiastically, marvelling as she did so that she could have given birth to such a ravishingly pretty girl.

Laura was petite and enviably slim. Even when pregnant she had only had a neat little bump, whereas Felicity remembered she had looked like a whale from the hour she conceived. Today Laura was wearing an off the shoulder pink top and a flowered skirt and pink espadrilles. Her dark hair was cut into an elegant bob that showed off her long neck beautifully.

At that moment Jamie came charging down the path gurgling 'Gaga, gaga'. Felicity would have preferred to be called Granny, but Gaga seemed to have stuck. Rather unfortunately close to the truth, she thought. She and Aunt Violet; Gaga and Great Gaga. Then, his sticky little hand in her own, they walked together up the path.

'You look nice.' Laura sounded surprised. 'You've done something different with your hair.'

'Venetia took charge – sent me to Roberto.'

'Wish she'd done that years ago. Then Daddy might not have ... '

'What?'

'Nothing, forget it.'

'No. I won't forget it.' She hadn't been in the house five minutes and already the atmosphere was charged with sparks. Gritting her teeth Felicity followed her daughter as they walked into the kitchen where Concepcion was ironing, a curtain of dark hair falling over her face. She didn't want to fight with Laura, but she really didn't see why she should be criticised every time she saw her.

'Pas devant les domestiques,' Laura hissed. 'Can you put the kettle on, Concepcion? We'll have tea in the conservatory.'

'Yes, Mrs Lancaster. 'Allo Mrs Fox. 'Ow are you?' The Spanish girl looked up and smiled, showing off her perfect, even white teeth.

'Fine thank you.' Jamie was still holding on to her hand.

'Fargin. Fargin,' he said eagerly, dragging her towards the conservatory.

'See you later, Concepcion,' she called over her shoulder.

'He wants you to see his new fire engine. Oscar brought it back from New York.' Laura picked up a plate of biscuits and

Felicity followed her out of the kitchen. In the middle of the conservatory was a large red fire engine almost as big as Jamie, who immediately sat on top of it and began ringing the bell.

'Laura, can we get back to what you said when I arrived?'

'Mum, I'm sorry. I shouldn't have said anything.' Laura's voice was contrite. She was like Henry sometimes, speaking without thinking.

'No you shouldn't. Maybe I could've made a bit more of an effort with my appearance, but your father wasn't perfect.'

'Don't spoil the afternoon. I've said I'm sorry. Please.' Laura's grey eyes looked pleadingly at her mother and then she smiled. 'Have a biscuit?'

'I shouldn't. My diet ... ' Felicity's hand hovered over the plate.

'How's it going? You're looking thinner.'

'I've only lost about five pounds – it's a bit up and down I'm afraid.'

'I think you're doing really well.' Laura was trying to make up for her earlier remarks. Felicity knew she wouldn't want her mother angry with her for long.

'How's Mark?' Felicity bit into a biscuit as she spoke and succeeded in covering herself in crumbs.

'So busy, you wouldn't believe. He's never home before nine and then he's completely knackered. He fell asleep in the middle of dinner the other night. I never see him – he leaves before seven.'

'How awful. It can't be good for him working those hours. He'll burn out.' Felicity hoped that was the right expression.

'Tell me about it. Every time I say anything he goes on about the mortgage and the bills.'

'What about selling this place and finding somewhere cheaper?' Felicity sipped her tea and helped herself to another biscuit.

'I've suggested that but he won't hear of it.'

'Or the country even?'

'I don't want to leave London,' Laura wailed. 'All my friends are here. And if I was in the country I'd never find any help. No decent au pair wants to be stuck out in the sticks. Concepcion loves being in London. She has a great time. One day perhaps, when the children are bigger.'

'Children?'

'I told you we're trying – though at this rate it'll be an immaculate conception.'

'Si, senora.' Concepcion appeared with a fresh pot of tea and a jug of squash for Jamie.

'It's all right. I was talking about something else.' Laura and Felicity laughed.

Concepcion gave them a baffled look, but she gave Jamie a glass of squash and a biscuit, and then sat down on the floor to play with him.

'So what's all this about you having a man living with you?' Laura half-whispered as she kept an eye on Jamie and Concepcion, although Felicity didn't imagine either of them would be interested.

'It's nothing. He's a chap, an old friend, a bit down on his luck. He's just staying with me for a few days.'

'You'd better watch out. He's probably after your money.'

Felicity gave a slight snort of derision, but perhaps Laura was right. Maybe she was being naïve.

'We had dinner with Daddy and Sally last week,' Laura announced with a slightly guilty look as she poured them both another cup of Lapsang Souchong.

'Really.' Felicity's voice was tight, but she forced herself to continue. 'How was he?'

'I knew you'd be like that.' Laura fiddled nervously with her wedding ring as she spoke.

'Like what? I'm pleased you still see your father.' Felicity didn't add 'in spite of what he did.' Much as she felt like it.

'I'm not sure he's all that happy.' Felicity hastily took a sip of tea to cover her confusion. She wasn't sure what she felt. She should be glad he was unhappy, but however badly he'd behaved she still didn't like to think of Henry being miserable. They'd been together for too long. He'd hurt her and she might hate him, but she couldn't help loving him at the same time. She sat down on the floor to play with Jamie in an attempt to hide her mixed emotions. Concepcion gave her a warm smile and Felicity thought wistfully of how much easier life had been when she was young.

CHAPTER 9

FELICITY FOUND IT HARD TO SLEEP THAT NIGHT, after her tea with Laura. Unwelcome images kept coming into her head. But it was no good thinking about Henry, imagining they could turn the clock back. Finally in the dark reaches of the night Felicity had had a wild fantasy that she and Darcy might have gone to the party dressed in matching navy suits. She could imagine them turning heads as they entered the room making Henry wildly jealous. In the cold light of day she realised it would only take the addition of a couple of bowler hats for them to look like Laurel and Hardy. And while she was all for everyone having fun, she didn't really want it to be at her expense. So she was forced to revert to her earlier plan.

She was feeling extremely nervous. It was the first time she had seen Henry and Sally together since the divorce. She visited Sadie to make sure her hair looked perfect and in the evening she took Rose's advice and did her makeup before putting on the freshly dry-cleaned cream silk tunic. Luckily the dry cleaners had been able to remove the stain. She allowed herself plenty of time to get ready and by thinking cool thoughts was able to complete her makeup without breaking into a hot flush. Darcy managed to look quite presentable in his suit with a clean shirt and tie and polished shoes. Felicity smelt a faint whiff of whisky on his breath, but decided to ignore it. They wouldn't have to stay long and if she could stop him from talking too much and keep him upright all would be well.

They found a taxi straight away and arrived fashionably late outside Annabel and Charles Cameron's large and expensive house off Kensington Church Street. Charles had inherited oodles of money and had gone on to make even more doing something in the City that made Felicity's brain glaze over just trying to understand. Every year they gave a lavish cocktail party for a couple of hundred of their closest friends. As the taxi stopped Felicity saw several people she knew chatting on the steps. She tried to convince herself this was going to be fun as she descended from the taxi after Darcy and he took her arm. She smiled graciously and waved cheerfully at Daisy who was just entering the house. Suddenly Darcy tripped and clutched frantically at Felicity to steady himself.

'You're pissed,' she hissed at him as she looked up to see Henry and Sally walking up the steps.

'Hi,' she forced herself to say through gritted teeth, as she and Darcy struggled to remain upright. She heard Sally say 'Typical, making an exhibition of herself,' as she swanned past with the merest nod of her head, and Henry raised an eyebrow but she could see that he was struggling not to laugh. Even through her embarrassment and fury Felicity noticed he was looking older and tireder than when she had last seen him. By now her cool facade had completely gone and she was puce in the face as she yanked Darcy, who seemed none the worse for his accident, with her and marched into the party. She was seething about Sally's remark, all the more so as she had a ghastly flashback of a few weeks after Henry had left when she had spotted Sally across a crowded street in Tetbury and had been unable to stop herself shouting 'You fucking bitch – how dare you steal my husband,' at her, which had been undignified, but satisfactory at the time. Together she and Darcy made a slow and deliberate ascent up the stairs to the first floor and into the double drawing room. Felicity thought without much resentment that you could fit the whole of her house in Battersea into this one room and still have space for a party. Charles and Annabel were standing at the entrance greeting their guests.

'Felicity darling, how wonderful of you to come. Looking as lovely as ever.' Charles smiled at her warmly, but Felicity had just heard him saying exactly the same thing to the guest in front of her.

'Thank you Charles, lovely to see you and Annabel.' She beamed at them both and added, 'You know Darcy of course.' She said this as a statement rather than a question.

'Of course.' Annabel nodded her perfectly groomed head but Felicity noticed that she and Charles exchanged a quick and practised glance. Darcy stepped forward with a little click of his heels and to Felicity's horror he gave a small hiccup then took Annabel's hand and planted a wet kiss on it.

'It's been far too long, dearest Annabel.' Annabel's expression suggested it would be a lot longer in future if she had anything to do with it. And Felicity noticed she surreptitiously wiped the back of her hand on her dress. Now Felicity looked round the room, desperate to find an ally. There were probably about a hundred people there already, but the room still looked empty, although the noise level was prodigious. Most of the furniture had been removed from the room and only a few chairs remained against the walls for the older guests. Without the heavy Persian rugs that normally covered the floor the polished wood reverberated with sound. Laura and Mark were standing talking to a distinguished-looking couple. When Laura saw her mother she turned towards her with a smile, which froze in disapproval when she saw Darcy. It was apparent that however hard she had tried to tidy him up Laura didn't think Darcy was a suitable escort for her mother. Felicity made some quick introductions and kissed her daughter and son-in-law.

Darcy kissed Laura's hand and remarked, 'It's obvious where you get your good looks from.'

Which as a compliment pleased Felicity only marginally more than it pleased her daughter; in fact Laura looked as though she might be about to consult her solicitor. The elderly couple turned out to be an important banker and his wife. Felicity grabbed Darcy's arm and just managed to prevent him doing his hand-kissing routine again. At that moment she spotted Venetia and Daisy standing by the French windows looking down on the garden and she went over to them as quickly as she could. She kissed them both and turned reluctantly to introduce Darcy.

'Dear ladies. A picture of loveliness,' Darcy proclaimed and gave a little bow.

'Darcy.' Venetia acknowledged him with a faint and distant smile, but Felicity could see the corners of Daisy's mouth twitching in amusement.

'Don't you dare kiss their hands.' Felicity glared at him. This was turning out to be a terrible idea.

Darcy, who had been about to do just that, contented himself with patting Daisy's arm and then looking hurt he clamped his arms rigidly to his side and spoke. 'I will go forth and procure refreshment for you all. Champagne, ladies?' Without waiting for a reply he set off unsteadily across the room towards a long table at the far end that was serving as a bar. As there were white-coated waiters circling the room with trays of glasses, and Venetia and Daisy both had drinks in their hands, this was hardly necessary. However, Felicity was just relieved to see him go. Now she turned to Venetia.

'Why?' she asked accusingly, 'Why didn't you tell me Darcy was the social kiss of death?'

Venetia, who was her usual elegant self, immaculate in a taupe trouser suit and a cream silk camisole, merely shook her blonde hair and smiled. 'I tried to warn you, but if you remember you refused to listen,' she said quite reasonably.

'What a pretty dress,' Felicity said to Daisy, to change the subject.

'Whose is it?' Venetia asked with her fashion editor's voice.

'I think it must be Rose's; I found it in the attic.'

'I meant what's the designer's name. Forget it.' Venetia was wearing perilously high-heeled mules that, Felicity thought, must account for her swaying slightly as they spoke. Looking round the room Felicity noticed it was filling up, but she could still see across to where Sally was holding court. Two or three people looked in her direction and laughed and Felicity had no doubt she was being discussed.

'It kills me to admit it, but she looks fabulous,' Felicity snarled, suddenly full of anger. 'Younger every time I see her. I don't know how she does it.'

'Collagen, Botox and plastic surgery – she's had the works,' Venetia said acidly.

'Is that why she looks as though Henry's punched her in the mouth and her eyes are about to pop out?' laughed Daisy, who looked gorgeous in a flower-print dress with spaghetti straps that showed off her firm, tanned and young arms. Not for her the pashmina, so casually draped over many of the older arms in the room.

'Oh watch out,' Felicity exclaimed. 'There's Jane Bignall.'

'Where?' Daisy was eager to see the famous Jane who she had heard much about, but never met. She followed Felicity's gaze.

'Who's that dishy man she's talking to? Her husband?'

'No. I don't know who that is? D'you Netty?'

Venetia looked at Felicity blankly for a moment, then pulling herself together she followed the direction of her friend's glances. 'Sam Tollard,' she said indifferently.

Felicity frowned. What was wrong with Venetia? She was the great party queen.

'D'you know any more about him?' Daisy asked, determined to include Venetia. But Venetia merely shrugged.

Felicity wondered what was wrong, she certainly wasn't in a party mood. And where was Andrew?

Felicity stopped looking at Jane. It was all right if you were married, she reflected bitterly, you could find attractive men to chat up at a party. She said as much to Daisy, who looked incredulous.

'Fifi, you've really got to get over this whole not having a husband thing,' Daisy told her. 'You've got a personality, you don't need Henry by your side, or Darcy,' she added.

Felicity looked wildy round the room as she remembered her guest. As she did so she noticed that Rose didn't seem to be here. She absently helped herself to a prawn wrapped in filo pastry from a passing wicker basket. The food at the Camerons was always delicious and she and Rose usually vied with each other to see who could spot this season's new trend-setting delicacy.

'Where's Rose? Isn't she here?'

'She's gone into hibernation,' Daisy confided. 'She simply won't leave home. Did you realise she hasn't been to London for over a year?'

'Not even to the hairdresser?' Felicity was astonished and mortified she hadn't noticed. Rose had been coming up to London to go to the hairdresser once a week for as long as she could remember. 'Not even to Warminster?'

Daisy shook her head. Felicity frowned. She was perturbed, Rose had always been so social, outgoing. She made a mental note to ring her first thing in the morning. But would it do any good? Rose was much better at talking about other people's problems than her own. Then as she looked around the room she realised she had something else to worry about. Darcy was still nowhere to be seen.

'Where's Darcy?' she asked Venetia. 'He should be back with champagne by now. I can't see him.' A waiter carrying a large silver tray of drinks came up to them at that moment and Felicity helped herself. Daisy shook her head as she gestured to her still-full glass. Venetia drained her own glass, stretched out an elegant hand and exchanged her now-empty glass for a full one.

'Probably finding it impossible to wrench himself away from all that free alcohol,' Venetia said, nodding towards the far corner of the room.

'I'd better go and find him.' Felicity set off in the direction Venetia indicated, but almost immediately she turned back. 'Oh, no,' she groaned as she spotted Jane marching purpose-fully towards them dragging a man with her. Unfortunately the man was not the attractive one she had been talking to earlier. This one looked more like Jane's usual type, red-faced and hearty.

'This is jolly, isn't it?' Jane exclaimed. 'I've brought a chap over to meet you. Can't have you standing here with all these women, when your ex is in the room. This is Bertie. He's married,' she added and then continued, 'but his wife's visiting her mother in South Africa. It's all right Bertie, you'll be perfectly safe with Felicity. We've known each other for yonks. Any trouble, just give me a shout. Just don't let her get started on the rugger songs.' She brayed with laughter at her own joke. 'Sally's looking terrific, isn't she?' Jane added. Then realising what she had said she made an apologetic face at Felicity who glared at her.

At that moment over Jane's shoulder Felicity saw Andrew standing at the bottom of the garden steps, by a gazebo, too close to Sonia. She was leaning back against an old apple tree and Andrew had his hand flat on the wall beside her. They were gazing into each other's eyes and talking with their heads close together. Felicity forced herself to stop looking down at them and turned back to Jane. She started to chatter wildly. She had to prevent Venetia seeing what was going on outside.

'What fun this is. So many old mates. Haven't enjoyed a party so much in years.' She could hear herself beginning to gibber, lying frantically and sounding just like Jane. Out of the corner of her eye she watched Venetia turn her face slowly towards the window. She stood silently, glass in hand, looking with an enigmatic expression on her face out at the garden.

The next moment there was a loud crash from the far side of the room causing a welcome diversion. Although any feelings of relief Felicity had felt dispersed when she realised Darcy appeared to be at the centre of it. They all turned their heads and at that moment the people in the middle of the room stepped back just in time for Felicity to see Darcy falling like a felled tree on top of a pile of glasses, that had undoubtedly caused the original crash, in front of the bar. What had possessed her to imagine he might behave, that he might be a suitable date for even one evening? To add to her humiliation Felicity saw Henry pick him up and drag him to the nearest sofa. Sally was following on his heels making the closest post-botox expression she could to a frown. Furious though Felicity was she couldn't help feeling quite affectionate towards Henry. Spoilt, lazy, unfaithful he might be, but he was kind and he had spotted a fellow sinner in trouble and gone to his rescue. Felicity left Jane with mixed feelings – she was glad to get away from her, but uncertain about the scenario that awaited her by the bar. She pushed her way through the crowd, passing Sam Tollard as she did so, but this was not the time to try and win him over with the power of her personality.

Thankfully by the time she got there Henry had got Darcy seated on a sofa and had organised a cup of black coffee for him.

'Never mind, old boy. You here with my wife?' he was saying to Darcy in a friendly manner, as Felicity arrived at his side, just in time to notice Sally flinch.

'Ex-wife now,' Felicity said automatically.

'Oh hello, Fifi. Trouble is,' he muttered out of the side of his mouth, 'he's so thin, he must get drunk on a thimbleful of whisky.'

Unlike me, Felicity thought, when it would take a whole barrel. Between them they ministered to Darcy while Sally stood, her face impassive, apparently too mindful of her recent expensive injections to risk pursing her lips, but her eyes were like flint.

'For heaven's sake Henry, leave him alone. *She* brought him,' she snapped. 'Let *her* deal with him.'

Felicity gave her a weak smile and wondered as she did so why she had had such a crush on her at school – had she gone for the strong silent type when she was young, or was it her performance as Mr Darcy in the school production of *Pride and Prejudice* that had done it?

As soon as her present-day Darcy opened his eyes and began to make a modicum of sense Felicity decided it would be better to take him home before any more disasters occurred. She looked round the room preparing to say her goodbyes and saw Venetia standing by the window, glass in hand and swaying slightly with a frozen expression on her face. Felicity craned forward and, looking down into the garden, saw Andrew still deep in conversation with Sonia. They were standing in the same place, heads still together, talking intently, and as Felicity watched Andrew brushed a strand of hair away from Sonia's forehead. Felicity gasped at the intimate gesture and turned towards Venetia. Her friend was walking rather unsteadily towards the bar.

'You deal with Darcy, I'll cope with Venetia.' Daisy was by her side.

'Thank heavens you're here – this is a nightmare. My date is out cold and my best friend is getting extremely drunk. All in front of my ex-husband. Perfect.'

*

Somehow or other, with Henry's help, Felicity got Darcy into a taxi and home from the party. He might have been skinny, but as a dead weight he was not a very manageable package. Once home she dragged him out of the car and half-pulling and half-pushing she eventually succeeded in getting him upstairs and into the spare room. Luckily the stairs were very narrow so she was able to wedge him once or twice when she needed to pause for breath. As far as she could see the only good thing about the evening was that she had managed to avoid introducing Jane and Darcy to each other.

It was still dark when Felicity woke up and heard the snoring next to her. For a brief moment she thought Cat had climbed through the window and got into bed with her. But something told her this was not Cat. Eyes still tightly closed she gingerly stretched out a hand and felt a bony arm. She opened her eyes and right in front of her face, with his head on the pillow next to her, was Darcy.

'Fucking hell!' she shouted in his ear. He sat up in bed and half-opened two red, unfocussed eyes. He turned his head towards her and then, as if the effort was too much, he slumped back on to the pillow and shut his eyes again. Felicity realised it would be hopeless trying to wake him up and instead got up herself. Even though Darcy was still asleep she was careful to hold her stomach in as she walked across the room. She wished that for once in her life she had bothered to put on her nightdress before going to bed. She might not want him in her bed, but she certainly didn't want him to see all her wobbly bits. At least he was wearing pyjamas, which meant she wouldn't have to see more of him than was strictly necessary.

Downstairs in the kitchen Felicity put the kettle on and, wrapped in her yellow cotton dressing-gown, she sat at the table, waiting for the water to boil and wondering why she had ever allowed Darcy to move into her house. She must have been mad. Feeling sorry for someone was one thing, but he could be a dangerous lunatic for all she knew. As for him getting into her bed, so far she hadn't got round to thinking about 'bed' in that sense. She'd imagined that sort of thing was over after Henry. If she had ever thought about it at all, she would have assumed he would be her one and only. Since the divorce, she might have allowed herself to imagine meeting someone, going out to dinner with them, the cinema, that sort of thing. But even in her own mind, she'd never got any further. And if she had allowed her imagination to go any further she would have hoped it would be someone more like Sam Tollard and not Darcy.

She shuddered, and drew her dressing-gown more tightly round her. She felt sick. What *had* happened with Darcy? Had anything happened? Why had he got into her bed? She didn't flatter herself it was anything to do with her desirability, more to do with Darcy's alcoholic state. But that was somehow just as irritating. It was one thing being fancied by someone one didn't fancy, but quite another being a blunder in the dark. She allowed her mind to flutter around the idea that something might have happened, but she quickly retreated from the image. She would know if she'd been ravished, wouldn't she? She hoped she hadn't been snoring, or dribbling or even worse, farting in her sleep. And how much of her had he seen and was he sober enough to remember anything? It had been one thing Henry seeing her in the nude – he'd had thirty years to get used to it. But someone new – she wasn't sure she was ready for that yet. And even if she had been, that person should very definitely not have been Darcy.

The kettle finally boiled and she made herself a welcome cup of coffee. Remembering the effort of holding her tummy in as she walked across the bedroom, she took a bottle of skimmed milk from the fridge and poured some into her coffee. Then sitting at the kitchen table she cupped her chin in her hands. She still felt sick. Maybe if she ate something she would feel better. Putting her mug on the table she got up and made herself some toast and spread it thickly with the last of her homemade marmalade. She'd made it every year at Upton; it was part of her routine, the rhythm of her life. When she had lived in the country the seasons of the year had come and gone, each of them with their own tasks. She was finding it difficult to settle into a pattern in London. She would have liked to talk to someone. She looked at the kitchen clock – it was five-thirty – not even Rose would be awake. Rose, that reminded her, she must ring her as soon as possible. There was something wrong, but what? What was it Daisy had said? Rose hadn't been to London in over a year and she had stopped going out. Felicity felt awful she hadn't noticed. What a bad friend she was. She had seen plenty of Rose and talked to her all the time, but it was true, she couldn't remember the last time she had seen her in London away from the safety of her own home.

Felicity tried to think about the problem. Rose was the one person she knew who had always seemed to have everything. Leo, who was the most wonderful man, adored her. Was he ill? Did Rose know something she didn't want to tell anyone? Or was it something to do with her children? She didn't see them very much, but they talked to each other on the telephone all the time, sent e-mails back and forth. Surely there wasn't anything wrong there? But perhaps as she got older she was missing them more. Even though it wasn't the same, she had Daisy and the boys living on top of her. And Daisy had always been like a daughter to Rose. She was surrounded by family and friends.

Round and round Felicity's mind it went – what was the problem? Felicity resolved to ring her as soon as possible and drive down to Hatch. She and Rose had always been close, but Felicity realised, yet again, that since her divorce she had become far too wrapped up in herself and her own problems. What a selfish cow she'd become. It seemed to her it was one of the most unattractive aspects of getting divorced – it made people so introspective. She had noticed it happening to friends in the past, but she had never thought it would happen to her. But then she had never imagined she would end up divorced.

She wished she could ring Venetia, but it was too early. Besides, judging by what she had seen last night Venetia had enough problems of her own. She had got very drunk last night and she had seen Andrew and Sonia together. But how much did she know? What was there to know? Andrew had always been an outrageous flirt, everyone knew that, but this seemed to be more serious. And what about the magazine, how were her problems there? It really was high time she stopped always thinking about her own life. Her friends had been patient with her while she got over the divorce. Now it was time to start looking outwards and getting involved in their lives once more.

Soon it got light, and after several cups of coffee she felt better and went upstairs to have a bath. She glanced into her bedroom on the way to the bathroom and Darcy was still fast asleep in her bed. Later on when she came out of the bathroom she tiptoed into her bedroom to pick up some clothes, but she needn't have bothered, Darcy was no longer there. Shrugging her shoulders she decided she would deal with him later in the day, when she hoped she would have worked out what to say to him.

*

Having bathed, dressed and left the house, she set off for the gym. Later that morning she walked briskly and cheerfully (she had weighed herself under the eagle eye of Terry and found that she had lost another three pounds) to see Venetia. When she arrived at her house the curtains were still drawn tightly, although it was now after ten. She rang the bell and waited. After a short time she heard footsteps and eventually the door was opened. Venetia was wearing a cream silk dressing-gown, her hair was unbrushed and for the first time in years Felicity saw her friend without makeup. She managed not to show the shock she felt, but at the same time, although she despised herself for having the thought, she made a mental note never to answer her own door without at least doing a modicum of repair work first.

'All right, Netty?' she asked, although it was obvious she was far from all right. Beautiful Venetia, was it just Andrew that had done this to her?

'I'm fine,' she croaked. 'Had a bit of a late night, think I had a touch of food poisoning, now I've overslept.' She looked as if she was about to burst into tears.

Felicity did not believe her. Judging by the state she had been in at the party last night, for food poisoning read hangover. She wondered if Andrew had come home with her, and if so had there been a row. Felicity was about to put out her arms to give Venetia a hug, although they had never had a very tactile friendship, but Venetia rebuffed her.

'Might just have a brandy to settle my stomach,' she said.

Felicity followed her into the drawing room and noticed how Venetia winced as she drew back the curtains and light flooded into the room. She pulled her dressing-gown more tightly around her and tied the sash. She was thinner than ever and despite herself Felicity couldn't help feeling a tad jealous. She might look ghastly, but at least she looked thin and ghastly, which was a shallow and unworthy thought when her friend was so obviously in trouble, but it popped into Felicity's mind nevertheless. Venetia suddenly slumped down into an armchair. Felicity, immediately full of contrition, took Venetia's hand. She perched herself on the coffee table beside her, hoping as she did so that it wouldn't break. She looked round the Kent-Fletchers' normally immaculate drawing room. It stank of cigarettes and there was an overflowing ashtray on the floor next to the music centre and a Leonard Cohen CD. On the marble slab in front of the fireplace an empty bottle of champagne lay on its side and a half empty glass with a cigarette end in it sat forlornly on the mantelpiece.

'Oh Venetia,' she said softly, 'what's up?'

'Actually, everything.' Venetia's voice was flat. 'The job's gone.' She ran the satin sash of her dressing-gown between her fingers repetitively. 'They call it downsizing. Want me to do freelance pieces – we all know what that means.' She coughed and lit a cigarette. 'Issuing a brave press release saying I'm leaving to spend more time by myself. Ha! Bloody ha! Certainly not with Andrew.' Her voice took on a bitter tone.

Felicity was silent. She could think of nothing to say. This was the last thing she had expected. She knew Venetia had been having problems at work for a while, but it had never occurred to her she might be sacked. She was a talented and respected fashion editor. Felicity felt terrible for her, Venetia was such a good friend and had always looked after Felicity, now she needed someone to be there for her. She tried to think of something helpful and encouraging to say and after a moment asked a question.

'What about the novel you always said you'd write one day? When you had time.'

'Huh – that's what journalists always say. Its just talk. Not going to happen. I'm too old. And don't you dare mention Mary Wesley.' Venetia poured herself another brandy, glaring at Felicity as she did so.

'Netty, d'you think that's going to help?'

'Obviously, yes. Don't look so disapproving. I'm not going to do this every day.'

'I should hope not, your liver'll collapse. Where's Andrew?' It was Sunday, so he should be at home.

'I don't know and I don't fucking well care.'

'Have you had a row?' Felicity asked tentatively.

'Why? What d'you mean?' Venetia was getting aggressive.

Felicity knew she had to be careful – she had no idea what Venetia knew about Andrew and Sonia. What was there to know? Was it a flirtation or were they having an affair? She had certainly seen them together last night and she obviously suspected something, but Andrew had always been a flirt, there was nothing new in that.

'I didn't mean anything, but you look so upset. I know you, it's not just the job, is it?' Felicity felt that she had to ask.

Venetia was immediately suspicious. 'Have you heard anything?'

'No, of course not. It was your tone of voice,' Felicity said hastily.

'I can deal with Andrew,' Venetia said grimly, but she looked very vulnerable as she sank back onto the sofa, and Felicity was worried she was near breaking point.

'Why don't I take you out to lunch – then we can go shopping,' Felicity said, desperately and inappropriately, but anything to try and cheer Venetia up.

'No, can't, got to get myself together and get into the magazine. Got a few things to pick up and a farewell party – what fun that's going to be,' she said bitterly as she dragged herself to her feet. 'Suppose I'd better get dressed now.' She swayed slightly and then steadied herself on the mantelpiece. She looked frail and Felicity wondered when she had last had something to eat. So much for her resolution to be a better friend.

'What about lunch at least? You've got to eat,' she said desperately.

'Not hungry. I'll get something later.'

Felicity was sure she was lying. 'Isn't there anything I can do?'

'What? Find me a new job perhaps?' The voice was bitter.

'No. Help you decide what to wear, that sort of thing.'

'Huh! *You*, help me?' Venetia didn't even try to keep the derision out of her voice.

Felicity realised there was probably nothing more she could do today. Venetia was the kindest person in the world under normal circumstances, but these circumstances were not normal. Like a trapped animal she was lashing out at all around her. Felicity would ring her tomorrow – perhaps

Venetia would want to talk and it would be Felicity's turn to listen.

As soon as Felicity got home she rang Rose, but her cousin claimed she didn't have time to talk. The chickens had red mites and she was off to dust them with powder. It was a perfectly normal thing for Rose to say and Felicity knew it would be useless trying to engage her in a talk about any worries she might have. Catching her at the right moment was vital. Felicity would just have to keep on trying.

CHAPTER 10

I T WAS STILL VERY HOT AND DUSTY IN LONDON following the Camerons' party. London, Felicity realised, unlike its continental cousins, was not a city suited to summer. It was happier in spring and autumn, she concluded, as yet one more person hooted angrily at her as she tried to park her car. She couldn't remember when she had been in London in August before now. After leaving Venetia at her house making a show of getting ready to face her work colleagues, Felicity made her way slowly back to Battersea to confront Darcy.

When she got home he was out, but the whole house was immaculate and he had left a note apologising so profusely that Felicity was left with the impression he was as horrified at ending up in her bed as she was at having him there. To her irritation she was both pleased and annoyed by this. She went into the kitchen and busied herself making gazpacho for supper. They would have to face each other sooner or later and she thought it would all be much easier over a meal.

Oscar was coming to pick her up at three o'clock so that they could go and see another possible premises he had found for his new shop. The architect had found too many problems with the one Felicity had looked at and Oscar had been searching frantically ever since. He had finally realised it was more important to find a suitable place than to swan off all over the country wooing craftsmen. Now he sounded very excited when he rang and she was excited too and a bit nervous. She really wanted to do well in this job. It wasn't just that it would give her something to do, but it might give her back some badly needed self respect.

It was a big shop on the Fulham Road, near Munster Road, and until recently had been a greengrocers. Felicity thought it would be ideal. There was plenty of space. The shop itself had large windows onto the street and the rooms at the back would be perfect for an office and storeroom. Inevitably there was a lot of work to be done, but it was in an excellent location. The architect had already had a look at it and pronounced it suitable. So Oscar and Felicity spent the rest of the day discussing where everything should be, what colour to paint the walls and even the name. Felicity was able to put Venetia to the back of her mind and concentrate on her son. When they finished measuring and making notes Oscar took her for a cup of coffee. They got quite giggly as they tried to think of names for the new shop.

'Crystal Balls?'

'Something for the Weekend.'

'The Dogs Bollocks.'

Things were getting sillier and sillier until Oscar finally said, 'How about "With Knobs On"?' and they were both agreed that it was a good name and were pleased with their own cleverness.

'How are you going to manage once the shop opens?' Felicity licked the last of the foam from her cappuccino off her spoon. They had not yet discussed other staff and Felicity was nervous Oscar might expect her to work there seven days a week.

'There's a wonderful girl, super efficient. Gillian.'

'Really?' Already Felicity didn't like the sound of Gillian. She rather doubted a super efficient girl would want to work with her. Not that she thought she was inefficient herself, but she had a mental picture of a super cool, supercilious blonde making her feel inadequate.

'I thought she could run the shop. The customers will love her.'

Now Felicity detested her. 'Where did you find her?'

'I met her with Barry last week. She grew up near his parents. But I want you to have a look at her. Hiring and firing the staff will be your responsibility.'

Felicity gave a sigh of relief. How stupid she was to feel intimidated by someone she had never met, particulary now she knew she wouldn't have to hire her if she didn't like her.

'Have you worked out exactly what everyone's going to do?'

'Of course. I'm Mr. Efficiency. Miles and Gillian to run the shop. I'll do the buying and you're in charge of administration.'

'Miles?'

'He's a gay friend of mine, and Barry's. We met him in New York, but he lives in London now. Do you have to do that?' Oscar frowned at his mother who was by now running her finger round her cup and licking it.

'Sorry darling, but it's the chocolate powder. It's delicious.' She paused for a moment savouring the taste of the chocolate. 'Can we have some more coffee and a piece of that cake?'

'I thought you were on a diet?' Oscar was looking disapproving. He wanted his mother to look her best and had so much self-discipline himself.

'I am, I've lost eight pounds. Well I had, but then I slipped a bit and put three back on, now I've taken them off again. So I'm having a day off. I'm starting again on Monday.'

'Why not have a black coffee and no cake – then you'll lose some more weight?'

'Don't be so logical. Everyone knows if you put weight on quickly it comes off quickly. It's a well-known fact. So if I eat lots this week, I'll start next week heavy and lose it all in the first few days, which will be good for my morale.'

'Women's brains ... '

'Don't be sexist.'

'All right, have a piece of cake, but I don't want you ringing me next week complaining about your weight.'

'I promise I won't.'

Oscar beckoned to the waiter who came over fluttering his eyelashes, making Felicity yearn for the days when good-looking Italian waiters fluttered them at her. Although she wasn't sure they ever had. He left them the menus and scurried off to a table full of young men at the back of the restaurant.

'Going back to the shop.' Felicity was scanning the menu as she spoke, looking for a suitably calorie-filled delicacy, 'how much of my time do you actually think you'll need?'

'I don't know. How does three days a week sound?'

Felicity smiled. That sounded perfect.

'How's Laura?' Oscar asked after they had chosen two suitably greedy slices of chocolate cake.

'OK, I think,' Felicity replied and then told Oscar about her tea party on Friday.

'She doesn't really blame you – but she was always Daddy's girl – she can't bear to think he could be to blame.'

Felicity thought how nice her son was. Even if he could be a wicked gossip, he was always ready to see the other person's point of view and she wondered where he got it from, certainly not from his mother. She gave herself a mental slap on the wrist. She must stop all this self-pity. She hated it in other people and now she was full of it herself.

'I know. But I wish she wouldn't take it out on me,' she continued.

'Did she have a go at you?'

'Almost – she started to say Dad left because I'd let myself go.'

'Well?'

'Don't you start!' Felicity groaned. She hadn't realised all her children had noticed her deterioration. 'I had my hands full with the B & B, the garden, everything.'

'I know, Mum. I'm not criticising you. You can't expect me to understand marriage. I find it difficult enough just sharing a house with someone during the week.'

'Barry?'

'Yes – he goes to his cottage every weekend, he's really into his garden and you know me and the country. All those birds waking you up at sparrow's fart and the dirt – my cream Versace jacket was ruined last time I went.'

'Why wear it in the country then?'

'Love, I suppose, still trying to create the right impression.'

'And that's where I went wrong. Stopped trying to create an impression.'

'Silly old bag.' Oscar leant over and squeezed her hand. 'It wasn't your fault. I think Dad was having some sort of mid-life crisis.'

'Hmm. That catch-all excuse, the male menopause.' Felicity felt she had heard that excuse once too often.

'And it's so draughty,' Oscar continued about the countryside.

'That's fresh air, darling. It's supposed to be good for you.' Felicity laughed.

'I hate things that are good for me.' Oscar lit a cigarette, inhaled deeply and changed the subject. 'Why doesn't Daisy have a man?'

'Well she has, sort of.' Felicity felt a delicious frisson of guilt as she finished her cake.

'D'you mean the horizontal date?' Oscar, noticing Felicity eyeing his plate, passed it over with half a slice still left.

'Does everyone know about him?' Felicity was surprised.

151

'Well, she's not exactly discreet. I meant a proper man of her own – not someone else's husband or a part-time shag.'

'Does she want one? She's always been such a free spirit.'

'I've just got a feeling she'd like to settle down, now the boys are getting older.'

'That's not what she said to me when we had lunch the other day.'

'No. It's not that she's said anything. Rather the opposite.' Oscar called for the bill and then continued. 'You know, protesting a bit too much.'

'There was that chap Geoffrey – he seemed keen. And he was nice, even though he didn't fancy me.'

'He's OK – he's been really helpful on the money for the shop. But Daisy says she won't go out with him – she's frightened of upsetting you.' Oscar glanced at his mother and then his watch.

'Well, she needn't be – I'm not interested in him and he's certainly not interested in me. Have you got to be somewhere?' Felicity tried to take the bill when it arrived.

'No ... well, yes, I've got a meeting with Miles and Barry.'

'About the shop? D'you want me there?'

'No, not this time. There's plenty of time for you to meet Miles. This is my treat.' Oscar grabbed the bill from the waiter who was hovering by the table.

'Are you sure?' Felicity was still surprised when any of her children paid for her – it was such a short time ago that she was handing out their pocket money every week. Being a mother was full of moments when you realised your children had grown up a lot faster than you were expecting.

'He doesn't want to admit he's made a mistake,' Oscar said suddenly as they were leaving the restaurant. 'She's an awful bitch.'

'Who?' Felicity asked in surprise, although she had a pretty good idea what he was talking about.

'Dad – Sally. I think he'd like to come back home.'

To her surprise Felicity felt a moment of panic, which must have showed on her face as Oscar raised an eyebrow.

'Don't you want him back?' The walked in silence for a moment towards Felicity's car.

'I don't know. It's not that simple. For one thing, there's no home to come back to.'

'Hardly an insoluble problem.'

'Too much has happened,' Felicity stammered. She had not been prepared for this.

Oscar gave his mother a hug as they stood on the pavement in front of the parking meter, then he stepped forward to call a taxi.

'Think about it,' he called as a taxi pulled up and he leapt in. Felicity waved as he drove off, imagining she would think of little else over the next few days.

*

As it happened Felicity tried not to think about Henry too much, at least not during the hours of daylight. She didn't see there was anything she could do at the moment. She could hardly ring Henry, even if she had wanted to, and ask him if there was anything wrong. And it seemed unlikely he would contact *her* – apart from anything else his pride wouldn't let him. Despite that she when she woke in the night her thoughts were whizzing round her brain like a manic Scalextric track. Had she let him go too easily? Why had he even thought of going? All that upheaval. Henry loathed change. At least the Henry she thought she knew loathed change, but perhaps she didn't know him. Oscar and Venetia said it was the male menopause. Was that it? Or was it her own fault? She'd taken him for granted, but worse, she had excluded him. 'Oh Henry, do go and find something to do ... do get out from under my feet ... ' She could hear herself. She'd emasculated him. Once the money had gone and she had had to become the breadwinner, he didn't have a role. She could see that now. How stupid she'd been. Now her children said he was unhappy. But as she couldn't contact him she wondered if there was any way of running into him. Unless they were invited to the same party again, it would be difficult. She could hardly start haunting the village where Henry and Sally lived or casually appearing in front of his tailor or hairdresser. She chased these thoughts round her head until morning.

In the cold light of day she turned her mind to Darcy, he was in her life in the flesh and was her most pressing problem. He had been living in the house for nearly two weeks. He was charming and attentive, had apologised a bit too much for stumbling into her bed, and he did try to be helpful. That was the plus side. On the other hand everything he touched seemed to break, he was incapable of understanding the burglar alarm, and on one occasion when he had cooked for her she had been violently sick during the night.

She also discovered rather late in the day that he had a serious drink problem. Yes, she had been warned and she realised he drank too much at parties, but otherwise it appeared to be fairly under control. He didn't fall over or throw up. He was too cunning for that. She started to notice things like the whisky bottle. Felicity wasn't a whisky drinker, but she liked to keep a bottle in the house for guests. One evening she noticed the bottle in the cupboard was nearly empty so she made a note to buy some more. The next night, when she opened the cupboard to pour herself a gin and tonic, she remembered she had forgotten to buy whisky. To her surprise she saw the bottle was now nearly full. The next night it was nearly empty once more and the following one, a miracle, it was nearly full.

As she no longer believed in fairies she had to assume it was Darcy. Then she opened the cupboard and noticed all those miniature bottles of strange liqueurs she had for making fancy puddings, and the guitar-shaped bottle of orange liquid, brought back from Ibiza as a joke, were empty. As she lived alone, apart from Darcy, there was only one suspect. She didn't think he had been like this when she had known him all those years ago, but perhaps he had. They had all drunk quite a lot in those days, and she had only known him on holiday. She knew she had to talk to him, but kept putting it off. It was quite nice having a man about the place, even a man as hopeless as Darcy. He was company in the evenings, someone to cook for. And it seemed less pathetic than living alone with a part-time cat.

'Darcy,' she accosted him one morning as they were both preparing to leave the house, 'could I have a word with you?' She felt a bit like a headmistress summoning a naughty child into her study.

'Can it wait? I'm meeting a chap about a job.'

'Really?' Felicity tried not to sound too sceptical, but it was hard to imagine that anyone in their right mind would offer Darcy a job.

'Chap I was at school with needs someone to manage his office.'

'And he thinks you'd be suitable?' Felicity knew she wasn't making a good job of stifling the note of disbelief in her voice.

'Why not?' Darcy was hurt, or at least pretending to be and he turned his back on Felicity. She only had time to call 'Don't forget about tonight' at his departing back as he went out of the front door, closing it firmly behind him. Felicity sighed. Another opportunity to confront him had gone. She used to think she was quite good with people, but there was no doubt that lately this skill had deserted her.

There wasn't time to think about it now. Tonight she was having her first dinner party and must get organised. In a moment of weakness she had asked the Bignalls and then persuaded the Kent-Fletchers to come and support her. Venetia seemed more cheerful and to have recovered, if only temporarily, from her fit of depression. Andrew was being attentive and, more importantly, being with Venetia. She had been offered some good freelance work, so on the surface it appeared that things were better. However, when Felicity had tried to have a more in-depth conversation with her, as they had always done in the past, she had cut her off abruptly. In the end Felicity had left it – it was obviously not the right moment. Andrew was busy cultivating Timmy Bignall, who he still wanted to put him up for Tuffnells, so he was delighted to be asked to dinner with them. She would have to keep an eye on Darcy, but apart from that it should be fine. She had already explained to Jane he was an old family friend who had fallen on hard times. Which was very nearly the truth.

One thing she did know how to do was throw a dinner party. Felicity enjoyed cooking and in the old days they had frequently sat down sixteen or more in the dining room. Six would be easy. She decided on iced cucumber soup to start with, as the weather was still so hot. For the main course she would do duck breasts in soy and ginger with Pommes Lyonnaise and mange tout and then fresh mango sorbet for afters.

First of all she had to go to the new shop and wait for the electrician to make sure he knew exactly what to do. The contract had been signed and Oscar was impatient to get on with things. He was on a buying trip in Italy and had trustingly left her in charge. Naturally everything took longer than it was possible to imagine and as a consequence she had to rush over the shopping. Just to be on the safe side she bought three copies of the *Big Issue*. She didn't get back home until nearly five o'clock. As she struggled in through the front door, laden with carrier bags, the phone was ringing. It was Jane Bignall.

'We're really looking forward to this evening, going to be jolly good fun.' There was a pause and Felicity wondered what was coming next. She didn't have to wait long.

'The thing is … ' There was another pause. Felicity remained silent. She was not going to help Jane out of a hole. 'Got a terrific favour to ask actually. The thing is,' she repeated, 'this great friend of ours is over from Hong Kong, she's staying with her brother. He's lovely, you'll adore him, he's getting divorced.' So that was the bait. 'We wondered if you'd come out with us, to a restaurant. She's only in London for one night, we don't want to cancel you, of course not, but we'd really love to see her.'

Naturally, Felicity insisted they should bring them to her house. The more the merrier.

By six-thirty she had the food prepared, the table laid with the silver gleaming and a crystal bowl of roses as a centrepiece. She had even put out the tray with coffee cups and a silver dish of chocolates on it ready for after dinner. She felt surprisingly calm and organised. Darcy came back at seven and Felicity decided she would go up to change in fifteen minutes. She just went to the cupboard to check she had some replacement candles when Darcy opened the passage door; the knob on the store cupboard door hit her in the face. Her front tooth went through her lip and her crown fell off.

'Oh Thit,' she lisped, and the thought crossed her mind that the *Big Issue* was losing its ability to ward off the banana skins of life. Darcy got an ice-cube from the fridge and attempted unsuccessfully to hold it to her lip as she scrabbled on the floor for her crown. Luckily it was intact so she rinsed it under the tap and tried to put it back into her mouth. She discovered it would only stay in place if she held it there with her tongue.

'What am I going to do?' she wailed as she put the crown into an envelope and stuffed it into a drawer.

'Wear a yashmak?'

Darcy wasn't being helpful so Felicity went upstairs to see what the damage was. She had a thick lip, but apart from that it really didn't look too bad, as long as she kept her mouth shut. It was a bit painful, but it was too late to cancel everyone, they would be here in a minute. She took a couple of paracetemol and found an old packet of Valium in the medicine cupboard. She took one to calm her nerves. She covered the swelling up as best she could with makeup and by the time she came downstairs she convinced herself no one would notice.

'How do I look?' she asked Darcy who was pouring himself a whisky.

'Fine,' he said carefully as he turned round. 'Now smile.'

Felicity reluctantly did so.

'Great Scot,' he staggered backwards dramatically, 'that is a truly terrifying sight. Not since I saw Macbeth at the National have I seen a more convincing witch.'

Felicity tried unsuccessfully to snarl at him but went into the drawing room and smiled at herself in the mirror above the fireplace.

'Fuckadoodle do. He's right.' She hurried back into the kitchen and retrieved the crown from the drawer by the telephone. She crammed it into her mouth and placed her tongue firmly against it to hold it in place.

'Ith's no good,' she lisped, 'I'm going have to thtay like thith all night. Oh Chritht. My firstht dinner party ath a thingle woman. What a thuckthess.'

At that moment the doorbell rang and the Bignalls arrived. Felicity told them what had happened.

'Have you tried super glue – it's awfully good for that sort of thing, I believe.' Jane was practical as usual.

'Haven't got any. In any cathe with my luck I'd thtick my lipth together.' Felicity was beginning to get the hang of speaking like this. She wouldn't be able to eat, but that would be good for her figure. A sort of DIY jaw-wiring job.

'What are your friendth nameth?' she asked.

'Sam Tollard and his sister Cicily.'

'Tham and hith thithter Thithily – thaths not pothible?' Felicity didn't know whether to laugh or cry when the doorbell rang again. Not Sam Tollard, that was too cruel. He was the attractive man she had seen talking to Jane at the Camerons' party.

'Darthy,' she shouted as best she could while leading the Bignalls into the drawing room. The word 'slapstick' came into her mind, but she felt it would be as well to keep it there and not attempt to say it. Somehow or other she was able to sort out the drinks while keeping a fairly calm exterior. Jane chattered relentlessly – trying to fill the awkward silence until Venetia and Andrew came into the room, followed by Darcy. He had obviously not explained the situation to them very well, because Venetia immediately went over to Felicity and grabbed her arm.

'Fifi!' Her expression spoke volumes. 'I hope that thick lip isn't the result of collagen injections, 'cos if it is you must sue.'

'Ith it that bad?'

Propelling her out of the room Venetia hissed in her friend's ear as they went into the kitchen. 'You're about to meet an attractive, available man with a swollen lip and a lisp. Only you, Fifi.' Venetia shrugged her shoulders as Felicity bent over the oven and peered through the door at the potatoes.

'If you know him tho well, how come you haven't introduthed him to me?'

'I was waiting for you to lose another ten pounds. He's also charming.'

'Why'th he available then?' Felicity was instantly suspicious. She stood up and divided a packet of peanuts into two glass bowls.

'The rumour is that his wife, Lavinia, fell in love with her brother.' Venetia poured some rice crackers into a shallow glass dish.

'Whoth brother?'

'Her own brother – well step-brother. But there was an awful lot of gossip. Everyone says they're getting divorced.'

Felicity opened her mouth and only just got her tongue under her tooth in time to stop it falling out on to the floor again. Sam was beginning to sound quite interesting as well as nice looking. She had rather unkindly imagined that if he was a friend of Jane and Tim he would turn out to be a crashing bore. He had looked attractive at a distance but the whole thing was academic now she had a thick lip and a lisp. She could see no earthly reason why he would fancy her even at her best, but he certainly wouldn't go for her like this. She decided she'd better not take any more Valium, but she found a bottle of Bach's Rescue Remedy in the cupboard and took a large suck from the dropper, then remembering that sweet chestnut was good for extreme mental anguish she had some of that as well. She was beginning to feel a bit better so picking up the bowls of peanuts she and Venetia went back into the drawing room just as the bell rang again. Leaving Darcy to answer it Felicity handed round the snacks and made sure everyone had a full glass. Hastily glancing round the room she felt quite satisfied. It looked charming in this light, the faded chintz of the curtains, the burgundy sofa, the fireplace filled with dry flowers, it all looked very attractive and inviting. What a pity she didn't.

Sam Tollard and his sister came into the room chatting happily with Darcy. Sam was a big man, with a round face and thick grey hair. He looked about sixty and he had a nice smile. His sister, Cicily, was almost as tall as her brother, but thin and angular. She gazed at Sam in adoration every time he spoke. 'Incest the Tollard family game', Felicity giggled to herself, wondering as she did so whether the Rescue Remedy had been such a good idea. She had a feeling it contained alcohol. Her mind seemed to be following most unsuitable paths. Incest. Inthest. Pity that it was a taboo word – particularly for Felicity tonight – or maybe not a pity. She didn't want a repeat of the Bignalls' party. At least female 'thircumthithion' was going to be a no-no.

'How d'you do.' Felicity brought her mind back to the present with difficulty and held out her hand to Cicily.

'It's awfully kind of you to have us to dinner. Super house you've got here. Jane was my absolutely best friend in Hong Kong. It's too awful now she's not there. I'm only over here 'cos Mother isn't well.' Cicily chattered on turning her back on Felicity halfway through and towards Jane, who had rushed at her shrieking , 'Cissy, Cissy. What fun!'

Felicity turned to Sam Tollard with relief. She thought his sister was rather tiring, and even though the evening had only just started it felt as though it had been going on for hours. What she'd really like to do, she thought, was to sit down on the sofa and have a little sleep. Unfortunately these people were waiting to be fed.

Smiling weakly at Sam she muttered, 'Excuth me. Kitchen dutieth.' She went back to the kitchen. The soup was already in the fridge in a white china tureen. On the table were several little bowls covered in cling film that contained croutons, chopped green, red and yellow peppers, cucumber and tomato. It all looked very pretty, lovely colours. Felicity started to sing tunelessly to herself 'Thom day my printh will come.' She was floating round the kitchen putting plates onto a tray. Suddenly she heard a cough. Sam was standing at the door.

'Excuse me,' he said politely. 'I wondered if you had any more ice?'

'Oh yeth, matheth. Whoopth.' Felicity had never realised how many words in the English language had 'S' in them until tonight. She giggled helplessly and swaying slightly sank onto a chair.

'Are you all right?' Sam looked concerned.

Felicity looked at him and closed one eye. That was better now there was only one of him.

'You gave yourself quite a knock on the head. Are you sure you're not concussed?'

'Thath another one. Concuthed. Concuthed.'

'Don't you think it would be better if you went to bed?'

'But we've only juth met.' Felicity's head flopped forward and she wasn't sure she could make the effort to lift it up again, her neck muscles had stopped working.

Sam smiled gently at her and bent to help her up. Tim Bignall came into the kitchen at that moment and between the two of them they managed to get her upstairs. Jane followed them and got her into to bed.

'D'you think we ought to ring the doctor? Or take her to A & E?' Sam asked. But it appeared that Jane had done a first aid course, and Felicity was dimly aware of her assuring everyone that everything would be all right.

'A bang on the head and then all those drugs. Silly girl.' Jane was as brisk as ever.

At that moment Felicity opened her eyes and looked up at the anxious faces looking down at her. 'Have you had any thoup Tham? Thoup Tham ... thoup Tham,' she repeated several times pleased with the alliteration and then closed her eyes.

CHAPTER 11

THE NEXT MORNING FELICITY FELT SURPRISINGLY WELL when she woke up. She did have a slight headache, but at least she didn't have a hangover. She hadn't had the chance to have a drink. What a waste of effort it had been. Her first solo dinner party and she couldn't remember anything about it. Perhaps it had been a ghastly dream. Her tongue felt for the tooth. It wasn't there. She sat up in bed and turned the light on. There was a knock on the door and Darcy brought in a cup of tea. He had obviously been waiting for the first signs of her stirring to tell her all about it.

'How are you feeling?'

'Not too bad. Head's a bit sore.'

'Nasty bump. We were all very worried.'

'Did you call the doctor?'

'Venetia called her chap. He lives near here so he popped round. Very jolly man. We all liked him enormously.'

'What did he say about me?' Felicity asked petulantly.

'Mild concussion. Rest. He said that was all that was needed.'

'So what happened to my dinner party?'

'It was a triumph,' Darcy paused and then continued, uncharacteristically tactful. 'Apart from your absence. You were naturally sorely missed.'

Felicity couldn't remember much after the guests arriving, but Darcy filled her in with all the gory details. Felicity groaned. Sam had seemed a nice, socially useful man. Perhaps someone she could have taken to the theatre, a balancer for her dinner parties? But now she would never know. Everyone told her there weren't many men out there for a woman of her age and she seemed to be using up her quota pretty rapidly.

164

Robin, the blobby bachelor, had practically run screaming from her presence. Geoffrey, the money man, wanted someone younger and slimmer. Now Sam, the latest divorcé, she had passed out on. The only one she'd had any success with was Darcy, a down at heel gentleman of the road. And she had an awful feeling she was going to be stuck with him for a very long time. But the first thing she had to do this morning was to get her tooth fixed. She couldn't go around alternately lisping or looking like a toothless hag. The moment Darcy had left her bedroom she had a bath and rummaged in her cupboard for something to wear. It was extraordinary, she had a wardrobe full of clothes, and yet somehow she never seemed to have exactly the right thing to wear on any occasion.

She rang the dentist and was able to get an emergency appointment that day. It was raining, after what seemed like weeks of dry weather, and Felicity had to hunt for her umbrella before going out, which delayed her slightly.

'I was under the impression it was an emergency. I'm not sure if Mr Jackson will be able to see you now.' The snooty receptionist looked up from her appointment book reluctantly when Felicity rushed in five minutes late.

'I'm tho thorry.' Felicity discovered it was impossible to lisp sarcastically, but she did her best. Opening her mouth, she removed the crown and plonked it down on the counter in front of the girl. The receptionist curled her lip, as if she imagined Felicity had done it on purpose. Once she was called into the surgery she realised why. Mr. Jackson was gorgeous. Sex on legs as Daisy would say. Tall, slim and young. He looked as if he was out from school, getting work experience. However he had a pronounced stoop from bending over mouths all day long, so she had to presume he had been qualified for some time. He was sympathetic, but annoyingly patronising.

'What have we been doing?' he asked.

Felicity felt like saying, 'I've been hit in the face by a door. I've no idea what you've been up to,' but naturally she didn't. She muttered something about an accident. He didn't even bother to make a quip about having a fight with her husband – did she have sad, single woman so clearly stamped on her forehead?

'Now I'm just going to take an X-ray. A picture of your teeth and gums.' He held a small white rectangle carefully between his gloved fingers. 'It's a bit difficult, but could you hold your finger just there. Now open your mouth nice and wide for me and then try to hold very still. Good girl. All done.'

Felicity remembered her great-aunt telling her one of the terrible things about old age was the way people assumed your brain had gone and talked to you as if you were a small, not very bright child. Felicity had listened sympathetically, never imagining it would happen to her. That was a few years ago, but now although she was only fifty-five it had already started. However, the dentist did manage to put a temporary crown on – it was rather startlingly white, but would have to do for ten days. At least she had stopped lisping, and as long as she didn't smile too much no one would notice. Before leaving the dentist she had been made to spend fifteen minutes with the hygienist, a terrifying sadist who had attacked her with metal probes. Felicity then had to endure the humiliation of being given a lesson in cleaning her teeth. Apparently she had been doing it the wrong way her whole life and, as the hygienist seemed to delight in pointing out, her gums were receding at an alarming rate. She really was long in the tooth.

*

'It's awful getting old,' she said to Rose later. 'You have to spend so much time just shoring things up.'

'I don't bother.' Unusually Rose was sitting at the kitchen table, mug of coffee clasped in her grubby hands which had large parts of Wiltshire embedded under her nails.

Felicity made a mental note to bring her some hand cream as a present next time she came to stay. I'm getting just like Venetia she thought. 'It wasn't really my finest hour. I thought doing a dinner party would be a doddle.'

'What was Sam like?'

'What I noticed of him, he seemed nice, but what with the tooth and the valium all I said to him was "More thoop Tham", then I relapsed into giggles.'

'Fifi, you are hopeless.' Rose gave her an indulgent look.

Felicity had been eyeing her narrowly and it seemed to her she looked a bit more relaxed, not quite so tired this weekend. She had to be careful as Rose had more than once asked her to stop staring at her.

Felicity was spending almost every weekend with Rose and Leo at the moment. And during this time she had sensed there was something wrong. She was worried about them, but she couldn't put her finger on what it was. Both the Blighs were relentlessly cheerful and maintained they were fine. Besides, even though it was nearly September it was still hot in London, and the summer was not a time to be away from Hatch. The garden was still looking lovely and Rose was busy harvesting, freezing, bottling and preserving. She always managed to have colour in her borders, whatever the time of year. Nasturtiums scrambled untidily out of pots on the terrace and Canna lilies flowered blowsily. About Rose herself Felicity wasn't so sure. She looked much the same, a bit older and more tired sometimes, but then so did Felicity. But there was an odd expression in her eyes when she thought no one was watching her. Despite the occasional momentary pause at the kitchen table she was more active than ever, filled with almost frenetic energy. Felicity tried to talk to her, but every question was fielded with reassurances, which did nothing to reassure.

'I'm fine Possum, just busy. So many people in and out … love it really. House full – nothing better.'

Rose whizzing round the kitchen making apple sauce for the deep freeze, baking cakes for the school fete, feeding Daisy and her boys, finding a book for Leo, raking up leaves in the garden. Rush, rush.

Felicity's offers of help were consistently refused. Once or twice she caught Rose looking intently at Leo. Was there something wrong with *him*? She wished she knew. He was getting older, but he seemed just the same as he always had.

'Just sit down and tell me all the gossip.'

Felicity sat down at the pine table covered in seed catalogues, farming magazines and a trug full of cooking apples.

'Shall I peel these?' she asked, wanting to be useful.

'Don't worry. I'm not ready for them yet. How are the children?' Rose's restless hands chopped a large bunch of mint as she spoke and the smell wafted through the kitchen.

Felicity looked forward greedily to having lamb for Sunday lunch, vowing as she did so not to have more than one of Rose's deliciously crunchy roast potatoes.

'Laura's fine,' Felicity knew her children were always a safe topic of conversation. 'She seems more cheerful at the moment – she looked lovely at the Camerons' party.' Felicity smiled, remembering her daughter who had been in her element that night. Although she couldn't help remembering Laura's expression when she met Darcy. Laura simply could not understand her continuing relationship with such an unsuitable person. But then Felicity wasn't sure she understood it herself.

'Why weren't you there?' She watched Rose carefully but could see no sign of embarrassment as she answered calmly.

'Troy cut his foot and had to have antibiotics. I couldn't leave him.'

Felicity could see Rose had the perfect excuse. Troy was her favourite black labrador and no one would expect her to leave him if he was ill. 'Is he all right now?' Felicity was sure of the answer, otherwise she would have heard all about it. In reply Rose gestured to the large basket in the corner where three black faces lay in a row.

'You're wonderful aren't you, precious one?' she said in the baby voice that otherwise sensible women use to animals. Three tails thumped hard on the stone floor and three pairs of liquid amber eyes gazed adoringly up at their owner.

'What are we going to do about Venetia? I'm worried about her.' Felicity tried another tack; perhaps talking about someone else's problems might allow Rose the chance to open up a bit.

They were having pasta in the kitchen, for once just the three of them. Rose placed a large earthenware dish of tagliatelli on the table and mixed in a sauce of tomatoes, onions, broad beans and aubergines.

'Well, at least Andrew's stopped his affair,' she said, licking the wooden spoon.

'Since when – they were all over each other at the Camerons. Right in front of Venetia.' Felicity watched as Rose grated fresh Parmesan over the dish.

'Since clever old Leo had lunch with him on Tuesday.'

'How come? Do tell.' Felicity was intrigued.

'Told him I'd blackball him. He's up for membership of Tuffnells. Terrible snob, Andrew, been longing to be a member for years.' Leo gave a slow smile.

'More than he longs to put his member into Sonia?' Felicity sniggered childishly.

'Apparently. He's always reminded me of Mr. Salteena in *The Young Visitors* – d'you remember, he was not quite a gentleman.' Rose started ladling out large helpings of pasta.

'Leo, you are clever,' Felicity said admiringly

'I know,' said Leo calmly and then added with a smirk, 'Of course, the man's such a shit, he'll be blackballed anyway. Upset too many husbands over the years.'

Felicity and Rose both laughed, rather unkindly feelings of sisterhood with Venetia surfacing as Leo continued.

'Since Charles Cameron caught him boffing his wife he's sworn to get even with him.'

'Andrew had an affair with Annabel Cameron?' Felicity's fork stopped halfway to her mouth. What a lot of things she didn't know about people who were supposed to be her friends. She certainly had been living in a cocoon.

'Not really an affair – it was in the South of France, about ten years ago. They were all on holiday together. Venetia had to go home, something to do with the magazine. Charles came back early from golf and caught them having a bit of a bunk up.'

'How awful. Poor Venetia. I'd no idea. But they were at the Camerons' party.'

'Of course, they know all the same people. It's perfectly civilised, but Charles is damned if he'll have him in his club.'

'They say revenge is a dish best eaten cold. Aren't I lucky to be married to such a devious genius?' Rose leapt to her feet as she spoke and fetched the salad bowl from the side.

Yes, you are lucky, Felicity thought, but she still had that uneasy feeling something was wrong.

*

170

Sleep evaded Felicity that night. She tossed and turned, not sure whether it was indigestion or worry keeping her awake. By the morning she had come to no conclusion other than that she would like to discuss it with someone, but with whom? Lying in the ancient hollow of the large sagging mattress of the bed in the best spare room she thought about what to do. She was so used to talking over all her problems with Rose she was left with a void, now that Rose was the problem. And Venetia had enough on her plate. More than she knew apparently. She listened to the birds start their early morning tune up. The cockerel crowed in the kitchen garden and from downstairs she could smell coffee and toast. Felicity heaved herself out of bed and had a quick bath. The speckled old mirror in the bathroom gave a kind reflection and once she had dressed she went downstairs. Leo was alone in the kitchen reading the *Sunday Times*. Felicity planted a kiss on his cheek and poured herself a mug of coffee. She was half reading the *Mail on Sunday* when Leo spoke.

'By the way,' he looked at her over the top of his glasses. 'I saw Henry the other day. I get the impression he's a bit down.'

'And I should care?' Felicity looked up, trying to look cross and nonchalant at the same time.

'Thought I would mention it. Between you and me, I think he's finding Sally a bit of a bully. All those piecrust promises.'

'Excuse me?'

'Made to be broken. Apparently she promised him he'd never have to lift a finger if he left you. Now she nags him constantly.'

Felicity snorted, feeling some sympathy for Sally for the first time. Henry would be only too happy to do nothing all day.

*

171

After a delicious and filling lunch, Felicity retired to the garden with a book. Rose and Leo had gone to see a potential bull they were thinking of buying. The afternoon was warm but autumnal, the air heavy with the smell of damp leaves and bonfires. Felicity thought that fall was a much better word than autumn as she watched the leaves drift down from the silver birch.

'Hi. What you reading?' Daisy appeared and looked over Felicity's shoulder.

'Betty Shine's *My Life as a Medium*.'

'I didn't know you were into all that.'

'I'm not. But I'm fed up with my life as a large. I thought it was a diet book.' They both laughed and then Felicity continued. 'What I don't understand is why people "on the other side" never come up with any really useful information. Like giving you the winner of the 3.30 at Ascot or telling you where you put Aunt Agatha's ring.'

Daisy slumped gracefully into a deckchair and stretched her brown legs out in front of her. 'Rose is into that sort of thing. Only don't tell Leo, he goes ballistic.'

'I didn't know that.'

'Yeah. She goes to see this old bat in Warminster. I took her once.'

'Is that the woman who cleanses auras?' Felicity asked.

'No. That was someone one of the school mothers told me about. She was a bit of a joke. This is something quite different.'

'Why does she go and see her?' Felicity was astonished. It seemed so unlike Rose.

'I dunno. She was really defensive. Said it was nonsense, but one had to keep an open mind.'

'Well, well. Who'd have thought it?' Felicity paused and put the book down on her lap. 'Do you think there's something wrong with Rose?' she asked Daisy. After all, if anyone knew it would probably be her half-sister. She saw her almost every day and they had always been very close.

'I know she's worried about Leo.'

'Leo? What's wrong with him?' Felicity felt full of concern.

'Nothing, I don't think. But he is getting old. I think it all goes back to when Dad died. She's convinced some sort of divine retribution will take Leo away.'

Felicity was beginning to realise there were a lot of things about Rose she didn't know.

Daisy pulled her chair closer to Felicity and, after looking round to make sure her sister wasn't anywhere to be seen, she spoke in a low tone. 'Do you remember Dad? He was your uncle, wasn't he?'

'Yes, but I only met him a few times.'

'Well, you probably didn't know he had angina – and he was the same age as Leo when he died. Mum had taken me to South Africa to see her family and left Rose in charge of Dad.' Daisy paused and looked round with a guilty expression on her face as if she felt disloyal talking about her sister like this. 'They had a stupid row and she didn't ring him. The daily found his body on Monday morning. She's always felt guilty about it.'

'I'd no idea.' Felicity could barely remember Rose's father even though he had been her uncle. There had been a family disagreement when he'd married Daisy's mother and her parents didn't really speak to him after that. Just polite formalities at weddings and funerals. 'What can we do? I can't bear to see her so worried. And this business of never leaving Hatch. Leo goes to London, why doesn't she?'

'I don't know. She just makes excuses. They're always quite plausible, but it's so unlike her. But at least she's gone with Leo to look at this bull today.'

'Perhaps I should talk to him about it.'

'Shh!' Daisy put her finger to her lips. In the distance they heard Rose calling the dogs as she came through the gate from the rose garden. Felicity got up to move her chair under the umbrella; the afternoon sun was burning the back of her neck. Hastily Daisy changed the subject. 'You know, Fifi, you're looking much better,' she said giving her an appraising look. 'Your whole shape has changed since you started going to the gym.'

Felicity grasped a roll of flesh round her middle and shrugged. 'I haven't lost much weight.' She frowned, but it was true her clothes did seem looser.

'Muscle weighs more than fat.' Daisy was an authority on exercise and diet, she was passionate about riding and always knew her own weight to the last ounce.

'So the more I go to the gym the heavier I'll get. Brilliant.'

'I don't know why you're so obsessed with your weight anyway. I think it's all genetic. Look at me, I can't put on weight to save my life, and my mother's the same And Leo – the more he eats the thinner he gets. Oh hello Rose,' she exclaimed as her sister flopped down on the grass beside them. 'How was the bull?'

'Leo's in love,' she smiled indulgently. 'But it's not true about his appetite. He doesn't eat at all. If I'm not here he doesn't touch his food.' She absently pulled the petals off a New Dawn rose she was holding in her hand. Her face had a worried look.

'There's nothing wrong is there? Has he seen a doctor recently?' Felicity tried gently.

'He won't. He hates doctors.'

'Make the appointment yourself and take him. That's what I used to do with Henry.'

'I suppose … ' Rose hesitated, then, as if uneasy at the way the conversation was going, she scrambled to her feet and set off towards the house. 'I might try that,' she called over her shoulder.

Felicity drove back to London in a reflective mood. It wasn't just her life that had changed in the last year, but the lives of those she loved. And not always for the better.

They were all in the process of evolving, but into what?

*

Felicity opened her eyes with difficulty. A bell was ringing. She struggled up through her dream. In the middle of the fog of sleep she heard the bell, but she tried to ignore it and drift back into unconsciousness. The ringing stopped, but it was no good, the spell had been broken. She lay in bed trying to recapture the memory before it dissolved completely. She was back at Upton, her beloved Upton, but it was no longer hers. She recognised the kitchen, or did she? It was her kitchen but the shape had changed. Where had that door come from? She had never noticed it before. Where did it lead to? She was on the other side of it, had floated through it and now she was standing in a big hall. It was the village hall. She heard the vicar speaking and turned round, but it wasn't the vicar, it was Henry, she went to speak to him, but someone grabbed her arm and she was flying across the hall with Sally, but Sally with long blonde hair. It was really important, they had to find something before the bell rang. As she was trying to work out what it all meant the bell rang again. Felicity stretched a hand out from under the duvet and fumbled for the alarm clock, realising as she did so it was the telephone ringing. Eyes wide open she grabbed it, terrified something had happened to one of the children.

'Hello, who's that?'

175

'Mum, it's me. Are you OK? You sound odd.' Laura's voice was shrill.

'Fine. I was asleep. What time is it?'

'Quarter to seven. I've been up for hours.'

'Well, I haven't.' Felicity realised she sounded rather cross so she added. 'Sorry darling. Is anything wrong?' She turned on her bedside light. Good Lord, it was practically the middle of the night. If only she and Darcy hadn't sat up half the night drinking red wine and talking rubbish.

'Concepcion's got 'flu. She's taken to her bed and she's just lying there groaning. And I've got to meet Mark at the airport. I don't know what to do.'

'D'you want me to come round?' Felicity knew the question was rhetorical, but was glad her children still needed her sometimes. Promising she would be there in half an hour, she dragged herself out of bed and pulled on some clothes. Reflecting that it was surprising how easily she had slipped into a new routine of getting up later she brushed her teeth vigorously. Too vigorously perhaps. She spat out blood, which reminded her that she must make another appointment to see the hygienist. That could well be the big event of her week. When she had the house to run and the B & B to manage she'd been up every morning at six o'clock, walked the dogs and seen to the chickens before breakfast. There had always been so much to do, too much she often thought. It was quite different now. She sometimes found herself still in bed at nine o'clock. But not this morning. Glancing at the weather she left the house grabbing her mac off the peg in the hall as she went. It looked as if the long hot summer was finally over and the heavy sky suggested rain later.

Driving to Laura's house she felt sorry for the Spanish girl. Laura, who was never ill herself, had very little patience or sympathy for anyone else. Concepcion was usually full of bounce and *joie de vivre*. She was gorgeous to look at, with thick dark brown hair and great limpid dark eyes. She appeared to have plenty of friends, was out all the time and constantly on the telephone. In fact that was the only real complaint that Laura had about her.

Felicity made good time on the drive across London from Battersea to Kensington. There was no traffic at this hour of the morning and she made a resolution to get up early every day. So much more would get done, on the other hand she didn't have that much to do, at least until the shop opened.

*

There was a black taxi with its engine running parked outside Laura's house, and Laura herself was waiting for her in their very grand first floor drawing room peering anxiously out at the street. She ran downstairs and opened the door before Felicity had time to ring the bell, grabbing her jacket from the chair in the hall.

'Thank goodness you're here, I've got to fly. Ring me on my mobile if you need to know anything.' And kissing her mother briefly, she leapt into the taxi and was gone. Felicity walked thoughtfully up the steps and into the house. When was Laura coming back? There had been no time to ask her as she ran out of the house. Jamie was in the kitchen trying to make the cat eat jelly.

'Don't do that darling,' she said absently as she started to clear up the breakfast things.

'Whoi?'

'Fluffy doesn't like jelly.'

'Whoi?'

Felicity had forgotten how monotonous early morning conversations with toddlers were.

'She likes cat food.'

'Whoi?'

177

'She just does. Now why don't you paint me a nice picture?'

'Whoi?'

Damn, she walked right into that one. She went to the cupboard under the stairs and pulled out a box of crayons and a block of paper.

'Do you want to draw a picture of Fluffy?'

'Okai.'

She sat him down on his little chair at his brand new drawing table. Tongue between his teeth he concentrated on choosing a colour.

'Jamie darling, do you know where Concepcion is?'

'Whoi?'

It was going to be a long day. He seized a black crayon and scribbled fiercely. She had noticed that he only ever seemed to use black. Was this something to worry about? Somehow, it had been much simpler when her own children were young.

'Concepcion! Concepcion!' she called as she went upstairs. On the first floor landing she stopped and listened. The sound of moaning came from behind the closed bedroom door on the right of the passage. She knocked gently.

'Concepcion, it's me, Mrs. Fox. Is something the matter?' Bloody stupid question, she thought as she asked it, but she couldn't think what else to say. There was silence for a moment and then the moans started again more loudly than before.

'Open the door, Concepcion. I want to take your temperature. See if you have a fever.' The sounds stopped and after a few seconds the door opened and a flushed face appeared.

'Oh Mrs. Fox. Ees terrible.' The girl came out hanging her head, her dark hair hanging in lank strands.

'Get back into bed. I'll bring you a cup of tea. Here's a thermometer. Do you know how to use it?'

The girl nodded and Felicity went back downstairs to make the tea and check on Jamie.

'What wrong with Ception?' James asked and Felicity wondered about his appalling accent. Yet another thing to worry about another day. Should she offer to pay for elocution lessons or would that offend Laura? She was beginning to feel like Scarlet O'Hara or possibly thanks to the menopause, Scarlet O'Face.

'She's not feeling well,' she answered briskly and stuffed a biscuit into his mouth before he could ask his favourite question. She believed in answering children's questions as truthfully as possible, but only within reason.

'Lovely cat – just like Fluffy. Now why don't you draw a picture of a dog? Because Granny wants to see a picture of a dog,' she added hastily anticipating him. She made a cup of tea for Concepcion and then took it upstairs, tucking the Spanish dictionary under her arm as she went.

'Now, how's your temperature?'

'Is normal. *Estoy muy constipado, senora.*'

'You're constipated. Oh, dear. How many days since you've been to the lavatory?' She smiled sympathetically and waited.

'No.' Concepcion giggled. 'Constipado, the nose.' She took a handkerchief and made blowing motions. Felicity had just found the word in the dictionary. Constipado – To have a cold. Well, they both made you blocked up. Now that misunderstanding had been resolved.

'You have a cold, not 'flu.'

'*Si.* A very bad cold.'

'Don't worry, you stay in bed and I'll look after Jamie.'

'Oy wanna do wee wee,' a small imperious voice announced as Felicity was coming downstairs.

'What a good boy for telling me.' Felicity beamed at her grandson. 'Do you need any help or can you manage on your own?'

'Oy'm big now. Oy can do it,'' he replied indignantly. However, Felicity thought it would be as well to accompany him to the loo.

'Oy got a winkle,' he said conversationally and then added. 'Daddy got a winkle.' Then after a pause he asked, 'Grandpa got a winkle?'

Felicity pondered the question for a moment before she spoke.

'At his age it's more a of a wrinkle, but you've got the idea,' she said with a smile.

*

Laura came back from meeting Mark at the airport and dropping him off at his office a couple of hours later. Felicity wasn't sure why he hadn't simply taken a taxi into his office, as he usually did, but Laura, bursting with suppressed excitement, said they'd had something important to discuss and she would tell her mother when it was a hundred per cent definite. She's pregnant, thought Felicity excitedly. By the time Laura walked in, the house had been restored to calm. Felicity had taken Jamie to his nursery school, with what she was sure was the wrong lunch. A packet of Hula Hoops and a banana didn't seem much, but she couldn't find any bread to make a sandwich. Concepcion was in bed; the groaning had subsided and all that could be heard was the occasional cough and sneeze. She had ventured down to open a tin of soup, but Felicity had shooed her back up to bed and taken a tray up for her. Concepcion responded well to being mothered, as Felicity clucked over her. After all, she was only eighteen and living a long way from home. It was hard enough being uprooted in your fifties and so much harder doing it in another language.

'You like it here in England?'

'Oh, yes. Is good, but I not make many friends, all peoples foreign like me. French peoples, Romania, Czech. Not good.'

'Why not?'

'I here for learn English.'

'And you haven't made any English friends?' Felicity enquired.

'Not so many. I need English boyfriend, to espeak English with me.'

Felicity smiled. Perhaps she could persuade Oliver to take her out as they were both at a loose end.

CHAPTER 12

'SORRY I'M LATE. I can't think why people say Battersea's so convenient.' Jane strode imperiously into the house, her industrial-sized handbag narrowly missing the last remaining Wemys pig that Felicity had inherited from her grandmother. Felicity put out her hand just in time and rescued it from the hall table. Jane looked Felicity up and down. 'I see I needn't have worried. You're not even changed yet.'

'I have. What's wrong with what I'm wearing?' Felicity was indignant. She had spent a long time before deciding on a pair of navy trousers and a blue and white striped cotton jumper.

'Haven't you got a dress? Or at least a suit – with a skirt? We're going to meet Timmy at the golf club, not going to the beach for a picnic. Besides,' she added, dropping the bossy tone and replacing it with a horrible simpering smile as she whispered conspiratorially, 'men like feminine women.'

Jane herself was wearing a dazzling printed navy silk dress covered in eye-achingly bright yellow flowers, with matching yellow shoes and bag. Jane bossy was bad enough, but Jane as agony aunt was even worse. Felicity glowered, but, realising resistance was useless, went upstairs to change. Halfway up she turned round and stuck her tongue out at Jane's back view, which made her feel a lot better. She knew Jane could be a monster and she despised herself for being bullied, but all the unwritten rules for single women over fifty meant having a husband scored more points than not having one. Even if the husband in question was Dim. She wished she didn't think like that. Daisy didn't think like that, but then Daisy was thirty-eight not fifty-five. Felicity did know life was possible without a man. In other circumstances she might have been more of a feminist. She knew that plenty of her contemporaries had burnt their bras, but none of them lived in her part of Wiltshire.

Some minutes later Felicity came downstairs dressed in a respectable, russet shift dress. A good safe dress, in a colour she knew suited her. She was ready for inspection. As usual Jane made her feel like a naughty schoolchild in front of the head girl, as she looked her up and down.

'That's better,' Jane replied.

'Have you got a vibrator?' Something about the other woman's disapproving face compelled Felicity to ask a question that she knew would make Jane really cross.

'That's typical of you, always trying to shock people by making silly remarks. I remember you used to do it at school. I should've thought you would have grown out of it by now.' Jane's tone was exasperated. Felicity knew she was being immature but couldn't help it. Jane had the knack of bringing out the worst in her.

'I just wondered. I didn't know about them until the other day.'

'Maybe that gay son of yours – his sort probably know all about that sort of thing.' Jane made the slight expression of distaste that always came over her face when she mentioned Oscar.

'What do you mean: *His sort?*' Felicity was immediately on the defensive.

'Those gay clubs, all that promiscuity and drugs and stuff. I've read about it. Maybe not Oscar, but they are like that. You know that.'

'No, Jane, I don't.' Felicity's face began to burn. 'Just because Oscar is gay it doesn't mean that he's like *that*, whatever *that* means. And sex toys are quite normal now, I'm told. We're just old-fashioned.'

She took her navy blazer off a hook in the hall and counted to ten. It served her right, trying to irritate Jane and now it had back-fired and she was the one who was furious. She took a deep breath and turning back to Jane she continued more calmly.

'It was just a thought. It's important to know what's going on.'

'As long as you've sorted that out, we've got to get going.' Jane cast another critical eye over Felicity and gave a small sigh as she looked down at her feet. Felicity followed her gaze.

'I'm changing my shoes, don't worry. These are just an old pair I use for gardening.' She opened the cupboard under the stairs and pulled out a pair of newly-polished navy pumps with a fashionable kitten heel. 'Will these do?' she asked, waving them in front of Jane's nose in exasperation.

'What's happened to your legs?' Jane frowned. She scarcely looked at the shoes, so intent was her gaze on Felicity. 'They're all blotchy. You'll have to wear tights.'

Felicity didn't bother to say a word as she stumped upstairs. She'd spent hours applying an expensive fake tan but she had to admit the result was rather strange. Her knees and ankles had gone bright orange. After a couple of attempts she found a pair of tights without a ladder in them.

Felicity was beginning to feel this whole expedition was going to be a mistake. She didn't like Surrey, hated golf and was more than ever convinced she had never liked Jane. She debated whether to develop a migraine, but that would not only be a lie, but rude as well. Lifelong habits died hard and Felicity had been brought up to believe that once you had accepted an invitation death was pretty much the only good reason to cry off.

Jane had been planning this outing for some time. The words 'golf club' were said with bated breath. According to

Jane it was full of men; healthy men who played golf, respectable men, vetted by the golf club committee. Suitable men who, unlike Darcy, owned their own ties and were solvent (apparently golf club subscriptions were not to be undertaken lightly). Felicity was rapidly learning it was not so much a sport, more a way of life. She was not at all sure it was a way of life she would fit into. However, she had agreed to have lunch with Jane and Tim, and as the carrot she had been promised an undisclosed number of men.

Jane had her large, four-wheel drive, off-road vehicle with its gleaming, mud-free wheel arches parked outside Felicity's house. It seemed unlikely it would be stretched to its full capabilities on the A30, unless the meteorological office had some prior knowledge of extremely hazardous weather that they were not sharing with the general public. But then everyone drove these enormous cars in London now. What did they call them, Chelsea tractors?

Once they left the town behind Felicity noticed how the last remaining leaves on the trees had all changed colour. Even though it was still hot autumn was very definitely here. She could smell it in the air. It used to be her favourite time of year. Until last year. It was this time last year Henry had dropped his bombshell. Yet again she reminded herself what an idiot she'd been. All the signs were there, so why had she refused to see them? Sally Pelham, her old school friend, now newly widowed, had rung her soon after buying a house in the area. Having your husband die on you was a much more socially acceptable end to a marriage than divorce and everyone had rallied round. Felicity hadn't seen Sally for several years and at first it had been fun catching up on old friends. And she looked wonderful. Had looked after herself. Expensive clothes and hair, beautifully manicured hands. Felicity had been impressed, but stupidly as it turned out, it had not occurred to her to be jealous. Sally flirted with Henry, but that was just her manner. Perhaps that was why Felicity had had a crush on her at school. She was flirtatious. It was too long ago, she couldn't remember. But there was no doubt Sally flirted with all the local men, even the vicar. Everyone said she didn't mean anything by it. But then again she did. She meant to have Henry.

It had started innocently enough. 'Hello, Sally here. I hate to be a nuisance, but does Henry know anything about boilers? There's something wrong with mine, and I'm so silly about that sort of thing. I simply don't know what to do.' The late, and apparently not much lamented Mr. Pelham had, it appeared, dealt with things like that.

Felicity was much more likely to be able to fix the boiler, or at least know a man who could, but Henry liked being appealed to like that. He had had too many years of living with a very capable wife. Felicity was aware she had taken charge of everything over the last few years. Henry made her impatient when there was always so much to do, and she had tended to take things from him. 'Let me do that, it'll be quicker. For heaven's sake, Henry, give that to me before you make a hash of it.' The recollection of the way she had been did not make for comfortable memories. If she had been guilty of anything it was of being complacent and smug. It had simply never crossed her mind Henry might leave her. Every time Sally had rung she had happily let Henry go off to see if he could help, glad to get him out of her hair for a few hours. She remembered only too well all the times Sally had rung. 'You are sweet letting me borrow Henry. I promise I'll send him back.' And then the silvery laugh, meant to reassure. Treacherous bitch.

Jane had been prattling on but Felicity hardly heard her. She had been lost in thoughts about her own life. Suddenly she was aware of Jane asking her a question.

'So do you think it's a good idea?'

'I'm not sure.' Felicity hedged, having no idea what she was talking about.

'Nor am I, that's the problem. I want to get my teeth into something, but I'm afraid that counselling may take up too much time. But on the other hand I think I'd be pretty good at it.'

'Being a councillor? You'd be brilliant. You're just the type. An assertive personality.' Felicity thought that was a tactful way of saying Jane was bossy. And it was true, the country needed people like Jane who were prepared to get involved.

'Really?' Jane sounded surprised.

'Yes. You'd be excellent on all those committees. Stop them waffling on.'

'Committees? D'you think there'll be much of that?'

'Lord yes, local government's full of them.'

'Whaua, whaua,' Jane laughed loudly. 'No, idiot, not that sort of councillor – I knew you weren't listening properly. Relationship counselling. I've been thinking about it for ages. I'm really a people person. I like helping with relationships. I'm good at that sort of thing, got a bent for it. Look how I've been helping you. I know it can be frustrating when people don't take advice, but I think we're getting there,' she snorted. 'Might even get you married off again if you listen to me.'

Felicity was glad Jane was driving and couldn't see the expression on her face. Like an out of control steamroller the other woman continued.

'I've met this very interesting person, Tabitha Macleod. Do you know her?' She looked briefly in Felicity's direction, but without waiting for her to reply she carried on. 'Probably not. I doubt you'd be her sort of person. She's very intelligent.'

'Thanks,' Felicity muttered, but she might just as well have spoken to the air.

'She thinks I've a lot of untapped potential. Tabitha runs an alternative healing centre near Tunbridge Wells,' she added by way of conclusion.

Felicity longed to get on her mobile to Venetia or Rose or anyone who knew Jane and tell them. Jane, a counsellor, heaven help the general public. Talk about taking a sledge-hammer to crack a nut. Felicity had a vision of already fragile people being driven into clinics, gibbering wrecks after a session with Jane. On the other hand, the prospect of another session with Jane might make for an instant cure.

Jane's driving was becoming more and more erratic as she warmed to her theme, waving her arms about as she attempted to convince Felicity and possibly herself she had at last found a way to fulfil her destiny. Suddenly she turned right, without any warning or use of her indicator. A man in the car behind hooted but Jane merely waved at him enthusiastically, and crying, 'Wonder who that was?' drove on up a long, immaculately kept drive. The grass on either side of the road was perfectly manicured as if with nail scissors and liberally dotted with small groups of people in garishly bright clothes. They had arrived at the golf club.

Felicity had always been grateful Henry was not a golfer, all those hideous, clashing outfits. He said he'd never played, because if he did people would give him nothing but golfing presents for ever afterwards, but Felicity suspected it was much more likely to be laziness.

Sunningworth was apparently a world-renowned course and there was a waiting list of seven years to become a member. Jane drove into a large car park and having parked the car, led Felicity past the wide flight of steps below the front door and round to the back of the club. There, they walked along a dingy alleyway to a mean-looking dark green door marked 'Ladies and Tradesmen's Entrance'. Felicity followed Jane into the gloomy interior feeling decidedly mulish. Why on earth had she agreed to this fatuous exercise? The chances of Jane producing a halfway decent man were pretty remote and even if she did, did Felicity want one who played golf? Come to think of it, did she want a man at all?

*

'Here we are. Isn't this fun?' Jane didn't wait for a reply as she marched purposefully ahead of Felicity into a large panelled room filled with dark heavy furniture. Even though the sun was shining and the weather outside was warm, a coal fire was burning in the large fireplace. The room was empty apart from a quartet of middle-aged women playing bridge, and the toad-like figure of an elderly woman covered in thick tweeds sunk deep into an armchair, half asleep in front of the fire.

It made Felicity sweat just looking at her. Perhaps one day when she was really old she would be able to wear cashmere and tweed again. Through an open door at the far end of the room Felicity could hear sounds of merriment and the clinking of glasses.

'Are we going through there?' she asked hopefully.

'Lummy no. We'd be shot. Timmy'd be thrown out of the club. Men only in the bar.'

'How do we get a drink?' Even Felicity could hear the note of desperation in her voice. She didn't care, she was going to need some alcohol if she was going to survive this.

'Don't panic. Tim'll be here in a minute. Surely you can wait?' Jane's voice was full of disapproval. Did she think that after one gin and tonic Felicity would stand on the table and sing a rousing chorus of the *Ball of Kirriemuir*? Would she ever be able to live down that dreadful dinner party? Happily Jane was distracted as she caught sight of something in the corner of the room.

'Oh look!' she cried in delight, 'It's Lady Trubshawe.' Dragging a reluctant Felicity by the arm she marched over to the old lady who was dozing happily in a comfortable armchair, newspaper falling over her lap.

'Lady Trubshawe,' she shouted.

The old lady opened her eyes with a grunt and peered up at Jane through thick spectacles. 'Who are you?' she asked curtly.

'Jane Bignall. We met last month. My husband Timothy was in a tournament with your son, Peter. You remember? And your niece Cissy's a great chum of mine, from Hong Kong.' Jane wore her eager puppy expression and Felicity half expected her to leap up and lick Lady Trubshawe's face.

The old woman shuffled in her chair, tugging at her tweed skirt that had rucked up. She put one hand under her jumper and adjusted her bosom. When she had rearranged herself she stared up at Jane.

'I can't say I remember you. One meets an awful lot of people. They don't all make an impression,' she said dismissively then she turned her attention to Felicity. 'Who are you?' she demanded.

'Felicity Fox.'

'Anything to do with Henry Fox?'

'My ex-husband.'

'Can't any of you girls hang onto your husbands?' she grunted as she gathered up the newspaper off her lap and dropped it carelessly on the floor. 'I knew his father, Charlie. Haven't seen Henry for years, not since he was a boy. Eyes were too close together. Not very bright.' She paused to pick something out of her teeth with a long red fingernail.

Felicity was torn between pleasure at being referred to as a girl and fury at the old bat's remarks about Henry. Was that all that was left when one was old; being rude? Felicity would have liked to have pointed out to Lady Trubshawe that she had a grey curly hair protruding from a large mole on her chin, together with some suggestions about dealing with it. But she didn't. For once, her own carefully tweezered chin did give her something, however small, to feel superior about in front of this insufferable old bully.

'Hurray! Timmy's here.' Jane's nervous bray made the bridge four look up disapprovingly as Timothy Bignall and a lanky man with thinning fair hair and glasses, who Felicity, judging by Jane's sycophantic expression, guessed must be Peter Trubshawe, came into the room. Timothy was carrying a tray of drinks.

'G & Ts all round. OK?' He placed the tray on a small round table and kissed Jane and Felicity.

Peter went immediately to the armchair. 'All right, Mumsy?' he asked solicitously. Things did not look as if they were going to improve.

'Are you warm enough Petey? There's a nasty wind out there. I don't want you getting a chill on your kidneys. You know how susceptible you are.' The caring, maternal Lady Trubshawe was, if possible, even more unpleasant than the frank, rude Lady Trubshawe. Petey got to his feet immediately.

'Mumsy's right, as always. Better not risk it,' he laughed indulgently. 'I think I'll just go and find another sweater. Back in a mo.' With that he lolloped out of the room.

Jane, torn between her love of a title and her disapproval of anyone who made an unnecessary fuss about their health, was standing with her mouth slightly open, unsure of what to say.

'What ho!' said Tim, filling the gap. 'Bottoms up!' He raised his glass and then noticing Lady Trubshawe did not have a glass added, 'Can I get you anything Lady T?'

She bared her teeth in an arch smile and simpered. 'You are a darling, a dry martini would be simply lovely.' She struggled to get to her feet.

'Don't you move.' Tim looked horrified at the thought she might be about to storm the sacred citadel of the Men's bar. He grabbed her arm and tried to force her back down into the chair.

'It's Satan,' she grunted, roughly shaking him off. 'He's been in the car for over an hour. He must have his walkies.'

'I'll take him,' Peter came back at that moment wearing a maroon and blue cashmere Argyle cardigan over his yellow polo neck. Together with his orange trousers it was a combination of colours that, perhaps wisely, few people would attempt to get away with.

'Nonsense darling. You must be exhausted. Perhaps one of these girls would do it.' She gestured towards Jane and Felicity as she slumped back into the capacious armchair. 'You, Felicity, you do it. You look as though you could do with the exercise.' She gave a barking laugh. 'The blue Bentley. It's all right,' she continued, seeing Felicity's face. 'He doesn't bite. Now where are the keys?' She picked up a copious black leather handbag from the floor and with stubby fingers covered in dirty diamonds she rummaged around, producing first of all a lipstick-covered lace handkerchief, a powder compact and lipstick. Then a mobile phone.

'So silly,' she smirked as she brandished it in front of her captive audience, 'but Petey likes to be able to get hold of me.'

Felicity would have liked to get hold of her too, preferably around the neck. What about Jane needing the exercise? She was at least two sizes bigger than Felicity. Well, one anyway.

'Here we are,' Lady Trubshawe called, triumphantly waving a large bunch of keys in the air. Despite the unpleasant insinuations about her weight, Felicity was glad to have a reason to leave the room. It was hot and stuffy and lunch promised to be an exhausting affair. Even if she had fancied Peter, she would never be able to compete with Lady Trubshawe for his attention.

*

Once in the car park she looked round for a blue Bentley. There was only one it could be; old and dignified, it was parked across two parking spaces with magnificent disregard for anyone else. On the parcel shelf a tiny Yorkshire terrier lay half asleep. When Felicity opened the door he raised his ears and looked at her, tail wagging.

'Satan?' she enquired expectantly. The little dog sat up. Felicity picked up a lead from the back seat and as the dog jumped down she attached it to his tartan collar. Together they set off down the drive. This was better than that frightful room. Satan squatted down. 'Good boy,' she said encouragingly. After a few minutes he was still squatting. Nothing seemed to be happening. Felicity crouched down beside him. She peered at his bottom; a hard, brown turd was protruding, stuck halfway out. 'Fuck,' she muttered as she stood up and looked round for a dock leaf or a stray newspaper. Of course there wasn't one in this perfectly manicured landscape. She fumbled in her pocket and found an old tissue. Putting on her glasses she got down on all fours once more as she attacked Satan's nether region.

'Felicity?' Just as she had the offending object clasped firmly between her fingers a man's voice made her jump. She leapt to her feet, trying to hide the tissue behind her back and saw Sam Tollard standing in front of her smiling. 'Thought it was you,' he said.

'Recognised my dignified position, I expect?' Felicity snapped. Her face was wet with sweat, her glasses had slipped down her nose and her damp hair was sticking to the back of her neck. This was so typical of the embarrassing things that kept happening to her at the moment. It was as if God had looked down on her and thought her life had been far too easy and it was time to chuck a few banana skins in her path.

'There's a bin over there,' Sam pointed to a tasteful green litter basket. 'I won't offer to relieve you of that object.'

Felicity, dragging the little dog behind her, deposited the tissue and its contents. How mortifying, why did something like this have to happen in front of one of the few nice men she knew?

'Is that your dog?' Sam asked.

'Certainly not. It belongs to some frightful old woman. Lady Trubshawe.'

'Aunt Maud?'

'Oh no,' Felicity moaned, talk about things going from bad to worse. 'I might have known – my big mouth. I think I might go and bury myself in a bunker.'

'Don't do that. At least your big mouth has its proper number of teeth once more.' He was still grinning and it was infectious, Felicity couldn't help smiling too.

'Yes, I managed to get it done the next day. But let's not go over that evening again. What a disaster.' She shuddered as she remembered. What an accident-prone fool he must think her.

'Nonsense,' he said briskly. 'It was a great evening. We all enjoyed ourselves hugely. The food was delicious, just a pity you weren't with us.'

'I'd no idea Lady Trubshawe was your aunt,' Felicity was floundering. 'I'm sure she's charming, when you get to know her.'

194

'Don't worry – she's frightful. Unfortunately she's extremely rich, so she's used to everyone toadying round her. I should have recognised Scrotum.'

'Scrotum?'

'The little rat you've got on the end of that lead.'

Felicity laughed. 'Poor little thing,' she said. 'It's not his fault.'

At that moment a sleek black BMW convertible drew up beside them and Sam turned round. As he recognised the occupant he walked towards the car with apparent eagerness, calling 'Hello darling.' He bent over and kissed the driver.

Felicity felt a stab of envy; the woman was everything that Felicity wasn't, but would like to be. Dark glasses, which stayed on her cool dry face, short blonde hair, showing off the slender and wrinkle-free neck. Long, evenly-tanned bare legs sticking out from a short, but not too short pale blue dress. Feeling very petty Felicity hated her on sight. A feeling that didn't go away when she flashed Felicity a warm smile as Sam introduced them.

'This is my wife, Lavinia,' he announced and Felicity winced.

Sam's wife, not ex-wife she noted crossly. Yet another tripwire on the road to life as a single woman – men who were supposed to be getting divorced turning out to be back with their wives. Felicity fixed a tight smile on her face as she greeted Lavinia. The only other Lavinia she'd ever known had been at school with her, she'd had spots and glasses and everyone had called her Lavvy. She very much doubted this one had ever been called Lavvy, even at school.

'See you in the club.' Waving gracefully Lavinia Tollard sped off up the drive.

Thank goodness she hadn't tried to shake hands with Felicity. Now she had to put Satan back in the car and wash the smell of his lavvy off her own hands. After that she would have liked to hitch a lift back to London and escape from the club house. But she knew she couldn't. The Bignalls had asked her to have lunch with them. And to be fair, it wasn't actually their fault the whole day was becoming more ghastly by the minute. Sam escorted her back to the club, by way of Lady Trubshawe's Bentley and the Ladies loo where she washed the smell of Satan's bottom off as best she could. Her reflection in the mirror did nothing to cheer her up. Where Lavinia Tollard was cool, slim and elegant she was hot, fat and frumpy. Lavinia had the perfect summer dress, teamed with the perfect matching blue cardigan. However, there was probably no question of them doing it in a size eighteen and in any case a fitted dress like that only looked good over the fitted figure that Felicity, despite her efforts at the gym, didn't possess.

As soon as Felicity and Sam arrived back in the club house Tim ushered them all into the dining room. It was as if lunch was only served between one and one fifteen, judging by the way they were all made to hurry on through. Lady Trubshawe immediately took charge, even though it was the Bignalls' party. Sam and Lavinia had been invited to join them and Lady Trubshawe grabbed Sam firmly by the arm.

'I'll have Petey one side and Sam on the other. Tim, you can sit near me and Lavinia, you go next to Tim.'

Jane, silenced for once in her life, sat down next to Felicity. After a moment she rallied. 'Isn't this jolly?' she cried, but nobody answered.

The food on the menu sounded all right, if on the stodgy side. But there was a ham salad so Felicity chose that, feeling rather virtuous. A disappointing plate of limp lettuce, pickled beetroot and soft, over-ripe tomatoes topped with two slices of plastic ham arrived, accompanied by a sachet of salad cream. Felicity was rather regretting not having ordered the steak and kidney pie, until it arrived. The pie itself didn't look bad, although Lady Trubshawe's dentures were defeated by several lumps of meat. It was the dish of grey brussels sprouts and disintegrating cauliflower that reconciled her to her salad.

Sam, seeing her face, hissed at her across the table, 'Probably been boiling away since breakfast.'

Lady Trubshawe gazed at her son in sickening adoration throughout the meal. 'You must have some greens Petey. Tim, can you ask them if they've got any spinach. You need to build your strength up. He never complains,' she said to the table in general, 'But he's never been strong.'

Tim tried valiantly to introduce a more appropriate topic but Felicity failed to follow tales of birdies, bogies and eagles, not having more than a very vague idea what they were. Lady Trubshawe was an old bully who was rude to the club servants and ignored Jane and Felicity. She snapped her finger at passing waiters.

'Bring me a glass of water. Did I ask for ice? Filthy American habit. Take it away.' But turning to Sam she positively cooed. 'How are you both? Did you have a wonderful summer?'

Felicity glared at Jane. Sam had definitely been introduced originally as virtually divorced and a potential date. Now it appeared he and Lavinia were very much together as they discussed their daughter Melanie's wedding at Christmas. Lady Trubshawe was lending them Trubshawe Towers for the reception.

'She's marrying such a charming boy. Used to work for the government, just left that to become a DJ, whatever that is.' Lady Trubshawe was determined to dominate the conversation.

'Not the government, Aunt Maud, the Ministry of Sound.' Sam was trying hard not to laugh.

'What do they need a Minister of Sound for?'

To put some tape over your mouth, thought Felicity. But almost worse than Lady Trubshawe's rudeness was that Lavinia was being charming, making Felicity feel like a bitch for wishing she and Sam were divorced. She alone went out of her way to include Felicity in the conversation about the wedding.

'Have you ever known anything more exhausting than being mother of the bride? I'm worn to a frazzle with it all.'

'I remember. Laura's wedding was a nightmare. We rowed incessantly from the moment she got engaged until the wedding day.'

'Oh I'm not rowing with my darling Melanie. She's being a poppet. It's the caterers, florists, the dressmaker. They're all so unreliable.'

'We must have been lucky,' Felicity murmured.

'You tell them something, give them quite explicit instructions, then they completely ignore you.' It appeared there was a very determined core beneath the charm.

'Who's making the dress?'

'Araminta Crossley, everyone said she was brilliant. I was at school with her aunt, so I thought she'd know what she was doing. But Melanie's had at least a dozen fittings and she still hasn't got it right.'

'Lavinia's got very firm ideas about what she wants.' Was Sam raising his eyebrows as he said that?

'Quite right. You can't let these people get away with anything.' Lady Trubshawe had finished the unequal struggle of trying to chew a piece of gristle. She extricated it from her teeth and, holding it between her finger and thumb, peered at it narrowly. 'The food here gets worse and worse.'

'Can I get you anything else?' Tim's reddening face was all concern.

'Pudding,' she demanded and Tim leapt to his feet to get her a menu.

When he returned Felicity made a point of telling him the salad had been very nice and was rewarded with a grateful smile. After all, the poor man had invited them to lunch and was paying for it all.

Once Lady Trubshawe had ordered herself some treacle tart she turned to Felicity. 'Do you do anything?'

Lavinia coolly took a tiny sip from her glass of mineral water. Felicity, feeling hot and flustered under the old lady's stare, took a large gulp of wine and looked at Lady Trubshawe with reluctant admiration. The very thought of treacle tart in this weather had made prickles of sweat break out all over her body. Trying to think of iced water and cool mountains streams she did her best to compose herself.

'I work for my son, in his shop,' she said with some pride. It wasn't exactly true – yet, but it sounded more interesting than doing nothing.

'A shop girl. How extraordinary.' Lady Trubshawe gave a mirthless laugh.

'Really? What sort of shop?' Sam asked sympathetically. He looked embarrassed by his aunt's behaviour.

'It hasn't opened yet. But it'll sell finishing touches for houses. The odd little things you need – curtain tie-backs, light switches, cushions, lampshades, that sort of thing.'

'You must tell me where it is – I'll need things like that.'

'Sam,' Lavinia hissed at him across the table.

'Right … well … um … one always needs that sort of thing.' Sam was stuttering.

'In my day gels looked after their families. None of this nonsense about going out to work. But then of course we knew how to keep our husbands.'

Sam's face was flushed and Felicity saw his knuckles were white. That made two of them itching to punch his aunt. On the other hand, she had jumped in and saved Sam from an interesting revelation that might have made for an awkward moment. Possibly the Tollards were not quite as happily married as they were acting.

CHAPTER 13

'D ARCY, DARCY.' Felicity called out the name, quietly
and then more loudly as she stood in the hall after
Jane had dropped her off. She listened for a
moment, but could hear nothing. 'Cat,' she called next, but once
again heard nothing. Lunch had been a nightmare, but in
retrospect it had its amusing side and she couldn't help
relishing Jane's almost total silence, such was her awe of Lady
Trubshawe. But now she wanted to be on her own, have the
house to herself. It was one of the few luxuries of being
divorced that she was accountable to no one. As she took off her
jacket and flung it over the hall chair she made up her mind
about one thing. She would *never* allow Jane to talk her into
anything ever again. At least, not until the next time. What was
it about the woman that made Felicity incapable of saying no to
her? Maybe she would be a good counsellor – it might start a
new vogue, the 'sort yourself out or else' school of counselling.

Felicity dropped her handbag at the foot of the stairs and,
kicking her shoes off, wandered into the kitchen. What was
really going on with the Tollards, she wondered? She liked
Sam, he was attractive and had a sense of humour, but was
there any point in dwelling on any possibilities there? Even if
he didn't think she was a lunatic, it seemed he was still
married and to an elegant, if possibly difficult, woman. The
last thing Felicity wanted to do was get involved, in any way,
with a married man. Not after her own experience. She had
asked Jane about this on the way home, but had not had a
satisfactory reply.

'I gather from Cissy they've decided to give it another go.
At least until after the wedding,' was all she was prepared to
say.

However, it was good to meet new people, people who hadn't known her when she was married to Henry. They were both nice, although she wasn't sure she and Lavinia could ever be friends. But she could ask them to dinner together. It would be good to show Sam, and his wife, how normal she could be, but maybe that was tempting fate.

In the kitchen she looked round for Cat, but the only sign of him was the remains of a sparrow on the kitchen floor. Likewise the only sign of Darcy was an empty bottle of wine and two glasses. Interesting. It appeared that her household was sleeping off its excesses, but she wasn't about to go round opening doors to see for herself. After heating up the remains of her breakfast coffee she sat down at the kitchen table and clasped the china mug with a photograph of Jamie on it, that Laura had given her last year.

It was nearly five o'clock on Saturday afternoon. She would have a nice relaxing bath and then it would be a good time to make a few telephone calls. People would probably have finished shopping, got back from lunch or other weekend chores and wouldn't have gone out again yet. Taking the pad from beside the telephone she made a list. Telephone Calls she wrote and then underlined it. Then she wrote a small list of names: 1) Rose. 2) Oliver. 3) Venetia. That would do for the time being.

She dialled the Blighs number, but there was no reply. She wanted to tell her all about the golf club and the unspeakable Lady Trubshawe. She knew Rose would enjoy hearing about that. It was typical of Rose and Leo that they had never got round to having an answering machine, so she couldn't leave a message. She thought for a moment the two of them might have gone out somewhere together, which was surely a good sign, but then she concluded that as it was still light, they were probably in the garden. She pictured Rose in her dirty dungarees digging potatoes and smiling with satisfaction as she filled her wheelbarrow. Leo she imagined wandering in the park with the dogs, stopping every now and then to look at the state of one of the old, and sadly decreasing number of oak trees. She would ring them later this evening. Oliver was next and she hoped she would have better luck with him. She rang his mobile and he answered it on the first ring.

'Hi Mum.' It still surprised her that telephones showed you who was calling. Her mobile did it too, but by the time she had got her glasses out to see who it was they had usually rung off. After a brief update of what had been going on in both their lives, Felicity asked Oliver about his last girlfriend.

'How about Anastasia? Not still yearning after her?'

'No, Mum.'

'And that other girl you mentioned?''

'Nothing serious. Why the sudden interest?'

'Darling, I'm always interested in your love life.'

'Not very interesting at the moment.'

'That's why I was ringing. You know Concepcion?'

'Yup.'

'Well, she's here to learn the language, and she's not learning that much. She needs to go out with some English people.'

'You're not trying to set me up with Laura's au pair? How sad is that?'

'Not set you up. Just ask her out for a drink or something. If her English improved she could do something about Jamie's accent.'

'Mum. Jamie's accent's fine. You're such a snob.'

'She hasn't got any family over here, and all her friends are foreign, so I'm trying to help.'

There was silence on the other end of the line.

'Are you still there?' Felicity asked after a moment.

'Just looking through my diary. I'll give her a call. She's quite fit. We could go and have a drink.'

*

Felicity went into the kitchen feeling restless and in need of more caffeine she made herself a cup of instant coffee, which had to be better than foraging in the fridge or worse, opening that packet of chocolate chip cookies she knew was lurking on top of the cupboard. She took the coffee into the drawing room and sitting down on the sofa drew her feet up underneath her. She took a sip from her mug and made a face, she should have made an effort to make real coffee. Leaning back into the sofa she closed her eyes. It was awful the way children disappeared from their parents' lives. One moment they were adorable little pink bundles and you were cooing over them and kissing their toes. The next they were all grown-up, going their own way, having children of their own and leaving their mother, and probably father, worrying about them in the same way as they always had, but having absolutely no influence or control. But these were pointless thoughts, life was just like that. What was that T-shirt philosophy? Life's a bitch and then you die.

*

Venetia was the next person on Felicity's list. She wanted to have a good gossip, discuss Lady Trubshawe's rudeness, Jane's plans to be a counsellor, Sam Tollard's marriage. Venetia loved a good gossip and nothing was more likely to cheer her up than to be able to impart some knowledge to Felicity. She would be sure to know all about Sam and Lavinia.

'Hello, shweetie.'

Felicity realised immediately Venetia had been drinking. 'Everything OK?' she asked cautiously.

'Wonderful. I've lost my job and my husband's having an affair.'

Felicity gasped and almost blurted out, 'I thought that was over', but she instead she managed to say, 'What happened? How do you know?'

'Sonia. The bastard's been having an affair with that slut Sonia.'

'Are you sure?'

'Bitch rang me up, told me, just like that.' Felicity was silent, she didn't want to say too much at this stage. She had been feeling guilty ever since she had seen Andrew lunching with Sonia. She should have said something ages ago. But after her conversation with Rose and Leo she'd thought the affair was over. But was it? Why had Sonia decided to tell Venetia about it? Trying to call Andrew's bluff?

'I'm coming round,' she said to Venetia and put the telephone down before she had a chance to object. Almost running into the street she tried Rose again on her mobile as she got into the car. No mean feat considering she had to get out her glasses to do so and what with car keys and mobile phone it took her quite a time to sort herself out. Unfortunately there was still no reply from Hatch. What about Daisy? Felicity tried her number too, but there was no answer. She drove recklessly across London and parked outside Venetia's door regardless of the yellow line. It was Saturday, so she hoped it would be all right, but they had a nasty habit nowadays of keeping everything for the residents until ten o'clock. She wondered whether she should put a note on the car; 'Emergency – visiting wronged woman.' But those heartless traffic wardens wouldn't care. With any luck Chelsea were playing at home and they would be too busy harassing football fans to bother with her.

*

Venetia answered the door after a few moments. She was wearing a grubby and creased, pale pink silk dressing-gown, her hair hadn't been brushed and last night's makeup was still clinging to her face. Swaying slightly she stood, cigarette in one hand as she held onto the door frame with the other.

'Hi,' she said looking faintly surprised. 'What you doing here?'

Felicity took her arm and manoeuvred her into the house. Two small boys watched from the street, with the cold unflinching stare of the very young, until their embarrassed mother dragged them away.

'Sit down,' Felicity said firmly as they reached the kitchen. She looked round her, it was a room that was very seldom used. Venetia never cooked. All their parties were catered and they went out to dinner several times a week. Now, however, Felicity thought they needed coffee. Venetia was slumped against the immaculate brushed-steel fridge. Felicity took her arm and sat her down on a chrome chair and started opening and closing doors in an effort to find the ingredients for making a simple cup of coffee. Finally it was done and she sat down opposite Venetia, who had not spoken since they'd come into the house, but had managed to smoke two cigarettes in the time it had taken Felicity to get the coffee together.

'Netty darling, don't go all silent on me. Try and tell me what happened.' Felicity placed a dark green coffee mug in front of her friend. She spooned in a couple of lumps of sugar and then sipped from her own mug.

'I know Andrew's not perfect.' Felicity jumped as Venetia suddenly started to speak. Her words were spoken slowly and deliberately. 'People think he's a shit. But I love him. I've always loved him,' she continued. 'He's had affairs before. I know that.' There was a long pause. 'But I didn't know. You know?' She ground to a halt, her mouth half open, as if the effort of speaking had been too much for her and no more words would come out.

'You mean you didn't know for sure?' Felicity tried to encourage her to go on.

After a moment, Venetia took a few shallow, gasping breaths and continued to speak.

'He's always been discreet. I'd suspect things, but they never lasted. It was only bed. All that sort of thing.' She slumped in the chair, her head falling forward and her hair hanging in a matted curtain.

'What was different this time?' Felicity asked solicitously.

'I thought he'd got over all that.' She pressed a hand to her temples. 'He can't get it up any more. I thought he was finished with all that sort of thing. But apparently, it's just with me.' Her mouth was set into a thin line of misery.

Felicity flinched. Talking about sex made her feel uneasy, especially with Venetia. Cool, elegant, perfect Venetia.

The voice continued in a monotone, eyes cast down. Now she gave a bitter laugh. 'Silly me, I was quite pleased. Always thought sex was over-rated. So messy. Last few times Andrew and I tried nothing happened.' Pushing her hair back from her face she tilted her chin and leant back into the chair. 'He mentioned something about Viagra. That was ages ago, I thought he'd forgotten about it.'

'Obviously not.' Felicity was furious with Andrew. Why were men so silly? Even at sixty he was still thinking with his cock. 'Sonia's had a lot of practice. Probably knows all the tricks,' she said tactlessly and immediately regretted her words.

Venetia shuddered and took another sip of the, by now, cold coffee. 'I don't want to think about that,' she sighed. But it was obvious she could think of little else.

'How long's it been going on?' Felicity spoke without thinking. Why on earth had she asked such a stupid question? She hoped the guilt she was feeling wasn't showing in her face.

'I don't know. Andrew says a few weeks. That slut,' she spat the word, 'says months.' There was despair in Venetia's voice.

Felicity ached for her friend, but at the same time she was afraid Venetia was going to ask her if she had known anything about it. She got up and examined a large abstract painting on the wall. Playing for time she squinted at it. It might be a sunset, or perhaps a bunch of carrots?

'You've spoken to Andrew then?' she asked at last.

'Yes. He's not denying it. Just says it's over.'

Perhaps that was why Sonia had made the telephone call. If Leo was right and Andrew had dumped her she might want Venetia to hurt as much as she did. Venetia lit another cigarette and placed it with deliberation, but very unsteadily, on the overflowing ashtray. She rummaged in her handbag for a mirror. As she pulled it out Felicity leant forward and gently took it from her friend.

'You don't want to do that now. Have a rest first.'

Venetia didn't need to see herself looking as she did at the moment, that would certainly put her straight back onto the vodka.

'As bad as that?' Venetia fumbled for the cigarette and sucked deeply on it, her eyes squinting against the smoke.

'No, you look fine, just tired. And you haven't got any makeup on,' Felicity added helpfully.

'No makeup!' Venetia was startled into activity. 'What time is it? I've rather lost track today.'

'Nearly seven o'clock. And I'm not surprised. You're probably in shock. Why don't you go to bed? Try and get some rest. Got any sleeping pills?' Felicity was very keen on legal drugs. After all if God had expected man to manage pain unaided why had he invented distalgesics?

'Try the bathroom cabinet. Andrew's got some.' Venetia was like a zombie already. On further consideration Felicity thought it would be wiser just to get her to bed and forget about the pills. Heaven only knew how much alcohol she'd had.

It proved remarkably easy getting her into her room. She stood up unsteadily, Felicity took her arm and steered her, gently but firmly, along the corridor to the bedroom. She noticed the bed was unmade and only one side of it had been slept in. She wondered where Andrew was now. She didn't want to ask Venetia for his mobile number, but it would be much better if he didn't come back until Venetia had managed to get some rest. In the end she wrote on a post-it '7.00 pm. Venetia asleep – Might be better to leave her until morning. Call me! Felicity.' and stuck it on the bedroom door. With a final look at Venetia, who was lying on her back, mouth wide open, snoring loudly, Felicity tiptoed out of the flat. She did hope Andrew didn't go barging in. Venetia would want to look her best before they met again.

*

Felicity spent a quiet but frustrating Sunday in bed with the papers and Cat. It was still an unaccustomed luxury not having to get up, but at the same time it made her feel guilty about all the other things she could have been doing. She had got up early, and then taken a tray back to bed while she tried intermittently to ring Rose and Venetia, but without success. She was sitting up in bed worrying when at about eleven Darcy had popped his head round her bedroom door to give her the Sunday papers and say he was off to the pub. Once she heard the front door close behind him she luxuriated in the fact that she was alone in the house. She did manage to get hold of Daisy eventually and she told her Rose had indeed been gardening the previous day and Leo had managed to persuade her to visit an arboretum he was keen to see today. Felicity left a message for Rose to call her when she got back. From Venetia's flat came nothing but the sound of the answering machine all morning but in the afternoon she finally spoke to Andrew.

'How's Venetia?' She tried to make her voice sound casual and caring at the same time, although she knew she wasn't doing a very good job of keeping her annoyance with Andrew out of her voice.

'Fine. Bit of a hangover. She's having a rest.'

'She was rather upset when I saw her yesterday.'

'She gets a bit emotional – you know Venetia. It'll all blow over.' And that was all he would say. The emotional constipation of the average British man never ceased to surprise Felicity. Henry had been just the same.

*

On Monday morning Felicity set off for the shop. Today was the day she was going to meet Gillian and another girl, Angela – Angel. Either her hot flushes were finally disappearing, or the long hot summer was over. She was glad of her pale blue pashmina, wrapped snugly about her neck. She walked along the road feeling quite pleased with herself until she saw a woman walking towards her also with a pale blue pashmina, but hers was draped fetchingly over her shoulders, not bunched up round her neck. Felicity immediately unwrapped hers and tried to make it look more fashionable, but after a moment or two she gave up the unequal struggle. When she got to the shop she was happy to see that the shelf-fitters had been in and the stockroom was nearly ready. It was very exciting to think they could be open in a few weeks. She debated whether to try and get hold of Venetia again, but then decided to leave it until lunch-time.

*

'Hello. I'm Gillian.' A dark, immaculately groomed young woman came into the shop at precisely fifteen minutes past nine. She was wearing black trousers with a matching jacket. 'Not late am I?' She glanced at an elegant gold watch.

'No, absolutely on time.' Felicity stood up and brushed the crumbs from her croissant off her skirt, noticing as she did so she had a ladder in her tights.

'Bother,' she said as she indicated the offending run.

'I always keep a spare pair in my bag.' Gillian looked round the showroom with a supercilious smile.

You would, thought Felicity as she offered her a cup of coffee.

'Have you got decaffeinated?'

Felicity felt obliged to interview her, but she was only going through the motions. She couldn't employ someone who always had spare tights in her bag and didn't drink real coffee.

'I've got one or two other people to see. I'll let you know.' As the door shut she felt a sense of relief.

Half an hour later Felicity was sitting in the back office familiarising herself with the new computer. She had tried to ring Venetia but yet again it was the wretched machine and even her mobile was switched off. She had left messages of support and there didn't seem much else she could do at the moment. The next thing she knew, the shop door had opened silently and Angel was standing in the room.

*

Felicity had met her the previous week when she had wandered into a shop selling decorated loo seats. Not that she wanted one, but in preparation for her new role as an

211

executive she thought it was important to see what competition was out there. In the middle of the shop was a loo seat adorned with a caricature of Margaret Thatcher. Felicity stared at it in horror. Imagine seeing that every morning, she'd thought.

'Gross innit?'

Felicity turned round to see a young girl standing beside her dressed in a pair of low-slung trousers and a T-shirt that proclaimed 'Girls Cheat too they just don't get caught', skimming her evenly-tanned stomach.

'I'm supposed to sell 'em. You looking for anything special?' she suddenly switched to salesgirl mode as if she just remembered what she was there for.

'Not really, I was just passing. Hadn't seen this shop before.'

'It 'asn't been 'ere long. 'Bout three months.'

'Is it just loo seats?'

'Nah. Stupid nail brushes like frogs and loo paper with crosswords and stuff.' Her lip curled slightly as she spoke. Then, after a pause, she pointed towards the back of the shop.

'We've got some neat hand towels. With flowers and animals and things.' Suddenly she became the complete professional as she propelled Felicity over to the towels. She was right, they were very pretty and as the girl pointed out, very reasonably priced. Felicity bought three of them. One with a cat on it for her downstairs loo and a couple covered in rosebuds for Rose.

'Do you do bigger versions of these?' she asked as she was paying for them.

'They make them, but *we* don't stock 'em.' The girl raised her eyebrows and glanced towards the back of the shop.

'You don't sound as if you're that keen on working here.' Felicity said as she looked at her reflectively. She was an unusual looking girl, with her long face and wide-set blue eyes, like someone out of a Burne-Jones painting. Apart from the clothes.

'What's it to you?'

'I'm sorry, that was a bit impertinent. It's just that I'm starting a shop, well to be strictly accurate, it's my son who's starting it, and I wondered ... '

'It's not bad here, it's a job.' The girl shrugged, but she gave Felicity a smile that encouraged her to continue.

'What's your name?'

'Angel. Angela, but everyone calls me Angel.'

'I can see why. You've got a sort of mediaeval angel's face.' Felicity smiled back.

'Shouldn't think any of my friends know anyfink 'bout mediaeval angels.' She laughed and wound a strand of her long fair hair round her fingers in an embarrassed way.

'About the shop. It's not open yet, but here's my card – if you decide to move, give me a ring.' There was something about her Felicity liked and she was glad when she rang a day or two later. And now here she was standing in front of Felicity waiting to be interviewed.

'Who's that? What a babe.' Angel picked up a photograph of Oscar from Felicity's desk. It was the one they were using for the brochure and she had to get it to the printer this week.

'My son, Oscar. He owns the shop. He and his partner Barry.'

'Bugger innit the way all the fit looking ones are gay?'

'I don't suppose gay men think so.' Felicity giggled, then felt this was not a very businesslike start to the interview. 'Did you bring your CV?' she asked crisply.

Angel rummaged around in her bag and produced an immaculately typed piece of paper with about five lines on it. Since leaving school she had worked in a tearoom in Essex, a few months in a bar in Ibiza, followed by nearly a year in a well-known department store.

'Ibiza must have been interesting.' It was a pretty feeble remark. Felicity's interviewing skills still needed a bit of polishing.

'There was this guy I fancied. I followed him out there.'

'Your boyfriend?'

'Nah. Just someone I shagged. You don't go with your boyfriend to Ibiza, Mrs Fox. You go with mates, see how many guys you can pull.'

'Really?' Felicity's eyes opened wide. Was she mad to even consider this girl for a job in the shop? She seemed honest, too honest perhaps?

'That was just a summer job, I suppose?'

'Sright. Then I went to Mathers. That was all right, but then they closed the shoe department. They said they'd try and find me another job but I thought it was time to go. Then I went to Lulu's Loos, then you came in, Mrs Fox.'

'Call me Felicity.' The modern workplace was no place for formality.

'Ooh no. I couldn't, you're older than my gran.' Ouch. Angel blushed. 'I'm ever so sorry, that was really rude. Anyway my gran's dead.'

What a strange girl who thought nothing of going on holiday to have sex with strangers, but found it difficult to call someone by their first name.

'She had a teashop in Colchester,' she continued, recovering her composure. 'I helped her after school and in the holidays and when she fell ill. She passed away last year. We had to sell it 'cos of the money. Me brother wanted his share. After that I come to London.'

'I'm sorry. Were you close to your grandmother?' And how old was she, was Felicity's unspoken question.

'She brought me up. My mum was only fifteen when I was born. She done a runner. But Gran was brilliant. Her dad was a right villain.'

'Really?' Felicity hoped she had an expression of polite enquiry on her face.

'Yea. Spent years inside.' Angel's voice was full of pride. 'Made sure his family was all right though. That's how come Gran had the teashop. Then she got cancer.' The girl's eyes closed and her long hair fell over her face. She pushed it behind her ear impatiently.

Felicity saw a tear slide its way down her cheek. She put her hand on the girl's shoulder. 'I'm sorry,' she said again.

Angel sniffed and ran both forefingers under her eyes. 'Sorl right,' she shrugged. 'Just one of those things.' After a moment she spoke again. 'I'd like to work 'ere. I'm good in shops. I wouldn't let you down. Dead reliable I am.'

'I'm sure you are,' Felicity said truthfully, there was something about Angel that made her think they would be able to work together.

Felicity showed her round. She was beginning to feel really excited herself. The whole thing was coming together now. It felt real. The office, *her office*, had all its cupboards and shelves. Her desk was an elegant sheet of smoked glass. Oscar said that it was passé, but Felicity had always wanted one like it, and as it was in the back office she'd been allowed to have it. Her brand new computer looked efficient and once she had mastered it Felicity felt she would be efficient too.

The stockroom, with its empty racks, paradoxically looked bigger now than it had before the shelves had been put up. The light fittings had gone in on Friday, making everything look bright and new. Filling the shop with light. You couldn't see any of the fittings, which had been cunningly hidden. Oscar had given Felicity a long talk about the importance of lighting. He said they had to use light as a neutral background as one of the main things they would be selling was lights and lighting. Lights of all types, old, new, ethnic, an eclectic mix. The lighting in the shop had to complement the merchandise, not dominate it. There was a whole range of switches so that the room could be lit in an infinite variety of ways. Felicity, who had been endeavouring to memorise Oscar's explanations, tried to demonstrate it all to Angel, trotting out her son's words, hoping she sounded more confident than she felt.

'This switch fills the shop with a soft diffused light,' she said as a couple of sharply focussed spotlights illuminated the two standard lamps at the far end of the shop. 'No, wait a minute, I think it's this one.' She turned another knob and the room turned blue. 'I haven't had much practice with this.' Felicity felt a bit sheepish.

'D'you mind if I try? I think it might be this one.' Angel turned another knob and all at once the room was bathed in a warm glow.

'Brilliant. How did you know that?' Felicity was impressed. She was even more confident she had chosen the right girl for the job.

'It says diffuser on the button.' Angel giggled. Felicity pulled her glasses out of her pocket. All became clear.

Later, over a cup of coffee they discussed salaries, hours, etc. and then Felicity dropped her off at Parsons Green tube station before driving home. The shop was definitely falling into place. Miles was the only missing component. For some reason, Oscar had not yet brought him into to meet his mother.

CHAPTER 14

FELCIITY TOOK ANGEL TO MEET OSCAR the following day, half hoping she would be able to meet the elusive Miles at the same time. But apparently he had nipped over to New York on some urgent personal business. Oscar and Angel took to each other at once and they all ended up going out for lunch together. It was agreed Angel would start work helping to get the shop ready the following week. She had already given in her notice at the other shop that morning and was looking forward to being part of the new team.

*

Felicity was feeling particularly cheerful as she caught the bus home. There was something about the top of a London double decker bus on a sunny day that was infinitely cheering. As it made its ponderous way along the crowded King's Road Felicity took pleasure from looking into all the shop windows and people watching. She decided she would hop off the bus as it passed Habitat and buy a waste paper basket for her new office. Unfortunately hop was exactly what she did, but the skip and jump that followed sent her lurching into a lamp post. As she tried desperately to keep her footing a strong arm grabbed hold of her and she heard a familiar voice in her ear.

'Hello,' Sam Tollard said with a grin.

'Oh shit,' said Felicity to herself. Why did life keep doing this to her?

'You must think I'm an accident-prone lunatic,' she muttered.

'Are you all right? You look a bit shaken.' Sam's voice was full of concern. 'Why don't I buy you a cup of coffee?'

*

Five minutes later Felicity found herself sitting opposite Sam with a cappuccino in her hands. She was still feeling a bit shaky, but wasn't sure it was the result of her stumble off the bus, or the fact she had lost the facility to deal with life.

'You'll probably find this hard to believe,' she sighed, 'but I used to be a really capable person.'

'Don't be so hard on yourself, I do believe you.'

'Do you?' Felicity was surprised. He certainly hadn't seen much evidence of it on the few occasions they had met.

'Did you ever have any of those awful, scratchy, hand-knitted jumpers when you were a child?'

'Oh yes, my Aunt Violet gave me one every Christmas. Why?'

'D'you remember when you caught the sleeve on a nail or branch of a tree and you'd pull the loose thread and the whole thing would unravel?'

'I'd forgotten that. I had a royal blue one and I got it caught on barbed wire climbing through a fence. I got into such trouble.'

'Well, don't you think life can be a bit like that sometimes? Everything's fine, and then one thing goes wrong and everything else starts to fall to pieces.'

'I do see what you mean.' Felicity smiled. 'So you think that's what's happening, my life is in the process of unravelling? That's certainly what it feels like, but it's not a very cheerful thought.'

'But I bet your aunt used the wool again to knit something else!'

'Gosh yes, she did.' Felicity leant back in her chair. The little café was full of people and she smiled as she thought of all their lives as balls of different coloured wool. 'That's a good way of putting it. It sounds as though you've thought about it a bit.'

Sam leant forward, elbows on the table and rested his chin on his hands. He looked at Felicity and gave a crooked little smile.

'Things have been a bit complicated recently. All I'm trying to do at the moment is to keep sane until after the wedding.'

As a result of bumping into Sam, Felicity arrived home rather later than she had intended. And no sooner had she opened the front door than the telephone in the hall rang. It was Daisy.

'Where've you been? I've been trying to get you all day. You're mobile's switched off.'

'What's the matter? Is it Venetia?' Felicity fumbled in her bag. She had turned the phone off during the interviews and had forgotten to turn it on again.

'No. It's Rose. She's had a heart attack.'

Felicity sat down abruptly on the bottom stair.

'When ... how ... what happened?' Felicity thought she was going to be sick as the questions poured out. She forced herself to concentrate as Daisy spoke.

'She's in the county hospital. We're all with her. Leo's here. She wants to see you.' Daisy was crying.

'At least she's talking. Is she going to be all right?'

'They don't say anything. It's too early. Is she going to die?'

Felicity could hear the quaver in Daisy's voice. 'No Daisy, of course she won't die. She's strong. With any luck there won't be any permanent damage.' Felicity tried hard to believe her own words. She was thinking rapidly. She would leave a note for Darcy. He could feed Cat. She'd ring Oscar from the car. And Venetia, she must try her again. She found an envelope on the table announcing she had won £100,000. She turned it over and made a list on the back. She tried to convince herself that she didn't have the beginnings of Alzheimer's but she knew if she didn't write everything down it would go straight out of her mind.

'Oh Fifi, please come. And keep your mobile on.' Daisy's voice was frightened.

'Of course I'm coming. I'm on my way – be with you in a couple of hours. And try not to worry, hospitals never tell you anything if they can help it.'

'You will drive carefully won't you? We need you here.'

In the midst of her misery, Felicity couldn't help smiling at Daisy's attempt to be motherly. As soon as she got off the telephone she packed a bag, although she had no idea what she put in it. She scribbled a note to Darcy telling him what had happened and got into the car.

'Venetia, it's me. How are you?'

'Ghastly. Head's still throbbing, eyes all puffy. I look like shit.'

'I've been trying to get you all day yesterday and today.'

'I went to the hairdressers this morning – trying to repair some of the damage – I meant to go for a facial and to the gym, but couldn't face it. Bought some new shoes instead.' She gave a dry laugh.

Felicity interrupted her.'Listen. Rose's had a heart attack. I'm on my way down there now.'

'My God. I can't believe it. Not Rose. She doesn't even smoke.' Felicity could hear Venetia inhaling triumphantly. 'Is she going to be all right?'

'I don't know. It's too early to tell, but she's conscious. Hopefully it was just a warning. But how about you? Is Andrew there?'

'He was. Gone out now, but we're having dinner together this evening. He wants to talk.'

'What about?'

'How the fuck should I know?' Venetia's voice was harsh.

'OK. I'll ring you tomorrow.'

'Love to Rose.'

'I will. Bye.'

Felicity's mind was racing all the way down to Wiltshire. Rose of all people. Felicity had never known her have a day's illness. She had always seemed to be as strong as an ox, but apparently she wasn't. Felicity just could not imagine her not being there. She was the rock they all depended on, Leo, Daisy, the boys and Felicity herself. How long had all this been going on? Had Rose suspected there was something wrong with her heart? Surely it hadn't just happened without any warning. Felicity felt she should have guessed. She knew something was wrong, but she hadn't been sure what the matter was. She'd been too wrapped up in her own life. But all the clues had been there; the not going out, the never coming to London any more. And no one had said anything or tried to do anything. That was awful. She had looked tired sometimes, but she always did so much, would never let anyone help her. And she'd been worried, unnecessarily as it turned out, about Leo. She had to get better, what would they all do without her? Oh, how selfish that was. Imagine thinking like that. But Rose mustn't die. She had to get better. Felicity's thoughts whirled round and round leaving her exhausted. She was relieved to reach the hospital, where she might at least be able to be of some practical use.

*

Felicity was shocked when she finally arrived. Rose was in a room of her own and was lying in bed attached to a battery of machines. Her eyes were closed and for a moment Felicity thought she had died. Leo, sitting on a black plastic chair by the bed, looked grey and shrunken. He struggled to his feet and hugged her but Felicity was not at all sure he knew who she was or what any of them were doing there. Daisy, apart from her red eyes, was looking as beautiful as ever, but her face was a picture of misery. Jonathan and Tom were sitting together on a chair bickering with each other over Nintendo.

'Have you spoken to the doctor? Do you know what's happening?'

Leo and Daisy shook their heads and Felicity had the feeling they were completely lost and were looking to her for a lead. Tom, suddenly bored with watching his brother, started to play with a handle on the bed.

'Stop doing that, you little sod,' Daisy yelled at him, startling them all. She dragged him away by the sleeve of his T-shirt.

'How long have you been here?' Felicity asked as she looked at their exhausted faces.

'I don't know. A long time.' Leo looked hopelessly at his watch.

'Daisy, why don't you take everybody home, get something to eat and some rest. I'll stay and try to talk to the doctor, find out what's happening.'

'Great, can we go now Mum?' Tom picked up the Nintendo and leapt to his feet.

'I'm sitting in front.' Jonathan struggled to get out of the door before his brother.

'Leo's sitting in front.' Daisy's teeth were clenched. 'And unless you behave, you'll be walking home.'

'Cool. Can we really walk, Mum? We could hitch.'

'Don't be stupid.' Daisy grabbed their arms and led them, still trying to punch each other, out of the room.

While all this was going on Leo was standing looking at his wife. At one point he put his hand out and gently stroked Rose's hair. After a few moments he drew back, as if afraid he might hurt her.

'Leo,' Felicity took his arm, 'go home. Come back when you've had some rest. I'll stay here, try and talk to the doctor. I'll ring you if there's any news.'

'Perhaps that would be best. Don't know what to do here. Not very good in hospitals. Feel a bit useless.'

As Leo shuffled off, Felicity thought this was the worst part, seeing a family fall apart because the most important member, the lynchpin, was lying helpless in a hospital bed. She sat down heavily on the chair vacated by Leo. It looked as if it might double as a commode and Felicity hoped that it was secure, she didn't want to be involved in an unfortunate accident. She sat and stared at Rose intently for a few moments. She didn't look like Rose. It wasn't just that she was pale and attached to tubes and lines, there was something else. All at once Felicity realised she had never seen Rose lying down before. Rose was the closest thing to perpetual motion in human form Felicity had ever known. That was the strangest thing, to see her cousin prone on a bed. It was rather like seeing her naked for the first time. Feeling embarrassed she picked up a copy of *OK!* and leafed idly through it. Who were all these people? She had never heard of any of them.

After a short time Rose opened her eyes.

'Fifi. I knew you'd come, Possum. It'll be all right now.' Her voice was low, slow and sleepy. She held out her hand and Felicity took it in hers.

'You're going to be fine.' Felicity wished she had confidence in her own words, but what else could she say? Rose drifted off to sleep again. Felicity stared gloomily at their two hands entwined on the bed. The crepey skin, the liver spots. These were old hands, past their sell-by date hands. Rose gave her a squeeze and let go, but Felicity continued to examine herself. Was it possible to have a hand lift? What inappropriate thoughts popped into one's mind at times like this. Possibly because the alternative literally did not bear thinking about.

She was still sitting staring at her fingers when a plump young nurse bustled in.

'Can you tell me how she is?'

'You'd best talk to Doctor Khan. He'll be here in the morning. You give him a ring tomorrow.' She spoke with a cheerful Irish brogue. She bent forward and took Rose's pulse. 'Now Rose, how are we feeling?' There was no response. 'Are you family?' She turned to Felicity.

'A cousin. I'm staying with Mrs Bligh's husband and sister. We'll come back in the morning. When's a good time to catch Doctor Khan?'

'Well now, he does his rounds at ten o'clock, but we don't allow visitors in the mornings. You could ring about lunchtime. He'll be sure to talk to you then.' She picked up the chart at the end of Rose's bed and scribbled something on it. As soon as she had gone Felicity picked up the chart, but she failed to make head or tail of it. She bent over and kissed Rose's forehead and was rewarded by her eyes opening for a second.

'Bye darling.' Felicity startled herself, she never called Rose darling.

She drove back to Hatch House on automatic pilot, she didn't notice the colour of the autumn leaves, nor the sunset. At the house she almost burst into tears. Leo and Daisy were sitting in the kitchen drinking cups of instant coffee. The breakfast dishes were still stacked in the sink. A bowl of dying dahlias looked forlorn next to a pile of unopened mail. From the study the television was blaring out, not quite drowning the sound of the boys squabbling. Felicity realised that although Rose had only been gone for a few hours the soul had gone out of this house. It wasn't going to be easy putting it back, but Felicity knew it would be up to her to try, she owed that much to Rose. She hung her jacket up on a peg in the hall, rolled her sleeves up and set to work. She went into the study and switched off the television and ignoring the howls of protest she offered Tom and Jonathan a pound each to take the dogs for a long walk. Going back into the kitchen she gestured at the table.

'Daisy, be a love, throw those flowers away and go out and find some others. Those are just too depressing.'

Daisy pulled her unbrushed hair back with one hand and taking an elastic band out of the pocket of her jeans wound it round the tangled tresses. Then she got wearily to her feet and after rummaging in the kitchen drawer for a pair of scissors she silently left the room and went out into the garden. Once she had gone Felicity turned to Leo.

'Will you please go upstairs and have a rest? You look exhausted.'

'I'm all right,' he said although he obviously wasn't.

'Leo, my darling, when Rose comes home, she's going to need you to look after her, not the other way round.' She spoke slowly as if to a child. It had the desired effect, for after a moment Leo got slowly to his feet and squeezed Felicity's hand.

'You're right,' he said with a sigh and left the room.

Felicity loaded the dishwasher and turned it on, she swept the floor and tidied the table. She had just finished when Daisy returned with an enormous bouquet in her arms. She had picked a mixture of dark red dahlias with black-berries, teasels and rose hips. Daisy herself looked better, the fresh air had put some colour into her cheeks. She found a large blue earthenware jug and as soon as the flowers were arranged in it, on the kitchen table, the room began to come to life again. Felicity went into the larder to see what she could find for them to eat. There were plenty of eggs, potatoes and onions, so she decided to make a large Spanish omelette. There were cucumbers, lettuces and tomatoes from the garden so she made a salad and took a large wholemeal loaf out of the deep freeze and popped it into the microwave to defrost. Daisy seemed invigorated and relieved someone else was taking over. Felicity realised that although Daisy was the mother of two boys she had never actually taken charge of her own life. First her mother and then Rose had looked after her. Now she was turning to Felicity. And it looked as though the others would do so as well.

She discovered Rose's two children in Australia knew nothing about her heart attack, so after supper she went to Rose's desk and looked up their telephone numbers. Although she had met them a couple of times in the past, she didn't know them well and she felt terrible having to tell them about their mother. They both offered to come over immediately, but Felicity thought it would be much better for Rose and Leo to go out there together for a long holiday once Rose was back from hospital. However she promised to keep in touch with them and let them know if there was any change in Rose's condition. Once she got off the telephone she felt guilty she had prevented them from coming – suppose Rose didn't get better? Just because she was refusing to entertain that possibility she had to be realistic.

*

The next morning Mrs P turned up early for once in her life. She was longing to hear all the latest news about Rose. She started talking as she was taking her coat off.

'My sister-in-law, she had the same thing. Ever so sudden it was. One minute she was moving the settee, next she was in hospital. Course she never came out.'

'That's very cheering. Thank you.' Felicity could feel her teeth clenching.

'I told Rose to take things a bit easier. She was always overdoing it. I warned her.' She sucked her teeth. 'I could see she was a bad colour, quite flushed a lot of time. I put it down to her age, or perhaps the drink,' she added as an after-thought.

'What are you talking about, drink? Rose is *not* a drinker Mrs P. The odd glass of wine in the evening, nothing more.' Felicity was gibbering with indignation and longed, as she often did when confronted with Mrs P, to smack her face, but now was not the time to disrupt the household any more.

'I've seen it.' She sucked in through her teeth again. 'I have to put the empty bottles out. You should see the collection she took to the bottle bank last week. Mark you, Mr P liked a drop of whisky. I can't touch the stuff, not with my dsylepsia.'

Felicity knew her face was flushed as she tried to control her temper.

'Still getting the hot flushes are we? I'd have thought you'd have been well over them by your age. Still you big women always have more problems. I was lucky, but my Cynthia ... ' Felicity picked up a saucepan and banged it down on the kitchen table. Then she turned the radio on very loudly, but it was too much to hope that Mrs P would take a hint. Was it possible, she wondered, the evil old bag was blackmailing the Bligh family? What other reason could there be for keeping her on? They all constantly affirmed that she was a character, but as far as Felicity was concerned she was nothing but a foul-mouthed gossip.

'They'll give her a peacemaker I expect.'

'Really.' There was no point in correcting her.

227

'They can do a lot for hearts nowadays, but women's problems, they don't want to know. My Cynthia used to suffer with them fibroids. The doctor said they were the biggest ones he'd ever seen. She had to have a hysterthingummybob.'

All this was rather more information than Felicity had ever wished to have about the absent Cynthia. She knew she would never stop the relentless stream of gloom, but to gain a temporary respite she announced she had to make some telephone calls and she went out into the garden with her list and her mobile.

*

Oscar was calm and reassuring. What a heavenly child he was and at least being gay meant that his mother was the most important woman in his life. He was adamant she mustn't think of coming back to London until Rose was better. The most urgent thing was the brochure and he would deal with that. He said he could always get Darcy in to hold the fort if necessary. Why not Miles, she wondered when she got off the phone. She must remember to ask Oscar what was happening there. What a strange quirk of fate it was that had led her to Darcy and now he was looking after her house, Cat and business. Perhaps it would have the same effect that making a particularly disruptive child at school a prefect could have. It should be interesting to see Darcy with a sense of responsibility.

'Netty? How are things?' Felicity was apprehensive. She had tried to ring Venetia several times with no answer and now the phone had rung about fifteen times before being answered.

'Who's that? What time is it?' Felicity was sure it wasn't her imagination, the speech was slurred. She was tempted to hang up without speaking, but Venetia was her friend so she forced herself to continue.

'It's me, Fifi. I wondered how you got on last night?'

'Wha happened last night?'

'I don't know. I'm asking you.'

'Why should anything have happened?'

'Is Andrew there?'

'Why you want to know? You fucking him too?'

Oh dear, this was going to be a difficult conversation. Maybe it was time she spoke directly to Andrew and made him discuss the situation whether he wanted to or not. Perhaps she could enlist Leo's help. He might be grateful for something constructive to do. She could get him to ring Andrew and arrange for him to call Felicity. She didn't dare ring him at home and risk getting Venetia again. But her friend needed help and it was about time something was done about it. But at the moment Rose had to take priority and Felicity didn't have the time or energy to cope with Venetia's problems on top of that.

She had always known Rose was the strongest force in the household, but she was beginning to realise just how powerful a force that had been. They were all rudderless without her. Felicity had never been conscious of Rose bossing everyone around, rather the reverse, she had always appeared to do everything single-handed. But it was apparent that without Rose as the axis nothing happened.

Felicity knew they were all in shock, and the only way she could think of helping them was to set each of them a specific task every day. When they were busy they were all fine, but no sooner had Leo come back from the bottle bank than Felicity would catch him sitting with his head in his hands, where he would remain, as if paralysed, until Felicity sent him off to the newsagents to pay the paper bill. The boys would come back from collecting eggs and unless Felicity sent them off to dig potatoes they would be fighting each other, shouting and kicking until Daisy came running from wherever she was and started flailing at them with whatever she happened to have in her hands. As more often than not this was a riding crop Felicity felt it was imperative to keep them out of their mother's hair. At least Daisy had the horses to keep her occupied and she alone was prepared to leave the house in the evenings and would frequently leave the boys with Felicity while she disappeared mysteriously. Felicity longed to know where she went, but since Daisy, usually so garrulous, was strangely silent, she didn't feel she could pry.

The longer Rose was in hospital, the more Felicity wondered how they were going to cope when she came home unable to take over everything once more. Leo missed her the most, but for an articulate man he found it very difficult to express his feelings. He belonged to a generation that kept their upper lips stiff at all times, but even he broke down in front of Felicity one day. She got up early and found him sitting sobbing at the kitchen table.

'Oh Leo, don't cry. I can't bear it.' She had been close to tears herself.

'Just needed a moment, I'll pull myself together now,' he said, producing a large blue and white spotted handkerchief from his pocket and blowing his nose loudly. 'Mustn't let the side down.'

'She is going to get better, you know.' Felicity tried to reassure him. 'But,' she continued, 'you're all going to have to pull your weight. She can't go back to doing everything or she'll be straight back in hospital.'

'I suppose I could learn to cook. Can't be that hard to follow a recipe.'

And true to his word, Leo spent his mornings poring over cookery books. Daisy and the boys gallantly praised his every effort and did their best to eat everything he set before them.

*

'Hello Possum. For God's sake, get me out of here!' Rose was up and dressed, looking much more like her old self and impatient to go home. She had been in hospital for just over a week and she was being discharged with strict instructions from the doctors and nurses not to try and do too much. Felicity had gone to the hospital to collect her.

'D'you need an arm?' It wasn't easy getting used to Rose as an invalid.

'Certainly not – walking's good for me. In fact I've got to do it every day.'

'Your poor old dogs, they won't know what's hit them. They're used to pottering around with Leo.'

Rose grabbed her overnight bag, but Felicity managed to wrestle it off her. The doctor told her she had been very lucky and should take this as a warning. He had given her a diet sheet, with orders to stick to it. Out went the double cream, the butter, the big fry ups for breakfast. Fish, lean meat, fruit and vegetables were the order of the day.

When Felicity brought Rose back to Hatch she could scarcely believe her eyes. Leo had prepared lunch of dressed crab with salad followed by baked apples. On the table was a vase of autumn leaves and berries picked by Daisy and the table had been laid, albeit slightly haphazardly, by the boys. Rose took one look at her kitchen and burst into tears.

'Steady on,' Leo muttered, enfolding her in a big hug, 'You'll start everyone else off.'

Throughout that first meal the whole family were on the edge of their seats. Rose only had to change position in her chair and one of them was on their feet demanding to know what she wanted.

'Really, Possums, I don't think I can stand much more of this,' she said finally. 'You're all going to have to relax.'

Over the next few days life did manage to get back to some sort of normality, but with the difference that there was no more of Rose doing all the work while her family and friends sat around the kitchen table, gossiping and drinking. Rose had to learn not only to ask for help, but to accept it when it was offered. And the others had to learn to help without being asked. Felicity found herself in her element, setting up rotas for washing-up, cooking, shopping, taking the rubbish out, walking the dogs. Much to everyone's surprise the boys, unnaturally subdued and tiptoeing around Rose, didn't complain at all when they were given a list of chores. In fact, once Leo had assured them that Rose wasn't about to die and had come to an arrangement with them about paying them for any jobs they did, they were extremely cheerful. Daisy had always been very hit and miss with their pocket money. Now they could organise their own money and Tom even opened a savings account at the Post Office.

*

The day after Rose came home, Felicity took the dogs out for a short walk before breakfast. There was a heavy dew on the grass and she was just regretting not having put on her wellies when she spotted Daisy leaning over the fence of the paddock staring into space.

'Hi,' she said cheerfully.

'Ooops! You made me jump,' Daisy squealed as she surreptitiously wiped her eyes and Felicity realised she had been crying.

'What's wrong love?' Felicity put her arm round the younger woman.

'Rose,' she muttered, her voice barely audible.

'She's going to be fine. Don't you think she looks all right?'

'Yes, she does. I'm just being silly. I think its relief. I was so frightened she was going to die.'

'I know, but she's not. And you're going to have your work cut out to stop her slipping back into her old ways.'

'Don't worry, we're all going to do everything for her. We won't allow her to lift a finger.'

Felicity couldn't help smiling at Daisy's earnest face.

'That might be easier said than done,' she said wryly. Then calling the dogs she squelched back to the house to dry her feet.

*

Felicity stayed for several more days after Rose came home, just to make sure everything was ticking over smoothly. It was amazing to see her cousin staying in bed until 7.30 in the morning rather than rising at six and doing a thousand and one things before the rest of the household had risen. But even Rose functioning at half speed was faster than most people, and Felicity found she had to be alert at all times in order to keep her from trying to do too much. One morning she had discovered her, garden fork in hand, attacking the herbaceous border.

'What d'you think you're doing?' she cried as she ran out of the kitchen still wearing her rubber gloves.

'It's no good Possum, if I can't put my borders to bed I'll never relax.'

'But you're not supposed to be doing heavy work. I'll do it.' Or find someone else – Felicity wasn't Rose, she couldn't even attempt to do all the things Rose normally did. No wonder she'd had a heart attack.

'You might as well let me do it Possum. The worry of seeing them like that'll only give me another heart attack.'

This was not going to be an easy job and there was no way Felicity would be able to go straight back to London. She rang Oscar again and much to her surprise he said Darcy was coping well – he had been going into the shop to meet suppliers. Turning up sober when he said he would. How nice it was to be proved wrong and be pleasantly surprised for once.

*

A few days later, when Felicity was beginning to think about returning to London, the telephone rang. Rose was still in bed, and Felicity was in the garden picking a bunch of dahlias for the sitting room. Mrs P answered it and came to find Felicity.

'That was your ex, Henry, on the phone. Asking after Rose, supposedly.'

'Does he want me to ring him?' Felicity found it very irritating that her heart started to race at the mention of his name. It was only habit. She was not in love with him any more.

'He's coming over. I asked him to lunch. Cheer Rose up.' She re-tied the bow on her apron and after a suitable pause for dramatic effect sucked through her teeth and added, 'He's not bringing that woman.'

Felicity was torn between relief she wouldn't have to face Sally and intense irritation that Mrs P should take it upon herself to invite someone to lunch. She began to think fast, one half of her brain wondering what they could eat. It was her turn to do lunch as Leo and Rose were going to a local nursery in the morning. She had only been going to do baked potatoes, with a slice of cold ham and a salad. It wasn't special enough for her first meal with Henry in over a year. On the other hand she didn't want to look as though she was trying too hard.

She walked with deliberate casualness into the house, but once inside, away from Mrs P's evil eye, she dashed upstairs. What to wear? She didn't have much with her – had been wearing the same pair of jeans since she arrived and borrowing sweaters from Rose as and when she needed them. The only other clothes she had with her was the very business-like suit she had been wearing when Daisy had telephoned her to tell her the news about Rose. Hardly appropriate for a weekday lunch in the country, besides which she would prefer to look faintly seductive rather than as if she was visiting her accountant. She knocked tentatively on Rose's door, not sure if she was still resting.

'Come in.' The voice sounded cheerful.

'I've come to raid your wardrobe. You must have some-thing big enough. Henry's coming to lunch.' Felicity was starting to gabble.

'Slow down, Possum. You know I'm not supposed to have too much excitement. I'll have another heart attack.'

'Oh Lord,' Felicity waved her hands anxiously in the air. 'Do you need a pill or something?'

Rose, who was sitting on the edge of her bed, wriggling her feet about looking for her slippers, laughed.

'Don't be silly. I feel fine. Borrow anything you like Possum.'

Felicity rummaged around the large cupboard in Rose's bedroom and pulled out several things that caught her eye. She and Rose then spent a happy half hour deciding what would be most suitable to impress an ex-husband one didn't fancy. Certainly not. But on the other hand would like to make him realise what he was missing. Unfortunately Felicity decided ruefully that what he was missing was a large, red-faced woman with a rather better haircut than the one he had left. Still she did at least feel tidier in a long-sleeved white cotton shirt worn over her jeans to cover most of her bulges and the unsightly stains that the jeans seemed to have acquired.

After looking through the fridge and store cupboards she decided to make minted pea soup followed by a warm quiche and a green salad for lunch. That was quite sophisticated yet didn't look as if she had gone to too much effort. As she was busy organising the meal she didn't have time to think about Henry's imminent arrival. At a quarter to one she was just making the salad dressing. Rose had to be banished from the kitchen because she found it impossible not to take over. Felicity had sent her out for a short walk with Leo and the dogs when they got back from the garden centre. Regular exercise and no stress, that was what was required. With her usual impeccable timing Felicity had managed to drop olive oil all down her front just as Henry walked in through the kitchen door.

'Hello old thing,' he kissed her clumsily. 'Where's the patient?'

'Walking in the park with Leo.' Felicity felt a frisson of irritation – old thing, accurate maybe, but she was willing to bet he never called Sally old thing. Not if he wanted to hang onto his testicles. She rubbed ineffectually at the stain.

'You're looking pretty fit,' he managed to say next.

Felicity had heard Oliver refer to girls as fit, but somehow she didn't think Henry meant it in the same way. Although it was true she was quite fit. The gym was paying dividends: perhaps if she ever found another suitable man she would be able to impress him by beating him at arm wrestling. But at this rate it would be zimmer frame races.

'Thank you, and you're looking well.' Felicity looked at him as she spoke and realised it wasn't true. He was still a very attractive man, but he was looking at least ten years older. His face was flushed and puffy. Drinking too much? What had

Sally driven him to? Part of her longed to take him in her arms and give him a hug but another part couldn't help feeling it served him right for walking out on her like that.

'How's Sally?'

'She's fine.'

Was it wishful thinking or did his face take on a haunted look when she mentioned that woman's name. At that moment three black Labradors bounded into the kitchen, tails wagging wildly, followed closely by Leo and Rose back from their walk.

'Got a drink yet Henry? Didn't think so.'

'That's women for you.' Henry kissed Rose carefully as though she might break. 'Never get their priorities straight – always want to waste valuable drinking time talking.'

Leo waved a bottle of gin in front of Henry who nodded. And Felicity noticed he had drained his glass before Rose and she had been given their white wine spritzers.

'Being kept on short rations at home are you?' Leo winked at Felicity behind Henry's back as he poured him another gin and tonic.

'Certainly not,' Henry spluttered. 'Just celebrating Rose's return to health. I must say you look all right. Sure it really was a heart attack?'

'I'm sure,' Rose said dryly.

Lunch passed off well enough. It felt strange to Felicity to be sitting in the kitchen at Hatch with Henry, as they had so many, many times in the past. On the one hand it felt familiar and comfortable and yet everything had changed. She had to stop herself from talking to Henry as though he was still her husband. And Rose looked the same as ever, but now she sat, albeit uneasily, while Felicity and Leo got the meal together. They decided it wasn't quite warm enough to eat outside, but they took their coffee into the garden afterwards and all four of them sat in an awkward silence watching the sun getting lower in the sky. Conversation hadn't exactly flowed throughout the meal. Every time they got on to a safe topic, one or other of them would mention a taboo.

'How's Venetia?' Henry had asked.

'Fine,' Rose, Leo and Felicity chorused in insincere unison and immediately tried to change the subject.

'Did you hear Charles Cameron's brother died?' Henry was doing his best.

'No. How awful. He wasn't very old. What happened?'

'Heart attack.' Whoops. Conversational u-turn. Try again.

'Have you seen Laura recently?' Felicity asked Henry.

'Yes, she came to tea last week. She's gone shopping with Sally today.'

'Nice try Henry – now shall we talk about Oscar's latest tattoo?'

'Another cup of coffee anyone?' Rose leapt to her feet. Felicity and Leo simultaneously pushed her back into her chair and then got jammed in the doorway as they tried to enter the kitchen together.

'You must relax Fifi. You'll be the next to have a heart attack.'

'Oh God. This is ghastly.' Felicity grabbed Leo's arm and they both burst out laughing.

*

The day after Henry's visit the sun shone brightly, a real Indian summer day and, knowing there wouldn't be many more of them, Felicity and Rose drove to the sea. In spite of a stiff breeze there were a few hearty people sheltering behind windbreaks and even one or two swimming. Rose and Felicity walked slowly along the sand talking to each other.

'Smelling the ozone always makes me feel as horny as hell.' Rose took off her shoes and dug her toes into the sand.

'God, I can't remember what that feels like,' Felicity said, not entirely truthfully, but she was surprised by Rose's remark. Although they had known each other all their lives and been the closest of friends since adulthood Rose was several years older than Felicity and they never discussed sex. It wasn't that Rose was a prude, she wasn't. Nothing shocked her, but she never discussed her own life.

'That was my downfall, all those years ago. I met Bruce on Bondi Beach. How corny can you get? I was young and impressionable and thought he was the sexiest thing on two legs. Before I knew it, I was married with two small children.'

'Do you miss them? You never say.'

'Of course I do,' Rose's voice was cross. 'I hate the fact they live in Australia, chose to go back there.' She bent down and picked up a rounded, pink pebble. 'But it's my fault. I made a mess of things. Married the wrong man, in the wrong continent.' She plunged her hand deep into her pocket and dropping the pebble there pulled out a large and rather grubby man's handkerchief and blew her nose briskly and noisily. 'All that hospital nonsense.'

'Nonsense?' Felicity leant her head towards Rose.

'Making one think about death. I'm getting my pension next year.' She bent down and, picking up a stone, threw it into the sea. 'Leo's over seventy. How much longer have we got?' She grabbed Felicity's arm. 'It frightens me. It feels as if we're all running as fast as we can to stay in one place.' She paused and caught at a wayward strand of hair, and pushed it roughly into the rubber band that held the rest of her hair back.

'I try not to think about it too much,' Felicity lied. She didn't want to encourage Rose with morbid thoughts. She was supposed to be helping her to recover from a heart attack, not encouraging her to dwell on death. Although Felicity knew the near brush with her cousin's mortality had made her think about it in the middle of the night.

'I used to think about death more when I was young and knew it was never going to happen to me,' she finally said in what she hoped was a reassuring voice.

Rose managed a weak laugh.'You've got it right Fifi.'

'Me?'

'You've managed to get a life for yourself, a new house, a job and all of it without depending on a man.'

'But you and Leo – ' Felicity jumped in, shocked, but Rose interrupted her.

'Don't worry, I adore Leo. He's almost perfect. But while I was lying in bed, with nothing to do but think, I began to realise I've spent an awful lot of years looking after everyone else. And if I haven't got much time left I'm going to start thinking more about myself.'

'But I thought you loved all that – being the centre of the family.'

'I do, it's like an addiction. My name's Rose and I'm a people addict.'

'What do you mean?' Felicity look at her cousin anxiously. She knew heart attacks could change people's personalities, but Rose had always been the least introspective person she knew.

'It goes back to my childhood.' She paused and looked at Felicity. 'Can you bear this?' She was suddenly anxious.

'Bear it?'

'Me yacking on about myself?' They had reached a low stone wall that jutted out onto the beach, the remains of an old breakwater. Rose sat down and as Felicity sat down beside her she continued to speak. 'I suppose it all started when I was a child. You remember my father?'

'Uncle Derek, of course, although I think I only met him once or twice.'

'Family rows, so silly. After Mum died I was really on my own with Daddy. He was always so busy, the only way I could have any of his time was if I did everything for him. So that's what I did. Cooking, cleaning, sewing. As long as everything ran smoothly I was his good little girl and got his praise and attention. I suppose it became a habit.' Rose sighed and Felicity put her arm round her and gave her a hug. 'Then Daddy met Deirdre and she took over all that. She took it all away. I ended up needing to be indispensable, having to be the one that did everything for everyone else.' Rose turned her head away, but not before Felicity had seen the brightness of her eyes.

'I'd no idea. You never talk about your childhood.'

'What's the point? It's all in the past. I haven't thought about it in years. I suppose it was the heart attack that clarified everything. I had too much time to think in hospital. All these drugs making one over-emotional.' Rose turned back to face her cousin and gave her a watery smile. 'Stupid load of psychobabble.'

'Is that why you got married so young? Because you felt you weren't needed any more?'

'That's a bit too deep for me. But it's probably what a therapist would say. At the time I was just in love. Maybe I fell in love because I was looking for love. It's awfully easy to look back and justify all one's foolish actions.'

'You've never been foolish Rose.' Felicity squeezed her arm. 'You're the only sensible person I know.'

Felicity had never known her cousin in this introspective mood and it made her feel uneasy. She didn't know how to cope with it. Rose shivered.

'What about a cup of tea? Universal remedy.' Felicity noticed the day had got distinctly colder and thought she ought to get Rose inside. They could continue their conversation in comfort. 'We'll get piles if we sit on this wall any longer.'

'What d'you mean, get piles? I've been a martyr to Preparation H for years.'

Laughing, they climbed up off the beach and along a sandy footpath back down into the village. The days were shortening and the sun was low in the sky as they reached the café.

'Just look at that skyline. I'd love to be able to paint.' Rose gestured to the horizon where a herd of cows stood silhouetted, heads down, grazing peacefully.

'Why don't you?'

'Why don't I what? Paint? I don't know how.'

'That's it,' Felicity was triumphant. 'You could go to classes, learn. That wouldn't be running around after other people. It would be doing something for yourself.'

'I don't think so. I'd be hopeless.'

'That wouldn't matter, you'd be doing it for yourself after all, not for anyone else, and you'd get better.'

Rose shrugged, but Felicity could see she was thinking about it. Perhaps an idea had been planted in her mind.

*

Inside the café the air was full of the smell of burgers and onions. The only empty table had a chipped formica top and was awash with spilt tea. A small foil ashtray was overflowing with cigarettes and topped with a lump of discarded chewing gum. There were also two empty cups and a used tissue on a plastic tray.

'You sit down.' Felicity was solicitous. She gathered up the debris and took it to the counter. 'Could we have two teas and a cloth to wipe the table down with?'

'We're closing in ten minutes,' the surly-looking waitress almost snarled at her. Felicity decided to ignore her.

'Could we possibly have two teas?' she repeated in a slow voice. 'We'll drink them quickly.'

'Tttt.' The woman made an unwelcoming noise, shrugged and reluctantly poured two cups, slopping tea into the saucer as she did so. Felicity noticed wearily that one of the cups had a lipstick stain on it, but she couldn't be bothered to complain. She would drink from the other side of the cup.

'Why do places like this exist?' she asked Rose as she sat down.

'Because people come here. Look at us.'

'We shouldn't. What a horrible impression it must give to tourists. Imagine all those bemused foreigners coming in here – not quite St. Tropez is it?' They sat in silence for a moment drinking their tea. Felicity suddenly noticed that on a chair at the next table someone had left a dirty disposable nappy.

'Revolting isn't it?' Felicity put her cup down in disgust. The tea wasn't very nice, but whether it was the surroundings that were polluting the taste or not, she wasn't sure.

'One thing you'd think the English could do would be to make a decent cup of tea.'

Was it in because of or in spite of her surroundings that Rose was looking better?

'Have you made any plans?' Felicity leant forward towards her cousin.

'What?'

'Going back to our conversation on the beach. Have you thought about what you might do?'

'I don't know. I can't be an invalid for long, that's for sure. It'd kill me.'

Felicity laughed. 'I certainly can't see you reclining on the chaise longue reading Barbara Cartland while Leo peels you a grape.'

'Darling Leo, he'd be willing to try, but I don't think he'd manage it very well. Besides I'm far too practical – why waste the peel of a grape?' They both smiled. 'We're going to Australia after Christmas for six weeks to see the children. I haven't stayed with them for far too long. We won't be with them all the time, we'll do some travelling, spend some time with each other.'

Felicity leaned forward and, elbows on the table, she cupped her head in her hands.

Rose twisted her wedding ring. 'It's not like me to talk about these things is it? Lying in hospital wondering if I was going to die. That's what did it.'

'Well you're not going to die, and that's that. We all love you far too much.' Felicity watched a drip fall from the bottom of her cup as she lifted it from the saucer. 'The trip's a great idea,' she continued. 'But what about your garden? Can you bear to leave it for so long?'

'I don't know, but I'm going to try. The garden's just one more dependant after all and I'm going to try and wean myself from all of them. Dr Edwardes is going to look after it. He says he's got too much time on his hands since his wife left.'

'No boyfriend then?'

'He's not gay. That's just Mrs P. She caught him buying aftershave once.'

'We're closing. You'll have to go.' The surly woman appeared with a tired J cloth, which she listlessly wiped over the table. She gathered up the cups and saucers, even though Rose hadn't finished hers.

'Excuse me,' said Felicity, 'My friend was still – '

'Don't worry,' Rose interrupted. 'I think we're done here.'

CHAPTER 15

T HE WEATHER HAD TURNED and there was a chill in the air when Felicity left Hatch a few days after her conversation with Rose. She was still worried about her cousin, but there wasn't much more she could do there. It was up to Rose now to find a way of fulfilling herself and up to her family to get used to living with the new Rose. They were all pulling their weight when she left and she could only hope they would continue to do so. Felicity sent off for a brochure about a painting and walking holiday in the Lake District. It sounded relaxing and interesting. It might be just the thing for Rose and Leo. She was sorry to leave the Blighs, but apart from worrying about the shop, she was quite anxious to get back to her house. Besides, she was sick of wearing the same old jeans and trying to squeeze herself into Rose's tops. Although what with all the healthy food she had been preparing for Rose, the work in the garden and the long walks they had been taking, she thought she had lost quite a few pounds. But perhaps the most serious worry was that she had left Darcy in charge of everything, house, cat and shop.

'Welcome home. I've prepared a sumptuous meal. Let me carry your bags.'

Felicity was instantly suspicious at being greeted so effusively by Darcy. But she had to admit he looked an awful lot better. Fatter and less shabby somehow. He was sober too, which was a nice surprise. She entered her house cautiously. There was a delicious smell of cooking.

'That smells wonderful.' She smiled encouragingly.

'Boeuf Stroganoff, the secret's in the herbs. I'm quite famous for it.'

Something had to be wrong – it was all too good. There were flowers in the drawing room – a vase of bronze chrysanthemums. What had he done? This all smacked of a guilty conscience. Felicity went upstairs and dropped her bag and then she inspected the house from top to bottom.

'I give up,' she said finally. 'You'd better tell me what you've done.'

'I am deeply hurt. What an unpleasantly suspicious nature you have.' Darcy managed to look cross and full of injured innocence at the same time.

Felicity knew she had been wrong-footed. 'I'm sorry. It's just that I'm not used to this new, responsible, hard-working Darcy. What's been happening in the shop? Tell me about it over dinner.'

In the end they had an extremely pleasant evening. Much to Felicity's surprise the dinner was, if not delicious, at least perfectly edible. Darcy appeared to be genuinely enthusiastic about the shop. He had been going there most days. Oscar had rung every morning with a list of instructions. They were due to open shortly and they needed more stock. Of the elusive Miles there was still no sign and Oscar, whilst frequently on the end of the telephone, had not put in many actual appearances. Not only had Darcy been left to supervise all the builders' finishes, but he had taken it upon himself to source quite a few new items, and much to his delight he had received Oscar's approval. He had found a potter making a whole range of one-off vases, pots and lamp bases.

'Oscar tells me I have an absolutely natural eye. Perfect taste. It doesn't surprise me. I've always been renowned for my flair.'

Felicity found it quite reassuring Darcy hadn't changed completely. The other nice thing was that he and Angel had developed a real rapport. She had been popping into the shop on her way home even before she actually started work.

But despite all this, Felicity still had an uneasy feeling he wasn't telling her everything.

'Where's Cat?' she asked after supper. There had been no sign of her when Felicity arrived home, but this wasn't unusual. She often spent all day roaming the streets of Battersea.

'Have some more wine.' Darcy picked up the bottle and poured some into Felicity's glass

'Cat?' she asked again.

'Er … Cats.' Darcy looked sheepish.

'What are you talking about?'

'It appears Cat has a friend. Very similar. In fact I think we may have been feeding two cats all along.'

'Oh well, it could be worse.' That was all she could find out, perhaps there was nothing more and she just had a very suspicious nature. It would have to do for now. Felicity went to sleep in her own bed with a sense of relief. In the morning she knew she would have to hit the telephone and life, which had been in abeyance since she had been at Upton, would now start up again in earnest.

*

A list. That was the thing. Felicity woke up at seven o'clock, went downstairs and made herself a cup of coffee. Cat One and Cat Two were curled up together in a basket. They were identical – perhaps they had come from the same litter. Felicity looked at them narrowly – was that really all Darcy had to tell her? Time would tell. Sitting at the kitchen table she took a discarded envelope from the pile of junk mail she had opened last night. She always approached her post with a sense of excitement, generally misplaced as all she got nowadays were those impersonal personalised letters and not the cheerful letters from a long-lost friend or an invitation to an exciting party. The only use for all this waste paper was for making lists.

THINGS TO DO she wrote and underlined it neatly. Underneath she wrote:

1) Unpack.

2) Ring Leo – she had promised to ring every day to make sure that all was well. It was no good ringing Rose as she couldn't be relied on to tell the truth about her own health.

3) Ring Venetia – she had already had several rather unsatisfactory conversations – now it was time to see her.

4) Andrew – she would ring him at the office this morning.

5) Laura – what was going on there? Laura had sounded full of repressed excitement the last time they spoke.

6) Oliver – he had taken Concepcion out for a drink? It would be nice if the girl made some English friends.

7) Oscar – there was a lot to discuss about the shop. She would go in this morning.

She was able to cross the first item off immediately. She liked starting a list with something she had already done – seeing things crossed off gave her an instant sense of achievement.

Leaving her list on the kitchen table, Felicity took her mug of coffee upstairs and had a long, hot bath. The mornings were getting colder and it was probably time to turn the central heating on. Sitting wrapped in her towel some time later and before she could get on with her list the telephone rang.

'Hello. Felicity, it's Tim. Tim Bignall. Didn't wake you did I?'

'Hello Tim. No, you didn't, I've been up for ages.' Felicity was surprised to hear from him. 'How are you?'

'Fine. Sorry to bother you, but Jane isn't there by any chance, is she?'

'Jane here? No. Did she say she was coming to see me?' Felicity leapt to her feet in panic. The last person she wanted to see at the moment was Jane.

'No. Um … mmmm … I … I must have misunderstood.' Tim was spluttering on the other end of the line.

'Maybe she is coming. I'll get her to call if she turns up, shall I?' Tim sounded really embarrassed. He wasn't accustomed to losing his wife. Come to think of it Jane had been strangely silent recently. She hadn't rung Felicity once while she was at Hatch. Interesting. Felicity put the telephone down thoughtfully and was on the point of picking it up to ring Venetia when it rang again. It was Henry. Most peculiar, but life was like that. The telephone didn't ring for days and then it rang twice in the space of half an hour.

'I was wondering if we could have lunch. I'd like to talk to you about Laura.'

'What's going on? I spoke to her last week, she didn't say anything, but I thought she sounded excited. Is she pregnant?' Why hadn't Laura rung her?

'Slow down, old girl. She's fine, not pregnant as far as I know. I'll tell you when I see you. How about lunch today? One o'clock at The Cow all right?' The Hungry Cow had been one of their favourite pubs.

'Yes, I suppose so.'

After she got off the telephone Felicity realised her hair was dirty and she hadn't done her nails for weeks. She quickly rang Sadie but she was fully booked all day. She'd have to wash it herself and hope it didn't go too frizzy. She wished she knew Sadie's secret formula for leaving her hair sleek and in place. Did she have time to do her nails? Probably not, better clean and unvarnished than smudged. All thought of her list went out of the window, she had to sort out something to wear. What was suitable for lunch with one's ex-husband?

Skirt or trousers? Trousers were safer, but she looked better in a skirt. On the other hand she didn't want to look as if she were trying to impress him.

She tried on every pair of trousers in her wardrobe, followed by every skirt. She was now hot and flustered and thinking linen. She put on a white linen skirt and jacket, then looked out of the window. Bugger, it was raining, besides it was November – she couldn't wear linen in November. What would Venetia say? Venetia, double bugger, she hadn't rung her. Triple bugger, the rain was going to turn her hair into an Afro. Could one wear navy shoes in November, or should she have gone on to black? She pulled off the white linen and found a lightweight beige skirt lurking at the back of her wardrobe. It seemed strangely loose, how unlike the cleaners to stretch one's clothes. Next she found a cream silk shirt, without any visible marks on it, then a navy blazer, finally a striped scarf. Neat and tidy certainly, but the overall effect wasn't what she had hoped. She looked like an ageing air hostess. Off came everything. Time was getting short and she was getting hot and sweaty again. A spritz of scent and another go with the deodorant. What about the russet dress she had worn to the golf club? It hadn't exactly brought romance into her life, but she hadn't felt too bad in it. She did her best with the makeup, and with heated tongs managed to get her hair into some sort of semblance of order. There was just time to ring Venetia.

'Hello.' It was Andrew.

'Andrew, It's me Felicity. Is Venetia there?'

'No. But I'm glad you've called. Can we talk some time? I'm worried about Venetia.' That was a bit of a turn up, Andrew wanting to talk to Felicity about his wife.

'I think that's probably a good idea.' She kept her voice calm, she didn't want to bolt him.

'How about lunch?'

Two lunches this week. Bang went the diet. 'Great. When?'

To Felicity's surprise Andrew suggested Sunday, but he assured her Venetia would not be around. Felicity felt that any conversation could wait until then so she just asked him to get Venetia to ring her when she came in.

Just as she was going out of the door the telephone rang again. It was Jane sounding very sheepish, which was most unlike her.

'I hate to do this, but could you possibly tell Tim I've been with you, if he asks?'

'He's already rung me – I told him I hadn't seen you. Sorry.'

'Oh lummy. I'll have to think of something else.'

'What's going on Jane?'

'Can't tell you at the mo. I'll ring you later in the week. Got to run now.' And she rang off. What a mystery. Could Jane possibly have a lover? Was there a man brave enough?

*

Felicity arrived at the Hungry Cow fifteen minutes late and was annoyed to see Henry had not yet arrived. The pub was almost empty so she ordered a gin and slimline tonic and found a table in the corner. It was almost warm enough to sit outside, but the black metal tables on the terrace were covered in fallen leaves and bird droppings, the umbrellas had been put away for the winter and the uncomfortable-looking matt black chairs were stacked in a corner. She had hoped to arrive after Henry and make a bit of an entrance. It was much easier to hold one's tummy in while walking. Oh well, there was nothing she could do about it. How typical of him to be late. She could feel irritation rising up. She was in the middle of taking some deep relaxing breaths when Henry appeared.

'What's the matter old thing? You're huffing and puffing a bit. Sounds odd.'

'Just practising my yoga deep breathing,' Felicity replied untruthfully.

Henry leant forward and kissed her. 'When did you start yoga?'

'I've been doing it on and off for years,' Felicity said airily but she could feel herself blushing.

'Want another drink?' Henry stretched forward to take her glass.

'I haven't finished this one yet.' Felicity was surprised to see this wasn't true. Her glass was empty. She hadn't been aware of drinking anything at all. Henry ambled off to the bar and returned with two glasses. He gave her a lopsided smile and she remembered yet again how attractive he was. 'What's the matter with Laura?' she asked the moment he sat down.

'Nothing. She's fine. Mark's been offered a job in America.'

'What? Why didn't she tell me? How come you know all about it?' The words were tumbling out of Felicity's mouth.

'Nothing's settled yet. They're not telling anyone until they've made a decision.'

'I'm not anyone – I'm her mother.'

'And I'm her father. They just mentioned it when I saw her. They're only thinking about it and it would only be for a few years.'

'When are they going? Where, New York? When did all this happen?'

'It's been brewing for a while. Mark's had a few meetings over there. It'll be New York, but I'm not sure of the timing, if they go.'

'When did you see her then? I thought you were tucked up in your love-nest in the country.' Felicity tried hard to put a pleasant smile on her face as she spoke. Venetia always said bitterness was very ageing.

'Sally and I had dinner there last week and it was discussed.' Was it her imagination or had Henry's eyes narrowed when he mentioned that woman's name?

'I hope you had a lovely evening.' Felicity's voice was tight.

'It was good fun. Rather amusing. Sally was telling us all about when you had a crush on her at school.' Henry laughed merrily at the memory.

They both took a sip of their drinks but Felicity remained silent. She was busy trying to find a witty way of suggesting she would like to drop Sally into a vat of boiling oil.

'You never told me. Didn't know you'd ever been a lezzie.' Henry's eyes were gleaming now. What was it with men and the thought of two women together?

'I wasn't a lesbian. I had a crush on Sally for a very short time after she played Mr Darcy in the school production of *Pride and Prejudice*,' Felicity said at last with as much dignity as she could manage.

'Did you do anything? Give each other a tickle?'

'Don't be prurient.' Felicity was flushing with embarrassment, which was ridiculous, it had all happened over forty years ago.

'What does prurient mean?'

'Taking an unhealthy interest in other's people's sex lives.' Felicity felt a momentary smugness that her vocabulary was better than Henry's. She hoped she was right and made a quick note to look it up when she got home. But that didn't really make up for the vision she had of Sally, Henry, Laura and Mark all sitting round the dinner table sniggering about her. Why hadn't her only daughter defended her?

'What d'you fancy to eat?' Henry, as always when the conversation got awkward, was ready to change the subject. 'They do quite a good Ploughman's here.'

'I think I'd rather have the smoked salmon.' Not only petty, but pointless, smoked salmon was so cheap nowadays it would probably have hit Henry's pocket harder if she'd had the Ploughman's. When Henry had ordered the lunch he came back with a bottle of white wine and a couple of glasses. Felicity watched him cross the room with his familiar easy, long-legged stride. His thick grey hair was still flopping over his eyes in the way it always had. Felicity thought how difficult it was to really understand this man was no longer her husband. She had been with him for more than half her life. Had been responsible for making sure his clothes were clean, his stomach was full, his dentist appointments made and kept. Had shared his bed, listened to him snore as she lay curled up in the small of his back. Now it was nothing to do with her. Sally was in charge of Henry's life.

'You've done something to your hair,' Henry said as he sat down. He didn't usually notice things like that.

Felicity smiled. 'Venetia's been making me go to the hairdressers.'

'Looks nice.'

'Thank you. You're looking well too.' This was absurd. Making small talk with a man she knew better than anyone else in the world.

'How's Rose?' he asked with genuine concern.

'She's getting better, finding it hard not to do too much. But they're all watching her like hawks.'

'Bet she hates that.' Henry laughed, then as if determined to flatter Felicity he continued, 'Oscar says you're a great help with the shop.'

'Have you seen him too?' Felicity was surprised. Oscar and Henry tended to meet at weddings, christenings and funerals, not for cosy lunches.

'No. We spoke on the telephone. He says he's very busy – but whether with the shop or that new friend of his, he didn't say.'

'His boyfriend Barry, or his partner Miles – have you met them?'

'Certainly not. I don't want to be involved in all that. But at least the shop seems to be coming along.'

'It's fun. Although I haven't been there much, what with Rose and everything. But I was really glad to have something to get my teeth into.'

'Apart from me you mean?' Henry gave his crooked smile. 'I didn't treat you very well, did I? Behaved like a bit of a shit.'

'You certainly did. I suppose it would be charitable to do what everyone else does and put it down to the male menopause.'

At that moment a waitress came over and put down a plate of crusty bread with chunks of cheddar cheese, pickled onions and salad, and a large plate of smoked salmon sandwiches.

'So do you think they'll go to New York?' Felicity tried to keep the anxiety out of her voice. She and Laura might not have the easiest of relationships, but America was still a long way away.

'I'm not sure – but Laura's quite keen. All that shopping. It's quite a lot of money, so I expect they will go for a couple of years at any rate.'

'Did she think I might try and stop them?' She tried to keep her voice light.

'No, I don't think so. She said she was going to ring you today.'

'So what's the real reason we're having lunch?' Felicity knew she was putting Henry on the spot, but she wanted to know. She was intrigued; she hadn't lived with Henry all those years without being able to tell when he had something on his mind.

'Thought it would be nice to see you. Clear the air, that sort of thing.'

'We saw each other at Rose and Leo's last week.'

'Not alone.'

Very interesting. Felicity noticed her glass was empty, but only for a moment and then Henry topped it up.

'What about this fellow Darcy? Is he still sniffing around?'

'He's not sniffing around, as you put it. He's staying in the house for the time being, and helping out in the shop. Apparently he's got quite a good eye, Oscar's letting him help with the buying.'

'No romance then?'

Felicity laughed. The idea was absurd, but she gave Henry a sideways look. Was it possible he was jealous? That was certainly not what she'd been expecting.

'You're looking pretty good, old bean.' Without any warning Henry squeezed her hand. Good Lord, he was making a pass at her. 'When I saw you at Hatch, I remembered ... well lots of things really. You always were very fanciable.'

'Thank you.' Things were taking a strange turn.

'I thought perhaps, for old times sake, we might ... you know?'

'No Henry, I don't know.'

'A bit of rumpy-pumpy. Mmmm? How about it?'

Felicity giggled nervously at his ridiculous choice of words, but at the same time to her annoyance she felt familiar stirrings in her nether regions. Henry had always had that effect on her.

'What about Sally?'

'She's gone to Cheltenham to see her mother.'

Really men were bastards. How many times had he cheated on Felicity, if he was doing this so soon after getting together with Sally?

'Is there a rift in the lute?' She tried to convince herself she was genuinely interested.

'Nooo.' He didn't sound very sure. 'She's a great girl.' He paused and took a sip of his wine. Then he examined his fingernails carefully. After a moment he continued. 'Quite tiring sometimes.'

Tiring, that sounded intriguing. Surely they were too old to swing from the chandeliers. Maybe she'd taught Henry a few tricks.

'More wine?'

Before she could answer Henry was on his feet. Felicity thought about going to bed with Henry. It had been a long time. It was rather tempting, a little bit of sex before she forgot how to do it. On the other hand, she hadn't shaved her legs and she was wearing a particularly nasty pair of grey, saggy knickers. Also, she still loved Henry. She didn't think she was still in love with him, but you couldn't spend that long without love. She had a horrible feeling that if they went to bed together it might make her fall in love with him properly all over again, just when her life was getting back on to some sort of level ground. She didn't feel like risking that at the moment, if ever. Things were slowly getting better and she would be a fool to ruin everything.

'It's restful being with you. Cosy like an old armchair.' Henry was back with another bottle of wine.

Felicity was feeling quite mellow and giggly, but whether it was the wine or the surprise of Henry's proposition, she wasn't quite sure.

'And Sally's more like that ultra modern chair I suppose?' Felicity indicated the chairs on the terrace of the bar. 'Without the bird shit, of course.'

'Mmm. And she's a bit too keen on giving instructions.'

'Instructions?'

'During sex. You know, left hand down a bit, change gear.'

'That's a bit disloyal discussing her like this.' Felicity was giggling. She thought she might be slightly tight. She had better get out of here before she did something she would only regret.

'No it's not really disloyal. It's you I'm talking to.'

'Exactly. I'm your ex-wife.'

'Technically, but I never think of you like that. Come on old girl. How about it? For old times sake.'

Felicity stood up, while she still could. She picked up her bag, and stooping down she kissed Henry on the top of his head.

'You really know how not to seduce a girl, don't you darling? I should have thought you'd had more practice. I'm afraid it's thanks, but no thanks.' And she walked, slightly unsteadily, but she hoped with her dignity intact, out of the pub. Really, Henry was impossible.

*

When she arrived home from the pub Felicity realised she was singing to herself. Always a bad sign and pretty unpleasant for anyone who happened to be listening. She was also shaking. The combination of Henry and wine at lunch time was very unsettling. The first thing she had to do was go upstairs and shave her legs. She didn't want to be caught out unprepared again. If there was to be a next time she wanted to be able to make her decision on a less frivolous basis. As she was mopping up the blood she sat and pondered, not for the first time, the curious habit of hair. Why did it change so much with age? The hair on her legs now grew in strange clumps with bare patches in between. As for her bush, once so luxuriant, it was now more of a deciduous shrub at the turn of the year, with a dusting of frost on the few remaining leaves. At least Henry had seen it all before. But somebody new? That was never going to happen.

After the blood had mostly stopped Felicity covered her legs with an attractive display of Micky Mouse sticking plasters she had bought for Jamie. Feeling rather tired she lay down on the bed and admired the colourful collage on her legs for a while. It was nearly four o'clock and she had an appointment with Oscar at six-thirty. Perhaps she ought to have a rest. She got up and started to take off her dress. As she undid the last button it fell to the floor.

Felicity bent down to pick it up and as she did so something glinted at her from under the bed. It was a bracelet, but not her bracelet. Who'd been sleeping in her bed? It was very peculiar, who had been in her bedroom? It also showed what a slut she was, she should have hoovered under her bed. This would all have to wait until later. Felicity needed to lie down. She threw her dress over the back of a chair and kicking off her shoes lay down on the bed. She tried to go to sleep, but thoughts were bouncing around her brain. Did Henry still fancy her? Or was he just bored with Sally already? Did she still fancy Henry? Was Darcy a cross-dresser? Had she had a female cat burglar, who had found nothing to steal and feeling sorry for her had, instead of taking anything, left her a bracelet? Or was this what Darcy had been up to while she had been away – sleeping with someone in Felicity's bed? If that was the case it was quite a relief, it could have been something so much worse.

The next thing Felicity remembered was hearing the doorbell ringing away. She opened her eyes and sat up groggily. When she was young it had been easy to have a couple of drinks at lunchtime to function in the afternoon, but not any more. She felt terrible, as she always did if she slept during the day. Her head was thick, her eyes were finding it difficult to stay open and the inside of her mouth tasted extremely unpleasant. She heaved herself off the bed, and dragging on the by now rather crumpled dress and stuffing her feet into her shoes she stumbled downstairs.

'Hi Mum. We're having a meeting, remember?' Oscar was standing on the doorstep carrying a briefcase and a large folder.

'Of course I remembered. I was doing something upstairs.'

'Not your makeup I see.' Oscar put out a finger and rubbed under each of his mother's eyes in turn. 'Nor your ironing,' he added, eying the russet dress.

'I suppose there's no point in trying to hide it. I was having a rest. I had a rather unsettling lunch with your father. I lay down to think and I fell asleep. Now I feel ghastly. Always do if I go to bed in the afternoon.'

'With Dad?' Oscar raised an eyebrow at his mother.

'Certainly not. What made you say that?' Felicity was surprised Oscar should even imagine such a scenario.

'I dunno, Dad and Sally – Laura says Sally's always complaining about him.'

'Laura seems to be very friendly with her.' Felicity was beginning to sense a conspiracy between her daughter and Sally, but possibly it was her paranoia about her rival speaking.

'They've got a lot in common. And its all right, there's no need to make that face. Sally's making an effort with Laura and Laura's lapping it up. You know Laura.'

'I'm not sure I do.' By now Felicity and Oscar were in the kitchen and Felicity was making coffee. As she set two mugs on a tray she asked, 'Changing the subject – has Darcy got a girlfriend?'

'Pass.' Oscar helped himself to a biscuit from the Jubilee tin on the table.

'I can always tell when you're lying. I know you've been seeing lots of him while I've been away. He keeps boasting about how brilliant you think he is.'

'Slight exaggeration, but he's not bad. Excellent natural taste.' He took another biscuit.

'So about this girlfriend? I found an alien bracelet under my bed.'

'As in belonging to aliens or as in not belonging to you?'

'Stop playing for time.' Felicity poured out the coffee and took a bottle of milk from the fridge.

'OK, you win. I was sworn to secrecy, but Darcy's met someone.'

'Good for him, but why the secrecy? Did he think I'd be furious they used my bedroom? I am, but in a way it's a relief to know. I guessed he'd been up to something.'

'Well, I think it was more that he thought you might be jealous.'

'What?' Felicity was indignant. The very idea. 'What would I be jealous about?'

'Darcy shagging someone else? Being unfaithful to you.'

'I don't believe this ... Felicity spluttered. 'He's not being unfaithful. Darcy and I haven't been to bed, we're not lovers.'

'Really?' Oscar gave a snort.

Felicity glared at him for a moment, but he was laughing so hard that after a moment she started to laugh as well. 'You horrible child. You didn't think I was having an affair with Darcy did you?'

'Your sex life is your own business. It's nothing to do with me. I washed my hands of you years ago.'

Felicity spluttered. 'Does everyone think we're having sex?'

'What d'you mean by everybody? D'you want me to make a list? Dad. Sally, Laura, Oliver … '

'Oscar. No!' She was aghast. How could this have happened? Darcy was a joke, her good deed, she was really insulted that people, people she loved, could possibly imagine she could be having a serious relationship with someone like Darcy. On the other hand, perhaps they thought she was lucky to have anyone, even Darcy. 'What am I going to do about it?'

'What d'you want to do about it?'

'I want people to know it's not true.'

'The more you deny it, the more they'll think it's true. Perhaps you could put a notice in the paper?' Oscar was still snickering.

'What did they all say about it?' Felicity had to know.

'Oliver said "I can't believe that my mother could be so undignified".'

'Your brother can be so pompous.'

'Laura says she thinks your hormones need re-balancing, actually she thinks you're bonkers. Sally muttered something about showing off. As for Dad, he looked quite cross.'

'So that's what he meant about Darcy sniffing around. Oh fuckadoodledo, that's not the worst of it. I've just realised everyone'll think the bastard's dumped me. Bad enough to have people thinking I'd have an affair with Darcy, but its too humiliating to have them thinking he's found someone better.'

Oscar leant back on his chair and let out a shriek of laughter. 'It's too much,' he wheezed. 'I love it, I really love it.'

'That's because you're a nasty, sadistic shit.'

But Oscar's laughter was infectious and Felicity couldn't help seeing the funny side of the situation. After all, it would only be a five-minute wonder.

Oscar concluded they were not going to be able to take any business discussion seriously that evening, and he was meeting Barry later, so he merely left a bulky folder that contained reams of figures and lists of items that were apparently stock Oscar/Darcy had ordered. Felicity decided she would have to look at all that tomorrow. However she did feel better now and calmer as well, although thoughts of Henry kept creeping into her mind. She wandered into the kitchen vaguely wondering what she should do. Lunch did waste a lot of the day, particularly if you had wine with the meal. She ought to know better at her age. She ran the cold tap until it was really cold and, filling a glass, gulped it down. London water had a particular taste all of its own. Felicity rather liked it. She stood looking out of the window at her tiny garden. Rose had been worried her borders had not yet been put to bed, but Felicity's minute one didn't look as if it had ever got up in the first place. She had managed to get the house into some sort of shape over the past year, but apart from planting a few bulbs, she had left the garden to tackle next year. Darcy had made one or two forays into it and had at least mowed the tablecloth-sized lawn from time to time. He did have some uses.

'Penny for them.'

Felicity jumped and turned round. Darcy himself was standing right behind her. She had not heard him come in.

'I was thinking about the garden,' she replied truthfully.

'You know, don't you?' Darcy squeezed her arm sympathetically. Felicity immediately brushed him off and poured herself another glass of water. She was aware she was not looking her best for this embarrassing encounter. She was feeling distinctly bleary eyed and crumpled.

'That you've got a girlfriend. Yes, and I think it's terrific.' She gave the brightest smile she could.

'That's one of the things I admire about you – your bravery.'

'Bravery?'

'I know I've hurt you. It's all right, I understand you hoped our relationship might blossom into romance.'

'Darcy, I promise nothing was further from my thoughts.'

'There you are, stiff upper lip. Putting on a good face. You'll be trying to make a joke of it next.'

Felicity wanted to say going to bed with you would be a bad joke, but she managed to bite her lip and finally said, 'I'm delighted for you Darcy, I truly am, but can I make one request?'

'Of course, my dear, anything.'

'Please don't use my bed.'

'Yes, I do understand, that must hurt.' Darcy gave her an understanding smile and made as if to take her arm.

Felicity stepped smartly backwards. 'It doesn't hurt, but it might have done, if I'd lain down on top of one of her earrings.'

'There, you see. I knew you'd make a joke. The fighting spirit.'

'Doesn't she have a bed of her own you could use?'

'Unfortunately, although it is a truism, the path of true love seldom runs smooth and the lady in question cannot be compromised.'

'In other words she's married.' Felicity's tone was crisp. She felt that this conversation had reached the end.

Darcy had other ideas. 'I understand you're upset, you've been wronged once and I didn't want to be the one to do it again.'

'Once and for all Darcy, I do not fancy you, am not interested in a romance with you and can only marvel that you have found a female foolish enough to fall in love with you.' As she spoke, Felicity knew she was giving Darcy far too much ammunition and she was right.

'Hell hath no fury, as they say.'

'Oh do shut up.' Felicity finally snapped. She had a headache as a result of sleeping in the afternoon and listening to Darcy pretending he thought she fancied him was making her extremely irritated. All she wanted was to go to back to bed and have a nice rest. 'And don't you dare say I understand again or I'll clock you one.' For the second time that day she tried to make a dignified exit. A short while later she heard the front door slam. Darcy off to see his lady love presumably. Felicity decided she had had enough of today and even though it was only eight o'clock she was going to go to bed. She wanted to go into the shop bright and early the next day. It was due to open all too soon and she was sure it needed her finishing touch to get it ready. Although she had a feeling that when she did go to the shop she would find Angel and Darcy between them had it all under control.

CHAPTER 16

THE NEXT MORNING FELICITY WOKE before her alarm went off, feeling thoroughly refreshed. It was amazing how restorative sleep could be. She leapt out of bed without a care in the world, but quickly realised her mistake as her creaking joints complained. She hobbled into the bathroom, regretting she had not appreciated her youth and suppleness more when she had had it. Her face was blotchy with too much sleep but she did her best to repair the damage with a couple of layers of moisturiser, foundation and concealer. Once downstairs she grabbed a cup of coffee and was just going out of the door when the telephone rang. It was Jane.

'I need to see you,' she said without bothering with any preliminary pleasantries.

'I'm on the way to the shop. Can I ring you later?'

'No. I really want to ask your advice.' Jane was almost pleading with her and despite herself Felicity was intrigued.

She agreed to yet another lunch, a salad and no alcohol this time. It was far too easy to waste days. She had promised herself she would go to the gym today. She hadn't been for ages and Venetia would want to know why. Or would she? Felicity still hadn't heard from her friend, despite all the messages she had left. It looked like she would have to curb her impatience until her lunch with Andrew.

As soon as Felicity walked into the door of the shop Angel came running towards her, a huge grin on her face. She was wearing a pair of bright pink cut-off dungarees with a lime green T-shirt and her beautiful long blonde hair was being tortured with a mass of tiny, multi-coloured clips.

'Oh, Mrs Fox, it's really nice to have you back. We've really missed you.'

'I don't think you have. You seemed to have managed alarmingly well without me.' Felicity saw Angel flush with pride. The shop looked great, completely ready for the opening. The granite shelves that ran along the back wall had been empty last time she saw them, but now they were covered in Italian lampshades of every colour, size and shape. The wall on the left was decorated with light switches, bell pulls, decorative painted and brass fingerplates from France, China, Indonesia. The opposite wall contained jewel-bright Indian curtain tie-backs and cushions. The whole place smelled new and every surface sparkled. It was almost a pity they were going to allow customers in to mess it all up.

'Come and have a look at your office.' Angel took Felicity by the arm and led her into the office at the back. On her desk was a bunch of fragrant pink lilies in a smoky grey vase.

'How lovely.' Felicity sank her nose into them, realising as she did so they hadn't had the pollen removed and she would now have an orange tip to her nose for the rest of the day.

'They're a present from me and Darcy.'

'That's really kind of you Angel. You shouldn't have.' Felicity fumbled in her handbag for a mirror. 'I hope Darcy gave you his share of the money,' she said sternly. She didn't like to think of Angel spending her money on expensive flowers.

'He's going to. I know he will,' Angel said with more faith than Felicity was able to feel. 'He's in love,' she added with a giggle and a quick look at Felicity.

'It's all right. I'm really pleased for him.' This was ridiculous. Did the whole of London imagine she was in love with Darcy? But perhaps this was the moment she could find out who the unlucky woman was. 'Do you know her name?' she asked Angel casually as she rubbed rather ineffectually at the orange smudge.

'It's Sonia – oooh. I don't think I was supposed to tell you that. He'll be ever so cross. Don't tell him. Please.'

'Don't worry, I won't breathe a word.' Sonia, could it be Slutty Sonia? Why on earth? What on earth? Felicity could hardly wait to grab a telephone and ring Rose. Sonia and Darcy. Was it possible? Felicity pretended to be engrossed in repairing her face.

*

'Rose – You'll never guess.' No sooner had Angel gone back into the showroom than Felicity had dialled her cousin's number. 'By the way, how are you?' she added as an afterthought.

'I'm fine. Lying on the sofa as we speak, knitting a jumper. What won't I guess, Possum?'

'Who Darcy's having an affair with.' Felicity had great difficulty in imagining Rose knitting, but on the other hand it was easier than imagining her watching daytime television.

'Slow down a moment. I didn't know Darcy was having an affair.'

'Nor did I until he told me yesterday.'

'You're not upset about it?' Rose's voice was full of concern.

'Not you as well? Why does everybody think I'm in love with Darcy? I suppose even as we speak Mrs P will be spreading the word throughout the length and breadth of Wiltshire, not to mention her transatlantic e-mails. I am not now, nor ever have been in love with Darcy. Do you understand?'

'All right Possum. I only wondered, but I told everyone you had better taste.'

'Thanks for that, I suppose. Anyway guess who he's having an affair with?'

'I haven't a clue. Why don't you put me out of my misery and tell me?'

'Sonia. Would you believe?' Felicity heard a small gasp at the other end of the line.

'I'm speechless. Sonia and Darcy. Who would've thought?' There was a pause. 'Although,' Rose continued, 'she probably likes the idea of his being a baronet. Promising to make a lady out of her.'

'It'd take more than a title to do that.'

'Meow, meow, your claws are sharp this morning,' Rose giggled. 'Well, there you are. I bet she's only done it to spite Andrew.'

'What d'you mean?'

'She's not going to forgive Andrew for dumping her. She'll be trying to make him jealous.' She laughed. 'It's quite funny when you think about it. Sonia, the deceiving bitch, being deceived.'

'What d'you mean?'

'He hasn't got a bean and he's never going to marry her when he finds out Humphrey's money is all in trust.'

'Poor old Humphrey.' Felicity didn't know Leo's brother very well, but she couldn't help feeling that he'd drawn the short straw with Sonia.

'I wouldn't worry too much about him. I think he's longing for an excuse to boot her out. He and Janet will be quite happy pottering along together.'

'Janet?'

'His housekeeper. Lovely woman, large, cosy and a brilliant cook. He'll be fine, but what about Darcy?'

'I don't care about Darcy. At the moment I feel rotting in Hell's too good for him. How could he let people think we were having an affair? How could he have thought I was in love with him?' Felicity's voice was getting higher as she warmed to the subject.

'Don't get too indignant – methinks the lady doth and all that,' Rose interrupted her flow with another giggle.

'You old cow. I thought you were on my side.'

'You musn't be rude to me. I'm not supposed to get upset, I might have another heart attack.'

'Blackmail is a dirty word … ' Felicity could hear Rose's voice change as she smiled when they slipped into their old bantering routine. It felt good. The healing process was well under way, they were both fighting back and they were going to survive. 'It is nice to have you back in rude good health. I need you at the other end of a telephone, ready to give wise counsel.'

'That's me Possum, a regular sage. Why rude health anyway?'

'No idea. Better ask Leo. He's the oracle.'

'The oracle and the sage, what a grand couple we make.'

'See you at the opening on Monday, you silly old bag.'

'Not if we see you first.'

'You're definitely coming then, are you?'

'I'm polishing the zimmer frame as we speak.'

Felicity was smiling as she put the telephone down. She had missed Rose, it felt good to hear her sounding more like her old self. She sat at her desk for a moment looking around. It was difficult to think that a few months ago she had been right at the bottom of the abyss, with all her old familiar life gone. She had not imagined then she would be able to build a new life for herself as quickly as she had.

*

After her conversation with Rose, Felicity made a determined effort and managed to get quite a lot of work done. She checked through all the delivery notes against the stock and found that Darcy and Angel had indeed done a very good job. Everything on her desk was in immaculate order, far better than it would have been if Felicity had been left to arrange it on her own. She was really enjoying herself and had completely forgotten the time when she suddenly heard the familiar booming tones of Jane's voice in the shop.

'It's all right, I'll go straight in. Mrs Fox is expecting me.' Even in her hour of need Jane's imperious manner didn't alter. Felicity hastily grabbed her handbag and ran a brush through her hair. Why did Jane always make her feel she was about to face a school inspection?

'Aren't you ready? I thought we said one o'clock.'

'You said one o'clock, and yes, I agreed. I *am* ready. Just sit down for a second.' For once Felicity had the upper hand, Jane wanted her advice. She was determined to take advantage of this. Very methodically she put a pile of delivery notes back into a folder and then filed them away carefully in her gleaming, new, navy blue filing cabinet.

'Right,' she said after a moment. 'Let's go.'

As Felicity spoke, she noticed Jane for the first time. She looked terrible, as if she had slept in her clothes. Her hair was tousled like a used pot scourer. What on earth could be the matter? Optimistically telling Angel she wouldn't be long she took Jane off to the wine bar round the corner.

Jane was uncharacteristically silent as they walked along the road. Felicity chatted about the weather. She had a feeling that when Jane started talking she would have to give her all her attention. The sky threatened rain so she debated inanely with herself, in the absence of any response from Jane, about whether they should have taken umbrellas with them. The wine bar wasn't very full. Felicity had chosen it because it did a better trade in the evening. There was a long bar with high stools, but Felicity didn't think either she or Jane would look particularly elegant scrambling their way up on to them, showing unnecessary amounts of thigh. There was a table in the corner next to a simulated log fire. The wall was covered in sepia prints of London street scenes of the twenties. Jane sank into a maroon velvet chair and nodded when Felicity suggested a glass of white wine. She went off to get them and came back carrying a tray with a bottle of mineral water, two glasses of white wine and a plate of prawn mayonnaise sandwiches. So much for her salad and no alcohol lunch.

'Well?' she said briskly as she sat down. She wanted to get this over with as soon as possible so she could get back to the shop. 'What's the matter?'

'I've left Tim.' Jane managed to look smug and ashamed at the same time.

'Why on earth? I can't believe it. When did this happen?' Felicity handed Jane a glass and after unloading the rest of the tray she sat forward, all attention. She certainly hadn't been expecting this.

'Yesterday. It's been building up. Tim doesn't understand, he thinks it's enough looking after him. He doesn't realise there's more to me than just being a wife and mother.'

'Oh, Jane, he does. You're a wonderful wife and he loves you, I'm sure of that.' Of course Felicity wasn't at all sure what Tim really felt about his wife, but now was not the time to say so.

'In his own way he probably does, but I don't think that's enough. Tabitha says we owe it to ourselves to reach our full potential.'

Somehow Felicity wasn't surprised to hear Tabitha's name mentioned at this point.

'Can't you reach your full potential, whatever that is, and still be married to Tim?' Felicity was feeling rather sorry for poor Tim, he worked hard and he had put up with Jane for the past thirty years, something most people might think put them in line for a medal.

'I don't think so. I can't go on like this, with no point or direction to my life.'

'I thought you got on really well, you always seemed so happy together.'

'We were in Hong Kong. I had a role there, but I don't have that any more.' Jane opened her handbag and pulled out a much-folded brochure.

She thrust it at Felicity, who held out her hand rather tentatively. She had a feeling this was not going to be something she approved of. *Tabitha McLeod's Road to Enlightenment* she read with difficulty as it was in silver writing on a multi-coloured page. *It is every woman's right to be fulfilled. For far too long our sisters have been oppressed and forced to submit to the slavery of marriage ...*

'For heaven's sake Jane, this is all rubbish. And you know it.' Felicity was exasperated. How could she be taken in by this nonsense?

'It's not rubbish. It sounds a bit strong in the brochure, but when you talk to Tabitha she explains it all so well. And it's true you know. I could have done so many things, and all I've done is be at the beck and call of others.'

'What could you have done?' Felicity asked curtly. She had never thought of Jane as a great intellectual but to be taken in by this was absurd.

'Tabitha thinks I could have been a healer. In fact I still could – she can feel the heat in my hands when I hold them over her.'

Felicity could imagine the heat in her own hands as she itched to slap Tabitha. Even though they had never met she could imagine just what she was like.

'What about you? What do you think?' Felicity appealed to Jane.

'I don't understand.'

273

'You keep saying "Tabitha says" or "Tabitha thinks". What about you?'

'I agree with her completely. She's an extraordinary person. She understands I'm a people person. I'm not like you, I'm a warm, giving person. I wasn't meant to live in an emotional vacuum.'

Felicity decided to ignore the insult. Jane was probably unaware of what she had said. Sipping her wine she took a good look at the other woman. Although she looked a mess, there was a light in her eyes. The light of fanaticism? She was beginning to think Tabitha McLeod was rather a dangerous person and not just some loony. It was getting hot in the wine bar and Felicity wanted to escape, but she couldn't leave yet.

'Tabitha's such an attractive, exciting woman,' Jane carried on in her usual steamroller fashion. It dawned on Felicity that Jane was in love, but she wasn't sure if she realised it yet, so perhaps it would be better not to mention it.

'So where does Tim come into this equation?' He might not be the most exciting man in the world, but surely he deserved better than this.

'He'll be fine. Be snapped up in a moment, I imagine.' Jane's forehead creased briefly. Was this another notion put into her head by Tabitha? She pulled herself together and continued. 'He might do for you. You want a new man.'

'Hang on a second, Jane. First of all, I'm not at all sure I do want a new man, even if everyone else thinks I do. Secondly, you were the great advocate of marriage. What happened to all that stuff you spouted to me about your vows? And, last but certainly not least, Tim might have something to say about all this.' Felicity paused to give her words time to sink in. 'I can't believe you're intending to walk out on him after all these years.' Felicity thought this was probably exactly the sort of thing that had been going on in Henry's mind when he

274

walked out on her, in other words a great desire to walk away from the problem and a complete inability to put himself in her shoes. Because Jane/Henry had ceased, whether temporarily or permanently, to feel anything for their husband/wife they just wanted it tidied away. Extraordinary.

'I've seen the light. Tabitha has opened my eyes. Our marriage was completely one sided. Wonderful for Tim, but there was no space for me to grow.'

Felicity looked at the all too substantial frame in front of her and reflected that this was not entirely true.

'So are you moving in with Tabitha? I hope you're not being too rash. How much thought have you given all this? How long have you known Tabitha? A few weeks?'

'Don't worry, I know what I'm doing.' Jane drained her glass and got to her feet. 'Let's have another drink.'

'Well at least Tabitha doesn't ban drinking.'

'Certainly not. Alcohol releases one from inhibitions. Frees one to be oneself.' Jane stomped off to the bar, her sturdy feet encased in clumpy sandals. Just why did Tabitha want Jane to lose her inhibitions? Felicity had a pretty good idea, but how to broach the subject with Jane?

'Here we are.' Jane was back in no time with another couple of glasses of house white. Bang went all Felicity's resolutions.

'Tell me,' Felicity began cautiously, 'is Tabitha married?'

'Huh.' Jane gave a derisory snort. 'Haven't you been listening to anything I've been saying? Didn't you read the pamphlet? Tabitha believes marriage is legalised slavery.'

'So does she have a boyfriend? Or a girlfriend maybe?'

'Why do you have such a *disgusting* mind? I remember you were just the same at school.'

Felicity felt this most unfair, she would never have imagined anything half as sophisticated when she was at school. In those days all her humour had been very lavatorial.

'I shall make sure you never meet Tabitha, she is a truly spiritual person,' Jane continued.

'Bollocks,' said Felicity, only she said it to herself and aloud she asked Jane the question she had been longing to ask for hours. Jane was clasping her chubby fingers together and leaning forward earnestly. For a dreadful moment Felicity thought she was going to pray. 'If everything's so wonderful, why did you need to see me?'

'I want you to go into the house and collect some clothes for me. I've been sleeping in Tabitha's spare room, but I've got nothing with me. It was a spur of the moment decision. I've made a list.' She pulled a shorthand notepad out of her handbag and tore off a sheet. 'Here you are.'

'Why can't you go?'

'Tim's there and I don't want to see him at the moment.'

Felicity couldn't believe how brisk and heartless Jane was being. She appeared to be dismissing years of marriage on a whim.

'I can't possibly go rummaging around your house, especially not if poor Tim's there.' Felicity was horrified at the very idea.

'Don't be so wet. Tim's not going to do anything. He never does.' She sounded bitter. Perhaps that was where the problem lay.

Half an hour later Jane had battered away at her resolve and Felicity found to her surprise she had agreed to go round to Jane's house the following morning and pick up a few items. She was certain that if Jane said her blue nightdress was in the second drawer down in her chest of drawers it would be. It reminded her she really must sort out her own cupboards. It would only add to their pain if any of her family had to scrabble about in the dirty laundry basket to find her a nightdress if she were to be rushed into hospital.

Eventually she managed to escape from Jane and her incessant ramblings about the wonders of Tabitha and get back to the shop. Oscar was due to arrive at half past three to discuss the details of the opening.

*

'We've got a real crisis on our hands.' She heard his voice from her office before she saw him.

'What's the problem?' Felicity got up and walked towards her son. He was looking flustered. Felicity didn't think she had ever seen him like this before.

'Only fucking Barry. He is so not going to do this to me.' Oscar flung his scarf onto the counter and clenched his fists in frustration.

'Hang on darling. Just tell me what the problem is.'

'I've only invited half of London to our opening and Barry said he'd take care of the catering. And has he fuck?'

'I'm sure he wouldn't let you down.' Felicity spoke with more confidence than she felt.

'He's been coked out of his brain for a week. Then I caught him and Miles ... I can't believe it. I thought we were all right. Oh fuck!' Oscar put his elbows on the glass counter and sank his head into his hands.

'Darling.' Felicity put her arms round him. It was too much to see him like this. 'It'll be all right,' she said as she patted him on the back. They were never too old for a mother to give them a cuddle. She could hear him sobbing quietly.

'Angel, would you be a love and take Darcy into my office for a minute?' Felicity looked over Oscar's shoulder and saw Angel and Darcy staring at them with their eyes wide open. As soon as they had gone she gently led Oscar to a black leather sofa that was intended for the customers to relax in while they made their big decisions.

'It's no good Mum. I don't think I can go on. I want to go back to New York.'

'You musn't make any hasty decisions.'

'It's not hasty. I've known for a while it wasn't going to work with Barry. I was just kidding myself we had a future. I've sorta suspected he'd got something going with Miles for a while, but I didn't want to let you down.'

'You mustn't worry about me. I'll be fine.' Felicity was trying to think as she patted Oscar's hand and handed him a tissue.

'We've got this fucking party on Monday. What are we going to do?'

'We'll have to cancel.'

'How can we do that? Everyone's been invited. Besides whatever happens, the shop'll have to open. I've got to get rid of all this stock. How are we going to have this sodding party? We'll never get a caterer at this short notice.'

'Don't worry, darling.' The mother in Felicity leapt to the challenge. 'I'll make a few things, buy a few things. Get plenty of champagne, no one will notice.' Smoked salmon, she thought, on brown bread – Angel and Darcy couldn't mess that up. She would make some quiches and a few savoury tartlets. It wouldn't be fashionable food, but it would be good. They would need a couple of people to serve. She would ask Angel, she might have some friends who could help. Her mind was racing at the same time as she was listening to Oscar.

'I thought it was going to be different this time. I really thought Barry and I would grow old together.'

'I'm so sorry darling, but it obviously wasn't meant to be.' Felicity ached for her son, she felt so helpless. She could help on the practical side, but he would have to mend the emotional wounds himself.

'I feel awful about the shop, though. Leaving you in the lurch like this.'

Felicity could scarcely bear to look at his worried face. 'Don't let's worry about that now,' she said reassuringly. 'We've got an opening to get through before we start thinking about a closing.' Did the shop have to close almost as soon as it opened? Why couldn't she take it on? Darcy seemed to have a flair for buying as long as she supervised him closely and made sure he didn't have a free rein with the company cheque book. She would ring Geoffrey and talk to him. He had said he was impressed with her when they met at the Blighs.

Eventually Oscar calmed down and started to talk quite enthusiastically about New York. It was a city he knew well and he had always had a good time there. Besides, it looked as if Laura and Mark would be there at the same time and he'd always been close to his sister. Laura would appreciate having him around as well. Felicity continued to make soothing noises, although she dreaded the idea of two of her children and her only grandchild moving so far away. But they had their own lives and the most important thing was that they should be happy.

'Right you two, it's all hands to the pump.' Felicity noticed Angel's blank expression and was just about to paraphrase when Darcy jumped in.

'It's rather an old-fashioned expression, used by people of Mrs Fox's generation, it means ... '

'It means we've all got to pull together to make this opening party a success.' Felicity glared at Darcy.

'You can rely on me, my dear. It's the least I can do for you, under the circumstances.' He gave Felicity a warm, sympathetic smile that made her want to hit him over the head with one of his fancy lamps. But she needed him, so she sat on her hands and promised herself revenge at a later date. Angel was confident she could get hold of at least four girls who knew how to serve drinks and food.

*

After Oscar went home Felicity called Angel and Darcy into her office to discuss what they were going to do. They were both enthusiastic about continuing the shop with Felicity in charge, so all that remained for her to do was to contact Geoffrey to make sure he was still prepared to back them. She knew Oscar hadn't decided anything yet, but she would never be able to relax until she knew what the situation was, so she rang Geoffrey.

'Geoffrey, it's Felicity Fox. Something's come up about the shop and I was wondering if I could talk to you about it.'

'It's lovely to hear from you. Shall we have lunch to discuss it?'

'Would you mind if we just had a regular meeting, with desks, in an office?'

Don't worry, I'm quite safe,' he laughed nervously. 'Actually I've been seeing quite a bit of Daisy. I hope you … '

'That's great,' Felicity interrupted, deliberately keeping her voice cool and businesslike. She didn't want Geoffrey to think she was interested in him or jealous of his relationship with Daisy. After the Darcy fiasco, that would be the last straw. 'No, I want a proper meeting because I'm lunched out. I seem to have been having a series of them and they take up too much time, not to mention the calories.'

'All right, that suits me. When shall we meet?'

'Any day after our opening. You are coming to the party on Monday aren't you?'

'Absolutely.'

Felicity sat down to write a list of things to buy for the party.

1) Paper napkins. Why hadn't Daisy told her about Geoffrey?

2) Cocktail sticks. Did she think Felicity would be upset?

3) Smoked salmon. Obviously everyone thought she was desperate.

4) Lemons. How humiliating.

5) Brown bread. Well, one man fancies her.

6) Butter. But he's her ex-husband, so it's better no one knows about that.

7) Nuts. Yes, she would be if she slept with Henry.

With a supreme effort she made herself concentrate on the matter in hand. She would have to try to sort out everything else later. She had to be organised for this party, she must make it a success, particulary if she wanted Geoffrey, or rather his money, involved.

CHAPTER 17

THE NEXT MORNING, SATURDAY, Felicity got up early to go shopping. She already had her list which, after many frantic late night additions, ran to several pages. There was no sign of Darcy when she went downstairs so she decided to go on her own. She didn't feel like waiting around until he appeared, she wasn't even sure if he was in the house with or without Sonia. Before leaving she grabbed the piece of paper Jane had handed her. She supposed she had better bite the bullet and ring Tim. But first things first, she had to get everything ready for the opening on Monday.

Feeling efficient she entered Sainsburys wheeling her trolley purposefully round the store. She was just contemplating the merits of the many different salamis available when she heard a familiar voice from the next aisle.

'Well, there are always problems in a new relationship, especially when you get to our age.' It was Sally Pelham. But who was she talking to? Felicity stood like a statue, her ears growing longer by the minute.

'I've always thought Henry was really attractive. Sexy too.' It sounded like Slutty Sonia.

'He's adorable, but it's much more difficult when one gets a rescue husband. They pick up such awful habits from their previous owners. I'm having to completely re-train him.'

Felicity heard an irritating tinkling laugh – it was definitely Sonia.

'Really Sally. You are dreadful. You knew he was married, so that's no excuse. You should have left him to Felicity.'

'Don't be silly. You know what they say, men are like houses, you have to bag the good ones before they come onto the market.'

'I'm off married men. They're nothing but trouble.'

'But you're still married, aren't you?'

Felicity, flushed with a mixture of rage and humiliation, crept towards the end of the aisle. She had to hear the rest of this conversation, but she musn't be seen. She was poised for a quick getaway. Sonia spoke again.

'Technically I suppose I'm still his wife, but Humph's much happier mouldering away in the country with that dreary housekeeper of his.'

'So what are you up to then? Not still seeing Andrew, I presume?'

'I wish. The bastard dumped me, Venetia's gone completely bonkers and he's checked her into the Abbey.'

Felicity gasped and almost dropped a whole liver sausage. She replaced it carefully then picked up a bratworst and pretended to examine it. Venetia in the Abbey. No wonder Andrew wanted to see her. And that explained why he was certain Venetia wouldn't be there on Sunday.

'So are you seeing anyone else?' Sally was obviously determined to find out all the dirt she could.

'Darcy Fitzgerald.' Sonia sounded triumphant until she heard Sally's cruel laugh.

'You can't seriously be going out with Darcy? He's just a joke.'

'He's hung like a donkey and he's a baronet, so I think the laugh's on me.'

Felicity dropped the large German sausage back into the chiller and didn't wait to hear Sally's reply. She had no wish to listen to any more of this. If Sonia was about to start on details of Darcy's sex life she was going to beat a hasty retreat. She continued her way round the store in the manner of James Bond, flattening herself at the end of every aisle in order to avoid the gruesome twosome. She managed to negotiate the checkout and unloading of her trolley into the car without being seen, although she had a nasty moment when she spotted an elderly man pointing her out to a burly security guard. Once in her car she crouched low in the front seat and telephoned Tim. She rather hoped he would be out, perhaps on the golf course with Sam Tollard. Why had his name popped into her mind? He was married, at least for the time being, and in any case she had enough complications at the moment.

'Hello.' The telephone only rang once when Tim's eager voice answered.

'Tim. It's Felicity.'

'Felicity. Hello. How are you? All right. Jolly good.'

'Tim, this is a bit awkward, but Jane asked me to ring.'

'Have you seen her?' His voice was expectant.

'Yes. She wants me to come and pick some of her things up.' Whoops, she hadn't meant to say it just like that. It sounded so stark. 'She'd like me to talk to you,' she added desperately.

'Is she all right?'

'Physically she's fine, but I'm not at all sure about her mental state.' This was not the way the conversation was supposed to go. She couldn't do this over the telephone.

'Really?' Tim clutched at this tiny glimmer of hope, some rational explanation for his wife's behaviour. 'D'you think she might be having a breakdown?'

'I've no idea, but she is behaving very out of character. Are you busy right now? Can I come round?'

'That would be splendid. I'd like to talk to you, get some answers. After all, you're one of her oldest friends.'

Felicity winced, but refrained from saying anything.

*

284

As she drove to the Bignalls' house Felicity pondered about the curious fact that a few months ago her life had been a total mess and all her friends had been busy offering her advice to get her life back in order, and now for some strange reason the tables all seemed to have turned.

Tim opened the door before Felicity had time to ring the bell. He looked exhausted with dark circles under his eyes, and his clothes looked as if he had slept in them. He led her into the blue and white kitchen and Felicity was mentally rolling up her sleeves preparatory to doing a bit of housework, but the house looked immaculate. Tim must have been cleaning and tidying ever since Jane left, and as they came into the room he picked up a cloth and started nervously wiping an already spotless surface. Perhaps Jane had a point; maybe he wouldn't be such a bad bet as a new husband.

'Coffee?' he asked, remembering his manners.

'Let me make it.' Felicity felt she ought to be doing something.

'No. I'll do it. I've got a tray already laid. Just the way Jane does it.' He asked politely about Felicity while he got the coffee organised. How was the shop? The children? Her house?

Felicity answered him equally politely. In a few moments he took the tray and led Felicity into the drawing room. Like the kitchen it was immaculate. There was not even a speck of dust on the top of the piano. Although Upton had never been a particularly tidy house Felicity usually managed to keep a semblance of order, but when she went away for even a day she knew she would come back to chaos. Henry used to leave a trail wherever he went, half-drunk mugs of coffee here, dirty plate there, can of beer beside the telephone. Felicity sat down on the overstuffed chintz sofa with its perfectly plumped cushions, and taking a cup of coffee from the tray she turned expectantly to Tim.

'Damn difficult, this,' he said. 'Not much good at talking about things, specially not with women.' He was sitting on the edge of the windowseat clasping his knees with his hands.

'Perhaps you should start with what Jane said before she left.'

'Women are queer cattle.'

'Jane said that? I suppose that's Tabitha's influence.'

'No. No. My father used to say that. Told me when I was a boy they're a different species. You think you understand them, then blow me, you don't understand them at all.'

He looked so like a dejected little boy who'd had his train set taken away that Felicity felt like taking him in her arms and promising him an ice cream if he was a brave little soldier. She suddenly felt very cross with Jane. Tim was a thoroughly nice, decent man. He hadn't run off with another woman.

'I'm sure it's only temporary, a little blip. I think Jane's been a bit bored since you got back to England.'

'It's my fault, I know. She's wanted us to do things together, talk about our feelings, things like that. Not really my cup of tea. She never used to be like that.'

'I think,' Felicity said gently, 'she's been finding things a bit empty. Now the children have left home and you don't do all that entertaining and stuff you used to do in Hong Kong. All those people coming to stay, all those committees.'

'I know, but I thought she was getting involved with things here.' He got to his feet, walked over to the mantelpiece, picked up a Dresden figurine and started carefully dusting it with his handkerchief. 'Have you met this Tabitha person?'

'No, and I don't want to. She sounds like a complete phoney to me.' Felicity took another sip of her coffee.

'Really?' Felicity heard the relief in Tim's voice. 'Jane told me everyone thought she was a genius.' He put the figurine down and turned to face Felicity.

'Who's everyone? A lot of bored, gullible and stupid women.'

'Jane's not stupid. She's highly intelligent. An amazing woman.' He was indignant now and he had a fire in his eyes at the thought of his wife. Felicity thought it was rather romantic, the way he was still so in love with Jane after all these years and very sweet the way he leapt protectively to her defence.

'Of course, I didn't mean Jane. I don't think ... she's just ... she's looking for something, some meaning in her life.' Felicity knew she was stumbling over the words, but she wasn't at all sure of her ground here.

'She's so energetic. I'm not surprised Tabitha wants her involved in this centre of hers. I'm happy for her if that's what she wants, anything as long as she doesn't leave. I'd be no good without her.' He paused and gulped, unused to talking like this. 'You live on your own, got your life organised. I admire that, but I'd never cope.'

'I'm sure you would.' Felicity looked round the immaculate room with nothing out of place in it. 'But even if the worst came to the worst and Jane did decide not to come back, and I'm sure she will, you'd be snapped up immediately. There'd be a queue of women round the block.' Odd how Tim seemed to think she had her life organised.

'Huagh, huagh.' The truffle hound laugh made Felicity jump. 'Not very likely anyone else would have me.' He really didn't seem to realise that an odd man, however odd, was always useful. But perhaps Felicity had better not plant the seeds of this idea into his mind.

'I'm sure it's not going to come to that. I expect she'll spend a few days there and come running back home.'

'So why didn't she come here today?'

That was perfectly logical but Felicity thought quickly. 'I expect she felt that if she saw you she wouldn't be able to go through with it.'

'Do you think so?' He sounded pathetically eager, clutching at any straw.

Felicity wasn't at all certain this was the reason, but she saw no reason to say this to Tim. No need to make him feel worse than he already did. He was pacing restlessly round the room, making her feel slightly seasick.

'Would you mind awfully sitting down? I can't think with you wandering around.'

'Sorry.' He parked himself on the edge of a green wing chair, leant forward and, clasping his knees between his hands, rocked backwards and forwards. 'You're so sensible. I think I need your advice about what to do now.'

Felicity wondered, as she often did whenever anyone requested her advice, why anyone in their right mind would imagine she could help them out of their predicament. Sensible was the very last thing she felt. They both sat for a few minutes lost in their own thoughts.

'I really don't know, Tim, but maybe you'll have to play a bit of a waiting game.'

'What d'you mean exactly?'

'Well,' Felicity took a sip of coffee. 'If you rush after her now, or try and pressurise her into coming back, I should think she'll just try and defend her actions and she might paint herself into a corner.'

'How long will it take?'

Oh Lord, Tim seemed to think Felicity knew what would happen. Had a trusting belief in her knowledge of human nature. A very misplaced trust in Felicity's view.

'I wish I knew, Tim. I'm really not very good at this sort of thing. My husband pushed off and he hasn't come back. But this is entirely different,' she added hastily as she saw Tim's anxious face. 'I'm sure it's just a spur of the moment thing, a moment of madness.'

'Really, what makes you say that?'

Felicity had no idea, she had been making soothing noises. She longed to be able to say something positive, but she wasn't at all sure about anything. Why indeed should Jane come back or why not? She and Tim had been married a long time, but Felicity knew to her cost that didn't mean anything. At least it hadn't to Henry. Jane was bored with her life, but would it ultimately be less boring with Tabitha? Didn't the solution to boredom lie within herself? And what about Tabitha? What did she want out of it all?

'It's not as if she's in love with anyone else,' Felicity said when she finally spoke and then added after a moment's thought, 'I suppose you could always starve her out.'

'What? Cut off her food? How could I do that?' Tim looked puzzled.

'Cut off her money supply, or does she have heaps of her own?'

'No, but we've got a joint account. She can take anything she wants. I couldn't allow her to go without money.'

'I'm pretty sure Tabitha's the one who's after money. She probably sees Jane as a cheque book on legs.'

'Ahh. I see what you're getting at. I'll have to think about that one. Don't want her to hate me.'

'No, that might defeat the object of the exercise. Perhaps it would be better to just stick it out, if you can bear to.'

'I'm supposed to be going to Singapore for a couple of weeks. I was going to say I couldn't go, but it might be just the thing. Get me out of the way.'

Felicity didn't feel she had been much help, although Tim thanked her profusely before she left. She could really think of no good reason why Jane shouldn't return to Tim, but then what did anyone know about another person's marriage? She was pretty sure Tim didn't beat his wife, but maybe he was terribly mean, or made awful sucking noises when he drank soup. Jane's wardrobe and cupboards were, of course, immaculate and Felicity was able to gather up all the items on the list with no problems, but she hated to leave Tim looking so desolate. She must try and get to the bottom of things with Jane.

*

It was nearly two o'clock by the time Felicity got home and unloaded the car. She piled Jane's three large suitcases in the hall, where they created an unnecessary obstacle course. She tried to ring Jane on her mobile, but it was switched off, so she could only leave a message asking her to come and collect them as soon as possible. Next, she carried all the bags and boxes from the supermarket into the kitchen. By the time she had done this there was no room to move. She stared at them, daunted by the prospect of unpacking everything and wondering where she could put it all and still leave herself a space to work. In order to put it off she made herself a cheese, ham and pickle sandwich and retreated to the drawing room. No sooner had she sat down than the telephone rang.

'Hello, Fifi. It's me, Venetia.' The voice sounded cheerful and upbeat.

'What a lovely surprise. Where are you?' Felicity put her plate down on the coffee table.

'In the Abbey. I'm surprised you hadn't heard.'

'Well … ' Felicity debated whether to tell Venetia about the conversation she had overheard while shopping.

'Never mind, it's not important,' Venetia's said airily. 'I don't care who knows. It's marvellous in here. The best place in London to meet interesting people, You really ought to book yourself in here for a fortnight.'

'Isn't it frightfully expensive?' Felicity eyed her sandwich longingly.

'Yes, but it's worth every penny.'

'Why are you there?' Felicity asked tentatively.

'I thought it was because I was an alcoholic, but actually it turns out I'm just mentally and physically exhausted and was using alcohol as a prop. I'm here for a rest. No booze of course, but plenty of other things. They keep us very busy. Terribly healthy, massages, facials, just like a health farm.'

'Has Andrew been to see you?'

There was a pause. Felicity took a guilty bite of her sandwich. After her session with Tim she was starving.

'Not yet. I don't want to see him at the moment.'

Felicity hesitated. She wasn't sure whether Venetia knew her husband was giving her lunch tomorrow. But she decided Venetia deserved her honesty this time.

'He rang and asked me to have lunch with him. Says he wants to talk.' Felicity heard a snort at the other end of the line.

'Andrew talk? Good luck, whenever we try one or other of us ends up leaving the room.'

'You don't mind do you Netty? I could cancel. I just thought it might help.'

'Of course I don't mind. It won't do any good,' she said gloomily, 'I just can't deal with him myself at the moment.'

Felicity took another bite of her sandwich and made what she hoped was an encouraging noise through a mouthful of bread. What a selfish, shallow person she was. Her best friend wanted to talk about her most personal probems and she was thinking about food.

'We have all this group therapy and one on one therapy. I really believe I'm learning about my marriage. I think this could be a growing experience.'

'That is psychobabble for what precisely?' Felicity had always admired the way Venetia threw herself into everything wholeheartedly and was ready to accept new ideas.

'I don't understand it all yet. I've always known that Andrew and I both suffer from low self esteem. That's one of the problems – we're too alike.'

'Really? I hadn't noticed you rushing around flirting and having affairs with people.'

'We're both perfectionists and we find it difficult to deal with imperfection. That's why Andrew is always searching for the perfect woman, while I'm looking for the perfect lipstick.' She gave a harsh laugh.

'Stop it Netty. That's not fair, it makes you sound like an air head, which you're most definitely not.'

'I'm only using lipstick as an example – I want everything to be just right, my job, my flat, my life.'

'I'm not surprised you couldn't cope with everything, what with losing your job and discovering about Sonia all at the same time.'

Venetia conceded that everything had piled up on her, but she was beginning to see a glimmer of hope, the chance of a brighter future, but not yet. For the time being she was staying put, safely ensconced in the Abbey.

*

After she finished talking to Venetia, Felicity tried to sort out the house. Fond as she was of her new home in Battersea it was at moments like these that she missed the huge kitchen and larder at Upton. The three large suitcases containing

Jane's essential items were still filling Felicity's hall. She had left several messages on her mobile, but had not heard from her. Tripping over one of the cases for the umpteenth time Felicity cursed her friend loudly. Felicity left one last message late on Saturday night. Where was Jane?

'Jane, it's me, Felicity. Unless you get those bloody suitcases out of my house asap I'm going to leave them in the street.'

*

Felicity spent most of Saturday evening preparing for Monday night. 'Getting ahead' was the key. She folded nearly two hundred paper napkins, polished two hundred hired glasses, put nuts and olives into bowls, sliced lemons and covered everything with cling film. She packed empty wine boxes with linen table cloths, jugs for water, soft drinks and all the flower vases she could find. She made several large quiches and cooked hundreds of little cocktail sausages in honey and mustard. She would warm everything up on Monday and take it all to the shop in insulated bags. It wouldn't be fashionable London party food, but it would be good and people would enjoy it. There did not seem to be much more she could do until Monday when she would buy flowers and take everything else to the shop.

At eleven o'clock Felicity kicked off her shoes and sank into an armchair in the drawing room, a large glass of Pinot Grigio in her hand. She lay back and shut her eyes, exhausted. She woke with a start as the doorbell rang.

'Who the hell?' Felicity stumbled to her feet and smoothing her apron over her skirt, staggered to the front door. It still didn't seem natural to Felicity to check who was outside before opening the door. In the country they had never even bothered to lock the door at night. Peering out she saw Jane standing there. Felicity groaned. Much as she wanted to be rid of the suitcases cluttering up her hall, she was feeling extremely tired, and the thought of having to face a long conversation with her friend was an exhausting prospect. Reluctantly she opened the door. Jane had always been quite a Jaeger sort of person, but living with Tabitha had transformed her. And Felicity's first reaction was that this was not necessarily for the better. Venetia was adamant that large women always looked better in well tailored clothes, and seeing the apparition standing in front of her Felicity was forced to agree. Jane barged into the house, past Felicity, her voluminous black cloak swinging dangerously. Felicity grabbed the Wemys pig. In her hair Jane was wearing a ribbon that hung like the remains of a party streamer over one ear. Felicity felt quite strongly there should be a law forbidding anyone over the age of fifty from wearing ribbons in their hair.

'Sorry to be so late. Tabs and I have been in Wales, only just got back. You look ghastly.' She gave Felicity a disapproving stare as she came into the hall.

'I've been busy, on my feet all day. I've only just sat down.' *And not as ghastly as you do.* The words pot and kettle popped into Felicity's head.

'I'm going to give you a crystal, they're very good for giving you energy.' So is sleep, thought Felicity as Jane dived into her handbag and came out with a small cardboard box. Dropping her bag on the floor she reverentially opened the box. Nestling on a bed of cotton wool were several small crystals.

'Here, have one of these. Tabitha energised them all while we were in Wales. It was quite fascinating.' Her eyes took on a dreamy look as she passed the rough amethyst quartz to Felicity.

'That's very kind of you,' Felicity responded automatically as she slipped it into the pocket of her apron. 'Would you like a drink or a cup of coffee?'

'Love a whisky.' Jane took off her cloak and draped it over the hall chair. Underneath it she was wearing a pair of very tight jeans with a multi-coloured peasant blouse, and on her feet a pair of men's walking boots.

'Won't Tabitha be waiting for you?' Felicity asked hopefully. Jane was was tiring at the best of times and at the moment all Felicity wanted to do was to go to bed.

'No. She had to go and see someone. You've no idea how many calls she has on her time. People ring her up day and night with all sorts of petty problems. And she's so kind she rushes off to see if she can help.' Jane's eyes glinted with fanatic admiration.

Felicity poured out a glass of whisky for Jane. She made it quite a small one as Jane was driving and also she hoped it would be finished quickly and she would have the house to herself. She hadn't seen Darcy all day. He had an uncanny knack of knowing when there were boring jobs to be done. Now she wanted to finish her glass of wine and get to bed before he came back. If he was coming back.

'Thank you for picking up my cases.' Jane opened the largest one and had a quick check through it.

'Why'd you need so much stuff? I thought you were only staying with Tabitha on a temporary basis.'

'I want Tim to realise I'm serious.' Jane plonked herself down on the sofa and stuck her sturdy shoes out in front of her. 'I had to borrow these from Tabitha. She does so much walking she needs a pair of proper walking shoes.' Her face took on a dreamy expression as she thought about Tabitha and her sensible shoes. Then she continued. 'I'm extremely cross with him.'

'Tim. Yes, I realise that but why? He doesn't seem to have a clue.'

'He wouldn't. That's part of the problem. The other night I just flipped. We were having a talk about what I could do with my life. Do you know what he said?'

'No,' Felicity said truthfully. 'Do tell me.'

'He actually suggested I might like to do up his dressing-room.' Her face was contorted with anger at the memory.

'What's wrong with that? You like doing things up.'

'But I'd just done it up,' she wailed. 'I suddenly realised it's pointless working my fingers to the bone, trying to do things for him. He doesn't notice me or anything I do.' She downed her whisky pointedly and put the glass down rather loudly on the coffee table.

'Would you like another whisky?' Felicity felt forced to ask.

Jane nodded, getting to her feet and following Felicity into the kitchen. She stopped on the way to examine her suitcases.

'You seem to have got most of the things I asked for, but I hope you remembered my velour dressing-gown. It was hanging up behind the bedroom door.'

'I did and I've borrowed some insulated boxes for the food on Monday.'

'Monday. What's happening on Monday?'

'It's our opening party. I hope you're coming.'

'I don't know, I'm not sure of my plans. Is Tim going?'

'I think he's busy that night.' Felicity lied. Somehow she would force him to be there, if he wasn't in Singapore. It would be a good opportunity to get them in the same room together.

'Busy doing what?' Jane's voice was imperious.

'I've no idea, but I can't imagine he'll have any shortage of invitations. An attractive man like Tim.'

'Attractive? D'you think so? You've never said anything before.'

'Well, one doesn't, not a friend's husband. Of course he's attractive.' Felicity crossed her fingers behind her back.

'You sound as though you might fancy him yourself.' Jane's voice was full of surprise.

'Naturally I do, but you're one of my closest friends and I have scruples, unlike most women.' Felicity hoped God would forgive her lies.

'Well obviously I'm not intending to stay with Tabitha for ever. For one thing her spare bed's extremely uncomfortable.'

Possibly intentionally in order to lure people out of it and into her own was Felicity's unkind thought. Although even if one was a lesbian it was hard to imagine Jane would be one's first choice of partner. However, there was no accounting for tastes.

'So you're not thinking of divorcing Tim?'

'Certainly not. It's very undignified to get divorced at our age.'

'Thanks.' Felicity winced.

'Oh lummy, I always make a bish with you. But you know what I mean. Better the devil you know and all that.'

In spite of her tactless remarks Felicity was determined Jane should come to the shop opening, a chance to meet Tim on neutral territory. Jane and Tim were a manageable entity, but Jane alone, on the loose, or with the unknown Tabitha, was a much scarier prospect.

'I don't want to be rude, but I'm exhausted. If you'd just take your bags then I could go to bed.'

'Oh, all right. I'd like to have a good talk with you, tell you all about the Centre, but I can tell you're overtired. The crystal will help all that. I'm full of energy.' Jane scrambled to her feet and put her glass down on the table.

Felicity followed her into the hall, covering her mouth with her hand as she yawned. 'Do come on Monday,' she managed to say, adding as tempting bait, 'the Camerons are coming.'

'Really? Well, I'll certainly try to be there, but I'm not sure I'll be able to persuade Tabitha to come with me.'

Felicity's immediate thought was 'Whoopee', but she did think she'd been quite clever in giving Jane an excuse to be there. The Camerons were her social apex. She helped Jane out to the car with her bags, hoping as she did so that Tabitha's spare room was good and small. Jane would get fed up even quicker if she was constantly tripping over all her stuff.

*

The next morning Felicity woke much later than she had intended. Darcy was apparently still out as he had not appeared with the Sunday papers as he usually did if he was at home. Pulling on a dressing-gown Felicity wandered sleepily downstairs. She made herself a cup of coffee and fed the cats. Standing at the kitchen sink she gazed out at the garden. It looked tired and depressed in the rain, distinctly damp and dishevelled. It was not an analogy she was prepared to dwell on this morning. She turned back to her bright little kitchen and felt instantly cheered. Next year would be the year of the garden. Now she had to get ready for her lunch.

An hour later she was sitting in the drawing room leafing through a magazine, hoping she would look like the picture of composure when Andrew arrived. Just as she was looking at her watch wondering where he was, the telephone rang.

'Fifi sweetheart, I'm running late. Can we meet at Gianni's? I'll be there in twenty minutes. I've booked a table.' And before Felicity had time to protest he had rung off. Grabbing her mac and umbrella Felicity found her car keys and battled through the gusting wind and rain to the car, which was parked several streets away. She drove to the restaurant and eventually managed to find a parking space about half a mile away. So much for looking svelte, well groomed and composed. She arrived looking distinctly damp and dishevelled and hastily repaired to the Ladies to make some improvements. After doing what she could Felicity walked into the bar. Andrew was nowhere to be seen. The head waiter ushered her to a low sofa. Felicity would have preferred an upright chair that would be easier to get out of elegantly.

'Darling Fifi, how lovely to see you, and you're looking good. I like that skirt, shows your legs off. You always had good legs.' Andrew arrived with a flourish.

'You look terrific too, Andrew.' And indeed he did, sunbed-tanned face, cosmetically enhanced teeth, and had he had a touch of botox? His face certainly seemed remarkably line free. He was wearing a beautifully hand-tailored suit of dove grey, which toned with rather than matched his hair, a pink shirt and maroon silk tie. All was perfect, a bit too perfect Felicity thought, as she spotted the gold cufflinks inset with large diamonds that twinkled out from underneath his cuffs. It was somehow typical of Andrew that he always went just that little bit OTT.

'Glass of bubbly?' He ordered two glasses of champagne without waiting for her answer.

'Just one,' she muttered feebly. 'I'm driving.'

Two glasses arrived a moment later and Felicity started to relax. Champagne always put her into a party mood, even at her advanced age. The restaurant was an old-established Italian one that had been around for years and was still much loved by middle-aged businessmen, who had enjoyed it when it was trendy in the seventies. The food was good without being too modern, the décor likewise.

'I spoke to Venetia,' Felicity ventured at last after they had exchanged an obligatory amount of small talk.

'I know. She rang me this morning. They want to see me this evening.'

'Sounds like you've been summoned to the headmaster's office.'

'A bit like that. Some sort of group therapy, lot of ghastly mumbo jumbo. But I suppose I'll have to go.'

'How did she sound?' Felicity took a sip of her champagne and looked encouragingly at Andrew.

'Good I thought. Much calmer and more rested.'

He took a gold swizzle stick out of his breast pocket and carefully twirled it round his glass. Felicity smiled, it was years since she'd seen one of those.

Felicity quickly took another sip of champagne and averted her head for a moment. Andrew was not a man who liked to be laughed at. 'Are you and Netty going to be all right?'

'I hope so. I can't afford a divorce. Damned expensive. Besides Venetia's my best friend. I adore her. We've always understood each other in the past.'

'She didn't know about your affairs.'

'She always had a pretty good idea. But she didn't appreciate Sonia rubbing her face in it.'

'Why do you have affairs?' Felicity was genuinely interested.

'I adore sex. Netty doesn't. She doesn't expect me to live like a monk.'

At that moment the waiter came over and took their orders. Andrew suggested the *insalata tricolore* followed by *vitello piccata* and Felicity was only too happy to agree. As soon as they were seated at their table Andrew spoke again.

'The trouble with Sonia is that she never understood the rules.'

'Forgive my naivety, I didn't know there were rules.'

'One forgets what a little innocent you are.' Andrew laughed. 'If you want to have an affair, and stay married, you have to stick to the rules. Always have an affair with someone who has no interest in rocking the boat, preferably someone who's happily married.'

'Not that happily,' Felicity remarked dryly. 'So what went wrong?'

'Sonia got ideas. I was stupid. I didn't realise she's longing to leave poor Humphrey. But she won't do it until she finds another victim.'

'Oh dear, poor Darcy,' Felicity murmured. 'You did know about Darcy, didn't you?'

'Of course. First thing she did was ring and tell me. I think she was trying to make me jealous.'

'And did she?' Felicity couldn't resist asking.

'No. I laughed, which made her furious.'

'I'm not surprised. As I said, poor Darcy.'

'Don't feel too sorry for him. Sonia'll do quite well out of Humphrey if she gets divorced. Keep Darcy in the manner to which he'd like to become accustomed.'

He laughed and despite herself Felicity joined in. Privately she thought Humphrey would be prepared to employ some very expensive lawyers to fight Sonia if she was too demanding.

Their first course arrived together with another glass of champagne. Suddenly Andrew leant forward and took Felicity's hand in his.

'How about you and me?' He gave her a slow smile.

'You and me?' Felicity gulped. Did he mean what she thought he meant?

'I've got a vacancy for a mistress.'

'What about your rules? I'm not married, happily or otherwise, in case you'd forgotten.'

'You're Venetia's best friend, sweetie. You wouldn't do anything to upset her.'

'I would have thought sleeping with her husband might upset her,' she said in her most sarcastic voice. She was on the point of indignantly removing her hand from under Andrew's when she was aware of the figure of a man standing beside the table. It was Sam Tollard.

'Hello Andrew,' he said. 'Thought it was you. How's Venetia?' he asked pointedly. Then he realised who Andrew's companion was. 'Oh, it's you, Felicity.' He looked embarrassed.

Felicity felt her face start to get hot. What on earth must he think of her? Too late she snatched her hand from the table and put it onto her lap.

'Andrew was just telling me all about Venetia. She's doing really well. She's coming home soon. Isn't that marvellous?' Felicity knew she was burbling, but couldn't stop herself. 'Andrew kindly asked me to lunch to tell me all about it. There's nothing more ... ' She ground to a halt. Never apologise, never explain – that was her mother's motto. Why couldn't she have kept quiet?

'How nice – for you both.' Sam raised a disbelieving eyebrow and gave them both a cold smile as he left the restaurant.

'Andrew, you really are a mega shit. You've dumped me right in it now.' Felicity was furious with herself as much as with Andrew, but Andrew merely laughed.

'Fancy Sam Tollard do you?'

'No I don't. Anyway he's married.'

'Not really. They're only staying together until their daughter gets married.'

'So everyone keeps telling me,' Felicity said crossly.

'You do fancy him. So I take it you're not prepared to have an affair with me?'

'You take it correctly.'

'Pity. Might have been rather enjoyable, for both of us. Oh well, I'll have to find someone else,' he drawled as he leant back in his chair. Felicity shook her head. Andrew was quite impossible, but at least he would never let one down, you could guarantee he'd always behave in the same way. Very badly.

*

After lunch Felicity drove home cautiously. She had only had two glasses of champagne, but she certainly couldn't risk losing her licence. Poor Venetia. Or was she poor Venetia? She and Andrew had managed to make their marriage work, after a fashion, for years and they probably would again. Andrew would have affairs, but might be more discreet now and Venetia would turn a blind eye. Other people's marriages were such a mystery. As for Sam, she cringed at what he must think of her. Her best friend was in a clinic and there was Felicity drinking champagne and holding hands with the said best friend's husband. And she had been told yet again that Sam and Lavinia were only together until after the daughter's wedding. But she had met him with his wife, and in any case she didn't want to be like Sally, moving in on a man before he 'came on the market'. But he was the only attractive man she had met since her divorce and she managed to blow it every time she saw him.

*

'Hello Possum. How you doing?' Rose rang that evening just as Felicity had finished the Sunday papers and was curled up on the sofa wondering whether there was anything on television she wanted to watch. Darcy had come and gone out again. He was still treading on eggshells round her, pretending he didn't yet believe she wasn't madly in love with him. Perhaps he and Sonia had been lent a flat. She didn't mind where they went, as long as they weren't using her office.

'Hi, Rose. How are you?' Felicity couldn't keep the solicitous tone, that she knew her cousin hated, out of her voice.

'I've just had another heart attack and I've rung to say goodbye.'

'My God,' Felicity gasped, half-believing it might be true.

'Idiot. I'm fine. I just can't bear the way people put on that soupy voice when they talk to me.'

Felicity giggled with relief, she had almost had a heart attack herself. She and Rose had been accustomed over the years to ringing each other on Sunday evenings to catch up on the minutiae of their lives.

'Don't do that to me, you old cow. Gave me quite a turn.'

'So what's been happening?'

'I had lunch with Andrew today and guess what?'

'He propositioned you.'

'Yes. He does it to everybody I suppose?'

'Yup. Even me!'

'Really. No accounting for taste. Did you do anything about it?'

'Fifi.'

'Why's he never made a pass at me before? That's not very flattering when you think about it.'

'I can give you three reasons.'

'Which are?'

'One, you're Venetia's oldest friend, two, he didn't have a vacancy and three, he's always been a bit nervous of Henry. Besides,' she added almost as an afterthought, 'you weren't looking as good as you do now.'

304

'Really?' Felicity smiled happily and she couldn't help fishing for more compliments. 'D'you think I look good now?'

'If you like that sort of thing.' Rose laughed. 'OK. OK. You're looking great, better than you've looked for years. Satisfied?'

'Wow, thank you.' Felicity stood up and craned to see her reflection in the mirror in the hall. She turned this way and that trying to look at herself objectively. She thought she looked much the same as always. Not too bad when she stood up straight, sucked her tummy in and tilted her head, and awful when she let it all sag. Still it was nice to have a compliment.

Half an hour later, when they had finished discussing all their friends and relations, they said goodbye. Rose was full of their plans for the forthcoming trip to Australia and it cheered Felicity to hear the genuine enthusiasm in her voice. The only thing Felicity didn't mention was the encounter with Sam. She wasn't sure why, but she was still embarrassed by the way she had behaved, like a stupid schoolgirl. She would see Rose tomorrow as she was coming to the party. Her first trip to London since her heart attack. It was a good milestone.

Although it was early, Felicity decided she would go to bed, as she wanted to be up early to get everything ready. But she could not sleep. Her mind was going over the day. Andrew's suggestion had appalled her, she would never consider doing that to Venetia, but he had said he was going to find someone else. With weird middle of the night logic she wondered if she should have agreed to have an affair with him in order to protect Venetia. And then there was Sam. What must he think of her? What did she think of him? One of the cats, annoyed by her mistress's tossing and turning, started kneading her tummy, trying to get comfortable. Then just as she was dozing off she heard Darcy come in. He was obviously in that state of inebriation where he was trying not to make any noise, but was stumbling on the stairs. Great. Felicity knew she was going to look like hell in the morning. Contrary to what everyone said, the older she got the more sleep she needed in order to function the next day.

*

'Hi Felicity.' Sadie greeted her warmly even though it was only eight-thirty in the morning. Being a hairdresser meant always being cheerful with your clients and listening to their problems, not coming to work overtired and overhung.

'I need you to make my hair bomb proof today.' Felicity said hopefully as she put on the charcoal grey gown. 'I've got a party this evening, but I've got to get all the food ready first.'

'No problem. I'll use plenty of gel. Get you shampooed in a minute. Coffee? Magazines?'

Felicity settled down with a cappuccino and a copy of *Hello!* She was leafing idly through the pages thinking that as the only soap she followed was *The Archers*, she knew less and less people in the magazine, when she spotted the photograph of someone with a familiar name. It was Tabitha McLeod, it had to be the same one, it was an unusual name. There she was, slim, young and very pretty and what's more she was smiling up at a very dishy man. That would teach Felicity to make prejudiced assumptions about people. She had expected Tabitha to be crop-haired and dressed in dungarees. She read the caption again, *Jeremy Foster, the radio presenter, with his fiancée Tabitha McLeod.* Well, at least that meant she wasn't after Jane for her body.

Felicity arrived home to a smell of burning. Darcy was at the kitchen sink when she got in. He had his shirt sleeves rolled up and was wearing a blue and white striped apron.

'What's burning?' Felicity rushed towards the oven and turned off the gas. 'What's the matter with you? Where's your sense of smell?' Felicity grabbed the pan and immediately screamed. The handle was red hot and she threw it on to the floor. Blackened quails' eggs rolled all over the kitchen. Darcy grabbed Felicity's hand and thrust it under the tap. She screamed again, the water was boiling hot. Darcy managed to turn the cold tap on and while Felicity held it there and tried to stop tears of anger and pain springing up in her eyes, Darcy found the first aid box. Some time later she was sitting drinking a cup of sweet tea, a drink she particularly detested but Darcy insisted it would be good for shock. Her hand was neatly bandaged, but extremely painful. How on earth was she going to get everything ready for tonight? In desperation she rang Laura.

'I hate to ask, but it's an emergency.'

'Don't worry Mum, I'll be right over.' Laura sounded cheerful and even enthusiastic about helping. 'Jamie's at nursery, so I could bring Concepcion too, if you like?'

'Great.' Felicity realised that she hadn't spoken to Oliver again about the Spanish girl.

'Good. I forgot to tell you Oliver took her out last week, she seemed to have a really nice time.'

They arrived within half an hour and Laura took charge completely. Felicity had forgotten how a crisis always brought out the best in her daughter. She had Darcy under control in a flash. He was given a series of simple, menial tasks, so that he couldn't get into too much trouble. Concepcion, her face wreathed in smiles, set off to the shops to get more quails' eggs. The girl was blooming and it looked as if her social life had improved. After a while Laura tried to insist Felicity go upstairs and lie down.

'You've had a shock. And you can't do anything here, not with your hand.'

'I think I'll get a taxi and go to the shop, make sure it looks all right. Check the flowers. That sort of thing.'

'If that's what you want to do, but do be careful, you don't want to spend the evening in A & E.'

*

Angel was hard at work when Felicity arrived, and everything seemed under control. The shop was full of lilies and Angel was carefully removing all the stamens to make sure none of their guests got covered in pollen. She had put an old sheet on the floor and was kneeling down concentrating hard. Felicity thought, not for the first time, she was very lucky to have found her. She had turned into a terrific employee. Conscientious, hardworking and very intelligent. Together they could make the shop work, they were a good team and surely between them they could keep Darcy under control.

Felicity didn't stay there for very long, her hand was throbbing and there was very little she could do one-handed. She tried to persuade Angel to go out to lunch with her; she needed something to do to fill in the time. There was no way she would be able to sleep even if she went to bed for the afternoon. In the end she went for a long walk in Battersea Park. Fallen leaves were blowing around or lying in piles. Felicity kicked her way through one of the bigger piles, thoroughly enjoying herself until she saw a park attendant shaking his fist at her. She hurried away, but not before she heard him shout, 'Stupid old woman.' That was probably a completely accurate description of her, but it didn't fit how she felt inside. Stupid possibly, but not old. People didn't get old any more. Look at Joan Collins, she didn't look like someone who had a bus pass. Felicity knew she would never look like Joan Collins, but did it matter? She had her own life, a life she'd made on her own, with a little help from her friends. That was the glue that held things together. She was jolly lucky. There was Rose, rock solid Rose, enfolding her with warmth, love and food. And now it looked as though she was going to be all right. There was Venetia, keeping her up to the mark, sorting out her hair, her figure, her wardrobe. She would be all right, her friends would rally round. That's what friends did. And finally there was Jane, maddening, bossy, but kind and so well meaning. She only ever wanted to help. Now she was in a muddle, but Tim was a determined man, in his own inarticulate way. He loved her, so perhaps they too would be all right. But tonight Felicity had to sparkle as the hostess of a party. Aiming a passing kick at another pile of leaves she set off for home.

*

In the event the party was a great success. The burn on her hand didn't seem to be as bad as she had feared. Everyone they had wanted to come, came: a sprinkling of press, some potential clients, a couple of influential designers and lots of friends. The shop became crowded and noisy. The champagne circulated well and the food disappeared. Oscar was there looking slim and handsome, if rather pale. Barry did not come, nor did Miles, so it looked as though Felicity was destined never to meet either of them. Oliver was there, looking well and happy. Concepcion was not there as she was looking after Jamie, but Oliver whispered to his mother that he was going round to see her later. Daisy came with Geoffrey. Felicity had never seen her look so pretty. She was aglow and she and Geoffrey were joined at the hip all evening.

Rose and Leo came looking a bit nervous, but glad to see so many familiar faces. Leo quickly found Rose a chair and she sat holding court at the back of the room. Tim arrived early, clean, scrubbed and hesitant. He positioned himself near the door so that he could spot Jane the moment she arrived. She came late with the Camerons, but Felicity noticed she spent quite a lot of the evening talking to her husband. Andrew came alone. Venetia was still in the clinic, but Andrew had

309

seen her and everyone was pleased with her progress. Sonia swanned in and entwined herself round Darcy. Andrew carefully stayed at the other side of the room. And Sam and Lavinia Tollard came with daughter Melanie in tow, Lavinia looking immaculate and Sam uneasy. They didn't stay long, but took a brochure. And last but not least, Henry came with Sally. Felicity was pleased to see she arrived looking cross and looked progressively crosser as the evening progressed. Henry looked a bit sheepish, but chatted merrily to Andrew and Leo, until he was dragged away.

After everyone had gone Oscar and Laura took Felicity out to a local Italian restaurant where they all tucked into large plates of pasta. Mark had already gone to New York to find them an apartment.

'It was great Mum.' Oliver beamed at her encouragingly, but Felicity knew he was still unhappy.

'I thought it went really well. Everyone said nice things about the stock. I hope a lot of them will come back.'

'Are you really sure you want to carry on once Oscar's gone to New York? It won't be too much for you?' Laura sounded genuinely worried.

'Too much for me? I'm in my prime.' Felicity laughed, not really believing what she was saying, but she wanted this challenge.

'And you won't be lonely without us?' Oscar's voice was full of concern.

'Oliver'll still be here. And I've got my friends, Rose, Venetia, Jane, they'll prop me up.' With a great effort Felicity made her voice sound cheerful. After all, it wasn't for ever and New York was only an airfare away.

'You mean the other way round,' Laura smiled at her, the prospect of a long absence perhaps making her fonder of her mother. 'You prop them up. Always have. You just had a bit of a hiccup when you got divorced, but you're back on track now.'

Felicity put her chin in her hands and grinned at her children. She was beginning to think life might go on getting better.

*

In the days following the party Felicity spent most of her time in the shop. They were surprisingly busy. It might be a novelty that would wear off, but Felicity was kept fully occupied serving customers as well as ordering more stock. Darcy had set off on a buying trip to Wales, with or without Sonia, Felicity didn't know, but she had Angel in the shop and in their few quiet moments they chatted companionably, each learning about each other's very different life. Darcy came back from his trip full of excitement with samples, photographs and sketches. There was no doubt about it, he had an extremely good eye. After the shop closed they all sat down in Felicity's office to go through Darcy's finds. After a certain amount of disagreement they settled on a range of cache pots and bowls in brilliant red lacquer. Finally Felicity told the others to go home. She wanted a little time to herself.

Felicity said goodnight to Darcy and Angel as they went on their way bickering happily. She heard the door close and she leant back in her chair. Peace at last. This was often the time of day she liked best. She had the place to herself and could enjoy the tranquillity after a hectic day.

Sitting down at her desk she considered her state of mind. She wasn't exactly depressed. Some aspects of her life were going really well. It was more that her life had taken so many unexpected turns over the last year. Firstly, it had never occurred to her Henry might fall in love. After the shock of that bombshell she had to adjust to selling the house, moving and living on her own. All her friends had seemed to think

311

what she needed was a new man, but what she had ended up with was a job, which was exciting, but no possible man in sight. She could have an affair with Henry. Was it technically an affair if one had been married? But that seemed like a very dangerous option. Sam was still with his wife, and despite everyone saying they were about to part, for all she knew they might be intending to stay together. As for her happily married friends – what had happened to them? Rose with her healthy country life had had a heart attack. Venetia with her perfect husband and perfect job was de-stressing in a clinic, and Jane with her conventionally smug married attitude to life had thrown her lot in with a crystal-gazing, alternative therapist. Life certainly kept on getting stranger and more interesting.

Felicity noticed her coffee was cold and it was after seven. She glanced at the pile of paper in the tray waiting to be filed. What better time to do it than now? She picked up a couple of folders and bent down to open the bottom drawer of the filing cabinet. In doing so she let out a most satisfactorily loud fart. This was one of the quirks of old age. She could remember when she was a child laughing like mad at Great Aunt Lily who had produced wonderful noises whenever she bent over to poke the fire. Now she was doing the same. She paused for a moment expectantly, waiting to see if there was another one brewing when she heard a cough. She looked up to see Sam Tollard standing the other side of her desk with a grin on his face.

'Very musical.'

'What the fuck are you doing here?' Felicity screeched in surprise as she got to her feet with as much dignity as was possible under the circumstances.

'Darcy let me in as he was going out. I came to ask you for a drink.'

Felicity, redder in the face than usual, thought for a moment. Her life was not going, as she had hoped, to end up in a safe and gentle harbour rocking gracefully towards a serene old age. Instead she realised it was going to lurch from burp, fart and other bodily malfunctions to the grave. Sod it, she thought as she smiled up at Sam.

'Right,' she said. 'Let's get that drink.'